BLOOD IN THE SAND

Two of Crowley's soldiers had seen the drone coming and shielded their eyes at the last moment. They had sprung from their hiding place and chased Ray Freeman as he ran toward his ship. Taking less than a second to aim, I hit one of them in the shoulder from over a hundred yards away. He spun and fell. His friend skidded to a stop and turned to look for me. I fired a shot, hitting him in the face.

Freeman's ship must not have been hidden very far away. Moments after he disappeared over the edge of the canyon, a small spaceworthy flier that looked like a cross between a bomber and transport rose into the air. Unlike the barge that Freeman had used as a decoy, the ship was immaculate, with rows of dull white armor lining its bulky, oblong hull. Gun and missile arrays studded its wings . . .

At first I thought Freeman had abandoned the base, but then he doubled back toward the barracks. I could see some of the guns along the wings glinting as I ran to view the fight. There was no hurry, however. Crowley's men were not prepared to fight a ship like this one.

The Gatling guns flashed. Some of the guerillas managed to escape, but there was no escape, not from Freeman.

Ken
Thank you for
reading my book.

THE CLONE
REPUBLIC

Hope you enjoy it

STEVEN L. KENT

— Father of the
author's beautiful
daughter.

ACE BOOKS, NEW YORK

THE BERKLEY PUBLISHING GROUP
Published by Penguin Group
Penguin Group (USA) Inc.
375 Hudson Street, New York, New York 10014, USA
Penguin Group (Canada), 90 Eglinton Avenue East, Suite 700, Toronto, Ontario M4P 2Y3, Canada
(a division of Pearson Penguin Canada Inc.)
Penguin Books Ltd., 80 Strand, London WC2R 0RL, England
Penguin Group Ireland, 25 St. Stephen's Green, Dublin 2, Ireland (a division of Penguin Books Ltd.)
Penguin Group (Australia), 250 Camberwell Road, Camberwell, Victoria 3124, Australia
(a division of Pearson Australia Group Pty. Ltd.)
Penguin Books India Pvt. Ltd., 11 Community Centre, Panchsheel Park, New Delhi—110 017, India
Penguin Group (NZ), Cnr. Airborne and Rosedale Roads, Albany, Auckland 1310, New Zealand
(a division of Pearson New Zealand Ltd.)
Penguin Books (South Africa) (Pty.) Ltd., 24 Sturdee Avenue, Rosebank, Johannesburg 2196, South
Africa

Penguin Books Ltd., Registered Offices: 80 Strand, London WC2R 0RL, England

THE CLONE REPUBLIC

An Ace Book / published by arrangement with the author

PRINTING HISTORY
Ace edition / April 2006

Copyright © 2006 by Steven L. Kent.
Map by Steven J. Kent.
Cover art by Christian McGrath.
Cover design by Judith Murell.
Interior text design by Kristin del Rosario.

ISBN: 0-441-01393-7

ACE
Ace Books are published by The Berkley Publishing Group,
a division of Penguin Group (USA) Inc.,
375 Hudson Street, New York, New York 10014.
ACE and the "A" design are trademarks belonging to Penguin Group (USA) Inc.

PRINTED IN THE UNITED STATES OF AMERICA

10 9 8 7 6 5 4 3 2 1

*I would like to dedicate this work to
Professor Ned Williams,
because he taught a bear to dance.*

ACKNOWLEDGMENTS

I want to thank my editors John Morgan (who moved on before this project could be finished) and Anne Sowards (who took over) for everything they have done to help me. Mark Adams, of Texas Instruments fame, helped out a lot with this project, as did my parents. My parents always help a lot.

Special thanks to Evan Nakachi, who gave me just the right encouragement at exactly the right moment to keep me going.

On the technical side, I need to thank Lewis Herrington, a former Marine colonel and a good friend. He spent a long time trying to help me understand the lifestyle, history, and tactics of the Marines—though his knowledge of cloning certainly left something to be desired.

Finally, I wish to thank my agent, Richard Curtis, because I am very lucky to have an agent like Richard Curtis.

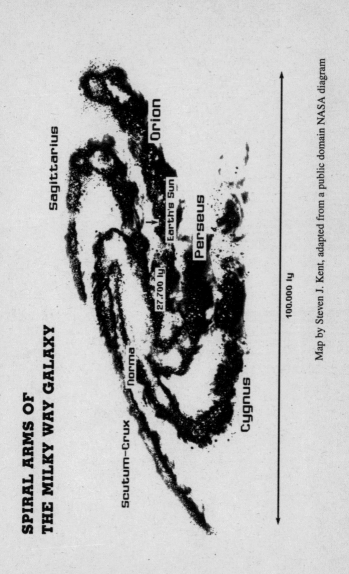

SPIRAL ARMS OF
THE MILKY WAY GALAXY

Sagittarius

Orion

Earth's Sun

27,700 ly.

Perseus

Norma

Scutum-Crux

Cygnus

100,000 ly

Map by Steven J. Kent, adapted from a public domain NASA diagram

"You had good reason, he said, to be ashamed of the lie which you were going to tell."

"True, I replied, but there is more coming; I have only told you half."

—Plato
The Republic, Book 3

INTRODUCTION

A.D. 2510
Location: Ravenwood Outpost; Planet: Ravenwood;
Galactic Location: Scutum-Crux Arm

"You picked a hell of a place to die, Marine," I told myself.

This planet had no economic value, no strategic value, and no scientific worth. The outpost, with its naked concrete walls, was just a primitive fort on a barren planet surrounded by plains and ice. Every Marine in every platoon that came to defend this spot ended up missing in action—a polite way of saying they were dead . . . gone to the halls of Montezuma. Semper fi, Marine.

As I walked through the halls of this shit hole, every boy stopped to salute me. "Ready at your post, Marine?" I would ask, pretending that it mattered.

"Sir, yes, sir!" they would shout, still naïve enough to believe that enthusiasm counted for something.

And I would grunt lines like, "Carry on, Marine," and salute, then move on knowing that nothing any of us did mattered. These boys were dead. Fresh out of basic, loyal to their last breath, and served up to die. I could not save them any more than I could save myself. In a couple of days, a patrol would come looking for survivors and find the base abandoned. The Corps would list us as missing in action, some officer would say, "Damn, not another platoon," and send the next forty-two men to replace us.

Legend had it that space monsters prowled the surface of Ravenwood. Most of my boys believed it was space aliens attacking the fort. Facing their deaths, these boys turned back the clock to the days when authors wrote books about alien invasions. But those authors were wrong. Once we entered space we discovered that we were almost alone in the galaxy. The only thing man had to fear was man himself.

Up ahead, a couple of my boys knelt in the shadow of a doorway and prayed. "You do that," I mumbled. "You pray. Why not?" *Once the guns are loaded and the troops in place, God and chance are all you have left.*

Even as I thought this, I realized that I didn't care what became of these boys. In fact, I did not care whether or not I made it off this planet alive. I had the urge to survive, but that was just instinct.

It was because of the lie. Plato's lie seems innocent, but it leaves you alienated from everything.

CHAPTER
ONE

A.D. 2508
Gobi Station

"Name?" The sergeant barked the question without bothering to look up from his desk. I heard the indifference in his voice and could not fault him for his callous attitude. Nothing important ever happened in dried-up stink holes like Gobi. Once you got assigned to a planet like this, your only option was to sit and wait for a transfer. It could take years. I'd heard rumors about Marines spending their entire careers on backwater planets praying for any excuse to leave, even a war.

"Private First-class Wayson Harris reporting as ordered, sir." I saluted, then handed him the sealed file that contained my orders.

I had shown up for this transfer wearing my Charlie Service uniform, not my armor. The uniform left me exposed to the desert air, and sweat had soaked through the material under my arms, not that this guy would notice. With his faded armor and stubble beard, this sergeant looked like he hadn't bathed in years. All the same, I could barely wait to change into my armor. It wasn't the protective chestplate and helmet

I wanted. It was the climate-controlled bodysuit, which had kept me cool in temperatures even less livable than this desert.

"PFC Harris," he echoed under his breath, not even bothering to look up. I shouldn't have saluted. Once you leave basic training, you only salute officers or Marines acting under command authority. You don't salute sergeants, and you certainly don't call them "sir," but it's a hard habit to break.

Having just spent three months living the spit-and-polish discipline of boot camp, I had come to fear drill sergeants for the gods they were. This sergeant, however, struck me as a heretic. His camouflage-coated armor had dulled, and there was sand and oil caked in the joints. His helmet sat on the ground beside his seat. I had never seen a Marine remove his helmet while on duty. If the job required combat armor, you wore the whole thing, or you were technically out of uniform.

The sergeant sat slumped in his chair with his armor loosened to fit his wilting posture. My drill sergeant would have given me a week in a detention cell if he saw me sitting like that; but I didn't think this guy worried about the brig. The brass doesn't punish you unless it catches you, and I doubted that any officers had set foot in this outpost in years. Why visit a place like Gobi Station and risk having a superior order you to stay. It could end your career.

"PFC Harris . . . PFC Harris . . . Let's see what we have here," he mumbled as he broke the red strip sealing my files. He flipped through the pages, occasionally stopping to scan a line. Apparently having found what he wanted, he spread the file on his desk and absentmindedly wrapped his fingers around his bristle-covered chin, as he browsed my records. "Fresh out of recruit training," he muttered. Something caught his eye, and he paused and mulled over the information before looking up at me. "A '1' in combat readiness?" He sounded like he wanted to laugh. "I've never seen anyone score under four hundred."

"It's a performance ranking, sir," I said.

He sneered when he heard the word, "sir." "You say something, private?"

"That number was my school rank. I drew top marks in hand-to-hand combat and marksmanship."

Godfrey cocked an eyebrow in my direction, then returned to my paperwork. "Son of a bitch, perfect scores," he whispered. "Why waste a perfectly good Marine on a shit-hole planet like this?"

He looked up at me. "You have a problem following orders, Harris?"

"No, sir," I said. I was, in fact, quite obedient by human standards. The military, however, had considerably higher standards. Most conscripts came out of clone farms that the government euphemistically referred to as "orphanages." Designed specifically for military life, the clones raised in these orphanages reacted to orders by reflex, even before their conscious minds could grasp what they had been asked to do. If an officer told them to dig a hole in the middle of a sidewalk, concrete chips and sparks would fly before the conscripts stopped to analyze the command. The clones weren't stupid, just programmed to obey first and think later. As a natural-born human, I could not compete with their autonomic obedience. My brain took a moment to sort out orders.

My inability to react to orders without thinking had caused me problems for as long as I could remember. I grew up in a military orphanage. Every child I knew was a clone. I might have entered Unified Authority Orphanage #553 the old-fashioned way—by having dead parents—but as a resident of UAO #553, I grew up with two thousand clones.

You would not believe the diversity that exists among two thousand supposedly identical beings. The Unified Authority "created all clones equal," taking them from a single vat of carefully brewed DNA; but once they came out of the tube, time and experience filled in the cracks in their personalities. Look at a mess hall filled with two thousand clones, and they appear exactly alike. Live with them for any length of time, and the differences become obvious.

"Your file says that you are slow following orders," Godfrey said.

"It's comparing me to clones," I said.

He nodded and flashed that wary smile sergeants use when they think you're spouting bullshit. "Did you speck some officer's daughter?"

"No, sir," I said.

"No," he grunted, and went back to my file. "Just wondering why they wasted a perfectly good recruit on a planet like this," he said.

"Random assignment, I suppose, sir," I said.

"Sure," he said, and his smile turned caustic. "Well, Private First-class Harris, I am Glan Godfrey. You can call me 'Glan,' 'Godfrey,' or 'Gutterwash.' Do not call me 'sir.' Gobi is pretty much a long-term assignment. Get sent here, and you're stuck for life. As long as you know that I am the sergeant and therefore the one you obey, you can forget everything they taught you in basic."

Growing up in an orphanage, you learn how to spot clones—they're all cut from the same helix. With Gutterwash Godfrey, however, I could not readily tell. He had sunbleached blond hair that nearly reached his shoulders. Every clone I had ever known had brown hair and an assembly-line flattop haircut. A decade on a desert planet could have fried the color out of Godfrey's hair, I supposed. But the loose armor and the thick stubble on his cheeks and chin . . . I thought that the spit and polish was programmed into their DNA. Could ten years on a desert planet bleach a man's programming the way it bleached his hair?

Godfrey pressed a button on his console. "Got a rack?" he asked, without identifying himself.

"Fresh meat arrive?" a voice asked back.

"Or a reasonable facsimile."

"Send him down, I'll put him in Hutchins's old rack," the voice said.

"Hutchins?" I asked, when Godfrey closed the communication. "Shipped out?"

"Nope," Godfrey said.

"Killed in action?" I asked.

"Nope. Suicide," Godfrey said. "Corporal Dalmer will meet you down that hall." He pointed ahead.

"Thank you, sir," I said instinctively, wasting another salute.

Godfrey responded with that sardonic smile. "The sooner you lose that, the better we'll get along."

I grabbed my two travel cases and started down the open-air hall. I had clothes and toiletries in one bag. The other bag held my gear—one helmet, a complete set of body armor, one body glove, one weapons-and-gear belt, one government-issue particle-beam pistol with removable rifle stock, one government-issue M27 pistol with removable rifle stock, and one all-purpose combat knife/bayonet with seven-inch diamond blade. Thanks to lightweight plastic-titanium alloys, the bag with the armor weighed less than the one with my clothes.

Halfway down the hall, I stopped to stare at my surroundings. After three months in the immaculate white-walled corridors of Infantry Training Center 309, I had forgotten that places like Gobi Station existed. No, that's not true. I never suspected that the Unified Authority set up bases in such decrepit buildings.

Judging by the name, "Gobi," I knew it was an early settlement. The cartographers used to name planets after Earth locations in the early days of the expansion. Back then, we settled any planet with a breathable atmosphere. That was before the science of terraformation passed from theoretical possibility to common practice.

The open-air hall from Godfrey's office to the barracks buzzed with flies. One side of the hall overlooked a stagnant pool of oily water surrounded by mud and reeds. I noticed the tail end of an animal poking out through the reeds. As I looked closer, I realized that it was an Earth-bred dog, a German shepherd, and that it was lying dead on its side.

"Don't worry, we run that through filters before we drink it," the corporal at the other end of the hall said. Like Godfrey, this man wore his armor and body glove without his helmet. The environmental climate control in the bodysuit must have felt good. I was perspiring so much that the back of my uniform now clung to the curve of my spine. Rivulets of sweat had run down the sides of my ribs.

"We drink that?" I asked.

"You either drink that or you buy water from the locals. The locals jack you. You could blow a full week's pay buying a glass of water from them. Only Guttman has that kind of money." He looked off toward the pond. "That sludge doesn't taste bad once you strain it.

"Name's Tron Dalmer," the corporal said as he stepped out from the doorway. "Whatever you did to get stationed here, welcome to the asshole of the friggin' universe. Did Gutterwash mention that we here at Gobi Station are the few and the proud?"

"No," I said, feeling depressed.

"This here is the smallest Marine outpost in the whole damned U.A. Empire."

I did not flinch, but Dalmer's use of the word "Empire" gave me a start. The commanders who ran both the orphanage and the basic training facility continually grilled us on the difference between expansion and imperialism.

"How many men?" I asked, not sure that I wanted to know. Most outposts had anywhere from three thousand to five thousand Marines. I had heard of outposts on isolated moons that only had fifteen hundred men. Judging by the size of this three-story barracks building, I guessed the population of Gobi Station to be at least one thousand.

"Including you, forty-one," Dalmer said. "The good news is that you don't have to share your room. The bad news is that if the locals ever decide they don't like us, they could trample our asses out of here. Of course, they barely notice us. Even with you we're one man shy of a full platoon. Besides, they are so busy with their own wars, they hardly notice us."

"So there is some action out here?" I asked.

Dalmer stared at me. "Fresh out of boot and in a rush to kill, eh?"

"I would hate to think that I wasted my time in boot camp," I said.

Dalmer laughed. "You wasted it, Harris. We have standing orders to stay out of local feuds." He led me into the barracks, an ancient building constructed of thick sandstone blocks with rows of modern dormitory cells wedged into its bulky framework. Each cell was designed to house four people, but no one lived in the cells on this floor. The doors hung open revealing dusty quarters. Gobi might once have played an integral part in the Unified Authority's grand expansion, but that time clearly had passed. A thin layer of sand covered the floor, and I saw twisting trails where snakes had slithered across the floor.

"You can have this entire floor to yourself if you want," Dalmer said. "Most of us prefer the bottom floor; it's cooler in the summer. Cooler in the winter, too."

"I take it this is summer?" I asked.

Dalmer snickered. "Boy, this is the dead of winter. Why do you think everybody's got their helmets off? We want to enjoy the cool air while it lasts."

He might have been joking, but I doubted it. He might have been hazing me. Maybe a battalion of grunts was hiding in some far end of the base watching me on a monitor and giggling as Godfrey and Dalmer dressed up in faded armor and tricked the gullible newbie into believing he had been assigned to Hell. My suspicions abruptly died when Dalmer brought me to the bottom floor. An entire division would not have cluttered the barracks so convincingly if they had worked on it for an entire month.

The only light in the chamber came from windows carved in the meter-thick walls. As my eyes adjusted, I saw hundreds of particle-beam pistols piled in one corner of the floor.

Dalmer followed my gaze and figured out what had caught my attention. "Broken," he said. "Sand gets in the housing and scratches the mirrors. Leaves 'em worthless."

On the open market, PB pistols sold for $2,000. Around the Corps, bullets were the ammunition of choice, but you could not count on them in low gravity or thin air. Particle-beam weapons were more difficult to maintain. You had to worry about prisms and energy coils—modular components that needed to be changed on a regular basis. "Why don't you change out the mirrors?" I asked.

Dalmer spit out a bitter laugh. "Fix them? Gobi Station used to be the outermost armory of the Cygnus Arm. We have a thousand guns for every man on this base." He stopped and thought for a moment. "Make that two thousand. We use them for shooting lizards. It's easier to grab a new gun than to requisition replacement parts. Hell, Harris, it's been two years since anybody's even been out to the firing range. This is Gobi."

He paused and stared into my eyes, probably wondering if I grasped his meaning. When I did not ask any questions, Dalmer continued. "Of course, we can't just throw broken weapons away, or the locals will steal them. Godfrey dumped a load once. I think we armed half the planet."

"Are there problems with the locals?" I asked.

"Not much. Some of them consider themselves gun-slingers, but it's all petty stuff. I doubt the Senate loses much sleep over Gobi." Dalmer turned and headed into the barracks.

Most of the windows opened to that pond in the court-yard. Flies and a sulfurous smell wafted in on the trace of a breeze. I could barely wait to snap on my helmet and breathe filtered air, but Tron Dalmer did not seem to mind the stench. Nor was he bothered by the rest of the squalor—uniforms left hanging off furniture, plates of stale food, un-made bunks. Looking around the floor, I would have thought that spoiled children manned this outpost, not Marines.

"That was Hutchins's cell over there," Dalmer said.

The door swung open at my touch, and I immediately knew that someone, likely Dalmer or Godfrey, had searched through Hutchins's belongings. His clothes were piled on the floor, his desk was swept clean, and his bed was stripped bare. Every drawer in the cell hung open from the wall.

"How long has this room been empty?" I asked. I wanted to ask Dalmer if he had found anything of value.

"Two, maybe three months," Dalmer said. "Did Godfrey tell you about Hutchins?"

"Only that Hutchins committed suicide."

"Put a goddamned particle-beam pistol in his mouth . . . Set his goddamned brain on fire."

Dalmer left and I set up my quarters. Using a blood-stained sheet I found wadded in a drawer, I wrapped the late Private Hutchins's belongings into a tight ball and stuffed them in a corner of the room. "Why am I here?" I asked my-self. "Why the hell am I here?"

The only time we met as a platoon was at breakfast. Once or twice per week, Glan Godfrey briefed us about recent com-muniqués from fleet headquarters as we ate. Nobody listened during Godfrey's briefings. We were as far from fleet head-quarters as you could get without leaving the galaxy, and nothing command had to say seemed of any significance out here.

On most days, the platoon divided up after breakfast. Godfrey and Dalmer generally hung around the base. God knows why. The rest of the platoon piled into a couple of trucks and rode into town. They generally returned before supper. I think they wanted to stay out later, but the locals closed shop before sundown.

I spent my first month jogging around the outside wall of the base, holding target practice at the firing range, and try-ing to convince other men to join me. Most of the men laughed at the idea of drilling. Godfrey and Dalmer would not even discuss it. One corporal, Lars Rickman, came out and trained with me twice, but he quickly lost interest.

After six weeks I gave up on training alone and took my first trip into Morrowtown. Godfrey congratulated me on having more starch than Hutchins. The last new recruit be-fore me, Hutchins, stopped training after less than one week. Life around the outpost became friendlier after I said I would go to Morrowtown.

Located a mere two hundred miles west of our outpost, Morrowtown had sixty thousand residents. On Gobi, it was the big league.

A word about our trucks—they were open-air transports with no armor and no guns. Beside the trucks, the only other vehicle in our motor pool was a dilapidated tank, generally referred to as "Godfrey's Go-Cart," that sat up to its axles in mud in the center of our courtyard. Oil trickled from the Go-Cart's crank case and seeped into the pond; but as Dalmer often reminded us, "It all gets filtered out."

Our trucks could have passed for farm equipment except that they had tank treads instead of tires. They were flatbeds with removable benches. Sizing up these twenty-foot-long Jurassic beasts, I could not begin to guess their age. They might have arrived with the first ship to land on Gobi.

"Shouldn't these have guns or rockets mounted on them?" I asked Rickman, as we loaded up.

"Why?" he asked, looking mildly interested. He was the

only man stationed on Gobi who even partially resembled a Marine. Not only had he at least attempted to train with me, he still polished his armor and carried a sidearm. When I did not answer his question about why we might want to carry a rocket launcher on the trucks, however, he mumbled something about hating fresh recruits.

Rickman was a clone, of course. All of the other Marines on Gobi were clones. Like Godfrey, Rickman had bleached hair and a gaunt face. The only Marine that Gobi had not made thin was Taj Guttman. Guttman had grown so fat that he no longer fit into his armor. He did not bother with his leg shields or boots; and he fastened his chestplate only at the top, wearing it around his neck like a stiff poncho. I doubt he would have bothered with armor if it were not for the climate controls in the bodysuit. Godfrey referred to Guttman as "Four-Cheeks," meaning he had enough ass for two men. The name stuck, and everybody used it.

As the new kid on base, I got to sit next to Guttman as we drove to Morrowtown. He only talked about one thing—poker. I had never played cards. No one gambled at UAO #553. We talked about gambling and how much we would enjoy it, but young clones are not much for breaking rules. As the lone human in the orphanage, I had tried my best to blend in.

We didn't play cards in boot camp, either. Until I arrived on Gobi, I assumed that all Marines trained hard and obeyed the rules. Of course, none of these Marines knew they were clones. Straight out of the tube, combat clones had brown hair and brown eyes, but through the miracle of neural programming, they thought of themselves as natural-born people with blond hair and blue eyes. That was how they saw themselves, too. When clones looked at themselves in the mirror, they saw blond hair and blue. God knows how the scientists pulled that off, but they did. And since clones were also hardwired not to speak about cloning among themselves, orphanages managed to raise thousands of clones without one clone telling the next he was synthetic.

Growing up, I used to eat in a cafeteria with thousands of identical cadets who never mentioned that everybody around them looked and sounded precisely alike. They could eat, shower, and shave side by side and not see the similarities they shared with the men next to them because of cerebral programming in their DNA. Even though they knew everyone else was a clone, they never suspected their own synthetic creation. Around the orphanage, people used to say that clones were wired to self-destruct if they ever understood the truth of their origin.

"Have you ever played poker?" Guttman asked. "It's a great game. Laying your cards and catching everyone flat-footed"—he grinned as if in ecstasy—"there's no better feeling."

"I've never played," I said.

"Stick with me, you'll make a fortune," Guttman said, sounding elated finally to have somebody who would listen to him.

Not having much to say to Guttman, I watched the desert as we drove. All I saw was sand and rock and clear blue sky. The ride lasted two hours—two hours trapped with Guttman. I was ready to hop off the truck and walk after the first hour. By the time we finally saw the city, my head hurt from all of Guttman's babbling.

Built almost entirely out of sandstone bricks, Morrowtown blended into its environment. I saw the shapes of the buildings long before I realized what they were.

"Here we are," Rickman yelled as he parked in a wide alleyway. Our muffler sputtered, and the chassis trembled as the engine coughed smoke.

"I hate these trucks," Guttman moaned.

With few words spoken, the platoon divided into groups. Some men went to a saloon where they got drunk on a daily basis. They could not afford clean water, but whiskey and beer were in the budget. Others quietly kept girlfriends in town. Not wanting a generation of half-clone children, Unified Authority scientists designed clones that were sterile, but that did not mean that they left out the sex drive. "The goal is to copulate, not populate," a drill sergeant once told me.

Guttman waited for me beside the truck. "Come with me. I'll get you into the best game in Morrowtown," he said in a secretive tone. Not having heard any better offers, I went with Guttman. "Leave your helmet in the truck. It makes you look silly," he added.

"I think I'll keep it on just the same." Okay, I was already absent without leave, technically speaking, but I saw no point in adding "out of uniform" to the list of charges.

"Suit yourself, but you're going to scare the locals," Guttman said, sounding a bit deflated. But nobody seemed scared of me. The people ignored us. Children played happily as we passed them on the street. A gang of teenagers stood on a sidewalk flipping coins against a wall. They paused to stare at us, then went on gambling.

It shouldn't be like this, I thought to myself. *They should be a little afraid of us.* Guttman, bobbing his head and waving at everyone we passed, clearly did not agree with me. His juvenile excitement showed in his chubby smile as he led me into a squat building that looked more like a bunker than a bar. Perhaps he liked the idea of showing off a new friend. Maybe he just loved playing cards. He came to this game every day and never grew tired of it.

"Ah, good, Taj Guttman. Excellent," a soft voice mumbled with an accent so thick that I could barely understand it. A short man with a round body and a head that was as bald as an egg approached us. He could not have been taller than five-foot-two. He smiled as if he was glad to see us, but something in his oily voice said otherwise.

"Kline." The name splashed out of Guttman's mouth.

"You are early today," the little round man continued, as I strained to decipher his words. This was the first time I had actually heard a Gobi native speak. He stretched vowels and slurred consonants so that when he next said, "And you have brought a friend," it sounded like, 'aaaant you heeef broood a fryent." He flashed his smile at me as he sized me up. "We have another visitor today as well." In Kline's thick tongue, the word "visitor" sounded like "fiztor."

Guttman turned to me, and said in an unnecessarily loud voice, "This ugly mutt is Kline." Up to this point in the trip, Guttman had struck me as being slow and stupid, but he had a way with languages. He matched Kline's accent perfectly when speaking to the locals, but had not a trace of an accent when speaking to me. Then he turned to Kline, and said, "And this is Harris. Sorry about the helmet; I told him that it makes him look silly."

"Harris" sounded like "Haaritz." "Silly" was "tziillie."

"I'm just here to watch," I said.

"Watch?" Kline asked as his smile faded. "This game is for players only."

"He'll play," Guttman said.

"Perhaps I should leave then," I said. "I've never played, and from everything Guttman tells me, this is no game for beginners."

"Nonsense," Guttman chimed in. "Of course he'll play."

"I wish you would," a soft voice said in beautiful Earth English. Someone had moved in behind me as Guttman and Kline led the way to the card room where several more players milled around a table. "I'm new at the game myself, and I hate the idea of getting swindled alone." A tall man with thinning white hair and a well-trimmed beard stepped out from the shadows along the wall.

"You must have money to burn," I said. "Guttman here is a card shark."

"Is he?" the man said, his eyes narrowing. His mouth was all teeth and grins, but the warm smile did not extend to his eyes.

Guttman giggled nervously. "It's all just fun."

"I'm living on enlisted-man wages," I said, "and my next check does not arrive for a week. I doubt I even have enough cash to buy my way into the game."

"You may wager your weapon," Kline said. "Sidearms are as good as cash at this table."

"What was that?" I asked in astonishment.

"Don't worry," Guttman said, giggling nervously. He stepped closer to me, and whispered, "I never come here with cash."

"I think I'm in the wrong place," I said, already deciding that I would report this to Godfrey the moment we got back to base. I had never imagined such insubordination.

"I have no objection to your watching the game," the bearded man said.

"They'll pass information over their communications

link," another player complained, looking at my helmet. "He'll tell Taj what we have in our hands."

"As I understand it, that link only works if both soldiers are wearing helmets," the bearded man said.

"What do you say?" Guttman asked Kline.

Kline considered. "Sit behind Guttman, and no walking around."

I agreed.

"And I insist that you check your weapon," said Kline, pointing at my pistol.

Seeing me hesitate, Guttman chimed in. "It will be safe. You cannot go anywhere in Morrowtown wearing your sidearm."

Though I did not like the idea, I unstrapped my holster and handed it to Kline.

The seven men closed in around a large round table. I sat in a chair behind Guttman and watched as Kline dealt each player five cards—two facing up and three facing down. Guttman slipped his pudgy thumb under the corner of the three downturned cards and peered at their values.

The card room had no windows. The only light in the room was the pale glow of a lamp hanging over the table. I would not have been able to read Guttman's cards had I removed my helmet. Our visors had lenses and filters designed for battle situations. Using optical commands, I activated a night-for-day lens that brightened my vision, then I used a magnification lens to get a better look at Guttman's cards. When he bent the corners to have a look, I saw that he had two threes and an ace on the table. The cards that had been placed faceup were a king and a six.

Guttman slid the ace, the king and the six forward. Kline collected each man's rejected cards and replaced them with cards from the deck. As Guttman fanned out his new cards, I saw that he had added a face card, a ten, and another three. He closed his hand and started bouncing in his seat.

The bids went around the table. When it came to Guttman, he pushed his pistol into the center of the table, and Kline handed him a tray covered with chips. I had no idea what Guttman's new cards meant, but judging by his happy wheezing, he liked them.

The man with the beard looked pleased as well. "Well, this is a rare pleasure," he said, and he spilled a stack of gold-colored chips on the table. The other players groaned as Kline circled the table again, gathering cards and replacing them with new ones.

"I'll raise you," Guttman said, and he carelessly tossed a stack of chips into the pot.

Some of the other players placed their cards on the table facedown and backed out of the game.

"Very aggressive move," the bearded man said as he matched Guttman's bid. "I have three kings."

Guttman sighed and leaned back in his chair as the man raked in his winnings, including the pistol.

I watched this with growing irritation. Guttman, apparently enthralled by this situation, looked back at me and winked. Fortunately, no one could hear what I was uttering inside my helmet.

"Do all soldiers carry these?" the man with the beard said as he hefted Guttman's particle-beam pistol. He did not touch the grip or the trigger. Instead, he treated the gun as if it might explode, gingerly pinching the barrel with his thumb and forefinger.

"Mostly we carry M27s," Guttman said, "like the one Harris was wearing. I prefer the particle beam though, it's worth a lot more money." He laughed and squirmed in his seat, apparently anxious to start the next hand and win his weapon back.

"Quite a hefty weapon," the man said. "It must be very sturdy."

"You'd think so," Guttman replied, "but they don't do so well in the desert. We have piles of broken guns lying around our barracks."

"Is that so?" the man asked. "Replacements must be easy to come by?"

"You kidding?" Guttman laughed. "Gobi Station used to be an armory. The place is a damned munitions depot. Isn't that right?" Guttman asked, turning in his chair to look at me.

I did not answer.

"I see," said the bearded man. He seemed to sense the tension coiling between Guttman and me. "So I shall need to take special precautions to keep this in working order."

"Can we get on with the game?" a player called from across the table.

Kline dealt another hand of cards. This time Guttman had two queens and a king facing down, with a four and eight facing up. From what I could tell, he was not happy with these cards. As he had done in the last game, Guttman pushed three cards forward, then tossed some chips into the center of the table. Everybody else followed.

Kline pivoted around the table a second time, giving Guttman two fives and an ace. A few of the other players grimaced. Kline tapped his cards against his tiny chin. Guttman ripped a thunderous fart, then feigned embarrassment while giggling under his breath. Throughout the last hand, he had kept one platinum chip hidden under his cards. When his third bid came, he selected that chip and slid it forward. "I call," he said.

Three of the other players grumbled and threw down their cards. Kline rolled his slow brown eyes. He looked at his cards, looked at the chips on the table, looked at his cards, and dropped his hand as well. "I'm out," he said.

The bearded man stayed in.

Silently, Kline proceeded to move around the table changing cards for the three players who stayed in the game.

Guttman took two.

So did the man with the beard. Whatever the man got, it made him happy. He grinned and threw a platinum chip and two gold ones onto the table. They jingled and spun as they settled on the pile.

Guttman's beefy hands hid his cards from my view; but I got the feeling he was strong. He started bouncing so hard in his chair that I expected it to splinter. He looked like a drowning man fighting for air. His chips were low, and I thought he might need to leave the game; but Guttman whispered something to Kline, and the dealer handed him another rack of chips. With a wicked grin, Guttman selected three gold chips and tossed them in the pot. Only then did I realize how Guttman had gotten that second rack of chips: He'd wagered my pistol.

I started to get up, but Guttman raised a hand to stop me.

"It's okay, Harris," he said. "I have everything under control."

I wanted to kill Guttman, but I couldn't. My pistol was gone, and the only chance I had to get it back would be if Guttman won the hand.

The bearded man's eyes positively sparkled now. He smiled across the table at Guttman. "You are quite the player," he said.

"How many?" Kline asked.

"Two," said Guttman, and he pushed two cards forward.

Kline leaned forward and took the cards, then dealt new ones. I saw what they were as Guttman inspected them—two queens. Guttman spilled two-thirds of his chips onto the table.

"Unexpected," the man with the beard said. "Wiser men . . ." With this he slid Guttman's blaster into the pot. "This sees and raises the stakes, does it not?"

Guttman pressed his fingers on the tops of his cards. "You must be pretty confident," he said.

I sure as hell did not feel confident.

Perhaps it finally dawned on Guttman that he might have to explain how he had lost both of our pistols. Perhaps, having no more guns to pawn, Guttman finally noticed the jagged edges behind the bearded man's smile. He gathered up the few chips he had left, and said, "Let's see what you have."

The mystery man showed all of his cards—three kings and two aces.

Guttman let out a long breathy whistle. "A crowded house? Nice hand," he said as he turned over his cards, showing four queens, "but I think the pot is mine."

He turned to grin at me, but his smile vanished when he saw that I had climbed out of my chair. "I would like my pistol," I said to Kline.

"Don't leave now," Guttman said. He jumped to his feet and walked over to me. Putting his hand by his mouth to block others from hearing, he whispered, "I'm just getting my stride. I'm about to clean these suckers dry."

Stepping around Four-Cheeks, I grabbed my gun.

"Listen, pal," Guttman said, grabbing me by my shoulder. Before I realized what I was doing, I spun and slammed my fist into Guttman's mouth. His legs locked and fell out from under him as he dropped flat on his ass. Rather than attempt to get up, he sat where he fell, wiping blood from his split lip.

"I'm leaving now," I said. This time, Guttman made no attempt to stop me.

CHAPTER
TWO

Old and sparse and dilapidated, Gobi Station did not have air-conditioning or any other form of climate control. It did not matter during the winter, when a cooling draft blew through the open-air corridors and enormous verandas, but winter ended so suddenly that it seemed like somebody switched it off. One day we had a breeze and the next morning the winds were withering. Daytime temperatures reached a dry 120 degrees. When the desert cooled after sunset, the temperature dropped to a tolerable 90 degrees.

Glan Godfrey continued making his cursory announcements every few days as we ate breakfast out of Meals Ready to Eat (MRE) tins. He didn't care if we listened or if we whispered back and forth as he spoke. A couple of weeks after my first visit to Morrowtown, however, Godfrey showed up for breakfast with a regulation haircut and a shave. He told us to put down our forks and pay attention.

Godfrey passed around a photograph. Someone called, "Pictures from home?"

"Shut up and listen," Godfrey said in an uncharacteristically severe voice. "The entire Central Cygnus Fleet is on alert. Command is looking for this man. His name is . . ."

Godfrey paused to check the bulletin. "Amos Crowley. Have any of you grunts seen him?"

"Doesn't he live in Morrowtown?" Lars Rickman joked with the man sitting next to him.

I was laughing with everybody else when Dalmer passed the picture my way. Crowley had intense dark eyes, white hair, and a thick white beard. I looked over at Taj Guttman squirming in his seat. We both recognized him, though Guttman clearly did not want to say anything. It was the man from the card game.

"What is he wanted for?" I asked.

"The bulletin doesn't say much about what he's done," Godfrey said. He held his notes up and read in a soft voice that almost seemed meant for a private conversation. " 'Crowley is sought for involvement in several seditious activities.' The brass in Washington labeled him an enemy of the Republic."

"He'll fit right in on Gobi; nobody likes the U.A. over here," someone bawled from the back of the room.

"Crowley was a general in the Army," Godfrey said. The laughing stopped, but I could hear men whispering to each other. "That makes him special. He was the highest-ranking general in the Perseus Arm before he disappeared. Now Washington wants a word with him in the worst way."

"He might be here," I said, and the hall went silent. "I saw him two weeks ago. One of Guttman's card games."

Glan Godfrey turned toward me. "Are you certain about this, Harris?"

"Yes," I said, suddenly feeling like a Marine again.

"What about you, Guttman?"

"It was a while ago . . ." he said. "I mean, I guess that looks like him, but I was . . ."

"You festering sack of eye pus," Godfrey said in a voice that echoed a dawning realization. "Did you bet your sidearm?" When Guttman did not answer, Godfrey's glare hardened. "Shit, Guttman, you lost your sidearm, didn't you?"

"I won it back with the next hand." Guttman sounded scared.

"Shut your speck-receptacle!" Godfrey snapped. "Fleet

Command is going to want a full report. I'll be surprised if we don't all end up in front of a firing squad for this, Four-Cheeks." He glared at Guttman for another moment, then turned toward me, and said, "Harris, come with me."

Taking short, brisk strides, and not saying a word, Godfrey ushered me to his office. He worked in a cavernous chamber that had probably once served as an entire office complex. The platoon could have bunked in the space. Real estate was never a problem on Gobi.

Godfrey's desk sat in a far corner. Light poured in through arc-shaped windows along the domed ceiling. "I need you to report what you saw to Fleet Command," Godfrey said, as we walked toward his desk.

"You want me to do it?"

"I'm not letting Guttman anywhere near Command. Harris, we're in trouble here. Admiral Brocius has taken a personal interest in this hunt. You think I'm going to show him that moron?"

"Brocius?" I asked, feeling numb in the knees. Vice Admiral Alden Brocius, the highest-ranking officer in the Central Cygnus Fleet, had a reputation for being hard-nosed.

Godfrey chuckled bitterly. "Brocius is personally directing the manhunt." He looked at me and smiled. "Don't worry about your career, Harris. You're on Gobi, you're already in the shits."

Godfrey crouched in front of his communications console and typed in a code. A young ensign appeared on the screen. He studied Godfrey for a moment, then asked the nature of the call. Godfrey said he had a positive sighting of Amos Crowley, and the ensign put the call on hold. When the screen flashed on again, Brocius, a tall and slender man with jet-black hair and brown eyes, stared back at us.

"What is it, Sergeant?" the admiral asked in a brusque voice.

"Two of my men spotted General Crowley."

"I see," Brocius said, sounding more interested. "You have a positive identification?"

"Yes, sir. One of the men who identified him is with me now."

"Let's have a word with him," Brocius said.

Godfrey saluted and moved back. I stepped forward and saluted.

"What is your name, son?"

"PFC Wayson Harris, sir."

"You saw Amos Crowley?"

"Yes, sir."

"Do you believe he is still on Gobi?"

"I don't know, sir."

"Do you have any reason to believe he has left the planet?"

"No, sir."

"Then you believe he is still on Gobi?"

"He did not tell the private his plans, sir."

"I realize that," Brocius said, starting to sound irritated. "Do you think he is still on Gobi?"

I did not know how to answer. I had no idea if Crowley was still on Gobi, and Brocius did not seem to care. It seemed like the admiral wanted me to say that Crowley was still here. I stole a glance at Godfrey and saw him nodding.

"Well, which is it?"

"He may be here, sir."

"I see. Very well then, put the sergeant back on."

Godfrey stepped up to the receiver. "Your man does not seem confident," Brocius said. "Still, if there is anything to it . . . I'll send someone to investigate."

Perhaps I overestimated Crowley's importance. I don't think that I expected the Central Cygnus Fleet to converge on Gobi, but I did expect a significant force. I expected marshals guarding the spaceport and a surveillance fleet blockading the planet . . . a full-blown manhunt. Admiral Brocius did not send any of those things. He sent one man—Ray Freeman.

Three days after my interview with Admiral Brocius, a beat-up barge appeared in the sky above our base. It was early in the morning, and the barge left a contrail of oily smoke in the otherwise immaculate sky. Lars Rickman and I happened to be standing in a breezeway enjoying the 90-degree morning chill when the ship first appeared. We watched as it touched down on the loading area beside our outer wall, its gear making a shrill grinding noise as it settled on the tarmac.

"What a wreck," Rickman said, as we trotted down for a closer look.

The barge had battered armor. Some of the plates around its cockpit had curled along the edges. There were rows of inset doors along its forty-foot hull that looked as if they might have housed an impressive array of weapons.

"This bitch has been through a war," Rickman said. He had a bemused smile as he looked back and forth along the spaceship's dilapidated hull. As we walked around the rear of the ship, the hatch opened, and Ray Freeman emerged— the biggest man I have ever met, standing at least seven feet tall with arms and legs as thick as most men's chests.

Freeman was a "black man." Understand that since the United States brought the world together in a single "unified authority," racial terms like "African," "Oriental," and "Caucasian" had become meaningless. Under the Unified Authority, the Earth became the political center of the galaxy. Most commerce, manufacturing, and farming were done in the territories, and the territories were fully integrated. I heard rumors about certain races refusing to marry outside of their own; but for the most part, we had become a one-race nation. So when Ray Freeman, whose skin was the color of coffee without a trace of cream, stepped out of his ship, it was like the return of an extinct species.

It wasn't just that Freeman was taller and several shades darker than any man I had ever seen. It was that his biceps were the size of a grown man's skull when he bent his arms, and his triceps looked like slabs of rock when his arms hung straight. And it was that you could see the outlines of those muscles through the stiff, bulletproof canvas of his sleeves.

Freeman's shaved head was so massive that it looked like he was wearing a helmet. A small knot of scars formed a paisley pattern on the back of his skull. He had a wide nose, which looked as if it had been broken several times, and thick lips. His neck was as wide around as either of my thighs. It completely filled the collar of his jumper, a garment that looked lost between Army fatigues and a pilot's uniform. Dents and scratches dotted every inch of the massive armored plate that covered his chest and shoulders. Judging by the scars and battered armor, I knew this man had enemies.

"Who commands this outpost?" Freeman asked.

"That would be Sergeant Godfrey," Rickman said, looking more than a little intimidated.

"Take me to him," Freeman said, in a soft and low voice that reminded me of gunfire echoing in a valley.

Without saying a word, Rickman turned and walked straight to Godfrey's office. Relieved to get away from the giant, I stayed back to examine this strange, old ship. When Rickman returned a few moments later, he mumbled something like, "tear off his friggin' head and spit in the holes."

"Who is he?" I asked.

"Don't know," Rickman said.

"I think I'll stay out of his way," I said.

"Don't count on it," Rickman said. "He sent me out here to get you."

"You're joking."

"No, I'm not. You get to go meet with Chuckles down in Godfrey's office."

I took a deep breath and headed for the barracks to grab my helmet. By that time, it occurred to me that Admiral Brocius might have sent the visitor, and I did not want to be caught out of uniform twice in one night. When I reported to Godfrey, I saw Freeman sitting cramped behind the sergeant's desk as if it were his own. Godfrey met me as I closed the door.

"Harris, this is Ray Freeman. He is here on orders from Admiral Brocius," Godfrey said, using the interLink system built into our helmets so that Freeman would not hear us.

"Here to catch . . . ?" I asked.

"He's a mercenary," Godfrey said, "and a real charmer."

"Two men saw Crowley," Freeman said in that same implacable voice.

"The other man was Private Guttman," Godfrey answered on his open microphone.

"Get him," Freeman said.

"Go get him, Harris," Godfrey said.

As I started to leave, Freeman said, "You go get him, Sergeant. I want to speak with the private." Suddenly I wanted nothing more than to go look for Guttman.

Sergeant Godfrey left without looking back.

"Remove your helmet," Freeman said as he placed a folder with the Central Cygnus Fleet seal on the desk. "This is the man you saw?" he asked, pulling a photograph from the top of the folder.

"Yes," I said. "I saw him enter a poker game in Morrowtown."

"You're sure this was the man?"

I nodded.

"Tell me about the game," Freeman said, with that low, rumbling voice. He listened carefully as I told the story, his face betraying no emotion. He did not say anything when I finished. Looking through me, he reached over and pressed the intercom button on Godfrey's desk, and said, "Send in the other one."

Godfrey and Guttman stepped into the room. Sergeant Godfrey retreated to a far corner and sat quietly.

Guttman, sweat rolling down his pale and puffy face, stood trembling before the desk. He had tried to dress properly for the meeting, but his armor would not cooperate. He wore his helmet, which no longer fit over his globe-shaped head, like a crown around his forehead. Guttman's chestplate dangled from his neck. He'd used belts to lash his forearm guards and thigh plates in place. If I had not known that Taj Guttman was a Marine, I would have guessed that he was a comedian doing a parody of military life.

Freeman seemed not to notice. No glint of humor showed in his face as he directed Guttman to a chair by the desk with a nod. Once Guttman lowered himself into his chair, Freeman showed him the picture of Crowley. "This the man?"

"I'm not sure. It may have been him. It could be him. I really did not get a good look at that man," Guttman twittered nervously. "I suppose Harris told you where we saw him?"

"He mentioned a card game," Freeman said.

"I see," said Guttman. "Whoever he was, he wasn't very good at cards. He won the first hand, then I cleaned him out on the second. He quit after the third hand."

"What were the stakes?" Freeman asked.

"Morrowtown isn't exactly a gambler's paradise," Guttman said, as sweat dribbled down his forehead. "You might take home $50 if the locals are feeling dangerous."

"I understand you can also win government-issue sidearms?" Freeman said.

Guttman turned completely white. He must have hoped that I would hide that part of the story. He glared at me for a moment, then turned back to Freeman. "Yes, I suppose. I don't think he had ever seen one before. He held it like he was afraid it would bite him."

"Is that the pistol?" Freeman asked, pointing down at Guttman's holster.

Guttman fished it out of its sleeve and placed it on the desk. Freeman picked it up between his thumb and forefinger, exactly as Crowley had done. Dangling from the mercenary's thick fingers, Guttman's gun looked like a child's toy. "Is this how he held it?"

"Yeah. Yeah, just like that."

"Idiot," Freeman said, placing the pistol back on the desk. "He shut off the charge guard outtake valve. This pistol will explode the next time you fire it."

Guttman looked at the weapon as if it had suddenly grown fangs. Spinning it in place rather than picking it up, he checked the energy meter, gasped, then moved his hands away quickly. "What do I do with it? Will it blow up?"

Freeman did not bother answering. Turning toward the communications console, he quietly said, "Take your weapon and wait in the hall." Guttman picked up his pistol and held it out in front of him as far as his arms could reach. Keeping both eyes fixed on the gun, he shuffled out of the office. I did not know which scared him more, carrying a sabotaged pistol or talking to Freeman.

"You wait outside, too," Freeman said to me.

I started to leave, then stopped. "Excuse me, sir," I said. "I remembered something else."

Freeman, who was now standing behind the desk, stared down at me. He did not say anything as he waited for me to speak.

"When Guttman lost that first game, he said something

about sand ruining these guns. He told Crowley that we had thousands of them around the base."

Freeman looked at me and nodded.

"That will be all, Harris," Godfrey said over the interLink.

"Don't go far," Freeman said.

As I left the room, I found Guttman pacing in the hall-way. He stormed over to me and stared into my visor. His pudgy face turned red, and his lips were blue as he snarled at me. "Great job, pal! Now I'm in deep."

"Guttman, that gun would have blown up in your face if you ever got around to shooting it," I said.

Guttman stopped for a moment and thought. His breathing slowed. "Yeah, I guess you're right." He pointed down the hall where his pistol lay on a table. "Do you know how to fix it?"

If there is one thing you learn in basic training, it's how to maintain a sidearm. All he had to do was open the buffer valve and discharge some gas. But Guttman had forgotten basic training. It must have been years since he had last stripped and cleaned a pistol.

"Drain the chamber," I said.

"Oh," he said. "Can you help me?"

The door opened behind us, and Godfrey peered out. "Harris. Mr. Charming would like another word with you."

As I stepped back into Godfrey's office, I saw Freeman talking to Admiral Brocius on the communications console. "What is your next step?" Brocius asked.

"I want to have a look around Morrowtown," Freeman replied.

"Keep me informed," Brocius said as he signed off. Freeman placed the photograph of Crowley back in his folder. Then he turned to look at me. "Do you have any civilian clothing?"

"Sure," I said.

"Dress down; I need you to take me into Morrowtown."

As we climbed into the truck, I said, "We'll save a couple of hours if we go in your flier."

Freeman glared down at me, and said, "We'll take the truck."

"Is there a reason I am wearing civilian clothes?"

"Yes," Freeman said, and he did not speak again for the entire two-hour trip. I tried to distract myself with memories of boot camp, but you cannot ignore a man whose very presence radiates intensity. I could feel him sitting beside me. I suppose he chose the truck to avoid calling attention to himself; but there was no way this black-skinned giant was going to slip into Morrowtown unnoticed. Just thinking about Freeman trying to be inconspicuous made the long ride pass more quickly.

The townspeople may have grown accustomed to Marines, but the sight of Freeman sent them running. People hurried out of our way as we walked through the streets. When we got to the gambling house, we found it locked tight. "Do you think anyone is in there?" Freeman asked.

It was late in the afternoon, but Guttman usually played well into the evening. "I don't know," I said.

"Good enough for me," Freeman replied. He drew an oversized particle-beam pistol from his belt and aimed it at the door. Without warning, he fired a sparkling green beam at the door, which disappeared behind a cloud of smoke and sparks. Then, lifting a massive boot, he kicked the smoldering remains out of the doorway.

"We could have knocked," I said.

Freeman did not answer as he disappeared into the smoke.

Kline had struck me as somewhat timid the first time I saw him. On this occasion, he went from timid to terrified. As I stepped through the doorway, I saw him standing beside the liquor bar inside the foyer, the same place he had been standing the time I came with Guttman.

Looking both scared and surprised, Kline stared unblinkingly at the remains of the door, then raised his hands in the air to show that he held no weapons. His gaze shifted in our direction, and he said, "May I help you?"

Freeman walked over to Kline and placed the photograph of Crowley on the bar. "We're looking for this man."

Kline looked down at the photograph and studied it for a minute. "He came in a month ago. That was the only time I ever saw him."

"What do you remember about him?" Freeman asked.

"He played a few hands and left; that's all I know," Kline said, trying to sound casual.

"Maybe this will jog your memory," Freeman said, pulling out his pistol and pressing its muzzle into the fleshy area between Kline's eyes.

Kline's eyes crossed as they looked up the barrel, but he remained composed. "I think he came here looking for soldiers. He asked me if any of the Marines from the base were coming and offered me $100 to let him join the game." Kline's voice trembled, but only slightly. Considering the size of the pistol pressed against his head and the damage that pistol had done to his door, I thought Kline remained amazingly calm.

"Anything else?" Freeman asked.

"That's everything," Kline said.

Never shifting his gaze from Kline's face, Freeman placed his pistol on the bar. He did so very gently, taking great care not to scratch the finish. Then he reached into a pocket below his chestplate. After fishing around for a moment, he removed a small silver tube.

"Your name is Kline, is that right?"

"Yes," Kline said, staring at the tube.

"Do you know how to kill ants, Mr. Kline?"

"By stepping on them?" Kline asked.

"Yes, you can kill one ant that way, but I mean a whole hill of ants."

Kline shook his head.

"You poison one ant with something slow and highly toxic. Kill it too fast, say, by stepping on it or using a fast poison, and all you have is a dead ant. But if you use the right poison, something that works real slow, that ant will infect his entire colony."

"Is that poison?" Kline asked.

"No, sir," Freeman said, shaking his head. "Just a little Super Glue." He pushed one of Kline's hands down on the bar with the palm up. Kline tried to close his fingers; but when Freeman squeezed his wrist, the hand fell open. "Now you keep that hand right there, right like that, Mr. Kline."

Freeman pulled the eyedropper out of the tube and

squeezed, forcing several drops of clear white liquid to ooze onto Kline's trembling palm. "See, that didn't hurt. A little glue won't hurt you."

Kline sighed with relief.

"Now this, this could hurt you." Freeman pulled something that looked like a lime from his pocket and pressed it into Kline's freshly glued hand.

Kline was no soldier, but he recognized the grenade the moment he saw it. "What are you doing?"

Freeman closed Kline's fingers around the grenade and held them shut as he quietly counted to sixty. When he released Kline's fingers, he wiggled the grenade to make sure the glue held fast. Then he pulled the pin from the grenade. "Ever seen one of these?"

Kline was speechless.

"This is a grenade. A high-yield grenade will take out a full city block. This here is a low-yield grenade. Small ones like this aren't nearly so bad. It might only destroy a couple of buildings."

"I see," Kline said, his composure gone.

"I made this one just for situations like this," Freeman continued. "This grenade senses body heat. As long as there are no temperature fluctuations, you'll be perfectly safe. You might want to use your other hand when you grab ice out of that freezer over there. Freezing air would set it off for sure. Don't pry the grenade from your palm. A change in temperature like that'll set it off, too. You wouldn't want to hit it with a hammer or drill into it, either."

"I see," said Kline.

"See that hole where I took the pin? If anything goes in that hole except this exact pin, that grenade will explode. Don't stick anything in that hole. You understand?"

"Yes," Kline stuttered.

"You might lose some skin when I pry the grenade out of your hand."

"When?" Kline asked.

"Think you can remember all that?" Freeman asked, ignoring the question.

"When will you take it?" Kline responded.

"The grenade is set to explode in forty-eight hours,"

Freeman said. "If I don't see you before then, I guess you can keep it."

Kline's generally nonplussed facade melted, and his lips pulled back into a grimace. "But . . . but how will I find you? Why are you doing this?"

"We'll call this an incentive, Mr. Kline. I think you know more information than you are telling me," Freeman said.

Kline looked at me for help, but only for a moment. "How will I find you?"

"I'll be at the Marine base, Mr. Kline. You come down and visit me if you remember something. But don't wait too long. Don't show up in forty-seven hours and fifty-nine minutes because I won't want to talk to you." With that, Freeman packed up his picture of Crowley and his gigantic pistol. He screwed the cover back on the tube and started for the door. I followed.

"What makes you so sure he's hiding something?" I asked, as we stepped out onto the empty street.

Freeman did not answer. Having reverted to his silent self, he walked to the next building. "Stop here," he said, ignoring my question.

The air was hot and dry. Since I was not wearing my climate-controlled bodysuit, the early evening felt like an oven. The sun started to set, and the sky above Morrowtown filled with crimson-and-orange clouds. The buildings, mostly two- and three-story sandstone structures, took on a particularly gloomy look in the dying daylight. Lights shone in some nearby windows. Freeman's khaki-colored clothes looked gray in the growing darkness.

"How do you know Kline is hiding something?" I asked again.

"I'm not sure he is," Freeman said. "I want to track him if he leaves town."

"In case he goes to warn Crowley?" I asked.

Freeman did not answer.

"So that wasn't a grenade? It was just a tracking device?" Suddenly Freeman seemed almost human. I laughed, remembering Kline's terrified expression.

"No, that was a homemade grenade. I placed a radioactive tracking filament inside the glue."

I did not see the point in gluing a grenade to Kline's hand. I believed him when he said that he did not know anything.

Despite his lack of social skills, Freeman knew how to read people. Moments after we left the bar, Kline popped his head out of the door. He spotted us and jogged over, carefully cradling his left hand, the one with the grenade, as if he were holding an infant.

"You won't leave Gobi?" Kline asked.

"Do you remember something?" I asked.

"No," he said, shaking his head but never taking his eyes off Freeman.

"I'll be at the base," Freeman said in his rumbling voice.

Freeman turned and walked toward the truck. I followed. "Do you think he is a spy of some sort?" I asked quietly.

"I don't trust him," Freeman said.

Freeman and I did not speak to each other during the drive back to base, but the silence did not bother me this time. He sat very still, his eyes forming sharp slits as he surveyed the moonlit landscape.

Perhaps I was slow. We were nearly back to Gobi Station before I realized that Freeman was looking for enemies. For all we knew, Crowley had an entire army on the planet, and he could easily ambush us on our way back to the fort. A lone soldier and a mercenary would not stand much of a chance in an ambush, but Freeman, well armed and always watchful, would not go down so easily.

If we drove past any enemies that night, they did not make a move. Except for the hollow cry of distant lizards scurrying along some far-off dune, I never saw any signs of life.

Gobi Station might have been the grandest building on the entire planet. Several times larger than any building in Morrowtown, the outpost had huge sandstone walls lined with columns and arches. A domed roof covered each corner of the structure. The first settlers on Gobi were probably Moslem—Gobi Station had a Moorish look about it. The outpost's sturdy walls and thick ramparts made for a good fortress. The yellow light of our poorly powered lanterns poured out from the outpost's arches and reflected on the gold-leafed domes. As we drove toward the motor pool, I felt warm relief in the pit of my stomach. We parked the truck, and I returned to my cell to sleep. Freeman headed toward Gutterwash Godfrey's office. I suppose he wanted to report to Vice Admiral Brocius.

Taj Guttman met me at the door of the barracks. At night, he wore a long, white robe that he cinched with a belt around his gelatinous stomach. The belt looked equatorial. "What happened in town?"

"Not much," I said, pulling off my shirt. I walked into my cell hoping to get away from Guttman. He followed. Trying to ignore him, I dropped my pants.

"Did you find Crowley?"

"No, but Freeman made quite an impression on Kline. That Freeman is a real prick. He glued a grenade to Kline's hand."

"He what?" Guttman sounded shocked. He made a whistling noise. "So do you think I'm going to get in trouble?"

"I don't think Freeman cares about you. I don't think he cares about anybody. Just stay out of his way. You'll be okay unless he decides to shoot you."

CHAPTER
THREE

Kline had a secret, and Freeman must have figured it out. Working with subtle clues that escaped my attention, Freeman pieced that secret together and shared it only with Admiral Brocius, leaving the rest of us unprepared.

Looking back, I should have seen it coming. A stockpile of military-grade weapons in a tiny garrison would be too easy a prize for a struggling army of traitors to ignore. Judging by Guttman and the other men who went into town, Crowley would expect little resistance if he attacked Gobi Station. Who knew how long he had had our base under surveillance. He had probably known our numbers, might even have been watching when Ray Freeman landed. Freeman's arrival probably worked like a catalyst, spurring Crowley to act sooner than he had intended.

Freeman knew that someone like General Crowley would not come to a backwater planet like Gobi for no reason. If Crowley was here and weapons were here, Crowley undoubtedly wanted the weapons. Freeman didn't share this useful information, however, because he had come on a bounty-hunting expedition and wanted to capture Crowley. If he had warned us, we would have prepared for the attack and Crowley would have seen us mounting guns and sending out patrols. He might have tried to flee the planet, and Freeman did not want that. Freeman had sized up the situation and decided to offer up my platoon as bait.

Crowley made his move the following morning. It started with a single explosion that shattered the silence and shook the desert like cracking thunder. The explosion came from the north side of the base, rattling the outpost's massive walls.

I jumped from my bed and looked out a window in time to see the last remnants of an enormous fireball dissolving into the sunrise. The bomb had demolished Ray Freeman's ship, cutting off our only escape route and destroying our only hope of air support.

Silence followed.

For the next ten seconds, the Gobi desert returned to its peaceful self. A burned red sunrise filled the horizon as the echo of the explosion rolled across the desert. I felt the last of the evening breeze through my window as I turned to throw on my armor. It took me less than thirty seconds to slip on my armor and helmet. I snapped the rifle stock on my M27 and exited my cell. Rickman came running from his cell and the others followed, including Taj Guttman, with his helmet stuck to the top of his head like a hat.

Their armor still worked. The smart-lenses in my visor registered signals transmitted by the other Marines' armor. When I looked at Rickman, Sarris, and Guttman, a computer in my helmet picked up signals from their armor and displayed their names and ranks in red letters. I heard several of the men asking questions over the interLink.

"What the hell was that?" Rickman shouted above the noise. Before I could tell Rickman about seeing the fireball, Sergeant Godfrey leaped down the stairs to join us.

"Everybody up top. Cover the entrances," Godfrey yelled. He carried a particle-beam pistol in his hand and used it to point up the stairs. I could hear men hyperventilating as they ran up and realized that I was about to go to battle with men who no longer had soldiering in their blood.

As we reached the top of the barracks, a rocket struck just

outside the arched entrance. A cloud of dust and smoke filled the open-air hallway leading to the main gate.

"I see them," one man shouted, firing wildly through an outer window.

I looked over his shoulder, but did not see anything. Even when I scanned the area using the heat-vision lens in my visor, I saw nothing, though the smoke and flames from the explosion almost certainly distorted my view.

Switching back to standard combat vision, I peered through the thinning dust cloud. A ring of small fires still burned around the ten-meter-wide hole that the rocket had left in our walkway. Constructed of massive sandstone blocks, the outpost could withstand gunfire, but not rocket attacks.

Looking at the jagged remains of the hall and hearing the chaotic chatter of the Marines around me, I did not feel scared or confused. I felt soothed. That must sound odd. It was the same feeling I have when I eat a favorite food or hear a familiar song. The world seemed to slow down, and my thoughts became clearer. It felt good. Everything around me was chaos, but I felt happy. It had never happened to me during the simulations back at the orphanage or during basic. If that was how it felt to be in a real combat situation, I didn't mind it.

"Sarris, Mervin, Phillips. Secure the main hall." Godfrey shouted orders over the interLink. Without so much as a moment's hesitation, three Marines pulled their pistols and charged down that shattered hallway. Automatic fire struck Sarris as he left the cover of the barracks. The first shot banked off the back of his shoulder plates, spitting chips of armor. Two more shots struck his head, shattering his helmet and spraying blood and brains in the air. He twisted and fell to the ground. Mervin and Phillips ran past him and sprinted through a volley of bullets and laser fire.

"Harris, go with them," Godfrey yelled.

Clones like Sarris reacted to orders by reflex, but I needed a moment. "Move out!" Godfrey shouted again, as I reached the door. I leaped over Sarris, landed on a layer of grit and debris, and slid, almost falling over. Bullets ricocheted off the walls around me. Clutching my gun close to my chest, I ran toward the crumbling ledge where the rocket had blasted through the walkway.

A few feet ahead of me, Mervin lay on the ground beside the shredded wall. He had been shot in the head and part of his helmet and visor littered the ground around him. I saw the singed skin and one brown eye, crazy with fear, staring at me.

"Harris, what are you doing?" Godfrey snapped. "What are you waiting for?"

"Mervin's alive," I said.

Rockets had destroyed the promenade around Mervin. I could not get to him without exposing myself. Judging by the way they hit Sarris and Mervin, Crowley had a dead-eye-dick sniper out there. I dropped to my stomach and pulled myself forward.

"Forget Mervin," Godfrey screamed. "I want that side of the base secured. Do you understand me?"

"I can get him out of here," I said.

Someone shot at me. A slug passed just over my back and tore into the wall behind. Rubble showered my head and shoulders.

"I gave you an order," Godfrey yelled.

Just then, I heard a hissing sound that I recognized at once. Rolling to one side, I hid behind a pile of rubble as a rocket slammed into the remains of the walkway about thirty feet ahead of me. My visor instantly polarized, shielding my eyes from the blinding flash.

Already weakened from the first blast, the breezeway collapsed. My armor protected me from shrapnel and flying fragments of sandstone as I fell amidst the rubble. I landed on my stomach, crushing the air out of my lungs.

"Harris. Harris!" Godfrey's voice rang in my ears, but I could not suck enough air into my lungs to answer.

"Damn," Godfrey said, but his grieving did not last long. "Phillips get to my office and contact Fleet Command. We need reinforcements, and now." Why Godfrey would ask for reinforcements from a fleet that was thousands of light-years away was beyond me.

I rolled from side to side, trying to draw air in my lungs and find the strength to stand. My back ached. My chest burned. My helmet protected my head from damage, not from pain. As I squirmed to lie on my side, my vision cleared. I saw the words "Theo Mervin, Private, First Class" superimposed over the cloud of dust to my right. As the air settled, I saw a pile of blocks and shattered tiles. A long crossbeam that must have weighed multiple tons stuck out of the top of the pile at a nearly straight angle. The top of Mervin's shattered helmet peeked out from beneath it.

The avalanche had dumped me in the courtyard. Kneeling, still dizzy from the blast and winded from the fall, I peered over the waist-high ruins of the outer wall. Increasing the magnification in my visor, I scanned the desert and saw four figures crouched along a distant ridge—three men in camouflaged fatigues and Kline, who had not changed out of his black-and-white card dealer's outfit. He still had that grenade glued to his hand. Clearly, Kline had not come to fight. He came to scavenge.

As Freeman had suspected, the grenade had worked like a catalyst, forcing Crowley to attack. If Kline had ever wondered whether or not to join forces with Crowley, Freeman's grenade had surely made the decision for him. There he was, watching the action, hoping to find the key on Ray Freeman's dead body and disarm the grenade.

"Harris?" Godfrey asked, likely having spotted me from a barracks window. "Harris, report."

"Just a little shook up," I said.

"Not your condition, you idiot," Godfrey said. "What do you see?"

"I see some of them . . . Four of them, a hundred thirty yards out." A tool in my visor measured the distance.

"There are three more a few yards to the east," Ray Freeman interrupted.

"I don't see . . . No, there they are. He's right." They wore sand-colored camouflage suits. Even after increasing the magnification in my visor, I did not know how Freeman had spotted them. There they were—Crowley and two other men standing around a table with a map and some kind of control console. Seeing the console explained a lot. Crowley hadn't come with an army, he'd come with trackers—motion-tracking robots that registered movement in a designated area and fired at that movement with incredible accuracy. Shaped like a barber pole, with radar equipment crammed into the ball at the top, one of these single-task devices cost almost nothing to build and could be used to fire anything from pistols to rockets.

"He's got trackers," I called out to Godfrey. "I can't see them, but I can see the control console."

"He has six trackers," said Freeman. "Four guarding the front wall of the base, one on the west, and one on the east."

"You're sure about that count?" I asked.

"Crowley has twenty men watching the west wall of the base," Freeman continued, "and ten to the east."

"Where are you, Freeman?" Godfrey asked. "Are you near the armory?"

Freeman did not answer.

"What is your position?" Godfrey repeated. What he should have asked was how the hell Freeman had tapped into our communications. The interLink was supposedly secure from civilian interference.

Freeman did not care about Gobi Station, defending the Republic, or protecting its Marines. Wherever he had hidden himself, he did not plan to go down with a platoon of clones. He was, after all, a mercenary, not a soldier. As far as I could tell, the only things he cared about were staying alive and capturing Crowley.

"Dammit! Where are you, Freeman?" Godfrey demanded.

Freeman said nothing.

"Do you have a clean shot at them?" Godfrey asked.

Still no answer.

I started to shuffle along the wall to get a better look at Crowley's position.

"Do not move, Harris," Freeman said.

"I see movement out the main gate," Rickman broke in.

Peering over the wall, I saw three Marines run toward a heap of rocks and dive behind it. They moved so quickly that I did not have a chance to scan their names. Two of the men took cover behind the massive front arch of the outpost and fired. They fired six quick shots, to which Crowley's men responded with a token spray of automatic fire.

"What the hell are you doing?" I screamed into the

interLink. The arch would offer protection from bullets, but a particle beam or a rocket would reduce it to rubble.

"Get your men out of there," Freeman said. But he was too late. The top of a tracker popped up from behind a sand dune; and before anyone could react, two rockets came flying toward the arch. At first I only saw the contrails, then a bright flash bleached the air around the arch where the men were hiding. The entire desert rumbled with reverberation. Rock chips and large chunks of pillars flew across the courtyard. A fist-sized stone struck my helmet. Adding to the cacophony, the domed roof of the main hall caved in. As the smoke and dust cleared, the jagged remains of the arch poked out of the ground in haphazard spikes. The rockets had destroyed the entrance and much of the main hall. From where I stood, I could look directly into Glan Godfrey's office. A huge block had fallen from the roof and crushed his desk, and I saw no sign of the communications console, our link to the outside world. Godfrey tried to raise Rickman and Phillips on his interLink, but no one responded.

"Harris, get to the armory," Godfrey said.

The armory was in the far corner of the base, just beyond the office. That last rocket had smashed most of the building, but the doorway to the armory remained standing. I started across the courtyard, cutting through the shallow edges around the stagnant pond area of the courtyard.

"Harris, stop," Freeman's voice shouted through the audio piece in my helmet. "Those trackers have you. Check for scanners with your radar sensors."

For a civilian, Ray Freeman seemed to have an incredible amount of information about Marine Corp combat armor. Our helmets included a sensor warning system that detected radar devices. I should have switched on the sensor the moment I knew there were trackers outside the wall.

I ran the scan and froze in midstep, still standing in the shallows of that polluted brackish pond. A blue ring appeared around the edges of my visor as the sensor kicked in. The ring remained blue for a moment, then turned yellow, then orange. The trackers were bathing the courtyard with radar, and they could only be looking for me. If the ring in my visor turned red, it meant that the sensors had fixed on my location. Orange meant they had detected me, but I had stopped moving before they could fire. A strong wind blew across the courtyard, shaking some reeds, and the ring around my visor turned yellow momentarily as the trackers homed in on the reeds. I dropped to the ground and felt my knees sink into the mud. My only hope was that the trackers would not notice me.

Moments passed slowly. In the air-conditioned comfort of my helmet, I felt both an odd elation and fear. Large drops of sweat rolled down the sides of my face, but kneeling in the mud and the reeds with trackers searching to find me, I felt strangely relaxed. I listened for the hiss of incoming rockets as the seconds passed and the ring in my visor fluctuated from yellow to orange and back to yellow again. It never turned blue or red.

"Harris, get to the armory," Godfrey yelled.

"Crowley doesn't care about the armory," Freeman said. "He wants the barracks." And Godfrey must have understood. Crowley wanted to keep the platoon bottled up in one place where he could hit it without risk of destroying the weapons he had come to steal.

"We need to attack," Freeman said.

"Are you insane?" Godfrey asked. "Harris, either get to the armory or get your ass back to the barracks."

They haven't located Freeman and they have me pinned down in the courtyard, I thought as I peered out through the reeds. *Everybody else is right where Crowley wants them.*

"Godfrey, you can't hide in the barracks," Freeman said. "You're playing into his hands."

"Harris, get over here," Godfrey ordered. "We'll cover you."

"Freeman, got any suggestions?" I asked.

Enemies around the west and north walls fired into the courtyard. Poorly aimed, possibly not aimed at all, their bullets chipped into the sandstone wall, making sparks and dust. They must have been hoping to coax me into running back to the barracks or returning fire.

"Make a break for the northeast corner," Freeman said.

I looked across the yard toward the northeast corner of

the outpost—the nearly disintegrated northeast corner where Rickman and Phillips had made their stand. The rockets had destroyed Phillips so thoroughly that his armor did not even register. "You're shitting me, right?" I asked, as I squeezed the rifle stock against my chest and prepared to run.

"I'll take care of the trackers," Freeman answered.

"You have a shot at them?" I asked. Even as I spoke, someone fired a spray of bullets along the wall behind me.

"Are you listening, Harris?" Godfrey piped in. "Get your ass over here."

"Leave them to me," Freeman said. "Move on the count of three."

"Got it," I said.

"It's your court-martial," Godfrey said.

"Get specked," I answered.

"One."

Some kind of strange creature shot into the air along the southeast corner of the outpost. I did not see it clearly, but it looked something like a giant flying snake as it jumped nearly thirty feet in the air, then darted behind a wall.

"Two."

Whatever Freeman had unleashed, it distracted the trackers. The ring around my visors went blue. I heard the hiss of rockets, but they flew well over my head and slammed into a wall along the back of the courtyard. In the wake of the explosion, a large rock slammed across the top of my helmet, almost knocking me senseless.

Three.

I did not hear Freeman count that last number. The impact of the rock hitting my helmet must have disabled my interLink circuit. In the echoing silence, I climbed to my feet and sprinted. Ahead of me, I saw Freeman leap to the top of a huge pile of rubble. He fired a grenade launcher toward the trackers, turned, then slid back down the mound for cover as men outside the outpost answered him with a hail of bullets. The shock wave of Freeman's grenade knocked me slightly off course. No one fired at me, and the sensor rings in my helmet remained blue. I dived headlong and joined him behind the rubble.

"Crowley has already left," Freeman said, as I sat up and pulled off my helmet.

"How do you know?" Using my rifle stock as a crutch, I pushed myself up and peered over the rubble. I saw nothing but open desert.

Freeman handed me a palm-top computer display that showed Gobi Station and the surrounding landscape. Freeman had either established a link with some satellite tracking our area or placed cameras around the outside of the base. The northern and western walls were ruins. The display showed people as small white ovals.

"You placed sensors?"

"Two days ago," Freeman said.

"You only flew in yesterday morning," I said.

"Don't you ever wake up?" Freeman asked. "I've been on this damned planet for three days now . . . came quietly with a second ship in tow. The one they hit was a decoy; my real ship is down there," Freeman said, nodding toward the canyon behind our base. "I can take you in the hold as far as the next outpost."

"I can't leave Gobi," I said.

"Have it your way." Freeman laughed and flashed a toothy smile. "Don't suppose you would cover me while I make a run for my ship."

"I suppose not," I said.

"The ship has missiles and a chain gun," Freeman said. "Help me get to my ship, and I'll fix this."

"I don't trust you," I said. I tried to peer around the rubble to get a look at the enemy. Somebody fired a wild shot that hit several feet wide of me.

"They're moving south. They will leave a few men to keep us pinned down while the rest of their force flanks the barracks," Freeman said, pointing at his display. "Godfrey could take them if he had any brains."

"He won't," I agreed.

A small trickle of blood ran down the side of Freeman's bald head. He didn't bother with helmets or battle gear other than the chestplate that was built into his fatigues. He placed one foot on a partially destroyed sandstone block and unloaded the grenade launcher he kept slung over his shoulder. He must have known that I did not trust him, but he also knew that I was trapped. I could either help him escape or pull him down with me.

"What do you have in mind?" I asked.

"They're gathering around the barracks." Freeman handed me his computer. Even as I watched, the little ovals representing Crowley's men moved toward the ridges along the barracks. "You storm them here, and I'll go get the ship."

"There are five men there," I pointed out.

Freeman took back his palm display and said nothing.

"Take out five men armed with a pistol?"

"How busted is your helmet?" Freeman asked.

"The sound is out," I said.

"Does the polarizing lens still work?" he asked.

"I don't know," I said placing the helmet over my head. The nonfunctioning interLink turned the inside of my helmet into an echo chamber. Using a few optical commands, I ran a diagnostic. "It works," I said, removing the helmet again.

No sooner had I said this than the strange flying animal that had distracted the trackers popped up from behind the far wall of the base. It skirted the top of the wall and dropped to the ground, traveling through the swamp and reeds. Only it wasn't an animal. It was a service drone that Freeman controlled with a small remote.

Dragging a ten-foot train of shimmering brown cloth behind it, the drone snaked toward us and stopped. Freeman unclipped the thermal blanket he had tied around it and attached a thin silver disc. "You'll want to cover your eyes in a moment," Freeman said.

Replacing my helmet, I watched the little drone pick its way through the debris that had once been the outpost's massive front wall. The drone zigged around broken pillars and scrambled through a large pipe. It disappeared behind the wall, but I could still see it on Freeman's readout as it approached the terrorists' bunker.

If Crowley's men saw it coming, they didn't seem to care. When the drone got within fifty feet of their location, the little sphere exploded in a chemical flash so bright that it drowned out the desert sun.

"Go!" Freeman yelled, and he slapped my helmet to make sure that I had heard him.

Even looking through polarizing lenses, I could barely see. The Gobi landscape looked faded and white. I felt as if I had been staring into the sun. Running half-blind, I did not see the knee-high ridge left from the broken wall. The toe of my boot jammed into the remains of a heavy sandstone block, and I lurched forward but managed to regain my balance without falling.

Over the top of the sand dune I saw three of Crowley's men squirming on the ground rubbing their eyes with both hands. One of the men heard me coming and patted the ground around him until he found a gun. He squinted as he aimed at the sound of my footfalls. I squeezed off two rounds hitting him in the face and chest. One of his friends screamed, "What happened?" I shot him and the other man.

Two of Crowley's soldiers had seen the drone coming and shielded their eyes at the last moment. They had sprung from their hiding place and chased Ray Freeman as he ran toward his ship. Taking less than a second to aim, I hit one of them in the shoulder from over a hundred yards away. He spun and fell. His friend skidded to a stop and turned to look for me. I fired a shot, hitting him in the face.

Freeman's ship must not have been hidden very far away. Moments after he disappeared over the edge of the canyon, a small spaceworthy flier that looked like a cross between a bomber and transport rose into the air. Unlike the barge that Freeman had used as a decoy, the ship was immaculate, with rows of dull white armor lining its bulky, oblong hull. Gun and missile arrays studded its wings. From where I stood, I had a clear view of the cockpit, but the glass was mirror-tinted and I could not see in. The ship hovered over me for a few moments, then launched across the desert in the direction of Morrowtown.

At first I thought Freeman had abandoned the base, but then he doubled back toward the barracks. I could see some of the guns along the wings glinting as I ran to view the fight. There was no hurry, however. Crowley's men were not prepared to fight a ship like Freeman's.

Its titanium-barreled chain guns made one continuous flash as they spent hundreds of bullets per second. Some of the guerillas tried to escape, but there was no escape, not from Freeman. Two men lunged into an armored truck. Before they could get the vehicle moving, he fired a missile that reduced it to flames and twisted metal. Freeman sprayed a dune with that chain gun, churning up sprays of blood and sand. When he finished, shreds of smoldering cloth floated in the air like autumn leaves. The only man left standing was Kline.

"Bastards!" Kline shrieked in his thick accent as I approached him. "You bastards! Are you going to kill me, too?"

Kline still cradled the grenade with both hands. His clothes were spattered and dripping with blood, none of it his own. He looked down at the pulverized remains of his allies. "Oh . . . goddamn . . ." he muttered.

Freeman hovered over the dune and landed his ship in a rippling heat cloud. He climbed out and came over to inspect his work. In the distance, Godfrey emerged from the barracks and started toward us.

Freeman stared at Kline with disgust. "Go," he said.

Kline looked down at his hand, then held the grenade out for Freeman. "Please?"

"Keep it," Freeman said. He turned his back on Kline and walked away. Kline cradled the grenade against his chest as he staggered into the desert. I didn't know if he would die of thirst or be blown to pieces, and I tried not to care. That useless moron had tried to sell my platoon for the slaughter, I told myself. But when he paused and looked back in what seemed like a plea for help, I felt a sharp pang of guilt. A moment later, he disappeared over a dune.

Any sympathy I might have felt for Kline disappeared when Godfrey uncovered a stockpile of gas canisters. Hoping to kill the platoon and leave the weapons intact, Crowley had brought three canisters of Noxium gas. Once he'd herded the Marines back into the barracks, he must have planned to fire the canisters into the building.

Readily available around the territories, Noxium acted like a gas, but it was really a microscopic life-form that was stored and used like lethal gas. It was really a swarm of particle-sized organisms that attacked living tissue. Upon release from a vacuum canister, the creatures would bore into anything that breathed. They were small enough to slip through combat armor and chew through flesh so quickly that it seemed to dissolve in their wake. Terrorists liked Noxium gas because it was cheap, easily stored, and cruel.

Admiral Brocius never came to Gobi, but he sent an envoy, Captain James Troy. Troy, with a small army, landed three days after the action ended. He sent troops to search Morrowtown, but he personally never left the safety of his ship.

One at a time, Troy called us all into his ship for ten-minute debriefings. He met with Glan Godfrey first, then detained him as he met with the other survivors. Freeman and I were the last men called in.

I walked over to where he was standing, and said, "You're going to be a hero, Freeman. You saved a platoon."

He smiled for a moment. It was the first time I had seen any emotion from him. "It won't come down like that. All Brocius cares about is that Crowley got away."

Godfrey appeared in the door of the ship wearing his faded uniform. He must have lost a lot of weight in his years on Gobi; you could not even see the shapes of his legs in his pants. "Think they'll leave him in charge?" I asked Freeman.

"Probably," Freeman croaked in that low rumbling voice. "After Gobi, life in a military prison would be a promotion."

"How about me?" I asked.

"You'll be the hero," Freeman said, with a bitter edge in his voice. "They don't want to talk about some mercenary saving the day. Harris, you never belonged on this planet in the first place. There are people watching over you."

I started to ask what that meant, but Godfrey called us over. He led us into Troy's flagship.

Freeman had not dressed for the occasion. He wore the same ugly jumpsuit. I suspected he would wear those clothes if he were invited to meet with God. As for me, I wore the Charley Service uniform I had worn when I first landed on Gobi. Except for some nicks from the fireworks, I looked precisely as I had when I landed on that godforsaken planet.

Troy sat behind a large black desk that shone like a mirror. The Cygnus Fleet seal hung on the wall behind him, just above a cluster of flags. He did not stand as we entered, but studied us with indifference. "You are the mercenary?" he asked. "Freeman, is it?"

Freeman nodded.

"I suppose you expect payment," Troy said. "As I understand it, you were hired to capture Amos Crowley."

Freeman said nothing. His face betrayed no emotion.

"Sergeant Godfrey says you routed the terrorists," Troy said. He glared back at Godfrey, who looked quite pale. "I can't imagine why we would pay you good money for saving this sorry pack. As I understand it, Admiral Brocius offered you twenty-five thousand dollars for capturing Crowley. You may continue your manhunt."

Freeman did not say anything.

By that time, I had a good idea about how Freeman's mind worked. The captain undoubtedly angered him, but Freeman would never give him the satisfaction of seeing that anger.

Troy leaned back in his chair. "You are dismissed, Freeman."

Freeman turned and left without a word. Standing at attention, I could not turn to watch him leave. I listened to his heavy boots as he trudged toward the boarding ramp. The room seemed to become cooler once Freeman left.

Troy turned to me, then pulled a piece of paper from his desk. After studying his notes, he said, "And you are?"

"PFC Harris, sir," I said.

"Harris. I understand that you are the only man on this planet who knows his ass from his knees. Sergeant Godfrey said that you ignored orders that would have resulted in the deaths of every man in the platoon. You are hereby promoted to the rank of corporal. I recommended giving you command of Gobi Station, but Admiral Brocius wants you transferred out."

* * *

Years later I had the chance to read my record and discovered that my promotion was based on misinformation. Whether he did it on purpose or he just did not know differently, Troy exaggerated my role in the battle. He said that I rushed an enemy gun emplacement, which was true, but he neglected to mention Freeman's role in the assault.

Unified Authority society was based on two documents—
the U.S. Constitution and the third book of Plato's *Republic*.
Two strata of U.A. society, the ruling class and the citizenry,
resembled life in the old United States. The third layer, "the
military class," was taken from Plato's three-tiered society
of rulers, warriors, and citizens.

The Unified Authority's government was a synthesis.
The U.S. Constitution called for a three-branch representative government with an executive branch, a judicial branch,
and a legislative branch. The framers of the U.A. Constitution kept the judicial branch of the former United States
intact, swallowing it whole into their government without
a single alteration. The political branches, however, were
greatly altered. Plato, that ancient sage, considered democ-
racy little more than rule by a mob and blamed it for the
death of Socrates, his mentor. That view suited the designers
of the United Authority, who, having conquered the rest of
the globe, did not relish giving every citizen an equal voice.
In the U.A.'s case, thesis and antithesis merged to create a
plutocracy.

In a nod to tradition, the Unified Authority retained its
capital along the eastern seaboard of the former United

States. It was the seat of all galactic politics and the home of all three branches of the federal government. It was also the home of the only voters that carried any authority. With it was the concession that progovernment historians might one day call "the great compromise" and the opponents "the beginnings of tyranny."

The Senate, clearly the most powerful political body in the Unified Authority, was not composed of members who were elected by popular vote. The House of Representatives, a far less powerful assembly, was. Analysts referred to the two chambers of the legislative branch as "the power and the politics." "The politics" was the House of Representatives, an odd assembly of legislators who truly represented their constituents back in the frontier worlds. "The power" was the Senate, an august body of lawmakers who had grown up among the population that Plato would have referred to as "the ruling class," the elite population of Washington, DC. Senators were not elected, they were appointed by the Linear Committee—which was the executive branch of the government. New senators were selected from a pool of well-groomed tenth-generation politicians living in the capital city—men and women who had attended elite schools.

The executive branch of the government was even more select. Called the "Linear Committee," this branch was made up of five senior senators. Analysts complained about the exclusive nature of this particular club. Looking back, I would have to agree. Only the Linear Committee could appoint new senators, and the Senate chose the members of the Linear Committee from among its ranks. I once read an article in which an author called the system "Royalty Reborn!" In that same article, she proclaimed, "America has finally attained a royal class." I do not know who that author writes for, but I have never seen her writings again.

In theory, the Senate ruled the Republic and the House was filled with figureheads. In truth, the House enjoyed so much popular support from the frontier states that a clever congressman could cause havoc.

Looking back, I can see why the Senate was so unpopular. The galactic seat was benevolent, so long as the member states did not openly challenge it. The individual planets could govern themselves as they wished, set up whatever sort of economies and industries they wished, and even create their own militias. What they could not do was break ranks from the Union. Any hint of sedition was dealt with harshly. As long as member states were seen as loyal to the capital, they had nothing to fear.

Along with the ruling class, Earth was home to the "warrior class." Washington eyed the growing power of the military with a wary eye; but as the Republic pushed deeper into the galaxy, Congress needed a strong arm to maintain order and protect the territories from external threats. Synthetic soldiers were deemed both more manageable and expendable than natural men, so Congress opted for an army of carefully engineered clones. That lent itself well to Plato's view of the military as a class of persons who would never know any life other than that of a soldier.

I think Plato would have approved of neural programming had it existed in his day. Through neural programming, U.A. scientists implanted algorithms into their soldiers' brains like code on a computer chip. Generals and politicians collaborated on the cloning project, hammering out the perfect specimen—soldiers who respected authority and who were strong, patriotic, and ignorant of their origins.

Once Congress and the Joint Chiefs had a mix they liked, they set the oven to mass production, cranking out an average of 1.2 million new fighting men every year. Of course, the soldiers did not come out of the vat fully formed. They needed to be raised, formed in the U.A. military's own image, and indoctrinated with the belief that God charged man to rule the galaxy.

Earth became the military-processing center, home to six hundred all-male orphanages, each of which graduated nearly two thousand combat-ready orphans per year. The orphanages were little more than clone incubators, though real orphans, like me, were sometimes brought in from the frontier.

We were the flatfoots, the conscripts. No clone or orphan ever reached officer status. The most we could hope for was sergeant. With the exception of some natural-born implants from frontier families, officers came from the ruling class. Children of politicians who did poorly in school or lacked "refinement" were shunted off to Officer Training School in Australia, a land that was originally settled as a penal colony. How ironic.

With three days of liberty before my transfer to the Scutum-Crux Fleet, I decided to visit the only home I'd ever known—Unified Authority Orphanage #553. That may sound dull or sentimental . . . maybe it was. I did not understand the concept of vacationing. They did not explain the concept to us in the orphanage or in basic. So with a few free days and a new promotion, I decided to go home and show the second triangle over my shoulder off to my instructors.

Located deep in the Olympic Mountains near North America's northwest coast, #553 sat between evergreen forests and a major waterway known as the Straits of Juan de Fuca. My home was a brick-and-steel campus with a five-acre firing range, a dome-covered parade ground, and a white picket fence. It was there that I spent my youth drilling, playing, and never wondering why my classmates all looked alike.

An "entrance by permit" sign hung over the main gate of the orphanage. I ran my identity card through a reader and the automatic gate slid open, revealing the long dirt road that led to the school. This was the veil, the hedge that separated the boys from the world. The ancients thought the world was flat, and the boys of #553 thought it ended outside the automatic gate.

Walking along the road, avoiding puddles, and surveying the woods, I let my mind wander until I reached the campus itself. In the distance, I saw dormitory buildings. Home. The road stopped at the door of the administrative area—a complex of red brick buildings surrounded by a beautiful meadow. Five- and six-year-old kids, all boys and all with the same broad face and brown hair, wrestled on the wet grass. The government maintained orphanages for girls, but they were on frontier planets.

Two boys paused to stare at me as I opened the gate. They studied my uniform, noting that I had two stripes on my sleeve, not just the single stripe of a private. "Are you a

Marine?" one of the boys asked in an almost worshipful tone. He knew the answer. Clone orphans learn uniforms and insignia in kindergarten.

I nodded.

"Whoa!" Both boys sighed.

I walked past them and entered the administration building. Nothing had changed at UAO #553 in the six months since my graduation. The windows sparkled, the walkways shone, the endless parade of slugs still clung to the walls. Groundskeepers squished them, poisoned them, and powdered them with salt; but still they came back, clinging to the brick like six-inch scars.

I walked past the administrative offices, down a hall past several instructional buildings, and past the cafeteria. None of those buildings interested me. I did not miss my math teachers or the counselors who held me hostage when I misbehaved. After passing the administrative building, I stepped onto the walkway that led past obstacle courses. Rifles crackled in the distance. A squad of students dressed in red athletic shorts and blue T-shirts ran across my path. Judging by their size, the boys may have been in their freshman year—fourteen years old and dying to leave the orphanage and begin boot camp. In another few years, they would report to the military induction center in Salt Lake City, where life really began.

Across a sloping hill, a squad of seniors entered the obstacle course. I knew their age because only seniors ran the course wearing combat armor. They needed it. I watched them scale walls, belly-crawl under electrical wiring, and fly across gullies using jetpacks. A line of instructors fired M27s with rubber bullets at the boys as they drilled. Armor or no armor, the bullets left inch-wide bruises wherever they hit. They would knock you senseless if they hit your helmet.

As I watched, an instructor shot down one of his boys. The kid's arms fell limp, and his jetpack cut off as he flopped to the ground like a wet towel. The instructors ignored him and started firing at other students. The boy would survive, but he would have a ringing in his ears for the rest of the day. Like every other kid at UAO #553, I had been nailed dozens of times.

After watching two more boys get shot down, I continued toward the Tactical Training Building. Located at the far end of the campus, the TT building looked like a two-story warehouse or possibly an aircraft hangar. The building had no windows, just double-wide steel doors. Some teachers called it "the shed."

You could not survive #553 without a mentor. Mine was Aleg Oberland—the man in charge of the Tactical Training simulations. Most cadets preferred the strapping sadists who ran the obstacle course—former enlisted men with frontline experience, battle scars, medals, and colorful stories. Oberland was the only retired officer on the teaching staff. He fought in historic campaigns—the kinds of wars that historians argue over, but he never talked about his time on the line.

He was six inches shorter than the other teachers and twenty years older. He had white hair that he kept in a thinning flattop. Most people thought of him as old and sullen, but they did not see what I did. What Oberland showed us was magic.

Oberland drilled juniors and seniors with holographic combat situations. His labs looked empty when you entered; but the moment you put on your combat visor, you would find yourself in a vivid and three-dimensional battle in a desert or on an enemy ship. Lasers in our visors projected the scenery into our eyes, painting it on our retinas, and Oberland had simulations of everything from territorial invasions to ship-to-ship combat. He even had programs simulating attacks on Washington, DC.

As I entered the dark front hall of the TT building I smelled the moldy air-conditioning, and my head filled with memories of the fear and rumors the building had inspired. Students were not allowed to enter the TT building until they turned ten, and even then, they only attended lectures on the top floor. We heard stories about what happened in the basement, but they were all false. Only students in their last two years at the orphanage could enter simulations labs, and they were not allowed to talk about it.

A spiral stairwell in the back of the building ran from the basement to the second floor. I squeezed down the stairs, brushing by dozens of students who stopped to admire my uniform. The stairs ended just outside Oberland's classroom. Glad to be back, I opened the door and went in.

Class must have ended just as I arrived. A crowd of students came up the steps and passed me while a few stragglers milled around their seats. Oberland stood on a dais at the bottom of the theater shuffling papers as I approached. He turned toward me as I came down the stairs. First he looked at my uniform, then he looked at my face. He squinted, and a flicker of recognition crossed his eyes, and his normal frown melted into a smile. "Harris?"

"Hello, Mr. Oberland," I said.

Oberland's gaze kept slipping toward my sleeve. "You're a corporal?" He looked up toward the ceiling as he did the math in his head. "You've only been gone for six months."

"A bit less than that," I said. "It's a long story."

"I just finished my last class for the day," Oberland said as he gathered his books and notes. "And I like long stories. Maybe we can talk about it over dinner."

"In the teachers' mess?" I asked.

"Unless you know someplace else." He stole another glance at my stripes as if to check if they were real. "What are you doing here?"

We started up the stairs. The last boys in the class ran past us. Oberland scowled at them.

"You haven't changed much," I said.

"I learned an important lesson in the Army, Wayson," Oberland said, in his usual gruff voice. "Just because people smile at you doesn't mean that they like you." He looked back down the hall. "I didn't come to #553 to make friends."

I thought about Amos Crowley. He had made friendly banter even as he rigged Guttman's gun to explode. "I know what you mean."

We went to the faculty cafeteria, a café-style eatery with square tables and an open buffet line. Though we were early, a few other teachers had already arrived. Oberland placed his books on a table and headed for the food. There were more than one dozen dishes to choose from—casseroles, soups, roast chicken, and salads. There was a dessert bar with fruit, cakes, and chocolates. "I didn't know you teachers ate so well," I said.

"We don't," Oberland said. "It isn't Earth-grown." Supposedly, Earth-grown meats and vegetables tasted better than foods grown on the frontier. Military chow and school food were made with Earth-grown ingredients, but I hadn't noticed much of a difference. From what I could tell, turnips were turnips and it didn't matter where they came from, they still tasted like shit. All of that Earth-grown hype was pure propaganda.

I slopped a scoop of beef casserole onto my plate, knowing it would taste better than the vacuum-packed Earth-grown MRE chow I ate on Gobi. I took a chicken breast and green salad.

"I just got my first transfer," I said as I placed my tray on the table.

"Transferred already?" Oberland sounded concerned. He sat across the table. "You can't have been at your last assignment for more than a few months."

"Four months," I said. "Have you ever heard of Gobi?"

Oberland thought for a moment. "Never heard of it, but that doesn't mean much. It's a big galaxy." He paused, and added, "Nice place?"

"Beautiful skies," I said, "a dilapidated base, and toxic water for drinking. Gobi Station is the Marine Corps' smallest outpost. Forty-one grunts stuck in the middle of nowhere. That was my first assignment."

"That sounds like the kind of place they leave you until you die," Oberland said, with a low whistle.

"I think that might have been the plan," I said, "but we saw some unexpected action. A band of malcontents led by a former general attacked our outpost."

"Was the general named Amos Crowley?" Oberland asked.

I nodded. "How do you know Crowley?" I asked.

"I served under Crowley," Oberland said. "You know about him, don't you?"

I shook my head.

"Amos Crowley was a brilliant officer."

"I don't know about brilliant, but he damned near wiped out Gobi Station. He would have taken us if it had not been for Freeman."

"Freeman?" Oberland asked.

"Ray Freeman, a mercenary. Cygnus Command sent him when we reported seeing Crowley."

Oberland's expression went flat, and he rubbed his chin. "A mercenary saved your platoon? Please tell me you're kidding."

I could feel tension welling up in my gut. "You never saw Marines like the ones on Gobi," I said, hating the defensive tone in my voice. "Men with long hair, men walking around without helmets . . . One of our guys was so fat he could not pull his helmet over his head. There was no discipline."

Oberland leaned forward, and whispered, "Were they clones?"

I nodded.

"I didn't know that could happen with clones."

"Mr. Oberland, these guys were on permanent R and R. They practically lived in the nearest town."

"Okay, so the mercenary saved the day. Why were you promoted?"

" 'Meritorious service,' " I said. "I helped Freeman while the rest of the platoon hid in the barracks."

Oberland smiled. "And you got a promotion and a transfer?"

"The transfer was the best part. I've been assigned to the Scutum-Crux Fleet, a fighter carrier called the *Kamehameha*."

"The *Kamehameha*? Not bad, Harris." He nodded. "That's Bryce Klyber's ship. He's got to be the most powerful man in the military today."

"He's not one of the Joint Chiefs?" I said. I would have known his name if he was one of the Joint Chiefs of Staff.

"Oh no, no, no." Oberland shook his head. "That would be Fleet Admiral Klyber to you, and he is much more powerful than the Joint Chiefs. They're just appointees; Klyber has friends and family on Capitol Hill. There are some interesting political goings-on in Scutum-Crux. One of the planets was just hauled before the Senate."

I shook my head. "Galactic news didn't seem all that important back on Gobi. Nothing ever happened there, and nothing that happened anywhere else mattered there."

"That's what they told you when you got there?" Oberland asked.

"That's what they told me."

"And you still believe them?" Oberland's smile turned acid. "Wayson, a renegade general from a different arm of the galaxy showed up on your planet and tried to blow up your base."

"Yeah," I said. "I guess so."

"You might have known who he was if you kept up with events, Wayson. You're going to be on the flagship carrier of the Scutum-Crux Fleet. Everything you do will have consequences."

"And Klyber?" I asked, wanting to change the subject from my own shortcomings.

Oberland leaned forward as if he wanted to whisper a secret, then spoke in a normal voice. "Admiral Klyber is the most connected man in the Navy. Perform a little meritorious service under his command, and you may be the first enlisted man to earn a commission."

CHAPTER
FIVE

On my last day of leave, I flew from Seattle to Salt Lake City, then took a military shuttle to Mars. Possibly the single most commercial spot in the universe, the Mars way station was not a colony but a conglomeration of stores, transport facilities, and dormitories. The first building constructed away from Earth, the ever-changing structure was always under renovation but never fully modernized—a sprawling structure with a gigantic military base and a civilian port filled with restaurants, shops, and overnight hotels. It was the Unified Authority's gateway to the galaxy.

I cut through the crowds and reported for duty at the military transfers' desk. A young corporal reviewed my orders and passed me through to a gate where I spent another two hours sitting around before boarding the long-distance transport that would take me to the Central Scutum-Crux Fleet.

All flights out of the Sol System passed through the broadcast station orbiting Mars. We had barely cleared the atmosphere when the "prepare for jump" sign flashed over the passenger compartment. Tint shields formed over the windows, but they only muffled the glare shining off the two gigantic elliptical discs that formed the broadcast station. The discs looked like giant mirrors; they were more than one mile across. Ships did not enter the discs, they merely approached and lowered their shields. The jagged electrical stream pouring out of the mirrors was so bright that glancing at it could blind you for life.

Though sending ships through the broadcast system cost nothing, keeping the discs powered was expensive. Private citizens paid a fifty-dollar-per-cubic-yard toll for entering the broadcast system. Corporations got lower rates when shipping products. Navy ships and government transports passed for free. A team of accountants probably spent their entire careers transferring funds to cover fleet movements.

The pilots cut the engines as we approached the broadcast discs. Our ship slowed to a glide while a silvery red laser scanned the outside of the ship, verifying our registration and checking for hazardous substances and weapons. The pilot said, "Prepare to jump," over the speaker system, and the sending disc, the one that translated ships into impulses and transmitted them, splashed its blue-white lightning against our hull. The air in the cabin began to crackle, and the electricity made my clothes conform to my body as if doused with water. Pressing my face against the tinted window for a better look, I got a quick glance of the orbital Army post guarding the disc before we flashed into the Sagittarius Arm.

The Unified Authority took broadcast station security very seriously, especially Mars Station security. Three F-19 Falcon fighters from the Air Force's Mars base patrolled the reception disc at all times and long-range cannons guarded the area from the surface of nearby moons. Lights illuminated every inch of the discs and the posts that guarded them. If there were some way to light space itself, I think the area around the disc station would have been lit.

It took us five minutes to travel the five hundred miles from the surface of Mars to the broadcast discs, and less than one second to travel nearly ten thousand light-years to the Sagittarius Arm. My trip from the Sagittarius Arm to the Scutum-Crux Arm took less than five seconds—just long enough for the transport to materialize and glide from the receiving disc to the transmission disc of the next station.

Using the broadcast corridor, you could travel from one galactic arm to the next in a matter of moments. Traveling within that arm to your final destination could take weeks.

The network did not rely on wormholes or black holes or any other natural phenomenon, it was purely devised by man. Sending discs emitted some kind of energy wave that absorbed matter and waves as they approached. The disc would simply communicate everything it translated to a receiving disc, where it could be turned back into its original form.

In theory, the disc orbiting Mars could have broadcast us to a disc near SC Command, but interLinking the galaxy would compromise Sol System security. To control broadcast traffic and prevent invaders from tapping into their system, U.A. engineers designed the broadcast corridor in a linear fashion. The Mars disc would only accept transmissions from four transmission discs—the two closest discs in the Orion Arm and the interarm transmitters in the Sagittarius and Perseus Arms. Transmissions from unknown sources were deflected into space and never materialized again.

Our final jump placed us in the center of Scutum-Crux, a mere 500 million miles from Command headquarters. Once away from the discs, most military vehicles were required to travel at a standard 30 million miles per hour. That meant approximately seventeen hours of flying time. Most of the other passengers on the ship were officers who chatted quietly among themselves. A corporal sat splayed across several seats in the row across the aisle from where I sat. I had seen him get on. He stowed his bags, dropped into his seat, and passed out, for all intents and purposes. I did not know if he was drunk or hungover, but he was dead to the world.

With nothing better to do, I decided to follow Aleg Oberland's advice and browsed the latest news broadcasts. I clipped on a pair of mediaLink shades and tapped the power button beside the right lens.

MediaLinks let you browse the news, send letters, or place calls. They were the basis of civilian communications, but their signal could not be secured. Enemies could tape them or jam them in combat. The shades worked very much like the visual controls in my combat helmet. Selecting topics and scrolling through menus by twitching my eye, I began searching for the Senate hearings that Oberland told me about. I selected the "News and Information" option rather than "Entertainment Programming" or "Correspondence." A menu appeared offering "Pangalactic Highlights," "Local News," "Sports," "Entertainment News," and "Business." I chose Local News for Scutum-Crux.

Stereophonic speakers along the sides of the shades rumbled a businesslike tune as two newscasters discussed big stories around Scutum-Crux, a backwater arm politically, with important strategic implications. The first story involved a planet called Ezer Kri sending a delegation to Washington to meet with the Senate.

At first glance, I thought I must have tapped into the wrong story. This was not about a planet that wanted to break from the Republic. All the people of Ezer Kri wanted to do was rename their planet. They held an election and a sizable majority voted to rename the planet "Shin Nippon." The report explained that "Shin Nippon" was Japanese for "New Japan." When the governor of Ezer Kri notified the Senate, he was informed that the name change was out of the question. The governor and a delegation of Ezer Kri politicians were summoned to DC to discuss the matter before the Senate. No arrests, no rebellion . . . why had this seemed important to Oberland?

I paused the broadcast. Though I had never heard of Ezer Kri, I remembered hearing something about a colony of Japanese people refusing to integrate. The rumors did not mean anything to me when I first heard them, but there must have been more to it. I scanned ahead.

When the Unified Authority first settled Ezer Kri, (I'm not sure what the name "Ezer" referred to, but "Kri" was a notation used for planets that had engineered atmospheres.) in 2303, the planetary administrator was of Japanese ancestry. Working quietly, he appointed several people of similar descent to his cabinet. When the administrator retired, he appointed his own successor. Not surprisingly, the new administrator was Japanese.

Over the next two hundred years, there was a Japanese

migration to Ezer Kri. While the rest of the galaxy integrated, 35 percent of the population of Ezer Kri was Japanese. The non-Japanese population complained about discrimination, but a U.A. investigation found that Ezer Kri was productive and law-abiding—a model planet with an excellent educational system and one of the best economies in the Republic. For some reason Oberland equated the proposed name change with sedition. So did the Senate, apparently. It meant nothing to me, and trying to reason it out gave me a headache. I switched off my media shades and went to sleep.

Including stops at several space stations, the trip took nearly twenty hours. By the time we reached SC Command, thirty new passengers had boarded and divided up by rank and phylum. Pilots and other officers sat in the front of the cabin. Tight clusters of sailors sat in the back. There were an even dozen Marine grunts on board.

"We're coming up on the *Kamehameha*," one of the officers said, waking me out of a light sleep. Hearing this, I looked out my window. All I saw was an endless field of stars.

The corporal in the row across the aisle woke up and stretched. He saw me pressing against the window and decided to help. "Do you see a pale gray star at one o'clock?"

There were a lot of gray stars. I felt the cramp in my back, heard my stomach growl, and knew that my patience had worn thin. Then I saw it. The other specks of light twinkled. The *Kamehameha* was a pasty gray dot.

"See it?" he asked.

"Flat-colored speck?" I asked. "It looks pretty small."

"It gets bigger."

It did indeed. As we approached, the bat wing shape of the hull seemed to stretch for miles. The top of the ship was so smooth that it looked like a running track. The top of the ship was the color of a shark, and its front face was lined with windows and weapons arrays. The bottom of the ship was beige in color. Huge antennae, at least fifty feet long and ten feet wide, protruded out of the top and bottom of the wing at each corner. During battle, these antennae emitted the magnetic currents that formed the ship's protective shielding.

The *Kamehameha* grew larger by the moment. Soon I could see blue-and-white plumes flaring from its giant engines. We might still have been fifty miles away when we slowed to approaching speed, but the old fighter carrier already looked considerably larger than the transport in which I had traveled. Another minute passed, and I could make out the individual gun placements.

"It's huge!" I said.

"First time on a carrier?" the Marine asked.

"Yes," I said.

"It gets a lot bigger."

Again, he was correct. I lost sight of the ship as we circled it from above to make our final approach. When we came around, we were less than a hundred yards from the rear of the ship. We could have landed our transport inside one of the dormant emergency engines, and the emergency engines were less than half the size of the main engines. Our pilot adjusted his approach, and we coasted onto a landing dock in the terraced rear of the ship.

Then something made sense. I had heard stories about these ships intimidating insurgents into submission, but I never understood. Teachers back at the orphanage told us the sterile facts about fighter carriers. They showed us holographic images. They cited measurements. Images and measurements meant nothing until you saw this ship in person; any impressions I formed listening to measurements and staring at images were dwarfed by its immense size.

"You won't even know you are on a ship," the corporal said. "It's not like being on a transport or a frigate. You won't feel it move or hear the engines. It's like living on base."

The corporal looked like a freshly minted clone. He had the stubble-cut hair of a young cadet but the small scars on his face and neck suggested he'd seen action. Military clones were a squat and powerful breed standing just shy of six feet tall. This man, however, clearly a bodybuilder, was wider than most. His shoulders and packed arms were not government-issue.

"You must have spent a lot of time at your last assignment," he said. "I've never met a corporal with less than two years' time on a carrier. This is my third, and I was lucky—I made corporal in five years."

The transport's booster rockets hissed as our pilot jostled the ship into position. I heard motors whine as electromagnetic skids dropped out of the transport, and locked us into place in the docking bay. Deckhands opened the hatch from outside the transport and the officers at the front of the cabin filed out.

"Unless I miss my guess, we'll probably end up in the same platoon," the corporal said. "I'm Vince Lee, just transferred up from Outer Scrotum." Seeing my confused reaction, he laughed. "The Outer Scutum-Crux Fleet."

"Wayson Harris." I said, standing up and pulling my gear from the locker above my seat. I followed Lee off the transport and into a large receiving area. Two officers, a young Marine captain and a slightly older Naval commander, stood on deck. The other passengers had already grouped by branch by the time we stepped down the ramp—the sailors proceeded on ship, the Marines and pilots remained. Lee and I took our spots at the head of the Marines.

Had I not recognized their uniforms, I would have guessed that the captain was the pilot and the lieutenant commander was the Marine. The lieutenant commander stood well over six feet tall and had the barrel chest and the intensity of a fighting man. I had trouble imagining him crammed into a cockpit. He called out the names of his pilots, and each responded, then he looked at his clipboard and smiled. "All accounted for."

Though I had not been told that these men were pilots, I had no trouble identifying them. Pilots were natural-born and came in various shapes and sizes. Being officers, they also did not carry duffel bags. You'd never see officers washing their own laundry or carrying their own bags. They left such menial tasks to enlisted men.

"I am Lieutenant Commander Mack Callahan," the lieutenant commander said as his new pilots stepped forward. "I run the fighter squads on this bucket." He approached one of the pilots and read the name tag on his uniform. "Where were you stationed last, Jordan?"

"Mars, sir."

"Mars?" Callahan nodded his head. "Some of you flew in from Orion? Long flight. I'll tell you what, Jordan, why don't you and the boys unpack, get plenty of rest, and report to my briefing room in thirty minutes." The pilots groaned, then followed Callahan off deck.

The captain stepped forward. "At ease." He reviewed at our ranks. "I am Captain Gaylan McKay."

From the side of my eye, I watched the pilots vanish down a gleaming hallway. I did not see so much as a finger smudge on the walls. Every light in every ceiling fixture shone brightly, and the floors sparkled. Captain McKay looked as if he had been polished, too. He was small for a Marine, certainly no more than five feet six inches tall with a wiry build. A strip of blond stubble covered the top of his head, and the sides were shaved clean. He had more of a smirk than a smile, but I liked the informal way in which he appraised us. He'd probably be a prick most of the time, but that came with the uniform.

"I'll take you to your quarters." As we followed McKay down the hall, he continued his orientation. "You boys are lucky," McKay said. "Marines get a good shake in this fleet. Admiral Klyber doesn't play favorites with pilots and sailors. Sea-soldier chow is as good as any on this ship."

McKay led us to a series of cabins in which bunk beds lined the walls. Reading from a list, McKay sent men to various barracks; but when he came to Lee and me, he said, "Let's talk in my office. Harris, I'll start with you."

He led me through an empty barrack. "Throw your bags on any rack."

I dropped my bags on the nearest bunk.

"Is your gear in working order, Corporal?" McKay asked.

No one had asked me about the condition of my armor since the battle on Gobi, nor had I thought about it. "No, sir," I said. "The interLink is out in my helmet."

"Bring it along, Harris," McKay called over his shoulder as he walked off. I quickly snatched my helmet and followed the captain down the hall. He entered a small office. I stepped in after him.

"Take a seat, Corporal," McKay said.

"We're starting up a new platoon. Your sergeant arrives tomorrow. He's transferring in from the Inner SC Fleet," McKay said with emphasis, as if that sector should have meant something to me. It didn't. "Admiral Klyber believes that something is going to break loose in outer Scutum-Crux."

McKay waited for me to respond. When I said nothing, he picked up my personnel file and began reading.

He turned a few pages, reading quickly, apparently taking in the details. "Ah yes, I remember your record. You were the one who made corporal in three months . . . Must be some kind of a record. Exactly what sort of meritorious service did you perform on Gobi?" As he asked, McKay closed the folder and watched me carefully.

"Terrorists attacked our outpost, sir. I . . . ."

"Attacked an outpost? Were you working out of an embassy?"

"No, sir," I said.

"You mentioned a problem with your helmet."

"Yes, sir. My interLink equipment failed during the battle."

"I don't know who designed this shit, but you can always count on something breaking when you need it most. My visor went black during a firefight, and I nearly shot my commanding officer." McKay smiled as if thinking about what might have been, then continued in a more businesslike tone. "Around here you turn your headgear in for routine maintenance after every battle. Fleet policy. We take maintenance seriously in this fleet. Show up for an engagement with a broken helmet, and you'll be lucky if the enemy gets you before I do. Got that, Corporal?"

"Yes, sir."

"You can bring your helmet back from battles melted to your head if you like. That's your business. But show up with broken gear, and I'll send you to the brig."

"Yes, sir."

"And, Corporal, in case you have not guessed, showing up to new assignments with busted gear makes a bad first impression."

"Yes, sir."

"Leave the helmet; I'll requisition repairs." Changing subjects, McKay pointed to the Scutum-Crux Arm insignia on the wall behind him—a fleet of ships in silhouette superimposed against the whirlpool shape of the Milky Way. "You have been assigned to the flagship of the Outer SC Fleet, Corporal. We don't put up with sloppiness on this ship."

He handed me a three-inch stack of papers. "Get this read ASAP. That will be all."

Without looking up, McKay added, "Send in Corporal Lee."

Until Amos Crowley's visit, the U.A. Marines maintained Gobi Station with forty-one men, one man shy of a full platoon. The bowels of the *Kamehameha* housed two full divisions of Marines—over twenty-three hundred of the Republic's finest.

Bryce Klyber's authority extended beyond the ship and even the fleet; every unit in the Scutum-Crux Arm was under his command. He was the only officer in the U.A. Navy to hold the rank of fleet admiral, a rank generally reserved for wartime.

Captain Thaddeus Olivera commanded the *Kamehameha,* and Vice Admiral Absalom Barry commanded the Outer Scutum-Crux Fleet. Klyber, who I soon learned was a notorious microcommander, preferred to work out of an office on the ship so that he could observe operations firsthand.

There were three fleets in the Scutum-Crux Arm, placing more than one thousand ships, more ships than the Earth Fleet, under Klyber's command. That did not mean he could stage a revolution. Unlike Caesar, crossing the Rubicon line as he brought his forces into Rome, Klyber would never be able to bring his fleet to Earth. Klyber's Rubicon was the Mars discs of the Broadcast Corridor, which were too small to receive or send capital ships such as fighter carriers and destroyers. The Broadcast Corridor ensured that Klyber's ships remained in place. Without the discs, it would take a thousand lifetimes to fly from Scutum-Crux to the Sol System in the Orion Arm.

The documentation McKay gave me described the protocol and command structure of the Outer SC Fleet. Most of the information was standard procedure, but I needed to relearn standard procedures and chain of command after three months on Gobi. Judging by the way Klyber ran the Scutum-Crux territories, he was the kind of commander who required his subordinates to march to his own drum.

As a young Marine, I did not know much about Navy workings. It struck me as odd that Klyber, supposedly a powerful admiral, retained an old ship like the *Kamehameha* for his flagship. The *Kamehameha* might have worked well as Klyber's movable command post, but it was obsolete as a fighter carrier. Klyber built each of his three fleets around a core of twelve fighter carriers. The *Kamehameha* was an old Expansion-class carrier, the only carrier of its class that was still in operation. All of the other carriers were Perseus-class, a newer breed of brute measuring forty-five hundred feet long and almost fifty-one hundred feet wide—nearly twice as long as their Expansion-class predecessors. Perseus-class carriers bore a complement of eleven thousand Marines, five times the fighting force that traveled on the *Kamehameha*. Perseus-class carriers stowed three times more tanks, transports, gunships, and fighters than Expansion-class carriers and had much quicker means for deploying units.

Lee and I spent our first night in half-empty barracks. Ten of the men assigned to our platoon had trickled in throughout the day, but most of the racks remained empty. Huddled in my bunk, I quietly read Scutum-Crux Fleet documentation well into the sleep period. Along with command structure and regulations, the documentation also laid out our daily regiment. Klyber expected his grunts to drill three hours per day, holding physical training, marksmanship drills, and practical simulations into the daily routine. After reading these daily requirements I sighed, and whispered, "Harris, you're a long, long way from Gobi."

Lee, laid out on the bunk next to mine, rolled to face me, and asked, "Wayson, what are you doing?"

"Reading regs," I said. "You finished reading already?"

"I don't need to read them," Lee said. "We had the exact same regulations at my last post. I was already under Klyber's command."

Travel had warped my internal timetable. Late as it was, I did not have a prayer of falling asleep. "I think I'm still on Earth time," I said, though I had no idea what time it might be back at the orphanage.

"I'm having trouble sleeping myself," Lee admitted. He rolled over on his side and checked his wristwatch, then quietly cursed. "Tell you what, you want to go have a look around the ship?" he asked.

"We can do that?" I asked.

"Damn, Harris! You're not in boot camp. Nobody cares what corporals do after hours," Lee said, sitting up and swinging his legs over the edge of his bunk.

"Boot camp wasn't that long ago," I admitted. "After basic I got sent to a planet called Gobi. Regulations didn't matter much there. I don't want to screw up."

"Okay, on behalf of Fleet Admiral Klyber, I formally give you permission to climb out of your bunk. You may grab a bite to eat, visit the bar, or have a look around the ship. Just keep out of restricted areas," Lee said as he pulled on his pants.

After numbing my brain with rules and command structure, the idea of a late-night walk sounded good. We got dressed and slipped out of the barracks. The ship had an eerie, abandoned feel to it. The hall lights burned as brightly as they did during the day, but the only footsteps we heard were mostly our own. I peered through the window of our chow area as we passed. The lights were turned low. Tables that had been crowded with Marines a few hours earlier now sat empty.

Our barracks and training areas were located amidships on one of the lower decks of the *Kamehameha*, not all that far from the docking bay. In the time that I had been on board, I had only seen the landing bay, the barracks, and the mess area. Lee, who had never served aboard that particular ship but had a working knowledge of carriers, had no problem conducting an impromptu tour.

We passed armories, a library, and file rooms—all

populated with skeleton crews. At three in the morning, even the bars sat empty. Lee led me to an elevator, and we went up three floors to the crew area. "This area is not restricted, but don't expect to spend much time up here," Lee said, as we stepped off the lift. "Sailors think of us as cargo."

It hadn't taken me long to strike up a friendship with Lee. After Gobi, I was glad to meet a Marine who stowed his gear properly and cut his hair to regulation. Like the clones back in Orphanage #553, Lee had created his own kind of personality. He did not know he was a clone, of course; and he thought one day he might be bootstrapped into the ranks of the officers. From there, he wanted to enter politics.

It was hopeless, of course. He was a clone; and because the Unified Authority did not recognize the potential of its own synthetic creations, Lee would never be promoted past master sergeant.

Unlike our barracks, the crew area showed signs of life. Duty officers patrolled the halls. We passed a mess area that smelled of fried eggs and meat. I peered in the door and saw sailors hunched over trays. A little farther, we passed a rec room with game tables, card tables, and a bar. I saw the marquee of a movie theater along the back wall. At that early hour, the recreation center sat empty and dark, but I could imagine it filled with lights and sounds and people during the early evening.

"They have a movie theater in there," I complained. "I'll bet my next paycheck that our rec doesn't have a theater."

"That's a good way to go bankrupt," Lee said. "Congress spares no expense when it comes to keeping its Marines entertained."

"You boys looking for something?" We turned around as a sailor approached us.

"We're new on the ship," Lee said. "Just having a look around."

The sailor was a clone, a petty officer with a single red chevron on his sleeve. He bore no more authority than Lee or I; but we were on his turf. "You must be new. This here is the crew area. We stow Marines below," he sneered. He grabbed Lee by the arm, then took a quick step back. Lee's arms and chest were thick with muscle.

"Didn't mean to intrude," Lee said with an easy smile as he turned back toward the elevator. "Not very hospitable. I thought we were all fighting on the same side."

Then Lee said something under his breath that struck me as very odd. "Specking clone."

I had only met Vince Lee earlier that day when he and I went to explore the *Kamehameha,* so I did not notice the anomaly then. With time I would notice that though he was friendly and outgoing with me, Lee did not socialize with the other men in our platoon. He and I normally found a table off on our own.

When Lee bought drinks, he purchased Earth-made beer. An avid bodybuilder, he asked for permission to work out in the officers' gym. In fact, he had as little contact as possible with other clones. No enlisted man saw himself as a clone, though most of them were indeed just that. Even so, antisyntheticism was rare among clones because they were raised with other clones, and the only people they knew growing up were clones. They did not know how to associate with natural-born people. But Lee, Lee was different. Like so many U.A. citizens, Vince Lee was quietly prejudiced against clones. He thought clones were beneath him. The difference was that other people were natural-born, Vince was synthetic. Many officers were antisynthetic; they despised their underlings. Vince was different. He despised his own kind.

The rest of the platoon arrived the following afternoon. That included our new sergeant—Tabor Shannon. As Vince might have put it, life aboard the *Kamehameha* became less "hospitable" the moment Shannon arrived.

Master Gunnery Sergeant Tabor Shannon landed on a late-afternoon shuttle. Shannon was the personification of the word "paradox." He was gruff, ruthless, and often profane. He openly favored the men who transferred in with him and even referred to them as "my men" because they came with him from his previous platoon. He was a belligerent and battle-hardened Marine. But I soon found out that Shannon's sense of duty added oddly smoothed edges to the jagged shards of his personality.

Captain McKay sent Lee and me to meet Shannon and the other men at the landing bay. We rushed down to the boarding zone. As the bay door opened, Lee said, "I bet he's a prick. What do you want to bet he's a real prick among men?"

We watched several officers disembark. Four pilots and a number of crewmen breezed past us without so much as a sideward glance. Shannon came next. He was tall and thin, with steep shoulders and a wiry frame. His fine white hair, the hair of an old man, did not match his sunburned face. Except for crow's-feet and white hair, he looked like a thirty-year-old.

Shannon walked up to us and paused long enough to bark, "Twelfth Platoon, you part of my outfit?" When we nodded, he dropped his bags at our feet, and said, "Stow these on my rack."

Under other circumstances that kind of arrogance pissed me off, but I had noticed something about Shannon's bags that left me too stunned to care. Lee saw it, too. The letters "GCF" were stenciled large and red on the side of the bag. When I was growing up, every kid in the orphanage knew what those letters stood for—Galactic Central Fleet. That was a name with a dark history. "You don't think he's a Liberator?" I asked.

"Damn, I heard that they were all dead," Lee said, staring at Shannon's back as he left the bay. Watching Shannon disappear down the corridor, I felt a cold shiver run down my spine.

The truth was that I did not know much about the Galactic Central Fleet or the special strain of clones that were created to fight in it. The history books called them "Liberators," but that was mostly because calling them "Butchers" seemed disrespectful.

The government deemed the battles in the Galactic Central War classified information and never released accounts of what took place. But the government could not classify the events that led up to war. Unified Authority ships began prospecting the "eye" of the galaxy—the nexus where the various arms of the Milky Way meet in a spiral—about forty years ago. That was during the height of the expansion. We had long suspected that we had the galaxy to ourselves, and exploration into the farthest and deepest corners of the frontier only increased the belief that the universe belonged to mankind. By this time we had traveled to the edge of the Milky Way but not to the center.

The media covered every detail of that first expedition to the center of the Galaxy, including its disastrous ending. Five self-broadcasting Pioneer-class vessels were sent. All five disappeared upon arrival in the Galactic Eye.

There was no information about what happened to the ships. Some people speculated that radiation or possibly some unknown element destroyed them as they emerged from their broadcast. The most common theory, of course, was that the expedition was attacked, but whatever really became of those ships happened so quickly that no information was relayed back to Earth. If the politicians and military types knew more than the general public, they did not let on.

Congress went into an emergency session and commissioned a special fleet to investigate—the Galactic Central Fleet, the largest and most-well-armed fleet in U.A. Naval history. The hearings and the creation of the Galactic Central Fleet were matters of public record. Reporters were taken out to the shipyards where the fleet's 200 cruisers, 200 destroyers, and 180 battleships were under construction. It took three years to build the fleet. During that time, the entire Republic braced for an alien attack.

Once the fleet was constructed, however, the news accounts stopped. This much I knew—that the Galactic Central Fleet was launched on February 5, 2455, and that it vanished. The ships were sent to the Galactic Eye and never heard from again.

I heard tales about the events that followed, but they were all gossip and myths. To avoid increased panic, the government imposed a news blackout immediately after the fleet disappeared. Then, two months after the disappearance, the Senate announced that the galactic core was under U.A. control. The only historical record of the event was a statement from the secretary of the Navy stating that a battery of specially trained soldiers conquered ground zero. Some time after that, a congressional panel announced that the men in the GC regiment were an experimental class of clones known only as "Liberators." There were no pictures of Liberator clones in our history texts; and though I searched, I never found any pictures on the mediaLink, nor did I ever find any information about the aliens that the Liberator clones fought in the Galactic Eye.

"The bag says 'GCF,' " I said. "You don't think he could be a Liberator?"

"You?" Lee asked, shaking his head.

"I don't know," I said. "I had a teacher who served with some Liberators. He said that they were taller and slimmer than other clones. He also said that they massacred entire planets."

"One of my teachers said that they enjoyed killing people and that they killed civilians when they ran out of enemy soldiers," said Lee. "That must have been an old rucksack," he added, though he did not sound as if he believed it. "He didn't look much older than us."

Like me, he had probably done the math in his head. If the GCF disappeared forty years ago, that would put Gunny Sergeant Shannon in his late fifties or early sixties. He looked bright-eyed, spry, and mean as hell. He was clearly a clone . . . a different species of clone, but still a clone. He had the same dark features as Lee, though he was a few inches taller. They looked like brothers.

"Like seeing a ghost," I muttered to myself. Having heard all kinds of rumors about Liberators in the orphanage, I should not have been surprised that Shannon looked so young. Liberators were supposed to have a synthetic gene that kept them young. Of course, I also heard that they had a fish gene that enabled them to breathe underwater and a slug gene that made them self-healing. I stopped believing the slug story by the time I was ten, but suddenly the youth gene seemed possible.

"We'd better stow his stuff," Lee said. "I would hate to piss him off."

Lee was too late. Just about everything pissed Shannon off. He marched into the barracks like a one-man wrecking crew, rearranging the racks and placing "his" Marines along the right side of the room. When Lee and I arrived, we walked into chaos. Acting on Shannon's orders, the newly arrived PFCs dumped other men's bags, books, and bedding to the floor. When one of the displaced privates asked Shannon what was happening, the gunny shouted a chain of obscenities and nearly hit him. "What is your name, Private?" Shannon shouted, strings of spit flying out of his mouth.

"Private First Class Christopher Charla," the private answered as he snapped to attention.

"Did the Congress of the Unified Authority award you that bunk, PFC Charla?"

"No," Charla mumbled quietly.

"I did not hear you, Charla. What did you say to me?" Shannon stood on his toes, his shoulders hunched, every conceivable vein puffed out of his neck.

"No, Sergeant," Charla bellowed back.

"Then this rack does not belong to you?" Shannon shouted. "Is that correct, Charla?"

"Yes, Sergeant."

Judging by the concern on Lee's face, I could tell that Shannon's was not standard sergeant behavior. All I had to go by was Glan Godfrey—and old Gutterwash did not give me much to go by.

Sergeant Shannon turned to look at Lee and me. "I told you to stow those bags in my office," he said, "then set up your racks. You sleep over there." He pointed to the farthest bunks from his office, and I realized that he had just demoted us to the bottom of the platoon.

My situation became worse the following morning.

Still unable to adjust to Scutum-Crux time, I woke up at 0500 and fidgeted in my bunk until I was sure I could not fall back to sleep. I noticed that Vince Lee's bunk lay empty. His clone frame lent itself well to bodybuilding, and he trained daily. My interests lay elsewhere. The one topic that interested me more than anything was battle-readiness. Weapons and hand-to-hand training lent themselves well to that preparation. After my discussion with Oberland, I had come to believe that knowing current events might also prepare me for battle. Knowing who I might have to fight and what they were fighting for had value. I put on my mediaLink shades to see if Ezer Kri was still in the news.

On-air analysts billed the Ezer Kri story as a crisis in the making. Apparently the Ezer Kri delegation asked the Linear Committee for a new senator. They wanted to hold a planetwide election and choose their senator by popular vote, the same way they elected their member of the House. According to the story, nearly every elected official on Ezer Kri was of Japanese descent. Though they were not stating it outright, the members of the committee seemed to want to excise everything Japanese from the planet. The request was refused. "Your request, Governor Yamashiro, is unconstitutional," the committee chair said. "The Constitution specifically calls for appointed representation."

Yoshi Yamashiro, the governor of Ezer Kri and the head of the delegation, next resubmitted a petition asking for permission to change the name of his planet from Ezer Kri to "Shin Nippon."

The chairman of the Linear Committee pointed out that "Shin Nippon" meant "New Japan," and refused to consider the petition.

At this point the story switched to video footage shot in the Committee chambers. The Ezer Kri delegation, made up of elderly men in black suits, sat at a huge wooden table covered with charts and computers. Their table faced a towering gallery packed with senators. The seven men in the delegation chatted among themselves in a language that I had never heard. Their voices rose and fell dramatically, and they did a lot of bowing. "Mr. Chairman," one of them said in a breathless voice. "We ask that the official language of Ezer Kri be changed to Japanese. That is the language spoken by a plurality of our population," he said, with a slight bow.

Angry chatter erupted in gallery.

"Governor Yamashiro," the speaker shouted, banging his gavel. "I will not entertain such a request. You are entirely out of bounds. Your behavior signifies contempt for this body."

The Japanese men spoke quietly among themselves. Yamashiro stood up. He was a short man with a stout chest and broad shoulders. He bowed. "I apologize for my offense, Mr. Chairman," Yamashiro said. The room calmed, then Yamashiro spoke again. "I humbly suggest that you change the name of the Republic to the 'Unified Singular Authority.' "

There was a moment of shocked silence, as if Yamashiro had performed some crude act that stunned every man in the room. Then hisses and angry conversation filled the chamber. The chairman pounded his gavel as the video segment ended.

The picture of the hearing faded and my shades now showed three analysts sitting around a table. One of them leaned forward. "This was footage of the Ezer Kri delegation's meeting with the Linear Committee this morning. After having several requests denied, Governor Yoshi Yamashiro suggested that the Unified Authority be renamed 'the Unified Singular Authority.' As you can see, the reaction was swift and angry."

"Jim," a woman analyst cut in, "that reaction was to Yamashiro's veiled suggestion that the government is really an extension of the old United States. The point of his comment was that we should take on the initials USA. Yamashiro made some good points," the woman continued. "The Linear Committee has been openly antagonistic toward the Ezer Kri delegation. We're not talking about a planet trying to break from the Republic, forgod'ssake, they just want to rename their planet."

"It's not just the planet name . . ." the first male analyst started.

"There are already planets named Athens, Columbia, Jerusalem!" another analyst added.

"Those are city names, and they do not have majority populations of Greek or Israeli descent. It's not just the name, it's the language. Governor Yamashiro wants to speak an entirely different language than the rest of the Republic."

"Jim," the woman commentator said, with a patient and all-knowing smile, "when was the last time you watched a broadcast from outside the Orion Arm? By the end of the century, linguistic scholars predict the dialects spoken in the outer arms will have evolved into unique languages. You cannot expect people who live ten thousand light-years apart to go on speaking the same language forever."

"And you think switching from English to Japanese is part of that evolution?"

"What I find most disturbing is the paranoia that is surrounding this entire issue," the woman said, ignoring the question. "It's as if the committee believes that switching the language is the first step to an invasion. It's ridiculous."

The woman made more sense, but I agreed with the male commentator. Perhaps it was my upbringing in a military orphanage, but I could not see how letting planets speak different languages would bring the galaxy closer together.

By that time I was losing interest in the story, so I switched off my shades. When I removed my shades, I saw a message light blinking over my bunk. Sergeant Shannon wanted me to come to his office. I climbed out of bed and dressed quickly, but Shannon was not in his office when I arrived. I found my helmet waiting on his desk.

Lee, just back from the gym, came into the barracks as I was stowing my helmet. "Hey, how was your workout?" I asked, as Lee passed my rack.

"Fine," he said, sounding brusque. I waited for him to shower and change, then we went to the commissary for breakfast. We had eaten almost every meal together since landing on the ship. I think we had sort of adopted each other. I hadn't yet figured out that Lee liked me because I was not a clone. As for me, after my time on Gobi, I was just glad to have a friend who truly fit the description "government-issue." Lee was acting odd and distant. I wanted to ask him what his problem was, but I figured he would cough it up in good time. As we walked toward the mess area, I saw a strangely familiar sight on some of the monitors along the hall—a picture of General Amos Crowley bent over a stack of poker chips, holding a particle-beam pistol. I recognized the table, the room, and the way Crowley pinched the pistol with his fingers. "Enemy of the Republic," was the headline. "Former general and noted terrorist Amos Crowley stands accused of sedition, rebellion, and murder."

I stared at the display hardly believing my eyes. "Son of a bitch," I mumbled.

"Do you know him?" Vince asked.

"I think I took that photograph," I said.

"You don't know if you took it?" Lee asked, suddenly interested in me again.

"I was at that card game, but I didn't have a camera. Neither did anybody else."

"Somebody had one," Lee said dismissively. "Do you play cards with traitors on a regular basis?"

I stared at the image for a moment, then continued down the hall. And then it struck me. All those gadgets packed into our visors . . . polarizing lenses, telescopic lenses, communications systems. Add a little data storage, and you could record everything.

"Do our visors record data?" I asked.

"Sure," Lee said, sounding as if I should have known that without asking. "How long have you been . . ." He paused to stare at me and laughed. "You wore your helmet to a card game? Harris"—he seemed to warm up as he sensed my embarrassment—"you're all right."

"Glad I've got your seal of approval," I said. I was again tempted to ask what was bothering him, but held back.

He looked back at the picture. "That's not your sidearm, is it?" he said, struggling not to laugh.

"No, it's not," I snapped.

"Just asking," Lee said, still sounding more than amused. The corners of his mouth still twitched. "Whose is it?"

"It belonged to a guy named Taj Guttman," I said, as we entered the mess hall.

"He wagered his firearm? I bet he wasn't wearing his helmet."

"No, he wasn't," I said.

"His goose is fried," Lee said.

We grabbed trays and moved to the chow line. Vince clearly wanted to ask more questions but had the good sense to wait until we had our chow and had moved to a quieter corner of the room. I felt a wave of panic. How many people knew what I had done—that I had lost my pistol to an enemy agent in a card game? I seriously doubted that McKay would keep the information to himself.

"Can't say I think much of a Marine who bets his pistol

in a card game, Harris," Sergeant Shannon sneered as he sat down at the table next to ours. "I don't think much of that at all."

Not many of my memories are associated with a particular day of the week, but I have no trouble recalling what day my helmet was returned to me. It was on a Sunday. I know that because later that day, hoping to get away from all of the questions about Crowley and the card game, I went to the rec room to watch a movie. Sincerely wanting to be alone, I chose the emptiest route through the Marine compound—and that took me by the chapel. Nobody went anywhere near that area on Sunday.

The military was always trying to push religion; but in my experience, fear of God was one of the things that science never managed to build into its neural programming. Many of the officers attended church services, but none of the clones I knew believed in God.

As I passed by the open door of the chapel on this day, however, I happened to catch a glance of somebody sitting alone at the rear of the chapel. His back was to me, but the tall wiry frame and fine, white old man's hair were unmistakable. There, wearing his dress uniform, was Sergeant Shannon . . . swearing, bullying, belligerent Sergeant Shannon.

CHAPTER
SIX

Some people say that the most glorious sight they ever saw was a beautiful moon or a perfect sunrise. For me, it was the three fleets of the Scutum-Crux Arm converging in orbit over Terraneau. Each fleet was set in array with its twelve Perseus-class fighter carriers set in a row like the jagged teeth of an enormous saw. Frigates and transports, awesome ships in their own right, seemed insignificant beside the mighty bulk of these dreadnoughts. The massive shadow of the fleets cast a discernible outline on the watery surface of the planet below.

Seeing so many ships huddled together fascinated me. I spent hours watching them from one of the *Kamehameha*'s observation stations. I watched attack wings of Tomcats and Harriers escorting transports between the capital ships and the planet below. With their black-and-gray finish and sliver-shaped hulls, the Tomcats vanished like ghosts in open space only to reappear as fast-moving specks when they sped across the bows of carriers.

"The U.A. Navy is awesome," I said to myself with pride. I wondered how anyone could hope to stand against it.

"I spent some time stationed on Nebraska Minor," Vince

Lee said as he leaned against a guardrail. "Ever heard of Nebraska Minor?"

"I cannot say that I have," I said.

"They do a lot of farming there. The whole planet is like one big farm," Lee said.

"Exciting assignment," I joked.

Lee thought about my quip for a moment, then chose to ignore it. "People on Nebraska Minor used to say, 'You should always kill the pig before you eat it.' You ever heard that before?"

"I feel deprived," I said. "On Gobi we had sayings like, 'You should never eat your children after they are six years old.'"

Lee pretended to ignore that comment, too. "It's a big fleet; a lot of firepower . . ." Lee's voice trailed off for a moment. "Greece and Rome weren't able to hold on to Europe, how can we possibly hope to control a whole galaxy? If there are planets that want out of the Republic, Wayson, I am not sure we should force them to stay in."

"I don't see how they can stand up to a fleet like this," I said.

"What happened on Gobi?" Lee asked as he followed my gaze out the window. "Crowley attacked a Marine base?"

A shuttle with a three-fighter escort silently approached our ship, drifting past the window. The ships passing by reminded me of fish in an aquarium. Lee's question did not surprise me; people had been asking about the Gobi story quite a bit lately. A team of security officers had given me an official debriefing, and Captain McKay had questioned me about it.

"You after the blow-by-blow?" I asked in a sardonic voice. He nodded, and I told him the whole story, including the part about becoming a corporal in three months. I think the promotion was the part that embarrassed me the most.

"The Unified Authority has long provided safety and prosperity for its member states. Now it has come to our attention that certain factions wish to divide our Republic. These terrorists would destroy the fabric of our society to satisfy their own selfish needs. Though their insurrection poses no significant threat to our great Republic, it must be dealt with."

I noticed two things about Fleet Admiral Bryce Klyber as I watched his high-definition image on the three-dimensional screen: his nearly starved physique and his overwhelming intensity. Klyber's cheekbones stuck out like ridges across his chiseled face and his skull looked dented at the temples. He had long arms that reminded me of twigs. The overall impression was that you could snap the man over your knee like a stick.

First fascinated by Klyber's skeletal appearance, I soon found myself mesmerized by the intensity in his icy blue eyes. He stared into the camera, seldom blinking as he plowed through his speech. When he paused to look at his notes, Klyber pursed his mouth so tightly that his lips formed a single line, and wrinkles formed on his chin.

"In future years, historians will look back upon the Unified Authority as one of man's crowning achievements. As a nation, we have conquered space. We have conquered the galaxy. Our progress will not be slowed by a band of hooligans."

The impact of Klyber's words was immediate and universal. Applause echoed through the *Kamehameha*. Klyber was speaking in an auditorium on Terraneau, but his speech was shown on every monitor on every deck of every ship in all three Scutum-Crux fleets. As he said those words, I have no doubt that all 2 million men under Klyber's command shouted with excitement.

"I have spoken with both the Joint Chiefs and the Linear Committee, and they have authorized me to subdue the enemy by all means necessary. As we speak, enemy strongholds are being targeted in all six galactic arms, and terrorist leaders are being sought out."

The platoon watched Klyber's speech on a small monitor hanging from the ceiling of our barracks. Everyone around me fidgeted with excitement except Shannon, who stood mute and slack-jawed with an expression that betrayed no emotion. His arms were folded across his chest, and he seemed to consider the weight of the challenges ahead.

"I will not discuss our tactics at this time, but every officer will be briefed. The details and goals of our missions will become apparent over the next few days.

"Dismissed."

The screen blinked off. As it did, the barracks began to echo with loud conversations.

"What do you think?" Lee asked me.

"Sounds like war," I said. "We will overwhelm them."

"If we can find them," Vince reminded me.

Like a crew heading into combat, we had the rest of the day to relax and think about the battles that might lie ahead. By the time Vince and I went to the sea-soldier's bar late that afternoon, it was already packed with noncoms. Tight knots of combat-ready Marines stood along the bar slapping each other across the shoulders and speaking in booming voices. They toasted Admiral Klyber and made dunderheaded statements about Congress.

A private from our platoon waved to us as we surveyed the bar. He came to us. "Lee, Harris, we have a table back there," he said, pointing with a frothy mug.

"I'm never quite sure, but wasn't that one of Shannon's men?" Lee asked, after the private left.

"Couldn't be. They don't talk to us."

Lee shrugged. "I suppose we should at least drop in on them."

"You find them, I'll get the beer," I said as I pushed my way through the crowd. I reached the bar and looked around. It was a big night. By all appearances, we were headed for a fight. The mood was wild. When the bartender asked what I wanted, I ordered two bottles of Earth-brewed beer.

"The best I have left is brew made with Earth-grown malt."

"That will do," I said handing him a twenty.

The bartender smiled and gave me very little change.

It took a few minutes to fight through the crowd and find the table. I handed Vince his beer. He looked at the label, and asked, "Earth-grown malt? I thought you didn't taste any difference?"

"I don't." I smiled, nodded, took a swig of my beer. "But you've sprung for Earth-grown so many times, I felt guilty."

Drinks did not come free on board the *Kamehameha,* but

they were pretty damn cheap. Even hard stuff like vodka and whiskey cost only one dollar per drink.

As far as I was concerned, the only difference between Earth-grown and outworld beers was the cost. The snobbish crowd said they tasted a difference, but I never did. For reasons I could not peg at the time, Lee preferred Earth-grown brew; but I had not bought the beer for the taste, I bought it for the occasion.

Most of our platoon sat around this table in two nearly concentric circles. "Guess we're standing," Lee said.

"Have you guys heard anything?" someone asked.

"You kidding?" a familiar voice burst out. "They're corpses. Corporals are always the last to hear shit." Just across from me, Sergeant Shannon sat with one leg up on the table. He looked relaxed, and his smile was almost friendly.

"We'll all know soon enough," Lee said.

The banter continued. We no longer seemed like a divided platoon. Shannon leaned back in his chair and listened to the conversations around him.

"Harris?"

Captain McKay, probably fresh from the officers meetings on Terraneau and still wearing his whites, tapped me on the shoulder. He smiled and spoke in a quiet tone that was just loud enough for me to hear him above the crowd. "Harris, I suspect that you are just about the most important person in the fleet right now."

"Begging your pardon, sir, I don't understand."

"That an Earth-grown brew you're drinking?" he asked, looking at my bottle. "The record from your helmet . . . that was the key to all of this. I showed it to Klyber, and he showed it to the Linear Committee.

"Do you know what Admiral Klyber told the Committee? He told them that our enemies 'no longer fear us.' 'No longer fear us,' that was what finally woke them up. That and your video feed. Life in the galaxy just got a little more exciting thanks to that goddamned helmet of yours."

"I'm not sure what to say," I said. I could not tell if McKay was angry or pleased. He sounded sarcastic, but I wasn't sure if he was joking or angry. He did not stay long, either. A moment later he waved to the platoon and disappeared into the crowd.

"We have our orders," Sergeant Shannon said as he called Lee and me into his office the next day. "Have a seat."

We pulled chairs up to his desk. Judging by the time mark on the communiqué, Captain McKay had sent the orders less than an hour earlier. "The *Kamehameha* has been assigned to a planet called Ezer Kri. Ever heard of it?"

"No, Sergeant," Lee said.

"We're invading Ezer Kri?" Lee and Shannon stared at me. "Ezer Kri has been in the news. I've been following the story."

"You know about Ezer Kri?" Shannon asked. He picked up a combat knife and wiped its blade on his forearm.

I began to feel self-conscious. "The story is all over the news. Ezer Kri has a large population of ethnically pure Japanese people who want to make Japanese the official language of the planet. The governor of the planet went to DC and the Linear Committee said no."

Shannon smiled. "Japanese? There's got to be something more. You can't invade a planet just because a bunch of people want to speak Japanese."

"I thought the old races disappeared," Vince said.

"You run into it a bit out here," Shannon said. "But I've never seen an entire planet like that."

"So we're sending a fleet?" I asked. "Are we going to blockade the planet or something?"

"I don't know what Klyber has in mind," Shannon said. "He is sending the *Kamehameha* and a few support ships."

"Is Admiral Klyber coming along for the ride?" Lee asked.

"I don't know if he returned to ship after Terraneau," Shannon said. "We're still six days out from Ezer Kri. Harris, see that every man in the platoon gets his armor shined and ready."

"Yes," I said.

"You should be keen on maintenance considering all the trouble your faulty helmet has caused," Shannon said.

"One other thing . . . I worked you both over when I got here. The whole deal changes now that we have an assignment. You understand? I'll be depending on you."

"Yes," Lee said.

"Understood," I said.

CHAPTER
SEVEN

The rain streamed down in sheets. Sudden gusts of wind slammed into the sides of the armored transport, battering it off course. I always hated ATs, steel-plated boxes designed with more concern about durability than aerodynamics.

We called the cabin area of armored transports the "kettle" because it was metal, potbellied, and had no windows. Inside this kettle, we heard wind rattling the cables that ran between the AT's tail and its stubby wings. The sounds of wind and rain were our only contact with the outside. I looked up through a hatch in the ceiling and saw the pilot flipping switches and pulling levers to smooth the ride.

The walls of the transport groaned as the ship touched down. Then the rear of the ship split open revealing a ramp for us to disembark. We had arrived.

They packed both of Captain McKay's platoons into one transport—sixty privates, sixteen corporals, and six sergeants. We came wearing armor and carrying minimal field supplies. Larger ships would bring artillery, vehicles, field hospitals, and temporary housing. For the time being, all of our equipment came strapped to our backs. I was not concerned. We had twenty-three hundred field-ready Marines on the ground, fighter craft circling the sky, and the only thing our enemy wanted was permission to speak a foreign language.

Shannon, his M27 braced across his chest as if he expected resistance, charged down the ramp shouting for the platoon to follow. He vanished into the glare of the landing lights.

We touched down on a temporary landing strip built by field engineers. Six other ATs landed around us. Above the brightness of the landing lights, I could see the deep black of the night sky.

"Line 'em up!" McKay shouted, his voice thundering over the interLink.

"Get a move on!" Sergeant Shannon yelled. The platoon assembled quickly, forming ranks and standing at attention. Shannon inspected the line, then took his place at the head of the platoon.

The rain fell in glassy panes, which splintered in the wind. Huge drops tapped on my helmet and shoulder plates. Out of the side of my eye, I could see steam rising from spots on the racks of landing lights.

Nestled in my temperature-controlled bodysuit, I felt warm. The temperature inside my armor was a balmy sixty-eight degrees.

Captain McKay crossed the landing pad to inspect the platoon. Dressed in his Charlie Service uniform, he looked cold and wet. His face was pale, and his shoulders were hunched. "Report, Sergeant?"

"All accounted for, sir!" Shannon said with a smart salute.

I heard the whirr of a wing of Harrier fighters doing a fly-over. Captain Olivera had orchestrated the landing by the numbers. First he scanned the area from the *Kamehameha* to find an appropriate drop zone. Next, he sent in a team of commandos to secure the area, followed by the field engineers who erected the temporary landing facility. Once the zone was secure and the facility was constructed, fighters were sent to patrol the skies. It all seemed like overkill for Ezer Kri. From what I heard, Governor Yamashiro had even offered to let us use the local spaceport.

McKay pulled a digital map unit from his belt and showed it to Sergeant Shannon. "Secure areas 7-J, 6-J, and 5-J, then set up camp at the perimeter—space W."

"Aye, sir," Shannon said, and saluted.

McKay returned the salute and walked off. The loud whine of turbines cut through the air as the transports lifted from the landing pad. More would arrive shortly.

Our drop zone was twenty-two miles outside of Hero's Fall, a city with nearly 2 million residents that served as everything but the government seat for Ezer Kri. The locals called Hero's Fall "the old city" because it was the planet's first settlement.

"Okay, gentlemen, we have a long night ahead of us," Shannon shouted over the interLink. "Let's spread out. Harris and Lee, your fire team can take the flank."

Marines do things in threes. Platoons have three squads, each of which is composed of three fire teams. Lee, as the senior corporal, was our team leader. I carried an automatic rifle. We had two privates on the fire team—a grenadier named Amblin and a rifleman named Shultz.

As the platoon divided into fire teams and formed a picket, we moved to the rear. We would remain to the right of the formation. When the shooting started, it would be our job to circle around the enemy. The formation worked well for scouting wide areas but would have left us exposed to sniper attacks in a less secure zone. But we were not walking into battle, and as far as I could tell, the only danger on the planet was that the locals wanted to tell us "sayonara" instead of "good-bye."

Klyber, however, saw our incursion as more of an unofficial occupation than an exercise. He deployed Marines to close the roads around Hero's Fall. Two thousand men might not be enough of a force to lay siege to a city the size of Hero's Fall, but we could certainly teach those Godless Japanese speakers a lesson.

As we left the glare of the landing lights, the lenses in our visors switched automatically to night-for-day vision that illuminated the forest in eerie blue-white tones. While the lens enabled us to see clearly at night, it also rendered us color-blind and hampered our depth perception.

"Keep the chatter down, gentlemen," Shannon said. "Call out only if you see something."

Shannon led us across the meadow and into the trees. The woods outside of Hero's Fall were filled with towering pines that reminded me of the grounds around my old orphanage. "Fan out," Shannon said. "Keep an eye on your team."

About forty minutes into our march, we located a paved road that ran through the woods—a highway leading to town. There were no signs of cars. The police had probably closed the highway to assist with our invasion. Shannon divided the platoon into two squads, which he marched on either side of the road.

"Harris, over here," Shannon called, as we marched.

I trotted to the front of the formation, sloshing through the damp pine needles and kicking up mud. Shannon had left the rest of the platoon and stood on a small ridge surrounded by a particularly dense growth of trees.

"Harris, what do you see in that stand of trees?" he asked, pointing straight ahead with his rifle.

The pocket of trees looked unremarkable. I used my heat-vision lens to see if someone was hiding in the brush. Nothing. Magnifying the view made no difference. "Trees," I said, sounding confused.

"Ever patrol a wooded area?" Shannon asked.

"Only as a cadet," I said.

"There's a trapdoor between those trees," he said. "See it?"

I used every lens in my helmet. "No, Sergeant," I said, beginning to wonder if he was playing with me.

"Stop looking for it. Listen for it. Use your sonar locator."

The locator was a device in our visors that emitted an ultrasonic "ping," then read the way that the ping bounced off objects and surfaces.

Using optical commands, I brought up the locator. A transparent green arc swished across my visor. In its wake, I saw four lines cut into the ground beneath a tree.

"Come here, Harris," Shannon said. He walked toward the door. As I followed, my sonar locator made a new reading, marking an oblong cavity beneath the ground in translucent green. "Damn," I whispered. "I never would have thought about a locator sweep."

"It's called a snake shaft," Shannon said. "You have any idea what it's used for?"

"No," I said.

"Neither does anybody else," Shannon said. "They're what you might call an anomaly. Let's go in for a closer look."

Sergeant Shannon pulled a grenade from his belt and set it for low yield. "Fire in the hole," he yelled as he tossed it into the trees. The grenade exploded with a muffled thud. When the steam cleared, I saw that he had blown a ten-foot hole in the top of the tunnel. Water poured down it as if it were a drain.

I stepped in for a closer look. It was so dark that even with my night-for-day vision, I could not see the bottom. "Who builds these?"

Shannon came over to me. "Mogats, I suppose. Nobody knows for sure. We found them during a battle in the Galactic Eye. That was the first time anybody saw them, I think."

I looked up from the hole and stared at Sergeant Shannon. Had Shannon let that slip, or was he trying to tell me he was a Liberator?

"They can stretch on for miles, and they're strong. I've seen LG tanks park right on top of one of these snake shafts and not dent the roof." LG tanks were low-gravity combat tanks—units that ran low to the ground and weighed in at as much as a hundred tons. "We used to dare each other to hide in the shaft while a tank ran over it. Far as I know, no one ever died doing it."

I stared down into that gaping black maw and watched water pour into it. "Should we check it?" I asked.

"You want to go down in there?" Shannon asked. He did not wait for me to answer. "Me either. I'll have a tech send a probe through it later. Might be something down there. Sometimes they're rigged to blow up.

"I want you and Lee to go scout the area for more of them. Make me a map." With that, Shannon returned to the platoon.

It took several hours to scour the area. Our search turned up eleven more snake shafts. Lee and I caught up with the platoon at Hero's Fall. I needed sleep, but that was not about to happen. Captain McKay and Sergeant Shannon hailed us. "Harris, Lee . . . Glad you could join us."

"We just got here, Sergeant," Lee said.

Across the camp, the platoons had already begun to assemble. I could see ranks forming. "Follow me," McKay said as he started toward the camp.

We set up camp in a large meadow just outside of town. By that time, the rain and wind had stopped. A pervasive stillness echoed across the grounds. The sun rose over the trees, and the wet grass sparkled.

Three Harriers and a civilian shuttle flew in from the west. The fighters formed a tight wedge and circled low in the air as the shuttle touched down. Once the shuttle landed, the fighters thundered over the city's edge and vanished behind a line of buildings.

Captain McKay called the two platoons he commanded to attention. When we were in place, the shuttle's hatch opened. Out stepped Captain Olivera, looking tall, gaunt, and dapper in his Naval whites. Behind Olivera came Vice Admiral Barry, the rather bell-shaped commander of the Scutum-Crux Fleet. Olivera and Barry met with McKay at the bottom of the ramp, and the three of them held a brief conversation. A few moments later, another officer disembarked, one whom I had not expected to see. Wearing a white uniform that seemed tailored to fit his skeletal frame, Admiral Klyber strode off the shuttle with what I would later learn was his distinctive long gait.

Klyber stood at least three inches taller than Olivera—the tallest of the other officers. Pudgy little Barry barely came up to Klyber's neck. Klyber conferred with Barry, asked McKay a question, and the entire party ambled forward.

"Let's have a look at the ranks, shall we?" Klyber said in a comfortable voice, but he paid little attention to the rows of Marines as he walked by. "Have you encountered any resistance?" Klyber asked.

"No, sir," McKay replied.

"No one challenged the air wings, either?" Klyber asked.

"No, sir," said Olivera.

"Have you found evidence of terrorist activity?" Klyber asked.

"One of my platoons sighted a large tunnel just west of town," McKay answered. "It was over three miles long."

"A three-mile-long snake shaft?" Klyber asked. "Religious fanatics, mobsters, racial segregationists . . . It's getting hard to tell the riffraff apart. I understand the Mogats have a large presence on Ezer Kri. Are your men prepared to lay down the law?"

"Yes, sir," said McKay.

"Then we have little to worry about, Captain," Klyber said, sweeping his gaze over the ranks. "This seems like a very pleasant planet; let's hope our stay is uneventful. Admiral Barry, I wish to conclude our tour of Ezer Kri within the month."

The name of the city appeared as "Hero's Fall" in our orders and in the mediaLink accounts of our operation, but as usual, we were misinformed. The local signage said "Hiro's Fall." Apparently the city was named after Takuhiro Yatagei, "Hiro" for short, the planet administrator who stocked the planet with people of Japanese descent. This was the spot where he and the original colonists landed—in legend talk, they "fell from the sky."

Searching for "riffraff" in Hiro's Fall proved to be problematic. The bureaucratic tangles began the first day. The mayor of Hiro's Fall complained to Governor Yamashiro, and Yamashiro formally inquired of the Senate if the Unified Authority was declaring "martial law" on Ezer Kri. The historic reference did not go unnoticed.

I wish we had declared Martial Law. I wish we had launched a full-scale invasion. Enemies do not demand their rights when you bully them, citizens do. Several shopkeepers refused to allow us to inspect their businesses. The president of a car manufacturer called his congressman in DC when Captain McKay sent an inspection team to visit his plant. The Hiro's Fall police department even arrested one of our fire teams for assaulting a local resident. When the police discovered that the victim was a burglar caught in the act, they let the squad go with a warning.

None of this should have mattered, but the more we

scratched the surface, the more we found evidence of deeply rooted corruption. An inspection of the port authority logs showed that the local police ignored smugglers. The Senate's problem might have been with the Japanese population of Ezer Kri, but the problem in this town was a Mogat infestation. The Mogat community had become so deeply rooted in Hiro's Fall that people referred to one of the western suburbs as the "Mogat district."

I had read more than a few stories about Mogats since taking Aleg Oberland's advice about following current events. The Mogats were a religious cult that took its name from Morgan Atkins, a mysterious and charismatic man who vanished about fifty years ago. I did not know anything about Atkins himself, and the only thing I knew about his movement was that it was the first religion created in space.

The U.A. government promoted Christianity, Judaism, and Islam. These churches had holy sites on Earth, and the government encouraged any activity that strengthened ties between frontier planets and Earth.

Atkins's beliefs were pangalactic. His preaching stressed independence, stopping just shy of outright rebellion. While the U.A. Constitution called for general freedom of religion, the Senate spun out a litany of obtuse laws designed to discourage Mogat expansion. The laws did not succeed. Protected by the courts, Mogat communes sprang like daisies across the frontier. News stories about the Mogat movement inevitably started with accusations about smuggling and ended with warnings about Mogat proselytizing and predictions that Atkinism would one day be the largest religion in the galaxy.

No matter what we found, Barry and Klyber seemed unwilling to do more than patrol the streets. We sent platoons on routine patrols through the Mogat district—an industrial area lined with warehouses and factories. We sent "peacekeeping" missions to monitor spaceports. Klyber wanted to make our presence felt without creating confrontations. His strategy worked. Most of the residents of Hiro's Fall resented our presence. We made ourselves hard to ignore.

I did not mind patrolling Hiro's Fall, though it was fairly

dull work. The town was not especially picturesque, but you could see the Japanese influence everywhere. A few downtown parks had pagodas with rice paper walls and fluted roofs. The canal running through the center of town was teeming with gold and white koi. Less than 30 percent of Hiro's Fall was Japanese; but if you were in the right part of town, you might see women dressed in orange-and-red kimonos. My sightseeing ended when the shooting began.

We began sending routine patrols into the Mogat district the night after we landed. These patrols were uneventful. We would hike past warehouses, steel foundries, and gas stations. Workmen stopped and stared at us. There was no way of knowing if these people were Atkins believers, though I suppose most of them were. One thing I noticed during a patrol was that few people in the Mogat district were Japanese.

Seven days after we landed on Ezer Kri, Staff Sergeant Ron Azor led the Twenty-fifth Platoon into the Mogat district for a late-morning patrol. The goal was to follow a random path, marching through alleys and small streets as well as main roads. Azor's path, however, was reckless.

Our combat helmets were designed for standard battlefield situations. They offered good visibility in most situations, but anything above a seventy-degree plane was a blind spot. Whoever planned the attack must have known that.

Azor opened his platoon up for an ambush by marching through a labyrinth of tall buildings and narrow alleyways. A four-story cinder-block building lined their final stretch. Walking beside that building, Azor's platoon had no hope of spotting the enemy that watched from above.

Just as the platoon reached the middle of the block, somebody fired two rockets from the roof of the building. Four men died instantly. Gunmen, hiding behind a ledge, picked off three more men as the platoon dashed across the street for cover.

Desperate to regroup, Azor shot the door off a warehouse. He and his men ducked in and radioed for assistance. Moments later, three rockets slammed into the warehouse. The corrugated steel walls blew apart as did a fuel pump inside the building. No one survived.

* * *

I was off duty when Shannon burst into the barracks and announced the attack. Every available man was called in. I threw on my armor and climbed into a truck. As we drove from the camp, I looked into a blue sky filled with feathery clouds, wondering how there could be an attack on such a beautiful day.

I asked that question again as the truck dropped us next to the pile of rubble that had once been a thirty-foot-tall warehouse. Twisted fingers of what once was a wall stood in the corners of the lot; everything else had crumbled. We were the third platoon to arrive on the scene. Men in green armor dotted the rubble. Shannon led us to a corner of the ruins, and we began pulling up metal sheets and concrete chunks by hand. I felt the urgency, but I knew that we would not find survivors. No one survives that kind of devastation.

I heard the thudding engines of gunships passing overhead. Long and squat and bulky, three Warthogs floated across the sky. They hardly looked airworthy, but there was something menacing about the deliberate way they scoured the rooftops.

The tension was thick. Had a pedestrian carelessly strolled down the street, we might have shot first and asked questions later. But the streets were empty. Perhaps they had been empty before the ambush as well. I wondered how many people knew that the ambush was coming.

"Dig," Shannon shouted over the interLink. "Any man who finds a survivor gets a three-day pass."

We normally would have located the bodies by looking for signals from their helmets, but the heat of the explosion must have destroyed their equipment. There were no signals, so we dug blindly through concrete, iron, and dust. As time went on, hope dwindled, and the rescue effort became less organized.

City engineers arrived on the scene with laser arcs that could cut through concrete and iron alike. With their help, we located twelve crushed bodies and the search became even more discouraging. Judging by the way the bodies were laid out, Azor must have told his men to spread out along the outer wall once they entered the warehouse. Perhaps they thought they needed to guard the windows and doors.

Sergeant Shannon came to check on me. He cursed softly when I mentioned my theory about the way the bodies were spread. "Fool," he said, yanking a metal sheet from under concrete so violently that it tore. "Clone idiot! The enemy shoots rockets at you, so what do you do? You don't hide in a fuel dump. Goddamn it!"

As Shannon spoke, a formation of fighters flew over us. Even though we were wearing helmets and speaking over the interLink, the noise of the fighters drowned out his voice. When they streaked away, I heard Shannon say, "So much for passive force. Klyber is going to make an example of friggin' Ezer Kri."

We did not find all of the bodies. In the early evening, as the sun set and a thick layer of clouds filled the sky, Captain Olivera spoke to us on an open interLink. "An entire platoon has perished here," the captain of the *Kamehameha* began.

As he spoke, three Harriers cruised low overhead—less than fifty feet off the ground. They rotated in perfect unison and banked as they made a hairpin turn. Perched on two crumbling piles of rock, I watched them. Suddenly the middle fighter in the formation exploded and dropped out of the sky. It landed in a heap of smoke and flames. Looking quickly, I saw a contrail leading from a nearby rooftop. Someone had sneaked up there and fired a missile. The two remaining Harriers broke out of formation.

"Spread out! Take cover!" Shannon yelled.

The Harriers zipped around a building, then charged back to the battle zone. Crouching, with my rifle drawn, I watched the roof from behind the knee-high remains of a concrete wall. No more shots were fired. Whoever hit that Harrier had slipped away after making his point.

CHAPTER
EIGHT

What leads men to make such foolish decisions? Admiral Klyber could never have touched the Mogats of Ezer Kri had they lain low. The government did not trust them, but our bylaws protected them. The daily patrols would have continued. We might have raided some buildings. Perhaps they had something to hide, or perhaps their separatist beliefs prevented them from waiting us out. Whatever possessed those Atkins believers to ambush our platoon, they had seriously miscalculated. Fanatics that they were, perhaps the Mogats thought they could take on the entire Scutum-Crux Fleet. But a few rockets and a massacred platoon did not intimidate Bryce Klyber. It irritated him. It showed him that the Ezer Kri government could not be relied upon.

With the *Kamehameha* at his command, Klyber had more than enough firepower to overwhelm Ezer Kri—a planet with a commerce-based economy and impressive engineering facilities but no standing army. Annihilating Ezer Kri would not have been enough for Klyber. He would have used Ezer Kri to send a message across the territories, and he would have made that message clear enough that every colony in the Republic would understand it.

The day of the massacre, the *Kamehameha* altered its orbit so that it flew over Hiro's Fall. As it made its first pass, the ship opened fire, leveling the entire Mogat district. More than fifteen square miles were thoroughly pulverized. Whatever it was that the Mogats wanted to hide, the *Kamehameha* vaporized it in a flash of red lasers and white flames.

A few hours after the demonstration ended, Captain McKay sent several platoons to the area to inspect the damage and search for survivors. It was all theatrics, of course. The destruction was total; nobody could have survived it.

I did not recognize the scene when I hopped off the truck. The sun had not yet risen, and in the gray-blue light of my day-for-night lenses, the urban Mogat district looked like a desert. Lots that once held buildings now looked like rock gardens. The heat of the lasers had melted anything made of glass and metal. It incinerated wood, paper, and cloth into fine ash.

We strolled around the wreckage for nearly an hour, not even pretending to search for survivors. Klyber sent us so that the citizens of Hiro's Fall would know that the U.A. Navy assumed responsibility for demolishing the offending district and that the U.A. Navy felt no regret.

"You see anything?" Vince Lee asked, as we walked over a sloping mound of pebbles that might have once been a factory.

Gravel crunched under my armored boot. "This is an improvement. If they planted some trees and built a pond, this could be a park," I said.

"You're not far off," Private Ronson Amblin said, coming up beside us. "That happens a lot. I've been on more than one assignment where we sacked an entire town, just blew it to dust. You watch. They'll build a monument to galactic unity in this very spot."

"And the bodies?" I asked.

"Bodies?" Amblin asked. "Harris, those lasers were hot enough to melt a truck. Anybody caught here was cremated."

By this time, the sun had started to rise above the skyline, and just as it cleared the tallest buildings, a motorcade approached. Four policemen on motorcycles led the way followed by four shiny, black limousines, with more motor-cycles bringing up the rear. The convoy drove within fifty yards of us and stopped.

Shannon spoke on an open interLink channel. "The local authorities." I detected disgust in his voice. "Fall in behind the other platoons."

Moving at a brisk trot, we lined up in two rows behind the other platoon and stood at attention. The doors of the first government car swung open. I had not been able to see into the cars with their heavily tinted windows, but I was not surprised to see Captain McKay, dressed in formal greens, emerge.

"Attention," Shannon bellowed in our ears, and we all snapped to attention.

I did not recognize the next man who climbed out of the car, but the third man out was Alan Smith, the mayor of Hiro's Fall. A couple of young aides climbed out of the second car and joined Smith. As Smith looked up and down the scene, I saw a set of meaty fingers grip the sides of the car as the rotund form of Vice Admiral Absalom Barry, wearing whites with multiple rows of medals, struggled to his feet.

Barry smiled as he looked over the landscape. Happy-looking wrinkles formed around his eyes. He approached the mayor and muttered something in a soft voice. I could not hear what he said, but Smith laughed nervously. He looked pale. As he passed our ranks, he stared down at our feet.

"I think a slight alteration in the town's name would be appropriate. Naming the town 'Heroes' Fall,' after the fallen Marines seems fitting, don't you think? And this spot, this destroyed area, would be a fine spot for a monument and park . . . with a statue dedicated to the memory of the fallen. That would go a long way toward showing your loyalty to the Republic," Barry said in a raspy voice, his pudgy cheeks glowing. "Nothing too fancy. Nothing over a hundred feet, just a simple monument surrounded by U.A. flags . . ." and then they were too far away to hear.

As the others left, Captain McKay remained behind to address the men. "Gentlemen, you have just witnessed the 'Bryce Klyber Urban Renewal' program."

EZER KRI: One of over 100 habitable planets in the
  Scutum-Crux Arm
POPULATION: 25 million (8.5 million of Japanese an-
  cestry)
LARGEST CITY: Hiro's Fall (4.5 million residents)
CENTER OF COMMERCE: Hiro's Fall
CENTER OF INTELLECTUAL ACTIVITY: Hiro's Fall
GOVERNMENT SEAT: Rising Sun
POPULATION OF RISING SUN: 3 million (2.5 million of
  Japanese ancestry)

Pulverizing the Mogat district changed the social climate
for us in Hiro's Fall. People who once pretended to ignore
our presence now feared us. Captain Olivera left three platoons to patrol "Heroes' Fall," then stationed the rest of us in
other major cities. My platoon was assigned to accompany a
diplomatic envoy visiting the capital city, Rising Sun.

We crossed the planet in two ships. Most of the platoon
traveled in the kettle of an AT. Vince Lee and I, and four
other lucky privates, stood guard on the second ship, a civilian cruiser on loan to the diplomatic corps.

The rest of the men flew in the belly of a flying drum that
barely looked fit to fly. They sat on hard benches with crates
of supplies and equipment around their feet. The main cabin
of the civilian cruiser looked like a living room complete
with lamps, couches, and a wet bar. God, I envied those
other guys.

Wearing greens instead of armor, two privates and I stood
guard around the main cabin. We stood like statues, pretending we did not notice as the bartender mixed drinks and the
waiter served meals.

The pilot flew the mission like a sightseeing tour, hugging close to mountains so that his passengers would enjoy
the vistas. That was another difference between the AT and
the cruiser—the cruiser had windows. From where I stood, I
occasionally saw our Harrier escort through those windows.
After the trouble in Hiro's Fall, we weren't taking any
chances.

Whenever I could, I stole a glimpse outside. The rain
around Hiro's Fall gave way to snow as we traveled north.

We flew over snow-glazed forests and frozen lakes, heading east into a brilliant red-sky sunset. The flaming horizon turned black, and we flew beneath a cloudless sky. As we continued on, the pilot lowered the lights in the cabin, and several of the passengers went to sleep.

When my detail ended, I went to a small cabin in the back of the cruiser to rest. Vince Lee took my post. As I entered the ready room, I noticed light under the door of an executive berth. I tried to figure out who might be behind that door as I lay on my bunk. Sleep came quickly.

Lee woke me a few hours later. "Harris," he said as he prodded my shoulder, "we're nearly there."

I dressed quickly and went to the main cabin. The bureaucrats were all where I'd left them, including one fellow who had camped out on a sofa and snored through half of my watch. Their suits were wrinkled, and a few had messy hair, but they seemed alert. As I moved to the front of the cabin, I looked out a window and saw the first glimpse of dawn—a small swirl of light just beyond dark layers of mountains. And there was Rising Sun, the most glorious city I have ever seen.

Rising Sun sat wedged between a snow-frosted mountain and a mirror-flat lake. Unlike Hiro's Fall, a city that seemed to embrace the past, Rising Sun was thoroughly modern. The streets were regular and straight. White-gold light blazed out of the buildings that lined those streets, illuminating the sidewalks. As we flew closer, I realized that the outer walls of the buildings were entirely transparent. The sight reminded me of a night sky filled with stars.

As our pilot banked the ship and came around for a landing, I stole one last glance out the window and saw the lake. The cruiser touched down softly and coasted toward a landing terminal. We taxied down the runway, the diplomats straightening their clothes and touching up their hair. They were not interested in the spectacular view, only organizing their briefcases and giving their computer files one final read.

When we came to a stop, I peered through the window and saw the armored transport landing a few yards away. Shannon would rush the men off the AT and line them up before our pilot opened the hatch. They were the lucky ones. They traveled in armor. Dressed in our greens, we would freeze our asses in that snowy cold air.

The hatch opened. Carrying my rifle poised across my chest, I led my soldiers down a ramp. We formed a line on each side of the ramp.

At the door of the terminal, a disorganized crowd of Ezer Kri politicians waited for our diplomats to deplane. There might have been as many as fifty of them. I could not tell if it was fear or cold air that made their jaws so tight and their skin so pale.

The first man out of the shuttle was Bryce Klyber, looking tall and gaunt, and wearing the same disingenuous smile that Vice Admiral Barry wore when he toured the Mogat district with the mayor of Hiro's Fall. Dressed in his admiral's uniform, Klyber looked severe despite the grin. He must have been cold in that uniform, but he gave no sign of it. He paused beside our ranks, pierced a few of the men with his gray eyes, then turned toward the terminal.

Yoshi Yamashiro, the governor of Ezer Kri, trotted out to meet Klyber. He wore a dark blue trench coat, unbuttoned and untied, over a charcoal-colored suit. Yamashiro was a stocky man with broad shoulders and huge hands. He was thick, not fat. There was no hint of softness in that neck or those shoulders.

Klyber and Yamashiro shook hands. Klyber said something in a soft voice that I could not hear. Catching himself too late so that it would seem more awkward not to finish, Yamashiro bowed. He made several smaller bows as he and Klyber waited for their limousine. Lee and I followed, taking our places in the front seat of that car.

"Admiral Klyber, we are honored by your visit." I heard Yamashiro's stiff banter as I sat down. Seeing him up close, I realized that Yoshi Yamashiro was older than I had previously guessed. Viewing the video clips, I took him to be in his forties. Now that I saw him in person, I thought he looked closer to sixty.

"This is a remarkable city," Klyber said, with a distinctly informal air.

"You are very kind," Yamashiro said, visibly willing himself not to bow.

As Klyber spoke, his diplomatic corps clambered onto a bus. These were the lackeys, the bean counters, the men who would give Ezer Kri a legalistic pounding. Once the lackeys were loaded, the entourage drove through town.

Isn't that just the way, I thought. *Klyber is all smiles and handshakes, but he comes with a fighter carrier and a complement of frigates.*

The car drove us to the west side of town, where the capitol building was framed by a backdrop of distant mountains. It looked like a glass pyramid with honey-colored light pouring out of its walls. There, we waited in the car while Shannon and his men lined up outside. Once the reception line was ready, aides opened the car doors, and Yamashiro led us up the walk to the capitol. Lee and I followed, trudging through shallow puddles on the way.

Lee and I were to remain with Admiral Klyber and maintain line-of-sight contact until relieved. As he led the admiral into the capitol, Governor Yamashiro glanced nervously over his shoulder at Lee and me, but his comfort was no concern of mine.

"This building is stunning," Klyber proclaimed, in a loud voice.

"Good thing it wasn't in Hiro's Fall; he would have bombed it," an aide whispered behind me. I looked back over my shoulder, and the three aides quickly turned down another hall.

"We are quite proud of our architecture," Yamashiro said.

"I have never seen anything like it," Klyber said.

"Then this is your first visit to Ezer Kri?"

"Yes," Klyber admitted. "I thought I had been all over this Arm. I've been assigned here for several years now."

Low-level bureaucrats peered out of office doorways as we walked down the hall. I worried about security even though the Rising Sun police had searched the building earlier that morning and there were guards and X-ray machines at every entrance.

For his part, Klyber focused his attention on Governor Yamashiro, pausing only once as we passed an indoor courtyard with a large pond and some sort of shrine. I saw several works of art around the capitol, but the best piece sat behind the desk just outside the governor's door. She stood as we approached, and I had a hard time staring straight ahead.

"Admiral Klyber, this is my assistant, Ms. Lyons," Yamashiro said.

I would have expected the governor to have a Japanese assistant, but this statuesque woman was cosmopolitan with brown hair that poured over her shoulders and flawless white skin. She had green eyes, and her dark red lipstick stood out against her white skin.

Admiral Klyber paid no attention to her. He walked past Ms. Lyons as if she weren't there and into the office.

She followed him, shuffling her feet quickly to keep up. She wore a short blue dress that ran halfway down her thighs. "Can I get anything for you, Admiral Klyber?" Ms. Lyons asked.

Klyber might not have noticed her, but Lee homed right in. He stole an obvious gander as he snapped to attention and pretended to take in the entire room.

"I am quite fine," Klyber said, without turning to look at the woman.

"We're fine for now, Nada," Yamashiro said.

"Very well," the woman said.

My first thought when I saw the woman was something along the line of, *Yamashiro, you sly dog*. But there was intelligence in her voice. I had misjudged.

Yamashiro's assistant turned to leave the room and stopped in front of me. She looked at me, and said, "Can I bring you gentlemen anything?"

With some effort, I looked past her and said nothing. When she turned to leave, I felt relieved.

Admiral Klyber might not have paid attention to Ms. Nada Lyons on her own, but our little exchange had not escaped him. He stared into my eyes until he was sure that I saw him, then he made the smallest of nods and turned his attention back to Governor Yamashiro.

Yamashiro did not retreat behind his wide wooden desk. Klyber sat in one of the two seats placed in front of the gubernatorial desk, and Yamashiro sat beside him.

"Okay, Admiral Klyber, the gloves are off. What can I do to prove my planet's loyalty to the Republic?" Governor Yamashiro asked, sounding stymied. "We have the entire Ezer Kri police force searching for leads. I have authorized the wholesale questioning of anybody affiliated with the Atkins movement . . . a sizable percentage of our population, I might add, and you still have no proof that the Atkins believers were behind the attack."

"I appreciate your efforts," Klyber said, still sounding relaxed. "All the same, I think the manhunt will go more smoothly if some of my forces help conduct it."

"I see," Yamashiro said, his posture stiffening.

"From what I have observed, Hiro's Fall was overrun by Mogat sympathizers. I understand that several Mogats held posts in the city government. I am sure you were aware of those problems, Governor Yamashiro." Klyber folded his hands on his lap.

"I see," Yamashiro said, looking nervous. "And you hold my office responsible for the attack?"

"Not at all," said Klyber, still sounding conversational. "But I will hold you personally responsible for any future hostilities, just as the Joint Chiefs will hold me accountable for anything that happens to my men.

"I will insist, Governor, that you remain in the capitol for the next few days. I have assigned one of my platoons to see to your protection."

"Am I under house arrest, then?" asked Yamashiro.

"Not at all. We are simply going to help you run your planet more efficiently."

"Then this is undeclared mart—"

"Martial law?" Klyber asked, his smile looking very stiff. "Friends in the Senate warned me about your gift for historical references."

Klyber leaned forward in his chair, and his voice hardened. His back was to me, but I imagined that his expression had turned stony as well. "This is not martial law, Governor Yamashiro. I'm trying to protect you."

* * *

Admiral Klyber retained five men from our platoon to guard his quarters, then set the rest of us loose on Rising Sun. He gave us full liberty so long as we remained dressed in battle armor. Apparently Klyber wanted to make sure that the locals knew we were there.

We, of course, used the occasion to acquaint ourselves with the bars.

Most of the men went out in a herd, but Lee and I got a late start. Lee was fanatic about his sleep. We had liberty, but we did not leave to try the local drinking holes until well past eight, and he insisted on trying the upscale institutions along the waterfront. When I told him that the rest of the platoon was checking out the bars on the west side of town, Lee responded, "Those clones may be satisfied with mere watering holes; we shall look at finer establishments."

"Asshole," I said, even though I knew the attitude was a sham.

We took a train to the "Hinode Waterfront Station." Everywhere we went, I saw signs referring to Hinode. Many of the signs were also marked with those strange squiggling designs that I understood to be the Japanese form of writing. It wasn't until the next day that I realized that "Hinode" was the Japanese word for "Rising Sun."

The bars we found were posh and elite, with swank names; some had Japanese lettering in their signs. The late-night dinner crowd strolled the waterfront streets. Men in business suits and women in fine dresses stopped in front of restaurant display cases to look at plasticized versions of the foods.

"This looks pretty expensive," I told Vince as I looked at a menu. "Yakisoba, whatever that is, costs fifty dollars."

"Maybe that's the name of the waitress," Lee said.

"Pork tonkatsu costs forty-five. If pork tonkatsu is the name of a waitress, I don't want her."

"How about over there," Lee said, pointing to a small, brightly lit eatery.

"That place is too bright for drinks," I said.

Lee ran across the street for a closer look, and I followed. The place was crowded. People used chopsticks to eat colorful finger foods off small dishes.

We entered, and the crowd became quiet. A man came up to us and spoke in Japanese. We, of course, did not understand a word of it. "Think he speaks English?" I asked Lee over the interLink in our helmets.

"Sure he does," Lee said. "This is why the Senate does not want them to have their own language."

After a few moments, I looked at Vince and shrugged my shoulders. The diners became loud again as we turned to leave.

I hated admitting defeat, but the Rising Sun waterfront beat me down. After a frustrating hour, Vince and I caught a taxi to the center of town. We found a likely-looking bar and went inside. The place was nearly empty. Three men sat slumped in their seats at the counter.

"This must be where the clerical help goes," Vince said.

Two Japanese women waited just inside the door. A hostess came and seated them. When Vince started toward the bar, she turned, and said, "Please wait to be seated."

After twenty minutes of waiting to be seated, we gave up and left to find another bar.

By 2300 *Kamehameha* time, Vince and I retreated to the west end of town. We were hungry, thirsty, and frustrated. In any other town, the bars would be the only lit buildings by that time of night. Not in Rising Sun. In this town every building's crystal finish glowed with the same goddamned honey-colored lights. At that point I wanted to stow my armor and walk into the next bar pretending to be a civilian; but if I took off my gear, I was technically AWOL.

As we explored the west end, we started hearing voices and music. We followed the sounds around a corner and found a crowded bar. Staring through the window, I saw several Marines. They had removed their helmets, which sat on the table. When I scanned the helmets, I recognized the names from my platoon.

"This must be the place," said Lee.

"I hope they have food," I said. I opened the door, and dozens of Marines turned to greet me. Sitting in the center of this ungodly pack, happily waving a cigar as he spoke, was Master Gunnery Sergeant Tabor Shannon.

One private placed his helmet over his head so he could

read our identifiers as we entered. "It's Lee and Harris," he said to the others.

"The illustrious honor guard has finally found its way," Shannon said. "Hello, Lee. Hello, Harris."

"Sergeant," I said.

"I'll get the drinks this time," Lee said.

"I don't get it," I said as I started to sit down. "Are we on duty or off?"

Shannon smiled behind his cigar, then uttered a few curses. "On duty. Klyber is using us as"—he considered for a moment—"as a diplomatic bargaining chip. He wants to show the locals how easy it would be for this visit to turn into a long-term occupation."

"Drinking sounds like a good occupation to me," one private said.

"Not occupation as in job, moron!" another private said.

"Oh," the first one responded.

"That's the kid that found the bar," Shannon said, pointing at the private with his cigar. "He's been soaking up beers for hours."

"So, are we on our best behavior?" I asked.

Shannon smiled. "In this case, bad is good." He nodded at the drunk private. "This boy's going to empty his stomach somewhere, probably right outside that door. Usually that would get him a night in the brig; but tonight, it will go unnoticed. Klyber wants to show the respectable politicos of Rising Sun just how much they don't want us around. A little puke leaves a lasting impression."

Shannon leaned forward. "Harris, did you know you have a friend in town."

"A friend?" I asked.

"Yeah," said Shannon. "It appears that the Japanese are not the only ones keeping their bloodlines pure on this rock." Shannon turned and gazed toward the far side of the bar. "That guy was asking about you."

I stood up and looked around the room. At the other end of the building, Ray Freeman sat with an untouched beer. The top of the table was level with the tops of Freeman's thighs. He looked like an adult sitting on children's play furniture.

"Know him?" Shannon asked.

"I know him. His name is Ray Freeman. He's the mercenary I met on Gobi."

Freeman looked over at me from his table. His eyes had their same dark intensity, but his mouth formed a cheerful smile. The overall effect was unsettling.

"You would not believe how much they charge for a damn beer," Lee said as he returned with two huge mugs. "For these prices . . ." He saw me staring at Freeman. "Friend of yours?"

"That's the mercenary that Admiral Brocius sent to Gobi," I said.

"Looks dangerous," Lee said. "Are you planning on talking to him?"

"He doesn't talk much," I said. "But I am curious about what he might have to say."

"I'm coming with you," Lee said.

"Do you think he wants trouble?" Shannon asked.

"If Ray Freeman came looking for trouble, I doubt I would have made it to the bar alive," I said. "He's worse than he looks."

"I don't know how that could be, Harris," Lee said. "He looks pretty bad."

Freeman stood and smiled down at me as Lee and I walked over. "Well, hello, Wayson. Been a long time. How is life in the Corps?" His voice had an overly friendly quality. First Barry, then Klyber, then Freeman. It was my day for seeing painted smiles.

"Is he always this chatty?" Lee asked over the interLink.

"What brings you to Scutum-Crux?" I asked. Freeman sat down and waved to the empty chairs around his table. Lee and I joined him. We must have looked odd, two men in combat armor sitting beside a bald-headed giant.

"I'm here on business," Freeman said.

"Anybody we know, Mr. . . ." Lee let his voice trail off.

"Sorry," Freeman said, still sounding friendly. "Call me Ray."

"Vince Lee."

"I guess Wayson has told you what I do."

"Sounds as if you do it well, too, at least if everything Harris says is true."

"I suspect Corporal Harris has exaggerated the story," Freeman said.

"He might have," Lee said. He removed his helmet. "No use letting my beer get warm. You're not drinking yours?" The head on Freeman's beer had gone flat.

"Actually, I only bought the beer to help me blend in," Freeman said.

"I don't think it's working," I said. "So is your target in the bar?"

"No, I came here looking for you. I heard your platoon was stationed in Rising Sun. This seemed like the best place to watch for you."

"What a coincidence," I said, not believing a word of it. "Both me and your target came to the same planet."

I took off my helmet and took a long drag of beer. "Are you still looking for Crowley?"

"I have a score to settle," Freeman said, "but that is not why I am here. I bumped into another friend of yours from Gobi earlier today. In fact, he's staying in the hotel across the street."

"Really?" I said. I took another drink, nearly finishing my beer. "Who is it?" Names and faces passed through my mind.

"I was hoping to surprise the both of you," Freeman said. "You know what would be funny, you and Vince can trade helmets, and we can surprise the guy. You know, so you don't have that identifier . . . just in case he's wearing his helmet."

Lee and I looked at each other. As far as I knew, the only people in Rising Sun with combat helmets flew in on the *Kamehameha*. Freeman had some scheme in the works, but I could not think what it might be, and I did not trust him.

"That doesn't sound like such a good idea," I said.

"Nothing is going to happen to you, Wayson," Freeman said, sounding slightly wounded. "It will be fun."

"Who are we surprising?" I asked.

"You wouldn't want me to spoil the surprise."

"I don't mind trading," Lee offered.

"Tell you what," Freeman said. He dug through his wallet

and pulled out a bill. "It's worth twenty bucks to me to have you guys trade helmets."

"I don't know about this," I said. The more Freeman tried to act breezy and conversational, the more ghoulish he sounded. I wanted to warn Lee over the interLink, but he had removed his helmet.

"You still don't trust me?" Freeman said.

"Twenty dollars?" Lee asked. He gulped down his beer. "What can it hurt?"

"Thanks," Freeman said, sounding pleased. "I'll pick up your next round, too."

"Don't worry about it, Harris," Lee said. "I'll just head back with the rest of the platoon."

Lee's hanging back with the platoon sounded good to me. I could not think of any reason why Freeman might want to hurt Lee, but I still did not trust him.

Lee grabbed my helmet, and I took his.

"Look, Wayson, I need to pay the check. Why don't you head across the street, and I'll meet you in the hotel lobby."

I took one last look at Lee, then put on his helmet. "Damn," I whispered. Whatever he'd eaten for lunch had left a foul-smelling ghost in his rebreather. I got up from the bar and walked toward the door. Shannon and a few other soldiers waved as I left.

The street was completely empty by that time. I checked for cars, then trotted across the street to the hotel.

The outside of the hotel was built out of that same thick crystal—very likely an indigenous mineral of some kind. The lobby, however, was not so elegant. Poorly lit and cheaply decorated, it had metal furniture and a scuffed-up check-in desk. The unshaved clerk at the desk watched me as I entered the lobby, but said nothing.

"Let's go," Freeman said as he joined me a few moments later. He no longer smiled or wanted to talk, that was the Freeman I knew.

"So who are we here to see?" I asked.

He did not answer.

"Is it Crowley?" I asked.

"Not Crowley," Freeman said.

Rather than take the elevator, Freeman ran up the stairs. We entered a dimly lit stairwell and climbed twelve flights. "You're still charming as ever," I said, as we reached the top.

Freeman pulled his handheld computer from his pocket and looked at it. "Hurry," he said. "Your pals are getting ready to leave the bar." He held the monitor so that I could see it. Apparently he had placed a remote camera under his seat. Looking at the monitor, I saw Shannon standing up. Some of the other men were already wearing their helmets and heading for the door.

We entered a red-carpeted hall with numbered doors. Freeman stopped under a hall light. He pulled a pistol from under his chestplate. He walked to room number 624. Pulling a key chip from his pocket, Freeman unlocked the door and let it slide open.

The only light in the room came from the glare of the street outside. We crept along the wall. We had entered a suite. Freeman pointed toward a bedroom door, and I stole forward to peer inside.

Looking across the room, I saw the pale moon through the top of a window. Someone was crouching beside that window, spying the street. I could only see his thick silhouette. In this dim light, he did not look human.

"He's watching the bar door," I whispered inside my helmet.

Using his right hand, the man brought up a rifle with a barrel-shaped scope. I had used a similar scope in training camp. It was an "intelligent" scope, the kind of computerized aiming device that offers more than simple magnification. "He's looking for . . ."

Then I understood. I sprang forward. Hearing my approach, the sniper turned around and started to raise his rifle. By that time, I had leaped most of the way across the room. I grabbed the rifle, spun it over my right hand, and stabbed the butt into the assassin's face. The man made an agonized scream and dropped to the floor.

I removed my helmet and went to the window. Raising the rifle, I looked down at the street through the scope. Most of the men from the platoon stood outside the door of the bar. The intelligent scope had an auto-action switch set to fire. The scope read the identifier signals from our helmets. The scope would locate a preset target, and the rifle would shoot automatically. In the center of the pack, Corporal Vincent Lee was clearly identified as Corporal Wayson Harris—me. The scope made a soft humming noise as it automatically homed in on my helmet.

"You owe me twenty bucks, Harris," Freeman said as he switched on the lights.

Lying dazed on the floor, the sniper moaned. One of his eyes was already starting to swell from the impact of the rifle, and blood flowed from the bridge of his nose. He reached up to touch his wounded face, and I noticed that his arm ended in a stub.

"Well, hello, Kline," I said.

Ray Freeman trusted the Rising Sun police enough to let them put Kline in a holding cell, but he insisted on watching that cell until military police signed for the prisoner. Freeman's wait would have been none of my business except that Captain McKay ordered me to remain with Kline until the MPs arrived as well. So the station captain placed a couple of chairs near Kline's cell and told us to make ourselves at home.

For me, making myself "at home" meant removing my helmet. Freeman made himself at home by pulling out a twelve-inch knife that he had somehow slipped past station security and cleaning his fingernails. The knife looked deceptively small in Freeman's large hands.

Admiral Klyber arrived with an intelligence officer as the first traces of sunrise shone through the wire-enforced windows. I jumped out of my chair and saluted, but Freeman remained seated. A slight smile played across Klyber's lips as he regarded us. He returned my salute, and said the perfunctory, "At ease, Corporal."

I was technically out of uniform. Looking down at my helmet, and feeling guilty, I said, "Sorry, sir."

"Not at all, Corporal. As I understand it, you caught the

prisoner while you were off duty." Klyber then turned to face Ray Freeman. "I understand you were instrumental as well."

Freeman said nothing.

"Sir," I said, not wanting to contradict the senior-most officer in this part of the galaxy, but determined to set the record straight.

Klyber interrupted me. "This is Lieutenant Niles, from Naval Intelligence."

I saluted.

He saluted back. "That's your bubble?" he asked, pointing to my helmet.

"Yes, sir," I said. *Bubble*, short for *bubblehead*, was Navy slang for Marines. And it was indeed mine. Lee and I had traded back after we caught Kline.

"Would you mind if I borrowed it? It could prove useful during my interrogation."

"Yes, sir," I said.

He took the helmet and excused himself.

"Why don't you stay for the interrogation," Klyber said, as Niles walked away. Freeman and I followed the admiral into a small dark room in which four chairs overlooked a bank of medical monitors and a large window. As we sat, a light came on at the other side of that window. Two policemen led Kline into the interrogation room and sat him on a small metal chair.

I must have been far too rough on Kline. No one had bothered to clean the dried blood from where I'd struck his face with the butt of the rifle. His left eye was swollen shut and purple. It looked wet and badly infected.

Niles entered the room carrying a large canvas bag in one hand and my helmet in the other. The policemen tried to cuff Kline's arms behind the back of his chair, eventually closing one manacle around his left wrist and the other around his right elbow. As they did this, Niles arranged several objects on a small table near the door. The policemen prepared to leave, but Niles intercepted them and whispered something. Niles smiled as they left the room, then he turned to Kline, and said, "You make a pathetic assassin."

"This is all a misunderstanding. An assassin?" Kline said. With his thick tongue, the S's in "assassin" had a harsh

sound—"azz-azin." "I came here for a vacation. I thought I
might do some hunting on Lake Pride."

"And this is your rifle?" Niles held up Kline's rifle and
peered through its scope.

"It's for hunting," Kline said.

"You sound like quite the sportsman, Mr. Kline." Niles
was terse but not unfriendly. He placed the gun back on the
table, then walked over to Kline, who shifted his weight on
the small metal chair. "Is it Kline or Mr. Kline?"

"Kline."

"I am asking if Kline is your first or last name."

"Only one name, I am afraid." Kline sounded distressed.

"Oh," Niles said. "So you are an Atkins Separatist. As far
as I know, only two kinds of people go by a single name—
Morgan Atkins Separatists and professional musicians. If
your right hand is any indication, I assume you are not a
musician."

"The term is 'believer,' not 'separatist,'" Kline said in a
sullen voice.

"My mistake," Niles said.

"Tell you what, Kline. Let's try an experiment. Let's pretend that I am you, and you are . . . Let's say that you are a
corporal in the Marines. We'll pretend that you are Corporal
Wayson Harris, for instance. Are you with me so far?"

Kline shrugged. "I don't understand the purpose of this?"

"Maybe this will help," Niles said, lifting my helmet
from the table.

"This is Corporal Harris's helmet." Niles stuffed it down
over Kline's head. Short and round, Kline was not made for
combat armor. The circumference of his skull was slightly
too large; but with some force, Niles managed to slam the
helmet in place. Kline screamed as the lip of my helmet
raked down across his wounded eye.

"Looks like a good fit," Niles said.

Kline slumped forward in his chair, hyperventilating.
Only the restraints around his arms kept him from falling to
the floor. "What are you doing?" he moaned.

"My experiment," the Intelligence officer said, sounding slightly offended. "You remember, we're conducting
an experiment?

"On the arrest report, it says that the scope on your rifle reads a frequency reserved for military use. That makes this scope contraband, and smuggling contraband between planets is a federal offense. And it gets worse. The report says that the auto-switch on this scope was set to go off when it located a specific signal. Now, why would the scope on a hunting rifle be set to read identifier signals in the first place? I'm sure this is all a colossal mistake."

Kline said nothing.

"According to the police, that specific signal would be the identifying code broadcast by Corporal Harris's helmet . . . the helmet you are wearing at this very moment. That would mean you came to Lake Pride hunting Corporal Harris.

"Me, I don't believe that a law-abiding fellow like you came to Rising Sun hunting another human being. So here is my experiment."

Niles picked up the rifle and walked behind Kline's chair. "First, I will load this rifle." He drew back the bolt. Deliberately fumbling the bullet so that it clanged against the barrel of the rifle several times, he slid it into the chamber and locked the bolt back in place.

"Now let's see what happens when I hit to auto-switch and point the gun at that helmet you are wearing."

"Don't!" Kline shouted.

"A problem with my theory?"

"You're going to kill me!" Kline's voice bounced and fluttered. He was crying inside the helmet.

Without a word, the Intelligence officer removed the bullet from the rifle and pocketed it. He placed the rifle back on the table, then wrenched the helmet off Kline's head. The prisoner whimpered and sat with his chin tucked into his flabby neck.

"You know, Mogat, I think you have some interesting tales to tell. And the best part is, chubby little speckers like you always talk. Always."

Niles headed for the door of the interrogation room, then turned back. "I'll have the police return you to your cell."

"He will cooperate," Admiral Klyber said quietly. "I doubt, however, that he will have any valuable information. Crowley would never trust anything important with such a weakling."

I felt as if I had just watched an execution. Klyber showed absolutely no empathy for their prisoner. The physiology monitors lining the walls of the observation room showed that Kline's heart pace had nearly doubled. His blood pressure rose so high when Niles placed my helmet over his head that a heart attack seemed imminent; yet I, too, felt strangely unsympathetic.

"I don't believe there was any particular bounty on Kline," said Klyber. "Does a reward of three thousand dollars seem adequate?"

Freeman nodded.

"Very good. I will see that you are paid by the end of the day, Mr. Freeman. I'm curious, though, why come as far as the Scutum-Crux Arm chasing a small-time criminal with such low prospects?"

"Little fish sometimes lead you to bigger ones," Freeman said as he stood to leave.

"I see," Klyber said, without standing up. "Well, fine work, Freeman. I hope you find the bigger fish you are looking for."

Freeman nodded again and left.

Admiral Klyber leaned forward and flipped a switch, turning off the sound in the next room. "Your name keeps popping up, Corporal Harris. Why should that be?"

I knew precisely why my name sounded familiar to Admiral Klyber, but I had no intention of dredging up my record on Gobi. I had other things on my mind, so as soon as Klyber and the Intelligence officer left the police station, I asked one of the guards to take me to Kline's cell. I found him lying on his cot and staring up at the ceiling, his swollen eye still oozing yellow pas.

"You should have a doctor look at that," I said as I entered the cell.

Kline said nothing. He continued to stare up at the ceiling.

"I can see you're busy, and I don't want to take up too much of your time, but I was curious how you survived Freeman's grenade," I said.

"Is that you, Harris?" Kline asked.

"It's me," I said.

"Did you watch the interrogation?"

"You didn't say anything about how you made it out of the desert with a grenade glued to your hand," I said.

Kline snickered and sat up on his cot. While returning the little mutant to his cell, the guards had finally washed the blood from his head, but the entire side of his face was swollen and bruised. He held up his left arm and let the baggy sleeve of his robe fall to reveal the stub. "How do you think I survived?"

"I'm guessing that the grenade was a dud," I said.

"I cut my hand off and left it in the desert, asshole. Well, one of Crowley's lieutenants cut it off for me," Kline said. "He found me wandering in the desert. Do you have any idea how much that hurt?" With that, he lay back down on his cot.

"So you decided to fly to Ezer Kri to shoot me," I said. "Why me? Why not Freeman? He was the one who glued the grenade to your hand."

"I wanted to go after Freeman, but Crowley said to go after you instead," Kline said without looking in my direction. "He said I'd never get a shot off if I went after Freeman. Freeman is a dog. You are just as bad as he is. You let him do this to me. You're just another rabid dog."

"And you are a terrorist," I said. "You are an enemy of the Republic."

"Everybody is an enemy of the Republic. I don't know anybody who likes the Republic," Kline said. "At least nobody who isn't a clone."

From what I could see, Governor Yamashiro sincerely wanted to cooperate. The mediaLink ran local news stories about the Ezer Kri police cracking down on all known Morgan Atkins sympathizers. Work crews began converting the ruins of the Mogat district into a park two days after the *Kamehameha* bombarded it. With local forces closing in on the ground and Klyber's ships blockading the planet, no one could leave Ezer Kri. Yamashiro only had twenty-four hours left to turn over the criminals. At that point, I thought he might make it.

* * *

The *Chayio* was one of fifteen frigates that accompanied the
Kamehameha on the mission to Ezer Kri. Small by capital
ship standards and designed for battling fighters and smugglers, frigates were approximately six hundred feet long and
outfitted with twenty particle-beam cannons. The guns on
frigates were perfect for downing the small, fast-moving
ships used by pirates and smugglers, but they would not dent
the armor on a capital ship.

They fit well with Admiral Klyber's philosophy. Since
the Unified Authority was the only entity with a navy in the
entire galaxy, he wanted the Scutum-Crux Fleets outfitted
for conflicts with smugglers and terrorists. After all, nobody
but the U.A. Navy had the capacity to build anything even
near the size of a battleship.

By spreading his frigates over the most populated areas
on Ezer Kri, Klyber formed a blockade that could stop ships
from leaving the planet. It was a good strategy. A single
frigate would have enough guns to shoot down any ship
parked in this solar system. On the off chance that a frigate
did run into that unforeseen enemy, the three nearest frigates
could converge on the scene in less than one minute. In theory, our net was impregnable and our ships unstoppable. But
in practice, our net had frayed along the edges.

The *Chayio*, for instance, guarded the space over a small
island chain, fairly boring duty. The captain of the ship was
not even on the bridge when the storm hit; his first lieutenant
had the helm.

The young lieutenant walked around the deck talking ca-
sually with other officers. Watching the video record that was
found in the remains of the ship two days after the attack, I
got the feeling that he did not take his duties seriously.

"Sir, I'm picking up increased energy signatures on the
planet," one of the communications officers called out. "It
looks like a fleet of small ships."

"Let's see what you've got," the lieutenant said, breaking
away from another conversation. He walked toward the
scanning station too slowly. Clearly he thought the sighting
was a nuisance.

"My reading just spiked," the communications officer said. "More ships are flaring up, sir."

"What?" The lieutenant sounded baffled. He leaned over the communications officer's shoulder for a better look; and then it happened.

There was a brilliant flash of blue-white light and two dreadnought destroyers appeared in front of the *Chayio*. At that point, our display screen divided in two. A small window in the corner of the screen showed the bridge of the *Chayio*, while the rest of the screen showed the scene as captured by a communications satellite orbiting Ezer Kri.

I had never seen ships of that make before. They bore the familiar sharp lines and forward shield arrays of U.A. Navy ships, but the hull design and size were completely foreign. The ships were several times larger than the *Chayio*. They had globelike bridges studded with cannons and firing bays. Their coloring was darker than charcoal—so dark that they seemed to blend into space itself.

"Forward shields, now!" the lieutenant shouted, demonstrating surprisingly quick reflexes.

The dreadnoughts hung silently in space for a moment. During that moment, the lieutenant at the helm of the *Chayio* called for his captain and sent a distress signal to all nearby ships. Neither the captain nor the nearby ships arrived in time.

One of the dreadnoughts fired into the frigate's shields.

"Do not return fire. Channel all power to the shields," the lieutenant ordered. He must have planned to keep a wall between his ship and the dreadnoughts until help arrived. His plan should have worked. With all of its power poured into the forward shield, the *Chayio* might have survived the battering for several minutes as it waited for help from the *Kamehameha*.

There was a blue-white flash behind the *Chayio*, and another destroyer materialized behind the frigate. This third ship took only a moment to stabilize before firing two torpedoes. With all power to its forward shields, the rear of the *Chayio* was unprotected. The little frigate exploded into a fireball that was quickly extinguished in the vacuum of space.

As I watched the frigate explode, I noticed streaks of light in the background. A swarm of smaller ships evacuated Ezer Kri and disappeared into space as the battle occurred.

Seeing the video feed, I knew that the fleeing ships would belong to the Mogats. Who else could they belong to? What other population needed to flee en masse? But I always thought of the Mogats as a bunch of crank religionists. Where the hell had they gotten a fleet of small ships? Another question: How had they gotten their hands on destroyers? As a Marine, my biggest question was, "Where are they going to next?" Wherever they went, I wanted to greet them.

CHAPTER
TEN

Though he would never have confided his feelings to his corporals, Sergeant Tabor Shannon must have sensed the upcoming war. Other platoon leaders let their men relax between patrols; Shannon had us dress in full combat armor and drill. He sent us on ten-mile hikes in the muddy forests north of Rising Sun. Three days after the attack on the *Chayio,* he took us for a predawn drill up the sheer wall of a nearby mountain. I could see the shape of the full moon in the clouded winter sky. Its distorted silhouette showed through the clouds like a smudge on a photograph.

Shannon dropped ropes from the top of the cliff; the rest of the platoon scaled up the face of the mountain to meet him. When we reached the top, he smiled and sent us rappelling back down. Our combat gear protected us from the cold, but nothing stopped the muscle burn in our arms and backs.

If there had ever been a layer of dirt covering the face of these cliffs, it had long since washed away. This face was rock and ice with a few stray ferns growing in its crags. As I dropped down the edge of the precipice, my boots clattered on the wet stone face.

"Move it! Move it! Move it!" Shannon shouted down at us.

My right foot slipped against the wet rock, and I struggled to find good footing. Like me, most of the troopers had trouble finding secure footing on the way back down. We did not practice rappelling on board ship. The last time I had done so was in the orphanage. We had jetpacks, why would we need to rappel?

"Too long! Too slow!" Shannon shouted.

"I'd like to see you do this," I said under my breath.

Shannon's cord dropped just to my right. I looked up in time to see him jump over the edge of the cliff. Taking long, narrow bounces, the sergeant plunged down the cord so quickly that it looked like a free fall.

"I could do that," I said to myself. "I just don't feel like showing off." I took a quick look over my shoulder. The lake filled the horizon. Craning my neck to look out, I could see the waterfront. In the daylight, the buildings looked like ice sculptures. I took a deep breath and prepared to drop faster. As I exhaled that breath, a bullet struck the cliff, shooting sparks and rock fragments that bounced against the visor of my helmet.

I blinked, though my visor protected me. Reflexes. At that same moment, I opened my fingers and let the cord whip across my armor-covered palms, dropping me into a loosely controlled free fall. As I reached the trees below, I tightened my grip to slow myself. I let go of the rope and dropped the last few feet into the mud. Standing a few yards away, Sergeant Shannon stood muttering to himself under his breath and firing live rounds at the cliff. He had removed his helmet. His face was spattered with dirt. The mud, combined with his all-tooth smile and wide, excited eyes, gave him a crazed look.

"You call that climbing?" Shannon yelled. "Move it, you dipshit maggots," he bawled with a string of accompanying cusses. "I did not bring you here to go sightseeing!" He fired his rifle, and two of the men crashed down to the mud.

"I'll bet that's Lee," Shannon muttered as he stared up at the cliff. "Hey, Lee, have a nice fall." With the butt of his rifle tucked under his arm, Shannon squeezed off two shots that severed the cords just above one of the man's hands. The man plummeted, bouncing off the face of the cliff before igniting his jetpack and lowering to the ground safely. Seeing what happened, the rest of the men rappelled down the cliff more quickly.

"Jeeezus sakes Christ!" Shannon yelled, looking over his panting platoon. "I could have picked off the whole friggin' lot of you. The whole damn lot. I thought I came to drill Marines, not take old ladies sightseeing. Hell, I could have cooked me a barbecue and called your next o'kin before I started shooting. Next time, I'm loading rubber bullets and bagging me some maggots. You sisters better wear your safety loops tight. Next time I'm shooting rubbers.

"And, ladies, when I say 'next time,' I mean after lunch."

All of us "ladies" groaned.

Lunch was no treat. It rained. We gathered around the truck and opened our MREs. No heated food to soften our bellies that day, just the standard mushy vegetables and pre-fabricated stew. Despite the vacuum packaging, everything tasted stale.

A white government car pulled up beside us as we ate. A pasty-faced bureaucrat in a shiny gray suit climbed out of the car. He had perfectly coiffed hair. With his clothes and grooming, the man looked completely out of place among the trees. He scanned the platoon, picked out Sergeant Shannon, and joined us.

"Can I help you?" Sergeant Shannon asked, with a wolfish grin.

"Sergeant Shannon?" the man asked.

"I'm Shannon."

The man held out an envelope with an SC Central Fleet seal. Handing his rations to another soldier, Shannon took the communiqué and opened it. "Harris," he called.

I walked over. "Sergeant?"

"Looks like you get to skip our next hike," Shannon said. "SC Command wants you to deliver your prisoner to the *Kamehameha*." He handed me the communiqué. I scanned it quickly and saw that I was supposed to get cleaned up and dress in my greens.

I rode back to camp in that posh government car. No hard wooden seats in that ride. When we got back to camp, my bureaucratic escort gave me ten minutes to dress and shower.

"We're on a tight schedule," he told me. "You need to report to the *Kamehameha* by three."

The Rising Sun police met us at the landing pad and turned Kline over to me in cuffs and manacles. I signed for him and walked him onto the transport. We had the kettle to ourselves, just Kline and me, alone, sitting near the back of the ship. His injured eye looked more infected than ever. The skin around it had turned purple, and yellow pus seeped out from under the closed eyelid.

He stared at me for a moment, then asked, "Harris?"

"Yes," I said.

We both sat silently as the ramp closed and the AT took off. Not wanting to look at that ruined face, I stared straight ahead at the metal wall of the kettle and let my thoughts wander. *Would there be war?*

"They're going to execute me," Kline said, his calm voice cutting through my thoughts.

"I suspect they will get around to it, sooner or later," I said.

"No," Kline corrected me. "They are going to execute me tonight. They will hold a tribunal. I won't even get a trial. You are delivering me to be executed."

"You cannot possibly expect me to feel sorry for you. You came to Ezer Kri to shoot me." I shook my head. "You should have stayed on Gobi. No one cared about you there."

Despite what I said, I did feel sorry for Kline. In the time that I had known him, he had led a band of terrorists to kill my platoon and attempted to "azzazzinate" me. My universe would be safer once he was gone, but there was something pathetic about this inept, one-handed fool.

"You soldiers are all alike," he said, probably not seeing the irony in his statement.

"I'm not a soldier," I said. "I am a Marine."

Kline shook his head but said nothing.

"I'm curious, Kline. Did Crowley put you up to this?" I asked.

"Did you read my final confession?" Kline asked.

They had interrogated Kline thoroughly over the last few days, but I had not seen the reports. "No," I said.

"It was my idea," Kline said. "I wanted to kill you. Crowley tried to talk me out of it."

"Did he?" I asked. "Did he tell you I was on Ezer Kri?" We must have been approaching the *Kamehameha*; I could feel the transport rumble as the engines slowed.

"He told me where to find you," Kline said, sounding a bit defiant.

"Did he arrange your trip?"

"Not himself. One of his lieutenants."

"And he gave you the rifle and the scope?"

"Yes."

"And he preset the scope to read my helmet signal?"

"Yes."

For the first time since takeoff, I turned and looked directly at Kline. "And you think it was your idea? He played you."

In the background, jets hissed as our ride glided up into the primary docking bay. The ship touched down on its landing gear, and the soft hum of the engines went silent. The rear of the ship opened, and a security detail of four MPs stomped up the ramp.

"Corporal Harris?" One of Admiral Klyber's aides followed the MPs. "Corporal Harris, we're on a very tight schedule."

"Is this the prisoner?" one of the MPs asked.

I looked around the cabin, pretending to search for a third passenger. *There are only two of us,* I thought. *I'm wearing a uniform, and he's wearing cuffs.* "This is the prisoner," I said as I gave the guard Kline's papers. The MPs formed a square around Kline and led him away.

"Corporal Harris," the aide said in a nervous voice. He was a lieutenant, and I was just a corporal; but I was Klyber's guest. This aide did not dare pull rank.

"Sorry, sir," I said.

"They are waiting for you on the Command deck."

"Yes," I said, my thoughts following Kline.

The lieutenant led me down the same corridor that Vince Lee and I had explored on our first night on the *Kamehameha*. Vince was considerably better company. This man strode in silence, staring coldly at sailors moving around the deck. At least nobody turned me back for being a Marine.

A voice in the back of my head said that I was far out of my depth as we approached the admin area. That was the holy of holies on most ships, officer country, but we were headed for far more hallowed halls than mere officer country. At the far end of admin were the six elevators that led to the Scutum-Crux Command deck. The lieutenant approached one of these elevators and rolled the thumb, pointer, and middle finger of his right hand against a scanner pad. The elevator call button lit up.

"Ever been back here before, Corporal?"

"No, sir."

The elevator door slid open, and we stepped in. I stood silent, watching numbers flash on a bar over the door, my mouth dry and my throat parched.

We stepped onto the twelfth floor. Staff members from every branch sat at desks. An Air Force major stood in front of a large glass map moving symbols. A colonel from the Army walked past us and ducked into a small office. No one seemed to notice us.

At first glance, SC Command looked very similar to the admin area at the base of the elevator, except that here you saw men in Air Force blue and Army green. The lieutenant led me past the cubicles and lesser offices, and the surroundings became much less familiar. Even the ceiling was higher on this part of the deck. We entered a large waiting room. The naval officer/receptionist glared at me. "Is this Corporal Harris?"

"In the flesh," the lieutenant answered.

"He is in conference," the receptionist said, "but he said for you to go in."

"In conference?" I asked.

"That means we need to keep absolutely quiet," the lieutenant whispered. We approached a convex wall with a double-paneled door. As the panels slid open, I heard Admiral Klyber speaking. The officer put up a hand, signaling me to stay outside as he peered into the circular room. A moment later, he turned back and signaled for me to follow.

Admiral Klyber and Vice Admiral Barry sat along the

edge of a semicircular table facing a wall with several screens. I recognized the faces on the screens from stories I had seen in the news. Admiral Che Huang, the secretary of the Navy, a member of the Joint Chiefs, spoke on one screen. Generals from the Army and Air Force, also members of the Joint Chiefs, showed on other screens, along with a member of the Linear Committee.

"You said Ezer Kri would not pose a problem, Barry," Huang said in an angry voice. His image glared down at Admiral Barry, his lips pulling back into a sneer.

"The planet has no standing military and no registered capital ships," Barry said. Clearly shaken, the vice admiral wheezed and snorted as he spoke. Beads of sweat formed on his mostly bald scalp. "Those ships could not possibly have come from Ezer Kri."

"I quite agree," said Klyber. "Admiral Barry had no reason to anticipate the attack on the *Chayio*." He leaned back in his chair, laced his fingers, and spoke in a calming voice like a mediator who had come to settle a squabble among friends. "As I read this, it appears that the reality of the Atkins threat is finally showing itself. Admiral Barry was only briefed about hostilities with the Yamashiro government."

"Atkins?" asked the member of the Linear Committee.

"We've all seen the record; those destroyers broadcast themselves to the scene," Klyber said. "Did you look at the design of those ships?"

"I'd need clearer pictures," the Committee member said. "I saw your notes; but after all of these years, I can't believe it."

"Fair enough," Admiral Klyber said. "But we do agree that those ships are of an obsolete U.A. design and manufacture? I am sure we agree that this was not an extragalactic attack."

The faces in the television screen nodded in agreement.

"We know that the Mogat population vanished after the attack on our platoon," Klyber continued. "A number of ships launched during the attack on the *Chayio*. Intelligence traced that launch to an uninhabited island. It seems safe to assume that the separatists massed on that island as they planned their escape."

"I am aware of that, Admiral," Huang hissed. "If those ships came from the GC Fleet, they would be hopelessly outdated."

"Not necessarily," Klyber said. "The *Kamehameha* was commissioned before we began exploring the Galactic Eye. They may have updated their ships just as we reoutfitted this one." He shot a furtive grin at Vice Admiral Barry, who fidgeted nervously and wiped his forehead with the back of his hand.

"So how do we proceed, assuming those ships were from the GC Fleet?" asked the member of the Linear Committee.

"There were hundreds of ships in that fleet," Klyber pointed out.

"Even if they reoutfitted it, I don't think the GC Fleet would be much of a threat," Huang said. "Not against a modern navy.

"The GC Fleet was a one-dimensional fleet designed for invasions, not ship-to-ship combat. It did not have frigates or carriers. It will be helpless against fighters." No one seemed interested in Huang's opinion, however.

"Perhaps we'd better double the patrols guarding the broadcast system," said the general from the Air Force.

"Would there be any way to track the fleet's movements?" asked the Committee member.

Klyber shook his head. "Once we get a psychological profile of whoever is commanding the fleet, we may be able to predict his steps. For now, the best we can do is to go on alert."

The Army general sighed. "It's the enemy that you can't see . . ."

"Do you think Crowley is behind this?" asked the Committee member.

"I've put a great deal of thought into this," Klyber said. "Crowley has a mind for tactics, but he has no skill for coalition building. He is no politician. If a civil war is brewing, Crowley will need allies . . . political allies."

The Army general smiled. "Thank God Morgan Atkins is dead."

"Atkins?" asked Admiral Barry.

"Is he?" Klyber said. "I don't know how we can rule Atkins out of the picture."

"My God, he would have to be a hundred years old," Barry said.

"I never call them dead until I see a tag on their feet," said Huang, who clearly enjoyed needling Barry on every topic.

"With the right ambassador, Crowley won't have any trouble finding plenty of support in the House of Representatives," said Klyber. "We will need to observe how the politics play themselves out in the House. Crowley's allies will expose themselves sooner or later."

"If he's tied in with Atkins, he'll have lieutenants on every planet," the member of the Linear Committee observed.

"We must choose our next step wisely," Huang said. It seemed like he was trying to regain control of the conversation by reviewing what everyone else said. "If you are right, Admiral Klyber, we have no way of knowing where or when Crowley will strike."

"What do we do about Ezer Kri?" Barry asked.

"We should make an example of Ezer Kri," said Huang, the faces in the monitors nodding their agreement. "Blast the planet until nothing is left. We cannot show any weakness in this situation."

Admiral Klyber leaned forward, placed his hands palms down on the table and took a deep breath. "If that is the consensus."

Huang made a weary sigh. "You have other ideas, Admiral Klyber?"

"The Mogat Separatists have already abandoned the planet, and the rest of the population seems sufficiently loyal to the Unified Authority. Governor Yamashiro is a smart politician; he knows he's in a fix."

"We cannot afford to appear weak," Huang said. "If we let Ezer Kri get away with attacking a U.A. ship, other planets will follow."

"Of course," Klyber said. "But we have already agreed that the attacking ships did not launch from Ezer Kri. Destroy the planet now, and you will only kill innocents. What kind of lesson is that?"

"And your suggestion?" asked the Committee member.

"Once we have captured the people responsible for the attacks, we return them to Ezer Kri for public trial and execution on their own home planet."

"We'll look like fools if they get off," said Huang.

"Rest assured," Klyber said, "these terrorists will be found guilty. We will see to it."

"Found guilty on their home planet; I like it," said the Committee member.

"Absalom Barry is a capable officer," Admiral Klyber said, as we walked back across the empty lobby toward his office. "He lacks vision, but he runs an efficient fleet. When I was transferred to Scutum-Crux, I put in a request for him."

I had not asked about Barry. I never asked one superior officer about another; such inquiries inevitably came back to haunt you.

We entered a short hall that led to Klyber's office—a surprisingly small room with a shielded-glass wall overlooking the rear of the *Kamehameha*. The galaxy seemed to start just behind the admiral's desk. While trying to speak with him, I constantly found myself distracted by the view of Ezer Kri or a passing frigate. His desk faced away from that observation wall, and, disciplined as he was, I doubted that the admiral turned back to look out often.

"Please, sit down," Klyber said. As he spoke, he picked up a folder that was on his desk. He studied it for a moment, then looked at me. "Our work on Ezer Kri is just about finished. I'll be glad to leave."

I said nothing.

"Corporal Harris, we're going to take on an important visitor over the next few days. The secretary of the Navy will be joining us. He has a mission he would like to conduct. In order for Huang's mission to succeed, we will need to draw upon your particular abilities."

"Sir?" I said, sounding foolish.

Klyber took a deep breath and leaned forward on his desk, his gray eyes staring straight into mine. "You grew up in an orphanage, Corporal?"

"Yes, sir."

"What did they tell you about the cloning process?"

Just hearing an admiral mention the word "clone" left me dizzy. I knew he had not brought me there for a casual chat. I felt a prickling sensation on my back and arms. Clenching the arms of my chair, I felt nervous, genuinely nervous.

"The teachers never discussed cloning," I said. "I heard rumors; we talked about it when the teachers weren't around."

Without releasing me from that intense stare, Klyber leaned back in his chair again. He picked up a pen in his right hand and tapped it against the palm of his left. "Tell me about the rumors."

I pried my eyes from his for a moment and stared out through the viewport behind him. I could see Ezer Kri, a blue-and-green globe with patches of clouds. I could see a frigate off in the distance. Far off in space, I could see the star that was the system's sun. "They never know they are clones," I said, fighting to take control of my emotions: I was not a clone. I had nothing to fear. "They can't see it. Two clones can stand side by side looking into the same mirror and not see that they look alike." I knew that—I saw it every day.

Klyber's mouth formed an amused smile. "Yes, the infamous identity programming—clones don't know that they are clones. Have you also heard rumors about their dying if they learn the truth?"

"I've heard that," I said.

"They weren't thinking about the works of Plato when they came up with the death reflex, but a similar idea is found in *The Republic*. Plato did not want mobility between his classes. I think he was most concerned about ordinary citizens trying to become warriors or rulers. Are you familiar with that?"

We had studied Plato when I was growing up in the orphanage, but I could not think at that moment. I shook my head.

"No? Plato said that if people challenged their station, you were supposed to tell them that they were made yesterday, and all that they knew was just a dream. Sounds ridiculous.

It sounds a bit like the death reflex. Plato thought you could control the masses by stripping them of all that they knew with a little lie . . . Plato's lie.

"The Senate wanted something a little stranger. If clones saw through the lie, the Senate wanted them dead. Putting guns in the hands of a synthetic army scared them. They wanted to make sure they could shut the synthetics down if they ever saw through the lie. I was against it. A mere scrap of neural programming seems like thin protection against a danger that could potentially wipe out our entire defense. The Senate debated it in an open session.

"The hardliners won out, of course. The majority argued that renegade clones would be the greatest threat to the Republic, and they had a point. They said that once the clones realized they were not human, there would be no reason for them not to rise up. Fear of the warrior class goes all the way back to Plato, himself.

"What else do you know about clones, Corporal Harris?"

His questions were torture. "How do they die?" I asked. I could not remember my mouth ever feeling so dry.

"What kills them?" Admiral Klyber gave me a benevolent smile. "A hormone is released into their bloodstream. It stops their hearts. It's supposed to be fast and painless.

"Do you know why Congress is afraid of its own cloned soldiers?" Klyber asked. The humor left his smile, and his gaze bored into me.

"No, sir. I don't." By then I felt more than dizzy; my stomach had turned. Arguments took place in my head as I considered the evidence that proved my humanity, then shot it down with questions about clone programming. I never knew my parents. Did that make me a clone?

"No, not because of a mutiny . . . because of me," Klyber said.

"When I was a young lieutenant, I oversaw the creation of a special generation of cloned soldiers. It was done during the troubled times, Corporal Harris. Our first explorations into the central region of the galaxy ended in disaster. A fleet of explorer ships simply vanished, and everyone feared the worst. That was the only time I can ever remember when the politicians stopped talking about expansion and colonizing the galaxy."

The words "central region" seeped through my whirling thoughts. I focused on them, considered them. "Were you stationed with the GC Fleet, sir?" I asked.

"No," Klyber said, putting up a hand to stop me. "I was safe on Earth, a recent graduate from Annapolis, with a promising career and some highly placed friends. My father was on the Linear Committee, Harris. I had guardian angels who kept me safe and put me on the fast track. I was assigned to oversee a special project. It was important that Congress not get wind of the project, or the Senate would have canned it. My father knew about the project, of course, but he was the only member of the Linear Committee who did.

"Morgan Atkins was the senior member of the Linear Committee at the time. The entire Republic worshipped him. Did you know that Atkins was on the Committee?"

So confused that I did not even understand Admiral Klyber's question, I shook my head.

"Atkins was big on manifest destiny. 'Humanity can never be safe until it conquers every inch of known space,'" Klyber said, lowering his voice in what I assumed was a parody of Atkins. "No one challenged Atkins. He single-handedly ran the Republic.

"The Galactic Central Fleet was Atkins's idea. He wanted a fleet that was so powerful that all enemies would fall; and when Atkins called for action, by God, people jumped. The problem was that Atkins's fleet had to be self-broadcasting. We usually sent self-broadcasting explorer ships to set up discs; but with explorer ships disappearing, he wanted a self-broadcasting fleet."

Klyber rubbed his eyes. "God, what a nightmare. The Galactic Central Fleet was just like they say—bigger and more powerful than any fleet ever assembled. Just building the broadcasting engines cost trillions of dollars. In the end, each ship cost five times what normal ships cost.

"It took three years to build the fleet. Three years, and all of that time the military was on high alert looking for any signs of an invasion."

Klyber stopped speaking for just a moment. His gaze seemed far away, but his eyes stayed focused on mine. "We tested for every contingency. The explorer ships could have been destroyed by some kind of broadcast malfunction, so we bounced the GC Fleet back and forth across the Orion Arm until no one knew where it was without daily updates.

"Once we were sure of the broadcast engines, we sent the fleet to explore the inner curve of the Norma Arm . . . the center of the galaxy. The ships flew near Jupiter. They initiated the self-broadcast, then they were gone. It was just like the explorer ships; we simply never heard from them again." Klyber sat up. "Atkins accompanied the fleet. It was his pet project."

"I don't understand, sir." I said. "Atkins went with the GC Fleet?"

"My father never trusted Atkins," said Klyber. "He had me assigned to research a new class of clones around the same time Atkins proposed his grand fleet. Congress never knew what I was doing. Atkins never knew. It was strictly a military operation."

"Liberators," I said.

"Liberators," Klyber agreed. "You've probably heard rumors about Liberators having animal genes . . . We experimented with genes from animals, but it didn't work. Liberator clones were not very different than earlier clones except that they were smarter and far more aggressive. We gave them a certain cunning. We made them ruthless. They needed to be ruthless. We thought we were sending them to fight an unknown enemy from the galactic core—something not human. Do you understand?"

Klyber did not pause for me to answer.

"One of the scientists came up with the idea of ideas . . ." Klyber smiled for just a moment, then the smile vanished. "Hormones. Classical conditioning. We mixed endorphins in their adrenal glands. The mixture only comes out in battle. A drug that would make the clones addicted to war. Only a scientist could come up with an idea like that, Harris. It never occurred to us military types.

"You need to understand, these clones were our last hope, and we had no idea what was out there. We were sending them into hostile space. Whatever was out there had annihilated our most massive fleet."

"An alien race?" I asked.

"No. No aliens, just a crazy bastard politician. It turned out that Morgan Atkins was behind the whole thing. He wanted to build a new republic, with no allegiance to Earth. He was the ultimate expansionist, pushing the idea that Earth was just another planet and not the seat of man. It sounded good. It sounded poetic and freedom-loving, but anyone with an ounce of intelligence could see that his views would lead to chaos.

"Even back then, Atkins had fanatical followers. We later found out that Atkins planted men on every ship in the Galactic Central Fleet. They put poison gas in the air vents and commandeered the fleet as soon as it arrived in the inner curve. Of course we didn't know that back on Earth. All we knew was that Atkins and his fleet were gone. We found out the truth after the Liberators arrived; but by that time, Atkins had a base, a hierarchy, and the strongest fleet in the galaxy. He didn't know about my clones, so he wasn't prepared.

"We sent a hundred thousand Liberators in explorer ships. Atkins's land forces never stood a chance. Atkins and most of his men got away in their self-broadcasting fleet. That was the last anybody saw of those ships. At least it was until now."

"I never heard any of this in school."

"Of course not," Klyber snapped. "This was the most classified secret in U.A. history. It was so damned classified that we backed ourselves into a corner. When communes of Atkins followers began springing up around the frontier, we couldn't arrest them. There would have been too many questions."

My head still spinning, I tried to understand where Admiral Klyber was taking me. That war ended forty years ago. An image came to my mind. "The sergeant over my platoon . . . Is he a Liberator?"

"Master Sergeant Tabor Shannon was in that invasion," Klyber said. "It wasn't really a war, not even much of a battle. Atkins's men had no idea what they were fighting."

Admiral Klyber took a deep breath, stood up from behind

his desk, and turned to look out that viewport wall. "Do you have any other questions, Corporal?" he asked. Then, without waiting for me to respond, he turned, and added, "You're not an orphan, Harris, you are a Liberator. A freshly minted Liberator."

CHAPTER
ELEVEN

Learning about my creation did not kill me. Identity-programming and the death reflex were components of modern cloning. I was a throwback, an early-production model that somehow found its way back on to the assembly line for a limited run.

"Do you understand what I am telling you?" Admiral Klyber asked me.

A few moments before, I had been wrestling to gain control of my thoughts. Suddenly I could think with absolute clarity. I felt neither sad nor confused. I nodded.

"You are a Liberator, and knowing it will not kill you."

"Yes, sir," I said.

"Perhaps we should stop for the evening." From behind his desk, Klyber stared at me suspiciously, the way I would expect a parent to examine a child who should be hurt but claims to be fine.

"I'm okay, sir," I said.

"All the same, Corporal, we have accomplished enough for one evening." Klyber stood up from his desk, and the meeting was over.

* * *

"It never occurred to us that we were anything but clones," Sergeant Shannon said as he choked back his first sip of Sagittarian Crash, easily the worst-tasting drink you could find in any civilized—or uncivilized—bar. They called the stuff "Crash," but it was really vodka made from potatoes grown in toxic soil. Congress once outlawed the stuff; but as it was the only export from an otherwise worthless colony, the lobbyists won out.

Shannon and I picked Crash for one reason—we wanted to get drunk. Crash left you numb after a few thick sips. "Damn, I hate this stuff," Shannon said, frowning at his glass.

"You ever wonder about . . ."

Shannon stopped me. "Knowing you are a clone means never having to wonder. You don't wonder about God—he's your commanding officer. Good and evil are automatic. Orders are good because they come from God. I even know where I'm going after I die." He smiled a somewhat bitter smile. "The great test tube in the sky."

"Isn't that blasphemous?" I asked.

"Blasphemous?" Shannon's revelry evaporated upon my using that word. "I'll be specked! I suppose it is."

"I thought you were the churchgoer?" I said. "You're the only one in the platoon who goes to services, and you're the one Marine I would think was the least likely to attend religious services."

"Least likely?" Shannon said, looking confused.

"You're the only Marine on this ship who specking well knows he's a clone. Clones don't have souls . . . Remember, man may be able to create synthetic men, but only God can give them souls. Isn't that what the peace-and-joy crowd is preaching these days?"

"If you are anything like me, and you are exactly like me, you don't really give two shits about what peace and joyers are preaching."

"I still don't feel like going to church," I said. "Do you believe that stuff?"

"Yeah," Shannon said, "I just don't know where I fit into it."

It was only seven o'clock. Most of the men were at the mess hall eating dinner. When Shannon saw me returning to the barracks, he had suggested that we drink our meal instead.

Except for the laugh lines around his eyes and his old man's hair, Shannon looked like a man in his midtwenties in the dim light of the bar. "How old are you?" I asked.

Shannon grinned. "There's old and then there's old. After the GC Fleet, the boys on Capitol Hill decided that they wanted kinder, gentler clones, so they opened up orphanages and raised them like pups. Now they have eighteen years to teach you good manners.

"Back in my day, you came out of the tube as a twenty-year-old. I got my first gray hairs as a ten-year-old or a thirty-year-old, depending on how you look at it. Nothing else has changed. I've seen my physical charts—nothing's changed."

"Are you the last Liberator?" I asked.

"I'd say you are," Shannon said. "I've heard rumors about Liberators in the Inner SC Fleet, but you're the first one I've seen. Klyber is partial to us. If there were other Liberators around, I think he'd be the one to have them.

"What I don't understand is where you came from. Why make another Liberator after forty years? They didn't make you by accident."

"An experiment?" I suggested.

"Maybe Klyber ordered you up special," Shannon said. "If it was him, he did it without telling the politicos. They hate Liberators on Capitol Hill. Whoever started you on Gobi was trying to protect you. Somebody wanted to keep you a secret as long as possible, but that went down the shitter the moment you were at a card game with Amos Crowley."

Shannon held up his drink and stared through the glass. He swished it around. "Watch this."

Shannon took a deep breath, then drained his glass. He shivered, and for a moment he slumped in his chair. Then he looked at the bartender, gave him an evil smile, and turned his glass upside down.

"Goddamn!" the bartender said.

"Another one," Shannon said.

"Another one will kill you," the bartender said.

"You try it," Shannon said to me. "One good thing about Liberators, we don't get shit-faced."

I looked at my glass. In the dim light, Crash looked like murky seawater. "Drink it in one shot?" I asked.

"Kid, he's trying to kill you," the bartender warned.

Closing my fingers around the glass, I brought it up to my lips and paused.

"Don't do it, kid," the bartender warned. "You'll pickle your brain."

Sergeant Shannon watched me, his eyes never leaving mine. Heaving a sigh, I put the glass in front of my mouth and tipped it. The syrupy drink spilled over my bottom lip and onto my tongue, leaving a numbing tingle everywhere it touched. I swallowed quickly.

"Whoa!" I said. First my throat felt painfully frozen, then my lungs burned, and finally I felt a flash of nausea; but all of those sensations went away quickly. I looked at the bartender, smiled, and turned my glass over.

"You want another one, too?" the barkeep asked.

"No," I said. "I really don't."

"Give him another," Shannon said. Sergeant Shannon fixed the bartender with a most chilling smile. He did not glare, did not snarl, did not do anything overtly menacing, but the bartender understood the unspoken message. He looked at both of us, shook his head, then took our glasses.

When he returned, he handed us our drinks. "I'll tell the infirmary to send a doctor."

I took my drink. "To the great test tube in the sky?"

"You kidding? They'll melt us down and reuse us just like any other equipment." Shannon picked up his glass. "You think you can handle it?"

I laughed. "I'm drinking it, aren't I?" I said, and I emptied the glass in one slug. Fighting the chill and nausea, I tried to sit straight on my seat and lost my balance. I almost fell but somehow managed to catch myself.

Shannon, watching me with some amusement, said, "Rookie," and drank his shot.

"You going for thirds?" the bartender asked.

"No!" Shannon and I answered in unison.

* * *

That night, before going to sleep, I slipped on my mediaLink shades and found an eight-thousand-word philosophical essay about the Platonic justifications for building the death reflex into clones. I barely finished the first page before I realized that the booby-trapping of clone brains meant nothing to me. Klyber's engineers had placed different glands in my head, and I no longer cared about what might or might not have been placed in other clones' brains. Closing the article, I noticed that there was a two-hundred-word synopsis.

Plato understood that the warrior class would envy the ruling class and that the ruling class would fear the warrior class. He sought to keep the classes in place with the most childish of lies:

Well then, I will speak, although I really know not how to look you in the face, or in what words to utter the audacious fiction, which I propose to communicate gradually, first to the rulers, then to the soldiers, and lastly to the people. They are to be told that their youth was a dream, and the education and training which they received from us, an appearance only; in reality, during all that time they were being formed and fed in the womb of the earth, where they themselves and their arms and appurtenances were manufactured; when they were completed, the earth, their mother, sent them up; and so, their country being their mother and also their nurse, they are bound to advise for her good, and to defend her against attacks, and her citizens they are to regard as children of the earth and their own brothers.

—*The Republic*
Book 3, Page 16

According to this article, Plato's deceit is made true in that the modern-day warrior class is of synthetic origin. Further, the death reflex is shown as analogous to erasing an individual's belief in his personal history and therefore his identity.

CHAPTER TWELVE

Captain McKay appointed me to a seven-member color guard, and I spent the next few days holding a Marine Corps flag as Bryce Klyber and Absalom Barry welcomed an endless stream of diplomats and politicians. The Senate sent a legal team to overhaul the Ezer Kri court system, and we lined up to meet them. The Federal Bureau of Investigation sent a team of detectives to hunt down any remaining Mogat sympathizers, and we lined up to meet them. Two members of the Linear Committee flew out with an army of reporters, and we lined up to meet them, too.

Every few hours, a group of VIPs arrived, and McKay sent us to hold up our colors. After five days of round-the-clock flag holding, I began to sleepwalk through the arrivals. I no longer cared who stepped down the ramp. At least, I thought I stopped caring.

The night we left Ezer Kri, McKay summoned the color guard to his office. I got the message late and was the last to arrive. When I pressed the intercom button by his door, he squawked, "Harris?"

"Sir?"

The door opened. "As I was saying, this is the big one. You have a problem, sailor?"

One of the sailors in the guard looked nervously to the other men for support. "We just received two members from the Linear Committee."

"Speck me with a hose!" McKay yowled. "Committee members aren't brass. They can't send your ass to the brig, boy. They don't even notice you. Hell, I could show up with my pants off and a flag dangling from my dick, and the only thing those committee members would notice was that the goddamned flagpole looks awfully long. If you so much as fart on this one, you're specked for life."

With that he dismissed the others and kept me behind. "Do you have any idea who our guest is this time?" he asked.

"No, sir," I said.

"Admiral Che Huang from the Joint Chiefs. Are you familiar with him?"

I nodded, feeling a new knot in the pit of my gut.

"I'm going to be straight with you, Harris. I tried to get you pulled from this duty, but Admiral Klyber wants you on it. You had a conversation with Admiral Klyber a few nights ago?" McKay's nearly clean-shaven scalp gleamed in the bright lights, but his brow formed a shadow over his eyes giving his face a skull-like appearance.

"Huang does not like clones, any clones."

I had heard that Huang was antisynthetic. "Especially Liberators?" I guessed.

"As far as he knows, you're extinct." McKay stood up and put on his hat.

"Thanks for the warning," I said.

"Don't mention it, Harris," McKay said as he started for the door. He turned back. "Klyber likes you. He's a powerful man, and he knows what he's doing; but just the same, don't draw any attention to yourself."

Klyber, Barry, and Olivera waited by the landing bay for Admiral Huang's arrival. I noticed nothing unusual about Admiral Klyber or Captain Olivera, but Admiral Barry looked like a man headed for a firing squad. His face was pale, and beads of sweat shone on his forehead and scalp. He mopped that sweat with darting dabs, then crammed his handkerchief back in his blouse. Klyber looked at him and said something that I could not hear.

A red carpet ran the length of the floor, ending at the hatch through which Admiral Huang would arrive. My color guard stood at the other end of the carpet, holding flags representing the Army, the Marines, the Navy, the Air Force, the Unified Authority, the Scutum-Crux Arm, and the Central SC Fleet. We stood as still and intent as our human legs would allow us. The officer of the deck did not need to signal us to attention, we were already there.

A light over the hatch turned green, and the door slid open. Nearly one full minute passed before Admiral Che Huang of the Joint Chiefs of Staff stepped into sight.

Huang appeared to be in his midfifties. He stood around six feet tall, with square shoulders and a narrow waist. He had his cap tucked under his left arm. I could see white streaks through Huang's thinning, brown hair. There was something about his neatly tailored uniform, or the tilt of his head, or the way he narrowed his eyes as he looked around the landing area, that suggested both breeding and contempt.

"Admiral Huang," Admiral Klyber said as he led Barry and Olivera to the hatch. "I trust you had a pleasant trip."

Huang stopped and stared down at the group of officers who had come to greet him. A thin smile played across his lips. "Admiral Klyber," he said in a stiff voice. The two men shook hands. "Have you read my messages?"

"Admiral Barry and I have discussed them at length," Klyber said. "I think you will be pleased with the plans we have made."

"Splendid. I wish to get under way as soon as possible," Huang said as he stepped away from the hatch. He looked around the hangar and his gaze seemed to lock on the color guard.

"We can start straightaway," Klyber said with an easy air. Beside him, Vice Admiral Barry managed a tight smile, but the stiffness in his shoulders was unmistakable. All of the blood left his face. As the officers turned to leave the bay, Absalom Barry drifted back and walked several paces behind everybody else.

"At ease," Captain McKay said, after the brass disappeared.

I was surprised to find Sergeant Shannon and Vince Lee talking when I returned to the barracks. They got on together professionally; but on a social basis, they did not have much use for each other.

I had come to realize that Vince, possibly the first real friend I had ever had, was an antisynthetic clone. I never stopped to think about why he befriended me so quickly after we transferred to the *Kamehameha*. Now that I did think about it, I decided he liked me because I did not look like every other enlisted man, no matter how subtle the difference. Later, however, I suspected that he had a special dislike for Liberators. That was why he had turned quiet around me when Shannon first landed. First he had thought I was natural-born, then, when he saw Shannon, he realized that I was not just a clone, I was a Liberator. The reason Vince and I were friends was because of a grandfather clause. He and I had already struck up a friendship when Shannon arrived. I suppose that having already struck up a friendship with me and not having any natural-borns to turn to, Lee decided I was okay.

For his part, Shannon simply considered Lee an "asshole of the highest order." Shannon called him a "synth-hating clone" and said that his quirks were bad for morale . . . pretty idealistic talk from the platoon sergeant who swept into the *Kamehameha* with all of the tact of a typhoon.

In this I think he was wrong about Lee. I think it was the reverse. For all of his bluster about bootstrapping his way into a commission and going into politics, I think Vince suspected the truth. I think he wanted to convince himself that he was not a clone and adopted an antisynthetic attitude as a shield because he believed it would protect him. As he well knew, confirmation about his clone origins would trigger the death reflex.

"I hear Admiral Huang is on board," Sergeant Shannon called out to me as I entered his office. "Was that who arrived on your last color detail?"

"In the flesh," I said.

"Goddamn," Shannon said. "Did anybody bother to mention what he is doing here?"

"Not that I know of," I said.

"Lee, you're going to be in charge of the platoon for the next few days," Shannon said. "Scrotum-Crotch Command has transferred Corporal Harris and me to a special detail for an unspecified period. Harris, why in God's name is high command asking for us?"

"I don't know," I said. "I'm not sure."

"Which is it?" Shannon asked. "You don't know, or you're not sure?"

"Do you know why Admiral Huang is here?" Lee asked.

"Unless SC Command is pulling one sergeant and one corporal from every platoon, I'm guessing that this has something to do with our being Liberators," Shannon said.

"You know you're a Liberator?" Lee asked me in a loud voice that echoed across the office.

"I should have figured it out on my own when he arrived," I said, nodding toward Shannon. "He's the first Marine I've seen who was my height and shape. Admiral Klyber must have thought I was an idiot for not finding it out on my own."

"Klyber?" Lee asked.

"He told me I was a Liberator."

"And you didn't die when you found out?" Lee asked.

"Holy Jeeeezus, Lee! He's standing in front of you, isn't he! What I want to know is why the hell an admiral is wasting time telling a corporal anything."

"They didn't build the death reflex into Liberators," I said.

"Harris," Lee said, "we need to talk."

"It's going to have to wait," Shannon said. "We're expected at Fleet Command." He paused and considered things. "I can't see anything good coming out of a visit with Admiral Huang," he said in a hushed voice, almost a whisper.

"I get the feeling that Klyber is looking out for us," I said.

"That's how I read it," Shannon agreed.

"Can Klyber protect you from the Joint Chiefs?" Lee sounded concerned. "I mean, Huang is as high as they go in the military."

"If the intel I hear about Klyber is true, his strings go a lot higher than military connections," Shannon said. He turned to me. "Pack up. We're supposed to report to the Command deck within the hour."

"This lift doesn't seem secure, does it?" Sergeant Shannon asked, as we entered the elevator to the SC Command deck. "I used to wonder why there were no guards." He pointed to narrow rows of vents lining the ceiling and floor. "You know what those are for?"

"Oxygen?" I guessed.

"Noxium gas," Shannon corrected me. "Last time I was assigned to the *Kamehameha* a disgruntled swabbie tried to make an unscheduled visit to Command, and I got to clean up afterward. He'd only been dead for a couple of minutes when we got here, but that was long enough. His arms and legs turned to jelly and squished through our fingers when we tried to lift him. We ended up washing him out with a steam hose."

The door to the lift opened, and I was glad to step out. We entered the large, unfinished lobby, and one of Klyber's aides led us to the conference room. The curved panels of the entryway slid open, and the aide motioned us in.

Admiral Huang, Vice Admiral Barry, and Admiral Klyber sat equidistant from each other around the round conference table. Huang turned to glance at us as we entered the conference room. He paused, and his quick glance lengthened into an angry stare. "The Senate has outlawed your bastard clones, Admiral Klyber."

"The Senate outlawed the creation of new Liberators," Klyber corrected. "Nothing was said about Liberators that already existed. Sergeant Shannon has served with distinction under my command since the Galactic Central War."

"The other one looks new," Huang snapped.

"He has distinguished himself in combat," Klyber said. "He has been a model Marine."

Huang's eyes hardened as he focused on me. I could feel the weight of his stare and sensed the heat of his anger. "These are the men you have selected?"

"Sergeant Shannon, perhaps you and Corporal Harris can give us a moment?" Admiral Klyber said.

Shannon led me out of the conference room. We stood just outside the door, waiting for Klyber to summon our return. "That Huang is a prick," I said after a moment.

"Whatever he is here for, Klyber wants us involved, and Huang wants us out," Shannon said.

The panels slid open, and the aide who had originally brought us to the room led us back in. "Sergeant, a squad of military police will arrive on deck momentarily. Please see that they escort Vice Admiral Barry to his quarters and detain him there," Huang said. As he spoke, I saw Absalom Barry gasping for air. His jaw hung slack, his eyes stared vacantly ahead, and he looked as if he might have a heart attack on the spot.

Huang sneered. "I think I may have finally found a good use for your clones, Klyber; they'll make good jailers." The room remained utterly silent until four MPs arrived. "Rabid clones and a half ton fleet commander . . . it's quite a fleet you've got here."

The MPs—Navy, not Marines—had their orders when they arrived. They surrounded Barry, who slowly rose to his feet and followed them out of the conference room, his egg-shaped head bobbing as he walked.

"That was wasteful," Klyber said. "Barry may not have . . ."

"We needlessly lost a frigate and an entire platoon," Huang interrupted. "The Joint Chiefs have ordered a board of inquiry. Until Barry's court-martial is complete, I suggest that you steer clear of him, Admiral Klyber."

"Barry acted properly," Klyber answered, his voice cold, his emotions still under control.

"The secretaries of the Army and Air Force disagree," Huang shot back.

Shannon and I followed Barry and the MPs out of the conference room. The panels closed behind us, sealing off the conversation.

"Do you think Huang came all the way from Earth for this?" I asked Shannon, as we waited outside the conference room for the third time that day. "He didn't come all this way just to arrest Barry?"

"No." Shannon smiled. "He didn't come out to Scrotum-Crotch just to arrest Barry. That was just a bonus."

The aide led us in to the conference room for the third time. This time Captain McKay sat with Klyber, and Hurricane Huang was not to be found.

"Sergeant Shannon, this is not your first tour aboard the *Kamehameha*?" Klyber asked.

"No, sir," Shannon answered. "I spent four years on this ship."

"I see." With Huang gone, Klyber took on an informal tone. He pointed to two chairs and had us sit down. "My first command was on this ship, more than twenty years ago, and she was already looking old. I thought it was a demotion at the time. I later found out that every secretary of the Navy for the last fifty years served on this ship. All but one—and that one wants to mothball the ship and retire the name."

With his icy gray eyes and his all-consuming intensity, Admiral Klyber could not hide his disapproval. He smiled, but his eyes still looked tired and angry. "Barring the further arrest of key commanding officers, I think we should discuss your mission." Klyber looked back to where Gaylan McKay sat. "Are you ready, Captain?"

There was an unmistakable familiarity between McKay and Klyber. They did not act like friends, but I heard the patient tone of a mentor in Klyber's voice. Captain McKay walked toward the wall with the conference monitors. The room darkened, and the image of a dark green planet appeared on one of the screens. "This is Ronan Minor," McKay began. "It is a stage three planet."

"Stage three planets" were seeded planets that were nearly ready for habitation. By the time they reached stage three, they had a detoxified atmosphere, stabilized gravity, and oxygen-producing rain forests. After twenty years at stage three, planets were, according to U.A. scientists, usually considered ready for colonization. Smugglers were not as patient. They often used stage three planets as bases for their operations.

"You may have been wondering why we have been favored by a visit from Admiral Huang," Klyber interrupted. "Here is your answer."

The planet disappeared from the screen and was replaced by the image of a man with a neatly trimmed, white beard. "Recognize him, Harris?" McKay asked.

"Crowley," I said.

"General Amos Crowley," McKay said. "How about these men?"

The picture switched, and we saw a video of three men holding a friendly conversation in what looked like a private living room. One of the men sat on a plush chair—Crowley. The other two, whom I did not recognize, sat on a sofa. The camera closed in on Crowley, then panned the others. When the camera reached the third man, the image froze, showing a slender man with dark skin and dark eyes.

"This is Warren Atkins."

"You've heard of his famous father," Klyber said. "Considering recent events on Ezer Kri, we were more than curious when Fleet Intelligence intercepted this video feed. Until now, we had no proof of a link between Atkins and Crowley."

"How do we know this was shot on Ronan Minor, sir?" Shannon asked.

"Good question," McKay said. He allowed the video to resume at a slowed speed. As the camera faded back to take in all three men, a window appeared along the right edge of the screen. McKay stopped the feed. He approached the screen and pointed to the window. "At present, the Department of Reclamation has thirty-five seeded planet projects in the Scutum-Crux Arm. Of those, only twelve are at stage three."

"Admiral Huang came all the way out here to oversee a mission with one-in-twelve odds?" Shannon asked.

"Not likely," McKay agreed. "Intelligence was able to lift a serial number off that climate generator."

"Not meaning to show the captain any disrespect, but is there any chance that they meant for us to intercept this file and locate the planet?" Shannon asked.

"You're asking if this is a trap?" McKay asked. "It may be a trap."

"Admiral Huang and I have discussed that possibility," Admiral Klyber said. "Sergeant, I should think that you above all people would recognize the importance of capturing Atkins."

"Find Atkins, and you find the GC Fleet," Shannon agreed.

"Something like that," Klyber said, looking not at us but at the picture of Warren Atkins on the monitor. "The Navy has improved its ship designs since launching the Galactic Central Fleet. Atkins beat a frigate with three dreadnoughts, hardly something to crow about. Had he run into a battleship or a carrier, the outcome would have been different."

I did not want to say anything, but I was not sure that I agreed. The attack on the *Chayio* had been smart and well executed. Somebody had analyzed our blockade and found a weakness.

"Are we sending a platoon to Ronan Minor, sir?" Shannon asked.

"Huang isn't taking any chances on this one," McKay said. "He brought a team of SEALs."

Shannon's lips broke into a sardonic grin. He looked from side to side as if hoping to see if the rest of us had caught the hidden punch line of a bad joke.

"Is something funny, Sergeant?" McKay asked.

"I know what our sergeant is thinking," Klyber said. "You are correct, Sergeant Shannon, but it cannot be helped.

"For now I suggest that you go get some rest. We'll be in position around Ronan Minor in five hours. Your transport leaves at 0500."

"Okay, what did I miss?" I asked, as we rode the elevator down.

Shannon smiled that same sardonic smile. "Huang has SEALs. Why do you think he asked Admiral Klyber for a couple of Marines?"

I thought about this for a moment. "I have no idea," I said, shaking my head.

"He's covering his ass," Shannon said. "If we run into an enemy army, he can say we led them into a trap. If Crowley and Atkins get away, he'll report that we specked the god-damned mission. And that, Corporal Harris, is why they call out the shit-kicking Marines."

There was something of the poet in Sergeant Shannon.

* * *

If Crowley and Atkins were down there, they did not have radar. Radar was a luxury fugitives could not afford. The Navy could detect a radar field from thousands of miles away. Having radar would have warned them we were coming, but it would also have confirmed for us that they were there.

Huang's orders directed us to land a full day's hike from Atkins's camp so that no one would see us coming. We would drop in the morning, cut our way through the jungle, and surprise the enemy at dusk. I liked the plan's simplicity, but I was nervous about working with SEALs.

Having only been on active duty for one year, I had never seen SEALs in action. All I knew about them was that they were not clones, nor were they, unlike the other officers, the errant sons of Earth-based politicians. SEALs were volunteers. Adventurous young men from around the galaxy applied to join. Only the absolute best were admitted into SEAL training school, and less than half of those who entered the school graduated.

The SEALs were already aboard the AT when Sergeant Shannon and I walked up the ramp into the kettle. This was the first time I had ever gone out with a team composed of all natural-born soldiers, and I was curious to get a look at them. Most of them were on the short side—between five-foot-six and five-foot-ten—with taut builds, clean-shaven heads, and alert eyes. As we boarded, they became quiet and watched us warily.

The SEALs traveled light. We had a twenty-mile hike from the drop site to the target zone. If we got bogged down in the jungle, Huang wanted us to stop for the night rather than travel blind. Shannon and I had brought packs. The only supplies the SEALs carried were what they could wear on their belts.

The rear of the kettle closed as our pilot prepared to take off. Hearing the hiss of the lifts, I placed my helmet on the bench beside me and rested my elbow on it. Shannon, who sat across the floor from me, continued to wear his.

As we rumbled out of the landing bay of the *Kamehameha*, the SEALs began talking quietly among themselves. They had clearly worked together before and spoke nostalgically about planets they had raided. I could not see into

Shannon's helmet, but I got the feeling he enjoyed listening to them. There had only been one real war in the last hundred years, and Tabor Shannon was the only man on our mission who was old enough to have fought in it.

One of the SEALs pulled a cigar from his vest pocket. As he lit it, I noticed a round insignia brantooed on his forearm. In the quick glimpse that I got, I saw the whirlpool pattern of the Milky Way with each of its arms stained a different color.

The brantoo process involved melting a pattern into the skin, then staining the burn with alcohol-based dyes. I knew plenty of Marines with tattoos. Some of the more rugged veterans around the *Kamehameha* had brantoos, but they were small, maybe the size of a coin, and single-colored. To make these brantoos, these SEALs would have suffered through the tinting process six or seven times. I wanted to ask the SEAL if he was awake when he got the brantoo, but I already knew the answer.

The SEAL looked at me. "See something interesting?" he said, in a way that was neither aggressive nor friendly.

"I noticed your brantoo," I said.

With a slight laugh, he rolled back his sleeve and showed me his arm. "We all have one."

I looked more closely. The insignia showed the Milky Way with red, yellow, blue, green, orange, and black arms. A banner over the galaxy said "NAVY SEALS." A banner under the galaxy said "THE FINAL SOLUTION."

Shannon removed his helmet, and said, "Let's test out your interLink."

I put my helmet on.

"They're not so tough," Shannon said over the interLink. "Don't let that brantoo shit fool you."

"It has six tints," I said.

"Keep focused, Harris."

"Six," I said.

"Harris, do you know why Admiral Huang got so angry when he saw us?" Shannon interrupted.

"Years of constipation?" I asked.

"He wanted Marines he could push around . . . grunts he could intimidate. He thought Klyber would give him a couple of normal jarheads. Instead, he got us."

"You think so?" I asked.

"Take my word for it, Harris. We're the scariest friggin' weapon in the Unified Authority arsenal."

I glanced at the SEAL who had shown me his brantoo. Nothing bound him to me, not even humanity. He was natural, I was synthetic. It might have been psychosomatic; but ever since my conversation with Klyber, I felt more and more disconnected from everyone around me. Was this untethering the reason the Linear Committee resorted to Plato's lie?

The SEALs passed small pots of green and black face paint among themselves. Dipping their fingers in the pots, they drew stripes and patterns over their faces until they covered all of their skin.

The walls of the transport shook as we entered the atmosphere. A few minutes later, a light flashed signaling that we had neared the drop zone. As we gathered our gear, Admiral Huang appeared on the overhead monitor. He spoke to the SEALs for a moment, then turned his attention to Shannon and me.

"You have been brought on this mission as a formality. You will do nothing unless so ordered by my men. If you get in the way, I will hold you personally responsible for the failure of this mission."

"Yes, sir," Shannon and I intoned, in perfect sync.

Huang turned back to his SEALs. "We need information, not corpses. I want them alive." With that, Huang saluted, and the signal ended.

Technicians aboard the *Kamehameha* had launched a surveillance satellite to view Ronan Minor long before our AT launched. They made a significant discovery—one part of the planet was infested with rats. The vermin offered an important confirmation. At that point in the seeded planet cycle, Ronan Minor should only have had plant life. Somebody had landed, and rats had escaped into a world with no predators and plenty of food.

As we left the ship, I noticed how well the SEALs blended into the jungle. The paint on their hands and faces, which looked so ridiculous in the all-metal environment of the armored transport, matched the leaves and shades of the jungle. We had learned about camouflage back at the orphanage, of course, but I had never seen it firsthand. The SEALs filed out in a column, with Shannon and me trailing a few yards behind.

My armor shielded me from the heat. I could see the way the humidity affected the SEALs. Underarm stains began to show through their uniforms within minutes of leaving the kettle. Drops of perspiration rolled down the oil-based paint on their faces.

"Those poor boys look uncomfortable." Shannon's voice oozed with mock empathy.

Though the SEALs used a proprietary channel to communicate with their headsets, I located a faint echo of their chatter on the interLink. They did not speak much, and the few crackling words I understood were all business. "I get the feeling that they're not thinking about the heat," I said.

When McKay first told us we would have a thirty-mile hike through the jungle, I envisioned one long, hot afternoon. The foliage grew thicker than I had imagined, and the SEALs cut ahead slowly, careful not to make unnecessary noise. Instead of trotting twelve-minute miles, we barely traveled two miles per hour. Since Ronan Minor, a small planet with a fast rotation, had sixteen-hour days, we were going camping, like it or not. We pushed to within four miles of the target zone, then stopped for the night.

When one of the SEALs told us that Shannon and I had drawn guard duty, I wasn't surprised. With heat vision and night-for-day lenses in our visors, we were the best choice to stand guard, but I could not help feeling snubbed. They were illustrious SEALs, and we were clones. While the rest of the team rested, Shannon and I sat on opposite ends of the camp.

About an hour after I settled into a nook beside a fern-covered tree, Shannon hailed me over the interLink. "See anything, Harris?" he asked, from the opposite end of the camp.

"Rats," I said. "Have you ever seen anything like this?" Using heat vision, I could see the rats' heat signature through the foliage. They looked like bright red cartoons with even brighter yellow coronas as they scampered back and forth along the ground.

"Do you see anything else?" Shannon asked.

"Negative," I said. "Am I missing something?"

"Look due west, all the way to the horizon. Keep using your heat vision."

We were at the top of a low hill, just a swell in the terrain really. The jungle spread in front of me, and I could see above most of the growth. Off in the distance I saw the dark red silhouette of the oxygen generator. Only the tops of its stacks were giving off heat.

"The generator," I said. "I missed it before."

"It's been shut down," Shannon said. "Stage three seeding—the plant life takes over the oxygen production at this point."

Thanks to my heat vision, I saw the aura of a rat running in my direction. I could not shoot it, of course. The noise would give us away. If the bastard came any closer, however, I was not above stomping it with my boot.

"Now look north of the generator. See anything?"

I looked but saw nothing. "This isn't some kind of trick question is it?"

Shannon laughed. "Use your heat vision. Look at the forest about one mile north of the generator."

"I still . . ." But I understood what he wanted me to see. Most of the forest looked velvety black through my visor, but there was a perfectly circular patch with a faint purple tinge. You had to look hard to see it, but it was there. "The Mogats?"

"The site's gone cold," Shannon said. "My guess is that they've been gone for months."

I stared down at the zone. Little yellow filaments of light dodged in and out. "No people," I said, "but there are plenty of rats."

"The happy little bastards have the planet all to themselves," Shannon said. "Maybe the SEALs will capture one. I would hate to see them go home empty-handed."

"Do we tell them that the target zone is cold?" I asked.

"Why ruin their night?" Shannon asked.

* * *

If we found the compound crawling with people, the plan was to radio the *Kamehameha* for backup. We did not make a contingency plan for finding it overrun by rats.

Night on Ronan Minor lasted nine hours, and the SEALs resumed their march an hour before sunup. Feeling a bit fuzzy-headed, I had a little trouble keeping up with them. Pushing through the unchecked vines and broad-leaved foliage was slow work. The air was thick as steam. Condensation formed outside my visor. I wondered how the SEALs managed to breathe.

The rats were not the only residents of Ronan Minor; the planet had a healthy cockroach population as well. We didn't run into many of them on the first day, but as we got closer to the Atkins compound, we saw them clinging to tree trunks and flying rather clumsily through the air. Several of them crashed into my helmet and fell to the ground. These were big roaches, maybe three inches long, with copper-colored bodies. I started when one crawled across the front of my visor. Nobody but Shannon noticed, but I had to put up with him laughing at me over the interLink for the next two miles.

We climbed over a rise and found the edge of the target. The entire site lay hidden under layers of camouflage netting.

"Sergeant"—the team leader motioned for Shannon to come—"do you have heat vision?"

"The compound is empty," Shannon said in a matter-of-fact voice.

"Son of a— Shit!" the SEAL said.

"You gonna tell him you scanned it last night?" I whispered over the interLink.

"Shut up, Harris," Shannon hissed.

"Any chance there is somebody hiding inside?" the SEAL asked.

"I doubt it. All of the machinery is turned off. If they had machinery going, I would pick up a heat signature from an engine or a generator."

By that time the entire team had gathered around Shannon and the SEAL leader. "We're still going in," said the SEAL. "Sergeant, you and the corporal wait out here."

Shannon saluted and slung his rifle over his shoulder. He turned to me, and said, "Let's just keep out of their way." We found a shaded spot overlooking the compound and sat and watched as the SEALS crawled face-first, rifles ready, under the edge of the camouflage nets.

I switched to heat vision and watched the SEALs' orange-and-yellow profiles through the netting. I lost track of them once they entered the buildings.

"Think they'll find anything?" I asked.

"Like what?" Shannon asked.

I did not have an answer. I continued to scan the compound with my heat-vision lens. Every so often I spied a SEAL dashing between buildings, but those glimpses were rare. "They're amazing," I said to myself, forgetting that Sergeant Shannon would hear me.

"Snap out of it, Harris," Shannon said. "They're no big deal. The only thing they have done is storm an abandoned compound, and you're already specking your armor. You watch, they're going to come up empty-handed, and Huang will blame us."

The SEALs spent hours searching the compound, giving me hours to consider Shannon's prediction. Roaches swarmed the plants around me, and I distracted myself by crunching some of them with the heel of my boot. The sun began to set in the distance, and the roaches became notably more aggressive. One marched right up to where Shannon was sitting, then tumbled onto its back when it tried to crawl over the top of his leg. He looked over and crushed it with his fist.

"So who is the dominant species," I joked, "the rats or the roaches?"

"The goddamned Mogats," Shannon answered. "They were the only speckers with enough sense to get off this rock."

Up ahead, I saw movement in the camouflage covering and switched to heat vision in time to see the first of the SEALs rolling out from under the edge of the net. Ten more were nearby.

"Look who's back," Shannon said a split second before the explosion. I just had time to take in the irony in his voice, then the very air around us seemed to turn white, activating the polarizing lenses in my visor. The explosion cut through the jungle in a wave. Its concussion knocked me flat on my back, but I quickly climbed back to my feet.

"GODDAMN!" Shannon yelled as he sprinted toward the clearing. I ran after him, rifle at the ready for no particular reason.

"Harris, find the ones who made it out. I'm going under the net to look for survivors."

There was no net, not where we were standing. Shreds of flaming camouflage netting floated down from the sky for as far as I could see. I saw Shannon running into the heart of the flames, dropping down a waist-high crater.

One of the SEALs lay with his back wrapped around the trunk of a tree at an impossible angle. I threw my helmet off and ran over to him. He was already dead.

Another SEAL lay on his stomach a few feet away. As I ran to him, I saw a streamer of flaming camouflage float over his shoulder. Brushing it away, I turned the man on his back. He was alive, but barely. A shard of metal the size of my hand was buried in his throat. Blood poured out of the wound.

He would die in a moment no matter what I did for him. I wanted to shake him. I wanted to yell, "What happened here? What the hell did you do?"

Shannon was wasting his time looking for survivors. Not even the rats and the roaches would have survived that explosion. The only survivors were the Mogats. "They were the only speckers with enough sense to get off this rock."

CHAPTER
THIRTEEN

Clones may come out of the tube identical, but experience takes over where genetic engineering and neural programming leave off. Most of the platoon followed soccer, boxing, and basketball. Gambling was rampant. But Vince Lee did not gamble or watch professional sports. He napped whenever he got the opportunity. He read books about self-improvement and told me that his time in the Marines would give him an excellent platform to launch into politics. He was a dedicated bodybuilder who started each morning lifting weights in the officers' gym. Of all of the clones I ever knew, Lee was the only one who openly worried about not being natural-born.

Lee was also the only man in our platoon who talked about retiring from the Corps. "When I get out," he would often begin a conversation, "I'm going to a frontier planet," he would say, "someplace where they appreciate hard work." Around the time we went to Ronan Minor, Lee sometimes talked about building a resort on the shore of Lake Pride, a few miles west of Rising Sun.

Ever since meeting with Oberland, keeping up with current events had become my hobby. It was an obsession, maybe even an addiction. I began each day with a quick glance at the headlines. I did so before crawling out of bed. If I found something interesting, I stopped to read it. I usually spent a good hour reading before tossing my mediaLink shades aside and heading for the mess. And after breakfast, I found time for more reading.

Two days after we left Ronan Minor I found a story with the headline: "24 SEALS LOST IN CRASH."

They don't release information when clones die. We don't have parents or relatives, so nobody notices. SEALs, natural-borns with families, merit a news story, even if it's completely fabricated. In this case, the official story was that twenty-four Navy SEALs were killed when their transport malfunctioned during a training exercise in a remote sector of the Scutum-Crux Arm.

"The accident occurred as the squad practiced landing maneuvers on an uninhabited planet." True enough, unless you count rats, roaches, and Liberators.

" 'The accident was caused by an equipment failure,' said Lieutenant Howard Banks of Naval public affairs. 'We are conducting a thorough investigation to determine the cause of the accident.' "

"There's already been a thorough investigation," I mumbled to myself. I knew that because my ass was on the line. Admiral Huang had Shannon and me held in custody while he and Admiral Klyber played back the data in our helmets. Huang called us a disgrace to the uniform and ranted about court-martials and executions; but in the end, we were cleared.

Other stories caught my eye. Back on Earth, the Senate seemed unaware of the war brewing in the outer arms while the House of Representatives seemed intent on stoking it. The big story out of the Senate was about a senior senator retiring and the party his friends threw to celebrate his years of service. The story listed the celebrities in attendance, and there was a side story critiquing gowns worn by politicians' wives. As far as the Senate was concerned, life on the frontier was just aces.

In the House of Representatives, congressmen were arguing about gun laws. Many powerful representatives wanted the gun laws preventing the private ownership of automatic weapons repealed. One congresswoman argued that citizens should be allowed to buy a battleship if they could afford it.

Delegations from the Cygnus, Perseus, and Norma Arms flew to Washington to meet with their congressmen. There was no mention whether these delegations also visited the Senate.

"Something's happening," Lee said as he entered the mess hall. "The fleet's moving." He had just come from the gym, and jagged vein lines bulged across his biceps and forearms.

"Moving where?" I asked as I took a drink of orange juice.

Lee, whose hair was still wet from the shower, smelled of government-issue soap. "I'm not sure where we are headed, but a guy at the gym said we're going to rendezvous with the Inner SC Fleet."

"Really?" I asked. "What about the Outer Fleet?"

Lee sat down next to me. "He says we're combining into one fleet.

"Wayson, I've never seen this before. You don't send twenty-four carriers to one corner of space for peacekeeping. This is war."

"That's drastic talk," I said. "How does the guy at the gym know so much? Are you sure he knew what he was talking about?"

It seemed like a fair question. When it came to the "need to know" hierarchy, we grunts were the bottom rung. I wolfed down the rest of my breakfast and waited for Lee to finish. Once he finished eating, we rushed to the rec room to look out the viewport.

We were no longer orbiting Ronan Minor. I saw an endless starfield and not much else. "Did your friend say anything about where we are headed?"

"Nope," Lee said. "Nothing at all."

"Do not learn the wrong lesson from Ronan Minor," Bryce Klyber said. He might have maintained a sparse office— the only things you ever saw on his desk were an occasional file and a set of pens—but his dining area was like an art museum. Track lighting on the ceiling shone down on a row of fine oil paintings along one wall. The outer wall of the room was a viewport overlooking the bow of the ship. Another wall was lined with two one-thousand-gallon aquariums.

One tank held schools of colorful fish that dived and darted among coral formations. The other tank was only half-full. A strange animal called a man-of-war floated along the top of the water. Perhaps it is an exaggeration to call a man-of-war an "animal," but I don't know what else to call it. It looked like a violet-colored bubble with long, silky threads dangling to the bottom of the tank.

"Do you follow the news? Have you heard the one about the twenty-four SEALs who died in a transport accident?" Klyber asked me in the kind of singsong tone you would use when asking a friend if he'd heard the one about the secretary of the Navy and the farmer's daughter.

"Yes, sir," I said.

"The Pentagon uses that story far too often." He shook his head. "One of these days, the Linear Committee will launch an investigation into AT disasters and learn that we haven't had a legitimate accident for thirty years."

I did not know if Admiral Klyber was serious. He sat by himself in an austere, uncomfortable-looking chair, picking pieces of chicken out of his salad. Klyber was the epitome of the aristocrat-soldier, elegant and well-spoken, sitting in his uniform at a table with fine wine in crystal goblets.

With his sunken cheeks and puny arms, he looked so fragile, but anger and intelligence radiated from his cold, gray eyes. "I suppose we shall never know if that compound was rigged or if Huang's SEALs blew themselves up."

"You don't think it was a trap, sir?" I asked.

Admiral Klyber mused for a moment, smiled, shook his head ever so slightly. "No. If Huang could not take prisoners, he would have wanted to leave bodies in his wake. Ours or theirs, it wouldn't matter to Huang as long as there were bodies." His mouth curved into a smile as he chewed a bite of salad. "Never occurred to you that those SEALs might have done it to themselves? Sergeant Shannon said that you were impressed by them."

"Yes, sir."

Klyber finished his salad. He laid his fork across the top of the plate and pushed the plate aside. Then he sipped his wine and turned toward his main course, a thick slab of roast beef.

"Corporal, I have served in the U.A. Navy for over forty years. I had my own command before Che Huang entered officer training school. In all of that time, the Liberators are the only blemish on my record."

"They won the war," I said, trying not to feel offended.

"Indeed they did," Klyber agreed. "Made the galaxy safe, didn't they? Unfortunately, history remembers them as unnecessarily cruel, and Congress outlawed them. You are going to help me prove otherwise, Corporal Harris. That is why I have taken such an interest in you. The climate has changed. We are headed toward war, and a fighting man with your talents will be recognized, clone or natural-born."

"Even a Liberator?" I asked.

"I believe so, yes," Klyber said as he sliced the meat on his plate. "Especially a Liberator.

"No clone has ever been promoted beyond the rank of sergeant. Only one quarter of the clone boys from your orphanage will become NCOs, Harris. You beat the odds in your first six months." He speared the prime rib with a quick stab and chewed it with small, mechanical bites. "Perhaps you and I can expand that field of promotions."

"Only natural-born are admitted into officer candidate school," I said.

Still chewing, Klyber neatly placed his utensils on his plate. He took a sip of wine and leaned back to savor it. "When I was at the academy, only Earth-born cadets were admitted. 'Earth-born, Earth-loyal,' that was the old saying.

"They've let that slide quite a bit over the years. Politicians have replaced tradition with political expedience. The citizens in the territories complained that they did not have all of the opportunities given to Earth-born children, so Congress used the military for a social experiment. They integrated and enrolled some out-born cadets," Klyber said, not even trying to mask the disdain in his voice.

"As you know, Huang saw fit to replace Admiral Barry. Our new fleet commander will be Rear Admiral Robert

Thurston, an outworlder born and raised in the Orion Arm. If an out-born can command a fleet . . ." Klyber looked at me and smiled.

Life on the *Kamehameha* settled into a schedule of drills and drinking. Something was brewing out there beyond the horizon, but nobody knew any details.

Two weeks after we left Ronan Minor, the *Kamehameha* rendezvoused with the rest of the Central SC Fleet in orbit around Terraneau. Two days later, the Inner SC Fleet joined our orbit.

Down on Terraneau, officers from both the Inner and Central SC Fleets attended meetings as Admiral Klyber created a new command structure. As bits of information trickled in, talk around the platoon was enthusiastic.

Most of the sea-soldiers I spoke with liked the idea of merging with the Inner SC Fleet. The combined fleet would have over a hundred thousand fighting Marines, a force that we believed capable of wiping out any threat.

None of the Marines seemed to care that a new fleet commander had replaced Admiral Absalom Barry. The name Robert Thurston meant nothing; and besides, he was Navy, we were Marines. As long as his boats brought us to the fight on time, we'd do the rest.

That indifference changed on the day that Thurston boarded the *Kamehameha*. Admiral Klyber took him on a tour of the ship. The last stop on the tour was our deck. A party of officers dressed in whites passed by our barracks, and we all caught a brief glimpse of the little troll.

Robert Thurston looked younger than most of the privates in my platoon. He had thick red hair and pimples; honest to God, pimples all over his face. He cut his hair to regulation length, but it stood in spiky clumps under his cap. I was most taken by his size. Thurston was five-foot-five at best, with a slender, almost effeminate build. Needless to say, talk at the bar was wilder than ever that evening.

"You see that kid? He's barely out of diapers," one clone shouted as he entered the bar.

"What do you think of Thurston?" Lee asked me as I found the platoon's watering spot for the night.

"I wonder if he drinks milk or Scotch," a private from the platoon joked.

"So he looks a bit green," I said as I downed half my beer.

"Yeah, he looks a little green," Lee agreed. "I'd hate to find myself nuked just because somebody's congressman-daddy pushed his boy up the ranks."

"I don't think you need to worry about that," I said. "From what I hear, Thurston earned his way up the ranks."

"Is that a fact?" Shannon asked, nosing his way into our crowd.

"That is a fact," I said.

Shannon, who knew damned well that I had met with Admiral Klyber the day before, considered my words. "That's good news," he said as he saluted me with his glass. "Did you all hear that? Harris heard that Thurston pulls his own weight, and Harris has good sources." Lowering his voice, Shannon added, "The boy must have one hell of a record."

"And there's something else," I said, moving toward Shannon so that no one else would hear me. "He's out-born."

I expected Shannon to spit out his beer, but he didn't. He stood frozen for a moment, then swallowed. "No shit?" he said. "Born off Earth? That little speck-sucker must really know his stuff."

FOURTEEN

The *Kamehameha* sat listless, while the frigates and fighters that surrounded her remained in constant motion. Nearly a dozen frigates orbited her hull, circling it in odd patterns. They would keep the flagship safe from fighter attacks. Of course, any fighter carrier, even an ancient one like the *Kamehameha,* had strong shields and powerful cannons.

The Inner and Central Scutum-Crux Fleets hovered along opposite hemispheres of Terraneau. For a moment, the two fleets looked like mirror reflections of each other; then the Central Fleet pulled back from the planet and arrayed itself in battle formation with six carriers launching fighters and six carriers in reserve. Harriers and Tomcats poured out of six carriers at the front of the formation like angry hornets defending their nest. The Harriers moved so quickly that they could not be tracked with the human eye.

Admiral Klyber, commander of the Central Fleet, attacked first. A wave of his Tomcats, fighters made for nonatmospheric conditions with particularly powerful missiles and particle-beam cannons, vanished from radar. When they reappeared, they were approaching the *al-Sadat,* the flagship fighter carrier of the Inner SC Fleet.

I watched the virtual representation of the battle in real

time on a three-dimensional holographic display. Floating in midair, the display looked like a glowing green grid with models of ships. Five meters long and three meters deep, it was large enough to show every detail of the battle.

"Man, that's fierce," Lee whispered to me.

"Shhh," I hissed. Everyone else in the room was silent.

Klyber's attack made perfect sense. The *al-Sadat* sat isolated from the other capital ships in the Inner SC Fleet. The nearest frigates were hundreds of miles away and headed in the wrong direction—toward what would likely become the front line of the battle. Klyber's fighters skirted that line, flanking Robert Thurston's formation and attacking an unguarded pocket near the rear. It would take a couple of minutes for Thurston's closest carrier to arrive on the scene.

Thurston commanded his forces from a simulated bridge in one corner of the auditorium. I had a good view of him from my seat.

"Shields," Thurston said, in a voice that seemed far too calm considering the situation.

"Should we take evasive action, sir?" a crewman asked.

"That will not be necessary," Thurston said as he paced the deck.

"Shall I signal for frigate support?" the crewman asked.

Admiral Thurston did not have the tactical advantage of watching the battle on a three-dimensional display. From my omniscient seat, I could see every aspect of the battle. I knew that Klyber had already launched a second wave of fighters. Thurston, with nothing more than a battle map that displayed in-ship radar readings, could not know what a forceful assault Admiral Klyber had planned.

"He's sunk. Klyber's going to end this fast," Lee whispered.

"Shhhhh!" I hissed. A few of the people sitting near us gave Lee and me some chilly glares.

On the other side of the room, where the officers sat, a loud cheer erupted. They wanted blood. "Bet the boy never saw anything like this at the Academy," one overexcited officer blurted in a voice that carried. With that, the officers became silent.

I glanced back at the 3-D display to see what all the cheering was about, but I was more interested in watching Admiral Thurston. He looked too young to command a ship. With his spiky, rust red hair and pimples, he looked like a teenage boy pretending to stand at the helm.

"A very aggressive attack," Thurston said, cocking a single eyebrow. "Either he intends to win early or he wishes to back us into a . . ."

I looked back at the full-battle display in the center of the auditorium. Klyber's fighters were closing in on the *al-Sadat*. Thurston showed amazing patience for a man whose ship was about to be attacked by 140 armed fighters. Warning lights flared along the ceiling and floor of the mock bridge. The sirens near the helm console blared so loudly that they choked my thoughts.

I doubted Thurston's grasp of the situation. Just behind that initial wave of fighters, half of the Central SC Fleet was in position for the second wave of the attack. Klyber had an unfair advantage—the *Kamehameha,* a thirteenth fighter carrier. She might have been old and small by carrier standards, but the *Kamehameha* still bore a complement of sixty fighter craft.

"Send the *Washington* and the *Grant* to sector 14-L. Tell them to launch fighters on my orders and power up shields on my mark," Thurston said as he studied his battle map.

"Sir, we are undefended," the crewman said.

"Prepare our pilots," Thurston said in a voice that made the order sound like a compromise, "but do not give the order to launch."

"Enemy fighters' ETA is less than one minute," another crewman yelled.

"What the hell is he doing?" Lee asked.

"Tell the captains of the *Washington* and the *Grant* to launch fighters . . . now!" Thurston's voice was emphatic. He looked so much like a boy in puberty that I expected his voice to crack, but he remained very much in control.

Two events happened simultaneously. Klyber's fighters arrived and commenced a meaningless attack. His Tomcats buzzed around the hull of the *al-Sadat,* but their pilots seemed uncommitted. Instead of firing missiles, they seemed more interested in flying defensive patterns. As they circled, the gun batteries lining the hull of the *al-Sadat* flashed green.

At the exact same moment, a much more important event took place on a distant part of the map. The *Washington* and the *Grant* launched fighters as two of Klyber's carriers and a complement of frigates entered the sector.

"Order the fighters in sector 14-L to attack the enemy carriers," Thurston said. "Have the Harriers concentrate their fire on their shield stations. The Tomcats can pick off any fighters they manage to launch."

"Yes, sir," the crewman said, a new note of excitement evident in his voice.

"Instruct the captains of the *Washington* and the *Grant* to attack the frigate escort. We can't allow those frigates to sneak up on our fighters."

"Yes, sir," the crewman responded.

Unlike the *al-Sadat,* which had its shields up, the carriers from the Central SC Fleet had lowered their shields so that they could launch their fighters. Thurston's Harriers fired missiles at the shield antennae on those carriers, quickly obliterating their best defense.

I watched as the tiny fighters moved in on the carriers like a swarm of ants. Their missiles would do little good against shielded carriers, but Thurston had timed the attack precisely right. Red lights appeared along the edges of the Central Fleet ships showing that their shield stations were destroyed. Having destroyed the shield antennae, Thurston's fighters suddenly became a serious threat.

Not far away, Admiral Klyber's frigates were completely mismatched against Thurston's carriers. In less than two minutes, the *Washington* destroyed five Central Fleet frigates and the *Grant* annihilated three more. Any frigates that survived this attack would limp away from the fight. Somehow Robert Thurston had peered into Klyber's mind and uncovered a weakness. The bulk of the Central Fleet's frigates fled back toward the protection of the fleet; but the Inner Fleet's Harriers and Tomcats continued to pummel the carriers, cutting off any hope of escape.

"How did he do that?" Lee asked.

Nobody shhhhed Lee that time. We all wondered the same thing.

Thurston began pouring out a steady stream of commands.

"Have the *Grant* send out bombers," Thurston said. "We need to finish those carriers before the rest of their fleet can regroup."

"Hail the nearest frigate," Thurston said. "Tell the captain that we require assistance."

"Only one?" the communications officer asked.

"One will suffice," Thurston said.

Until that moment, I had not noticed the toll that the *al-Sadat*'s cannons had taken on the Inner Fleet's fighters. They began their assault with 140 Harriers; now fewer than 50 of those fighters remained. As I tried to count the fighters, two large flashes lit up a far corner of the map. Thurston's bombers made short work of the trapped carriers.

"Excellent," Thurston said. I still expected his voice to crack. It didn't. "Recall the attack wings to the *Washington* and the *Grant*."

Thurston's fighters broke off their attack as Klyber's ships stuttered back to their end of the field. "They're running!" the communications officer yelled, no longer trying to conceal his excitement. "They're leaving their fighter escort stranded!"

"It would seem so," Admiral Thurston said.

I stopped to consider the tides of this battle. The Central Fleet had begun the fight with thirteen fighter carriers, sixty-five frigates, and nine hundred fighter craft. The fleet still had eleven carriers. According to the scorecard at the base of the holographic display, Thurston had destroyed more than three hundred of Klyber's fighters.

The war was won. I waited for Thurston to send his ships in for a final assault, but he sat silently watching his battle map.

"Admiral, the Central Fleet is preparing to evacuate," a deck officer said.

"Yes, it is," Thurston said.

"Shall we attack?"

"No. Let them go."

A stunned silence filled the auditorium. Moments later, a door near Thurston's mock helm slid open, and Admiral Klyber, flanked by several aides, stormed in. "You allowed my fleet to escape, Admiral Thurston?"

"Yes, sir," Thurston said.

"Explain yourself," Klyber demanded.

Robert Thurston sighed. "In its current configuration, the Inner SC Fleet is designed to win battles, Admiral, not wars."

"You had my fleet at your mercy," Klyber snapped. "You should have finished us."

"If we pressed the attack, we would have joined you in a battle of attrition—my twelve carriers against your eleven," Thurston said. "If we went in for the kill, I would have lost ships unnecessarily."

Klyber smiled. "Sensible decision, Admiral. How would you reconfigure the fleet?" Klyber sounded interested, but there was something dangerous about the way he stared at Thurston. Sharp teeth hid behind his smile.

"Fighters and frigates are excellent ships for repelling enemy attacks," Thurston said. "Having neutralized one-third of your fighters, I would need battleships and destroyers to finish your fleet."

The simulation took place in the largest briefing room on the *Kamehameha*, an auditorium capable of seating three thousand people that was only used for important occasions. A more-than-capacity crowd had packed in. Once the seats were filled, lines of people squeezed in along the walls. We had come for theater-in-the-round.

Klyber asked several more questions. When he finished, Thurston's three-man crew stood up from behind their computer consoles and applauded. Klyber and his aides clapped as well. Soon the theater erupted in applause.

Our new fleet commander nodded to his crew and walked briskly from the stage. He strode out of the auditorium without so much as a sideward glance. The applause, however, continued.

If his legend was to be believed, Klyber had never lost a combat simulation, not even as a freshman cadet. Of course, good records have a way of becoming unblemished when there is little chance of verification. Whether or not he was truly undefeated, prior to that match, Bryce Klyber was generally considered unbeatable in simulated space battles.

Over the next three weeks, the seemingly tireless Robert Thurston visited all twenty-five carriers in the Scutum-Crux Fleet. He took on all but one of the captains in simulated battles. (Captain Dickey Friggs of the *St. Ignatius* complained of fatigue and said he was in no condition for a fight.) The simulations always ended quickly and decisively, with Thurston on top.

Admiral Klyber's campaign to legitimize Robert Thurston succeeded in every corner of the fleet except one. Walking toward Bryce Klyber's office on what would turn out to be my last visit, I saw signs of open disdain toward the new fleet commander.

Everywhere else in the fleet they called him Admiral Thurston; but on the command deck, he was "Bobby, boy genius" or sometimes simply "the boy." In the time that I spent waiting to meet Admiral Klyber, I heard jokes about "the boy's" voice changing, his testicles dropping during battle, and a pretty good one-liner about him offering spiked milk and cookies to his officers so that they would let him stay up past his bedtime.

Sitting in the waiting room, I listened to the bits of humor in silence. What kind of jokes did they tell about clones? And another question—If Thurston hadn't wowed these people with his strategic skills, what would impress them?

The door to Admiral Klyber's office slid open, and he entered the doorway. "Corporal Harris," he said.

As I followed Klyber into his office, I heard an aide whisper, "The admiral's pet clone." It took real effort to pretend I had not heard it.

"Your mercenary friend is making quite a name for himself," Klyber said, as we crossed his office. "Freeman is walking a very fine line. He does a lot of piecework in this arm. According to the local authorities, some of his clients are worse than the hoodlums he brings in."

Klyber sat down behind his desk. I looked over his shoulder for a moment and stared out the viewport behind him. The *Kamehameha* had entered an odd phase of its orbit. I could not see Terraneau, just the blanket of space and an occasional frigate.

"Sit down, Corporal," Klyber said, pointing toward one of the chairs before his desk. As I took my seat, he asked, "What do you think of Rear Admiral Thurston?"

"He knows his way around a combat simulation," I said.

"I've never seen the like," Klyber agreed. "I hear there is a rumor going around that I let Thurston win. I would never stage a loss, not even to improve fleet morale. I don't see how my losing could possibly boost morale."

"No, sir," I said. I had not heard that rumor, and I doubted that anybody outside SC Command had. Rumors like that only existed among ass-kissing officers vying for a promotion. As far as I could tell, Thurston's victories had gone a long way toward improving ship morale.

Once the topic shifted to Thurston, Klyber spoke in short bursts. He leaned over his desk as he spoke, then sat back in his chair and drummed his fingers on the armrests of his chair when I answered his questions.

"That was a very unorthodox move, leaving a capital ship unguarded during a fighter attack. Moves like that can cost an entire battle."

"Did he tell you how he knew where to send the *Washington* and the *Grant*, sir?" I asked.

"Yes," said Klyber, sounding aggravated. "Yes, he did. He said that my flash attack meant that I wanted to put him in a defensive posture. He said my opening attack was either the wasteful move of an amateur strategist or an obvious attempt to herd an enemy out of position. The cocky little prick told one of my aides that he gave me the benefit of the doubt."

Klyber paused, giving me a moment to respond; but I did

not say a word. "Thurston read my attack as a move to spread the battle to three fronts. The bastard was exactly right."

"He figured that out from your opening attack?" I asked.

"Apparently so," Klyber said.

"Luck?" I asked.

Klyber smiled, taking my question as welcomed flattery. "I thought it was luck, but he's taken every captain in the fleet. The captain of the *Bolivar* managed to last the longest—twenty minutes; but he spent most of the simulation running away." Thinking of this match brought a wicked grin to Klyber's narrow face. "I sent a video record of the match to the Joint Chiefs. Che Huang may have something to say to Captain Cory about his tactics."

"Are you going to act on Thurston's suggestion about adding new ships to the fleet?" I asked.

"You must be joking," Klyber snapped. His demeanor changed in a flash. His eyes narrowed, and he pursed his lips so hard that they almost disappeared. Sitting with his back as rigid as a board, he said, "You give this man entirely too much credit. He won a simulation, nothing more than a game. That is a far cry from proving yourself in battle."

Knowing that I had touched a nerve, I nodded and hoped the moment would pass.

"We don't need new ships," Klyber continued. "Unless you have been briefed about some new enemy that I don't know about, the Unified Authority is the only naval power in the galaxy. We are the only ones with anything larger than a frigate."

"Yes, sir," I said. I thought about the three dreadnoughts that attacked the *Chayio*, but had the good sense to keep my mouth shut.

Klyber stared angrily at me for another moment. "I would not give that frontier-born mongrel the satisfaction," he hissed. Having said this, Admiral Klyber relaxed. His shoulders loosened, and he leaned back in his chair.

"People feel the same way about clones," I said.

A glimmer of Klyber's earlier humor showed in his smile. "I wouldn't hold my hopes out for a seat on the Linear Committee," Klyber said, "but, all in all, I think a clone is more readily welcomed into proper society than a prepubescent from the frontier. After all, clones are raised on Earth and are entirely loyal to the Republic. Can anybody really know where a frontier-born's loyalties lie?"

"But no clone has ever become an officer," I said.

"As I have said before, we may be able to change that, you and I." He turned to look out of the viewport. None of the other ships from the fleet were visible at the moment, so he turned back toward me.

"It's been forty years since the Unified Authority has seen a full-scale assault, Corporal. That is about to change. I am placing your platoon on point. If you perform well . . . Let's just say that I will be able to open new doors for you."

Klyber did not tell me the details at that time. Polished brass ran through his veins, and I was still a corporal. The details became apparent soon enough, however. Admiral Thurston cut the orders the following day.

We filed into the briefing room and sat nervously. People spoke in whispers that steadily grew louder as we waited, and more and more Marines packed into the room. By the time Captain McKay began speaking, four platoons had squeezed into a holotorium that was barely large enough for one.

McKay strode up to the podium alone. Sitting one row in, I was close enough to see the way his eyes bounced around the gallery. Then the lights went out. The holographic image of a dark planet appeared. The planet spun in a slow and lopsided rotation. No sunlight showed on its rocky surface. It did not appear to be a moon, but I saw no signs of plant life or water.

"Naval Intelligence has traced the location of the Mogat separatists who attacked our platoon on Ezer Kri," McKay said. His voice was low and commanding and tinged with poorly concealed excitement. "The insurgents have set up on a planet in the uninhabited Templar System called A8Z5. For purposes of this mission, we shall refer to A8Z5 as 'Hubble.' "

McKay spent the better part of an hour laying out the tactics we would employ to invade Hubble. When he finished, he opened the meeting for questions.

"Excuse me, sir," a Marine from another platoon asked. "Is that a moon?"

"Hubble is a planet," McKay said.

"God," Sergeant Shannon whispered, "what a pit."

CHAPTER
SIXTEEN

I knew the paradise Hubble once was and the hell it had become. One hundred thousand years ago, Hubble, the garden planet of the Templar System, had lakes and forests, mountain pastures and ice-capped peaks. Colorful birds once flew across its skies. During our briefing, they showed us video footage of the very spot on which the battle would occur. It was a paradise.

But Hubble no longer had a sky, per se. The noxious, oily gases that passed for its atmosphere could kill a person as surely as a bullet through the head. A thin film of gas swirled overhead, blurring my view of the stars. No sunlight warmed the planet's rock and powder surface. No plants grew through the hard crust that covered so much of Hubble's scaly ground.

On Earth, they still saw Hubble as an outer space Eden, but Earth was sixty thousand light-years away. The astronomers who named Hubble's solar system after an ancient religious order had no way of knowing that they were looking at an extinct vision. The images they saw were older than civilization.

Viewed from observatories in the much closer Sagittarius Arm, Hubble was a scene of grand destruction. From their telescopes, scientists watched as Templar, the eponymous central star of the Templar System, expanded. Once a benevolent sun, Templar died as suns often do, swelling until it devoured half of the solar system around it. Before collapsing into itself, Templar engulfed A8Z3, A8Z2, and A8Z1, its three closest neighbors. Those planets vanished entirely.

Fifty thousand light-years away, the flaring red surface of Templar had just begun to spread into the orbits of the next neighboring planets. I have watched video images of it melting entire mountain ranges and boiling seas into steam—images of a fifty-thousand-year-old apocalypse that are still viewable fifty thousand light-years away.

A8Z4 and Hubble (A8Z5), the fourth and fifth planets from Templar, were not completely destroyed, though the dying sun scorched their surfaces. A8Z4 now existed as a wisp of dust particles and gas. You could fire a missile through it. The once-rich soil of Hubble was cooked to ash, and its atmosphere became toxic.

The kettle opened to reveal the rim of a sweeping valley. As the platoon hustled out of the armored transport, I looked across the panorama and noticed how the black sky and gray landscape seemed to stretch forever.

During our briefing, Captain McKay described the full extent of this invasion. Within the hour, armored transports would land thirty thousand Marines on this desecrated planet with another seventy thousand Marines waiting in reserve.

The outer skin of Hubble's atmosphere was formed of combustible gas that exploded in harmless flashes when heated by rocket engines. We had so many ships passing through the atmosphere that the sky looked like it was on fire.

"Positions, men," Sergeant Shannon bellowed. "Fan out. Secure the area."

We knew the drill. Shannon had trained us well. He had rehearsed every step of securing a landing area with us hundreds of times.

"You heard the sergeant," I said to my fire team. The four men on my team formed a diamond, and we headed south to the ridge. The ash crunched and compressed under my boots. I did not sink; it was not like stepping into water or quicksand. It felt more like walking on dry leaves.

The sun that burned up this system might have burned out, but it still generated heat, over two hundred degrees. The planet's landscape spread before us as a perpetual nightscape. On other worlds I sometimes regretted the way our night-for-day vision blotted out color; but it didn't matter on a desolate brick, like Hubble. Everything was gray or black except for the amber-colored condensation that formed on my visor. I wiped at it with the tips of my fingers, leaving a translucent swirl. Fine beads of oil hung in the air of the planet like steam after a summer rain.

The first of the barges landed no more than thirty yards from where I stood. Jets of fiery exhaust flared from its engines. The blast blew dust that stuck to the oil on the front of my visor. I tried to clean it, but the hardened plastic on my battle armor only smeared the film. When I looked back at the barge, the smear obscured my view of a column of low-gravity tanks rolling out of its hold.

LG tanks were ten feet tall and thirty feet long—built long and low to take advantage of any available gravity. They were iron beasts carrying artillery, particle beams, and missiles. Weighing nearly two hundred thousand pounds each, they sank six inches into the clinker soil.

"Holy shiiiiit," Lee gasped over the interLink. "Sergeant Shannon, Harris, you'd better have a look at this." Lee stood at the edge of the valley. I joined him.

"What are you looking at?" I asked.

"Ping it," Lee said.

Shannon let out a litany of four-letter words.

Using optic commands, I initiated the sonic locator. My helmet emitted an inaudible ping that bounced across the landscape. One moment, I saw the valley below me as a wasted desert with cinder for soil; the next moment, the sonic locator overlaid that scene with a network of translucent green trenches. Hundreds of snake shafts crisscrossed the ground in nonsensical patterns. I did not know what the excavations could be used for. When I discussed them with veteran Marines, I used to get a shrug and a tired look. To them, snake shafts were as baffling as the giant stone heads

on Easter Island, something that religious fanatics built for
the sake of building. I thought that there had to be more to it
than that.

"Those can't all be snake shafts," I said. "There are too
many of them."

My sonic locator sent out another ping as the ghosts of
the first ping faded. An identical pattern appeared.

"The Mogats could not have dug those," I said. "They
only left Ezer Kri a few weeks ago."

"Then somebody has been digging into this planet for
years," Lee said. "Think they knew they would hide here
someday?"

"I don't know what to make of it," Shannon said as he left
to return to his squad.

As Lee and I debated the improbabilities of the snake
shafts, a gust of wind blasted so hard it almost pushed
me over. I looked back to see the gray hull of another barge
touching down. The barge's oblong body settled with a loud
creak, then made a loud mechanical whine as the cargo
bay doors opened. It carried Cobra gunships—low-flying
units used to cover ground troops. With their giant racks of
guns and rockets, Cobras looked more like gigantic bumble-
bees than snakes. The gunships' engines kicked into gear as
a conveyor belt moved them to the front of the cargo bay,
and they launched into the air.

My vision remained clouded. I tried brushing the oil-
based mud from my visor with my glove again, but that only
smeared it more.

By that time, over twenty thousand Marines crowded the
ridge with another ten thousand on the way. I looked across
the scene and took mental inventory of the men and tanks.
"Lee, gunships, tanks . . . this is a full-scale invasion," I said.

"I've never seen anything on this scale," he agreed.
"Shannon is probably the only active Marine who has."

The oil mist that passed for humidity in Hubble's atmosphere distorted sounds, but it did not smother them. A wing
of ten Harriers zoomed over our heads. Two seconds passed
before the roar of their engines tore through my helmet. By
the time the sound caught up to us, the Harriers had slowed
for a methodical sweep of the valley. As the fighters

approached the horizon, I heard the thunder of missiles and saw tiny bubbles of light along the valley floor.

"Move out!" McKay's voice bellowed over the interLink.

"Gentlemen, let's roll!" Shannon shouted.

That was our call. The first wave of the attack consisted of thirty thousand Marines, a mere five hundred tanks, and thirty gunships. The Harriers that preceded us pounded the enemy's gun placements, bunkers, and air defense. Whatever ships and airfields the Mogats possessed, would now lie in ruin.

As the Harriers wove their fire, our job was to cause chaos. We would breach the Mogat lines and scatter their defenders so that the rest of our landing party could deliver a killing blow. The Mogats were the men who had massacred our platoon. We owed them.

"Lets go!" Lee yelled to his men over a platoon-wide open channel on the interLink.

Lunging over the precipice, we used our jetpacks to glide down the sloping valley wall. Our packs set off small fireballs in the gassy air. From above, we must have looked like a swarm of locusts with exploding asses. Once we reached the valley floor, we dropped to our feet and trotted toward battle.

From an observation craft far overhead, one of our commanders signaled us to break into a picket line by illuminating a formation symbol in our visors. We rushed to comply. Forming diagonal lines with our fire teams, we stretched the width of the valley.

"There cannot possibly be any living people on this planet," I said to Shannon over the interLink.

"Shut up, Harris," Shannon said. "Keep the Link open." Shannon's words sounded harsh, but a certain lilt in his voice suggested agreement.

The ground started to vibrate under my feet. I looked back in time to see rows of tanks reaching the bottom of the valley wall. "Skiing" with our jetpacks, we had easily outpaced the heavy LGs down the slope; but now they were catching up to us quickly. Seeing their approach, I radioed my team to pick up speed.

I wiped the glass with the side of my forefinger, scraping

the dust and grease as best I could; but the stiff plates that
formed my gloves just would not absorb the oil from my visor. The landscape around me remained out of focus.

"Platoon leaders, report," Captain McKay ordered. He
took their reports over the open link so that everyone in our
platoon could hear them.

Tim Grayson, the sergeant over the Thirteenth Platoon,
responded. Sergeant Shannon said nothing. McKay waited
for his report then called, "Sergeant Shannon, report."

"Have you run a sonic sweep?" Shannon asked.

"Affirmative," McKay said, in a voice that was both au-
thoritative and efficient. "We are aware of the tunnels. We
have scanned the tunnels for enemy personnel and equipment as well." He sounded impatient. The ships orbiting
Hubble had much more sophisticated equipment than the
scaled-down sonic locators in our helmets.

I looked back and saw Shannon kneel with one knee in
the ash soil. "All clear in this sector, sir," Shannon said. I
could tell he felt frustrated by McKay's cool response, but
his voice hid it well.

The odd atmosphere continued to distort sounds. In an
oxygen atmosphere, the rumble of the LG tanks would have
rattled my armor. During field exercises on Earth, I could
hear gunships from hundreds of yards and could tell which
direction the sound came from. On Hubble, I did not hear
the gunships until after they had flown past me, and the
growl of the tanks seemed to come from all directions.

"Watch yourselves," McKay shouted over the interLink.

The tanks caught up to us. A less rigid formation flashed
in my visor, and my team fell back, keeping pace with the
tanks. We moved at a fast jog, maybe six miles per hour. You
had to watch your step in the low gravity. We had weights in
our boots; but it was easy to stumble. If you fell in front of a
tank . . .

An LG rumbled past me. The tops of its spools were just
about even with my head. The dust it kicked up stuck to my
visor, and I was temporarily blinded. I did not dare stop
with tanks rolling past, so I stumbled forward as I scraped
at the dust with the side of my finger. When I removed my
hand, I saw something on the tank that left me numb. The

words "PFC Harold Goldberg" appeared over a muddy spot in the tread. The tank must have run over Goldberg, crushing his helmet into fragments, some of which were trapped in the tread.

Ahead, at the end of the valley, I caught a clear view of Harriers circling in the air, dropping bombs and firing missiles. Three gunships flew low overhead, skittering into the distance and joining that battle. Suddenly the night sky boiled as dozens of fighters burst through the combustible outer atmosphere.

"They're launching ships!" McKay yelled over the inter-Link. "They're trying to escape."

Reality had finally caught up to the Morgan Atkins colony of Ezer Kri. They had caught a platoon unaware in Hero's Fall, then outsmarted a frigate, but now the U.A. Navy had them trapped. They would pay for their aggression.

"You're not going to get away this time," I whispered to myself.

Another minute passed, and I caught a quick glimpse of the battle ahead. A spark of light lit a distant ridge for a moment. The flash was so fast that I almost missed it. Slowing to a trot, I switched my visor to telescopic lenses. My dirty visor obscured my view, and Hubble's dark atmosphere made a clear sighting almost impossible, but I caught a glimpse of Harriers swarming the air above a lofty fire.

"Lee, have you seen what's going on up there?"

"I just saw a specking LG run over one of Grayson's men," Lee panted over our team frequency. "Stay alert."

I do not know if I sensed a shift in the ground or simply sensed the danger. For some reason I stopped and turned to watch the LG that had pushed up ahead of me. The ground in front of the tank rumbled and several columns of ash spun into the air. Those twenty-foot twisters were the only warning. As they dissolved, the ground in front of the LG crumbled, leaving a deep trench in its place.

Riding so near to the ground, the low-gravity tank was an easy target. It teetered on the edge of the trench for a moment, but its momentum and weight sent it forward, and it tumbled nose first into the hole. The ground shook, and a flash of flame shot into view.

"Holy shit!" Lee shouted into the interLink.

Until I saw the tank topple into that shaft, I had not felt the hormone rush that I had experienced during the battle on Gobi. Suddenly I felt the warmth running through my blood. The feeling was soothing. It was more than soothing. It felt good. "The bastards rigged their friggin' snake shafts to cave in," I shouted.

I heard Sergeant Shannon. "Command! Command! Stop all movements! Stop all movements!" But Shannon's warning came too late.

Looking around the valley, I saw the ground crumbling in all directions as dozens of trenches appeared. To my left, an LG tank struggled to reverse itself before it rolled into one trench, then backed into another. The men piloting the tanks did not wear breathing equipment. If they evacuated, they would be strangled by Hubble's toxic air.

"Stop all movements! Repeat, stop all movements!" Shannon continued.

Another tank to my left tried to pivot around a trench, but the powdery soil beneath it caved in. A group of men walking beside it fell in as well. Several more vehicles had fallen farther back; I could see their useless hulls leaning out of the trenches. Flames burst through their armor.

"Repeat, halt all movements!" Shannon bellowed then fell silent. By this time endorphins and adrenaline coursed through my veins.

The officers commanding the invasion would have known about the snake shafts. At least those who were alive would know. Some field officers were stationed aboard a mobile command center that more likely than not was now lying ass up in a ditch.

The invasion force ground to a stop, giving me a moment to survey the damage. I counted sixty-three destroyed tanks, but I might have missed some in the dust and smoke. There was no way of estimating how many men had fallen when the shafts caved in beneath them.

Across the scarred field, the tanks that had not fallen into trenches remained perfectly still. The men within them were trapped. Any movement might send them over a ledge.

"Gather your men," Shannon ordered his fire team leaders over the interLink.

"Fall in," I called to my men. Only one man answered.

"Amblin? Schultz? Respond," I called out. When they did not reply, I hailed them twice more.

"Sergeant," I said, hailing Shannon.

"What?"

"I'm missing two men," I said. "Amblin and Schultz. Requesting permission to look for them."

"You can look; but, Harris, do not drop in the snake shafts," Shannon barked back. "Even if you find one of your men in a shaft, do not go in after him."

"Understood," I said, though I did not understand.

"You have ten minutes to look," Shannon said. "Find them or not, in ten minutes get back to the platoon."

I called to my remaining team member. "You heard him. We have fifteen minutes to locate Amblin and Schultz."

We split up. I turned toward the rear of our stalled forces. What had once been an endless and empty strip of land now looked like a junkyard. The fire-blackened tails of low-gravity tanks poked out of the ground like scattered rocks. The oily Hubble atmosphere had smothered the fires that had erupted out of the ruined tanks, but smoke still rose from their hatches.

I passed a trench and stared down the hull of a derelict tank. It had fallen nose first, smashing its turrets under its own immense weight. Pausing to wipe the grease from my visor, I looked at the wreckage. Under other circumstances I might have hopped on to the back of the tank for a closer look; but with the crew still inside, I did not want to take a chance of making things worse.

A layer of sludgy, brown fog filled the bottom of the trench, obscuring the nose of the tank. As I looked more closely, I saw the bodies of dead Marines along the edges of the snake shaft. At first I thought that they might have jumped from the tank, but there were too many bodies, and most wore armor. Some of the bodies were burned. My visor did not register the identity signals from any of them. Whatever the fog inside the trenches was, it destroyed the electronics inside their combat armor. I did not want to know what it might have done to the men wearing the armor.

Amblin's armor still gave off its identification signal. As I looked across a collapsed snake shaft, I saw him. He must have caught on to a ledge as the ground collapsed around him. He lay sprawled, facedown, over the lip of the trench like a man hanging off the edge of a swimming pool. But Amblin was not moving.

I knelt beside him. When I touched his helmet, it rolled away from the rest of his armor. A layer of darkened blood sloshed around inside his visor. Shocked, I stumbled backward, my attention still fixed on the maroon liquid that seeped out from his shoulder pads.

"Dammmnnn!" I bellowed inside my helmet. Amblin and I had never been friends, but we trained together. I'd known I could depend upon him.

I remained sitting on the cinder soil for another minute, fighting to regain my composure. Everything had gone so wrong. Our invading army sat in a morass. How had they done it? How did these Mogat hoodlums, these small-time criminals and religious fanatics, outsmart our fleet?

"Lee, Harris, come on back," Shannon said.

"I found Amblin," I said.

"Is he okay?" Shannon asked, his voice perking up.

"He's dead," I answered. "There's some sort of toxic gas in the snake shafts."

"I saw shit like this during the Galactic Central War," Shannon said. "You find it on scorched planets."

"I hate this place," I said.

"Then I've got some bad news for you," Shannon said. "Our Harriers destroyed their ships."

"That's good," I said, feeling brighter. "I forgot about the air battle."

"The speckers ran into caves at the far end of the valley," Shannon continued, ignoring my comment. "We're going after them, Harris. We're going underground."

SEVENTEEN

The pleated cliffs surrounding the far edge of the valley had nearly vertical walls made of a black, obsidian-like rock that reflected light. From our gathering point a few hundred yards back, we did not have a good view of the dozens of caves in the craggy walls. They might have been formed by erosion, or bubbling heat, or carved by the same Mogat hands that dug the snake shafts.

At the moment, our invasion looked more like a rescue operation. Teams of corpsmen brought breathing gear to men trapped in LG tanks, and evacuation teams pulled the crews to safety. From what McKay told Shannon, our engineers had not yet figured out how to pull the surviving tanks off the battlefield. At a hundred tons each, the tanks weighed too much for personnel carriers to lift, and the ground was too broken to land barges. Vince Lee made a joke about building dozens of bridges and rolling the tanks to safety, but that seemed like the most plausible answer.

While engineers and evacuation crews cleaned up after the first stage of our invasion, wings of ATs flew in another regiment to replace the dead and wounded. Captain McKay had his two platoons regroup along one side of the Mogats' launchpad. We had lost twenty-one men—just less than half of our men, and our platoon had one of the lower casualty rates because we were at the front of the attack. We had almost been across the field by the time the shafts caved in.

We were not the only ones who had suffered. The broken hulls of so many Mogat cargo ships littered the near side of the canyon that I did not bother counting them. Our fighters and gunships had left a smoldering graveyard in their wake. The wrecked ships, strewn like broken eggshells across the ground, glowed with small fires that burned inside their hulls. The flickering flames were only visible through portholes and cracked hatches.

The Mogats had cargo ships of various sizes in their fleet. Clearly the enemy wanted to escape, not fight. I saw no sign of the dreadnoughts that had destroyed the *Chayio*, just lightly armed cargo ships and transports.

"I am sending coordinates over your visor," Captain McKay said, over an open frequency on the interLink. "We've been ordered to secure a cave."

McKay's mobile command center had survived the trap. His pilot had managed to swerve around three shafts and drive the vehicle to safety. With the airspace over the battlefield secured, the officers overseeing the invasion now commanded us from one of Klyber's diplomatic cruisers.

"Maybe they could command us from a penthouse in Washington, DC," Lee joked. "There aren't many snake shafts around Capitol Hill."

"Watch your mouth," Shannon said, his voice snapping like a whip. "Now roll out." Shannon, always duty-bound, did not let his men criticize officers.

The shortest way to our sector was straight across the launch area. We followed a path through the destroyed ships with our particle-beam rifles raised and ready, prepared to fire at anything that moved. We needn't have bothered. It quickly became apparent that our pilots had more than evened the score. I passed a large freighter with an oblong, rectangular front and sickle-shaped fins. Two-foot-wide rings dotted its sides, marking the spots where particle beams had blasted the hull. When I got closer, I noticed that the armor plating under the blast rings had blistered. Most of the ships had not even lifted off the ground when the attack started; and their shields were down.

As I walked by this particular wreck, I saw the fatal wound. The engines at the back of the ship, now little more than blackened casings and fried wires, had exploded. The thick and unbreathable Hubble air stifled the fire outside the freighter, but the inside sparkled with dozens of tiny flames. I peered through the open hatch and saw fire dancing on the walls.

I also saw people. If the ship was full at launch, at least three hundred people died inside it. In the brief glimpse that I got, I saw men slumped in their seats like soldiers sleeping on a long transport flight. One dead man's arms hung flaccid over the armrests.

"Are they all dead?" I asked Lee.

He did not answer at first. Just as I prepared to ask again, he said, "I hope so, for their sake."

We pushed on, weaving through the wreckage. I passed by a small transport—a ship capable of carrying no more than seven people. It had apparently lifted a few meters off the ground when a missile tore its tail section off. The ship crashed and settled top side down, bashing a hole in its nose section.

I looked in the cockpit and saw the pilot hanging from his chair, his restraint belt still binding him into place. The man's mouth gaped, and blood trickled over his upper lip and into his nostrils. More blood leaked from the tops of his eyes, running across his forehead in little rivulets that disappeared into his thick, dark hair. The pilot's arms dangled past his head; the ends of his curled fingers rested on the ceiling.

I could not tell if Hubble's gases had killed him or if he had broken his neck in the crash. I had no problem identifying what killed the copilot hanging from the next seat. A jagged shard of outer plating hung from his neck. From what I could see, that bloodstained wedge had sliced through the man's throat and become jammed in his spine.

A hand touched my shoulder and I jumped. When I looked over, I saw Shannon's identifier.

"Don't get distracted," Shannon said.

"Remind me never to piss off the U.A. Navy," I said.

"That's not the worst of it." Lee approached us and nodded toward the body. "His pilot's license was revoked."

"You're a sick man, Lee," I said.

We turned and continued through the wreckage. After a while, one ship looked pretty much like the next, and I no longer bothered to peer inside. The passengers were dead; that was enough.

As we reached the edge of the landing area, I noticed piles of melted netting and wires—the ruins of a camouflaged hangar. These people were so desperate to live that they had colonized an uninhabitable planet. No sane person would have ever searched for life on a rock like Hubble, but our intelligence network found them just the same. Perhaps a recon ship just happened to spot them or maybe a loose-lipped friend let the information slip over a drink. In any case, they were trapped.

We stopped a hundred yards from the cliffs. I had to ping the wall to locate the caves—night-for-day lenses are not good tools for spotting dark caverns set in jet-black cliffs. The ground was black, the cliffs were black, the sky was black, and the dust and oil on my visor were not helping. My sonic locator outlined the opening with a translucent green orifice, but I still could not tell what machinery might be hiding inside.

"Are we going in?" I asked Sergeant Shannon when I spotted him and his men.

He did not dignify the question with an answer. He stared ahead at the cave, his hands tight around the stock of his gun.

"They fight harder when they're backs are up against a wall like this," Shannon said. "They'll be more angry than scared."

I thought about what he said. "They're bound to have a few more tricks."

"No," Shannon said, sounding resigned to the situation. "They're at the bottom of their deck. They could never have expected us to find them here. We've finally closed every back door unless their friends have enough ships to overwhelm an entire fleet."

I followed Shannon's gaze back to the cliffs and the barely visible mouth of the cave. "We could wait them out. They're going to run out of food and air . . ."

"We'll take the battle to them, Harris. You want to know why we have all-clone enlistment? It's so that we can throw an infinite supply of men into any fire and not worry about the public outcry."

"Clones are equipment," I echoed.

"Standard-issue, just like guns, boots, and batteries," Shannon said. Through most of our conversation, Shannon stared at the cliff; then he paused and turned toward me. "We're still on point, and McKay's going to give the order soon."

I nodded and turned. "Lee," I called over the interLink. "Shannon says it's almost time to roll."

Lee came to me and held out his hand. He held a swatch of black cloth. "Wipe your visor, friend," he said.

"Where'd you get that?" I asked.

"I swiped it from that ship," he said, pointing toward a small cruiser that had broken wide open. "It's from the upholstery."

"Clever," I said. "Thanks for sharing."

"No problem," Lee said. "You'll do a better job of watching my back if you can see where you're going."

"Ha," I said.

By that time, the reinforcements were positioned all along the valley walls. We had enough men to cover every cave. No matter where they tried to evacuate, the Mogats would run into Marines.

"Okay, Lee . . . Harris," Shannon called out, "I just got the word. McKay wants us to secure the entrance."

That was just a courtesy call. The next message, sent over the platoon frequency, was the actual order. "Okay, gentlemen, secure this area and stay within the goddamned lines!" Shannon barked.

Along with missiles, fighters, and tanks, the Unified Authority Marine Corps utilized more subtle technologies. Command divided the battlefield and sent platoon the coordinates of their attack in the form of a visual beacon—a signal that drew virtual walls around our zone in our visors.

Looking straight ahead, I saw the black face of the cliffs. If I turned to the right or the left, however, translucent red walls appeared.

Lee and his team took the left edge of the target zone. Shannon sent my fire team to the right edge. He and the rest of the men ran up the middle. Shannon led the charge, leaving small clouds of dust in his wake as he moved forward in a low crouch. There was no cover for hiding, just flat, featureless soil.

With the next man crouched ten paces behind me, I sprinted along the right boundary of the target zone. Keeping my finger along the edge of the trigger guard, I pointed the barrel of my particle-beam gun at the cave.

The mouth of the cave—a broad, yawning keyhole in the side of the cliff—was twenty feet high and maybe ten feet wide. If the inside of the cave was as narrow as the mouth, we would be vulnerable as we funneled through it.

Somebody fired at me. Had he used a particle beam or laser, he might have hit me. Instead, he used a regular gun—a weapon that was somewhat unpredictable in the oil-humid air. Instinctively reacting to the first shot, which clipped the dirt near my feet, I jumped to my right and rolled. The world turned red around me. I had left the target zone and entered the no-man's-land outside the beacon's virtual walls. I heard more bullets strike the ground in front of me; but with the red light from the beacon filling my visor, I could not see where they hit.

I climbed to my knees and lunged back to the target zone, jumping forward, slamming my chest and face into the soft ground. My helmet sank deep into the ash, which caked onto glass. As I rolled to my left, staying as flat to the ground as I could, a coin-thick layer of ash clogged my sight. Moving slowly to avoid attracting attention, I reached up and tapped my visor with one finger, causing most of the ash to slide off. Then I pulled the swatch of cloth from my belt and wiped away the grime and ash.

Using heat vision, I peered into the cave and saw six gunmen hiding in the shadows with three more on the way. As I rolled on my back again, I saw red streaks flash through the air above my head.

I wanted to fire into the cave, but I did not dare. If I'd turned to shoot, I would have made an easy target—the enemy had pinned me down. They had pinned all of us down as they hid behind the entrance of the cave.

Of the forty-two men in our platoon, only twenty-one had survived to make the assault, and I suspected the casualties were mounting. Suddenly there it was, that sweet clarity. My body was awash with endorphins and adrenaline. My fear did not disappear, but it no longer mattered. I could see everything clearly and knew that I could handle any situation. The hormone left me feeling in control. I rolled to my left to get a shot, but a laser bolt struck the ground near me. Apparently the Mogats intended to make us earn every inch of ground we took.

Two bullets flew so low over my shoulder that they clipped my armor. One of the other men was not as lucky. As a seemingly endless wave of laser fire flew overhead, the interLink echoed with his scream.

Shannon shouted for him to stay down, but the wounded man did not listen. I turned in time to get a glance of him, though not in time to read his identity. The laser must have grazed the front of his visor, superheating the glass, which melted and splashed on his face. He managed to climb to his knees before a combination of bullets and laser bolts tore into his face and chest blowing him apart.

Seeing what was left of the soldier collapse back to the ground, I felt that strange, soothing tingle. Some hidden corner of my brain automatically took over, shutting out the panic. "I think I can get a grenade in there," I called over to Shannon.

"No grenades!" Shannon shouted.

"I can get it in the hole," I said.

"I said no, goddamn it!" Shannon said. "You hear me, Marine?"

CHAPTER
EIGHTEEN

I did not answer as I released the grenade I was pulling from my belt. At that moment, lying in the soil with bolts and bullets streaking over my head, I wondered if Sergeant Shannon might not be the real enemy. Rolling over on to my stomach, I held my gun in front of my face and squeezed off three shots. The men in the cave responded with a hailstorm of laser fire.

If anybody had asked me to guess who would break up the stalemate, I would have said "Shannon." But he was in a worse predicament than I. He was pinned down under heavy gunfire directly in front of the cave.

It took Vince Lee to turn the battle around. Suddenly pushing off the ground in a cloud of dust, he sprinted toward the mouth of the cave and leaped forward, squeezing rapid shots from his particle-beam rifle. Firing blindly, he managed to hit three of the Mogats guarding the cave. Using my heat-vision lenses, I watched them fall.

Lee landed face-first and slid into a cloud of dust just in time to dodge the return fire. I do not know if Lee and Shannon coordinated their attack on a private frequency; but as the Mogats concentrated their fire on Lee, Shannon rose on one knee, aimed, and fired.

Undoubtedly using heat vision for a clearer view, Shannon did not fire blindly. Each shot hit its mark, and the last of the Mogats fell dead. I expected more shooters to come, but the mouth of the cave remained empty.

"Cover me," Lee called, over the interLink. Keeping his rifle trained on the cave, Lee stooped into a crouch and cautiously walked toward the foot of the cliffs. He pressed his back against the obsidian wall, then inched his way toward the cave. He came within arm's reach of the opening and paused. "See anything?" he asked Shannon over an open channel.

"All clear," Shannon replied.

"Great work, Lee," Shannon said. "Okay, everybody, stay put. Captain McKay is sending a technician to check for traps." Shannon and I joined Lee just outside the mouth of the cave, but we did not enter it. Shannon took a single step into the fissure. He patted a clump of obsidian with one hand. Glancing back at us to make certain that no one was too close, he fired into the wall.

"Sergeant?" I said, rushing over to see what happened.

"It's nothing, Harris," Shannon said. "I'm just testing a theory."

An AT hovered toward us, hanging low over the valley and landing in our zone. The kettle opened, and a Navy lieutenant came down the ramp wheeling a bell-shaped case behind him. The engineer wore a breathing suit. It was not stiff like our combat armor, but it protected him from the environment. Shannon met the lieutenant at the bottom of the ramp. I followed.

"What's that?" I asked Shannon.

"That, Corporal Harris, is our eyes," Shannon answered. "Right now we have the enemy trapped in these caves. We're going to send in a recon drone to make sure our positions do not get reversed."

"A recon drone," I repeated. "That makes sense."

The case looked like it had been made to hold a tuba. It was three feet tall and wide on the bottom. The metal wheels under the case clattered as they rolled down the ramp.

"Are you the one that requested a drone?" the lieutenant asked. "What's the situation?"

"There are hostiles in those caves, sir," Shannon began.

"I know that, Sergeant," the lieutenant interrupted. This was no fighting man. He was a technician, the lowest form of engineer—but he was also an officer, and he had all of the attitude that came with wearing a silver bar on his shoulder.

"The enemy had several men guarding this entrance, sir," Shannon said. "My men were able to neutralize the threat. We want to send your drone to look for traps and locate enemy positions before going in, sir."

"Playing it safe, Sergeant?" the lieutenant quipped in a voice that oozed sarcasm.

"Yes, sir," Shannon responded.

"I didn't know you Leathernecks were so squeamish," the man mused. "I suppose I can help." He opened his case.

"What an asshole," I said over the interLink.

"Steady, Harris," Shannon answered in a whisper. "He's not just an asshole, he is an officer asshole . . . a second lieutenant. They're the buck privates of the commissioned class; and they always have chips on their shoulders. Besides, we need this particular asshole."

"Heeere's Scooter," the tech said to himself as he opened the bottom of the case. Scooter, a chrome disc on four wheels that looked like a slightly oversized ashtray, scurried out of the case. This demented officer treated the robot like a pet, not equipment. He'd painted the name "Scooter" across its front in bright red letters, and he stroked its lid gently before standing up.

"I do not believe I have seen that model of recon drone before, sir," Shannon said in a respectful voice that would certainly curry favor.

"It's a prototype. I built it myself," the man said. I could not see his face clearly through his breathing mask, but the lieutenant's voice perked up. "Let's have a look in that cave, shall we."

The lieutenant pressed a button on the outside of the case, and a four-inch video monitor flipped out of its lid. When he turned on the monitor, I was amazed by the panoramic scope of Scooter's vision. The silvery top of the robot was a giant fish-eye lens, offering a 180-degree view. Looking at that screen, I saw the case from which Scooter had emerged, the cliffs, and everything in between. The camera caught everything, and the monitor displayed it in stretched, but accurate, detail. This engineer was both a dork and a brilliant engineer.

"Impressive little specker," I said over the interLink for only Shannon to hear.

"Stow it, Harris," he replied.

Issuing the command "Scooter, enter cave" into a small microphone, the tech sent the drone on its way.

"Audio commands only?" Shannon asked.

"I programmed Scooter myself. He uses onboard sonar to find the best paths. He has dedicated self-preservation circuits. The only thing a human controller can do is slow him down."

Judging by what I saw on the monitor, Scooter used the same basic night-for-day vision technology we used in our visors. He was a stealth drone with no lights or weapons.

Skirting around rocks and holes, Scooter sped toward the cave like a giant, silvery beetle. The men in our platoon stopped and watched as it scampered by. When it reached the lip of the cave, it paused. For a moment I thought the little tin can might actually be scared.

"It's taking a sonic reading," the lieutenant said, as if reading my thoughts.

"Damn," Shannon said, with respect.

Pulling a small stylus from his case, the lieutenant said, "Sergeant, take this. If you want a closer look at something on the monitor, tap it with the stylus. That will send a message to Scooter."

The monitor turned dark as Scooter hurried into the cave. The little robot had a good eye for stealth. It traveled in cracks and crevices along the side of the wall, well concealed from enemy eyes.

That was good for Scooter, but not so helpful for Shannon. Even with enhanced night-for-day photography, Scooter was not showing us what we needed. It was showing us the safest path for creatures that were less than four inches tall. Also, Scooter moved too quickly. A squad patrolling such terrain might creep along at one or two miles per hour, but Scooter covered it at a steady fifteen miles per hour. Images flew across the monitor. Five minutes into its patrol, Scooter stopped and ran another sonar scan.

"Okay," the lieutenant said, "the Mogats are at least two miles deep into the caves."

"You've located a path to them?" Shannon asked.

"Sergeant, they're two miles down," the technician said, sounding shocked and mildly offended. Scooter has scanned for traps, and the entrance comes up clean. He's also verified their campsite."

I turned to look at the cave in time to see Scooter motoring out of the shadows. The lieutenant must have programmed it to think like a puppy when it was not performing a mission. The goddamned little robot detoured into a crowd of Marines milling near the cliffs and ran circles around their feet. When they did not respond, it returned to the lieutenant and parked itself beside his foot.

"But you did not locate the path to the enemy's position?" Shannon asked.

"Scooter could not get to them; they're too deep in," the technician said.

"Does Scooter have a map that leads to their locations?" Shannon asked, his irritation beginning to show.

"If you mean a map to their doorstep, that is out of the question, Sergeant. I am not going to risk a valuable proto-type reconnaissance unit."

"I know a safe dark place where we can stick his drone," Lee muttered over the interLink as he came up beside me.

"But you're willing to send in an entire platoon," Shannon added. "My men . . ."

"Clones," the technician corrected.

Shannon made one last attempt to explain himself. "I am not going to lead my men into that cave blind," he said in a reasonable tone.

"I've done what I can, Sergeant," the lieutenant said as he bent down to pick up his robot.

Shannon grabbed the man by his shoulders, pulled him straight, and then slung him backwards against the hull of the transport. "I don't agree, sir," Shannon whispered in a dangerous tone. "I think you can do more. I think you want to do more, because if that is all your useless bug-shit robot can do, I'm going to smash it. Do you understand me?"

"I'll have you in the brig for this." The lieutenant clutched the robot to his chest. His voice trembled as if he was about to cry.

Shannon picked up his particle beam and pointed it at the robot. "Right now, the safest place for Scooter is in that cave. Do you understand me, sir?"

The lieutenant's show of officer anger faded, and behind it we saw the scared technician. "I spent a lot of time programming Scooter," he pleaded. "If you want to locate hostiles, you can requisition a combat drone. That's what they are made for."

"I'm tired of arguing with you," Shannon said as he reached for the robot. "If you aren't going to send that bug into that cave, then it's useless to me."

"You're insane," the technician said.

"Even worse," Lee said to me only. "He's a Liberator."

"Get specked," I shot back.

"Sorry."

Staring at Sergeant Shannon, the technician must have realized that he had no options. Shannon was out of control, of course, and there might be a court-martial awaiting him when he returned to the fleet. But for the moment, with no available help, the lieutenant had no choice but to do as he was told. He passed Scooter over to Shannon.

Taking great care to be gentle, Shannon placed the robot on the ground.

"Scooter, enter cave," the lieutenant spoke into the microphone in a pouting voice. He turned to Shannon. "You will have hell to pay."

"No doubt," Shannon mumbled.

Shannon, Lee, and I bent over the monitor to follow Scooter's progress. The little robot zipped past our men and into the cave, then resumed its original path. The lieutenant kept his microphone close to his lips, issuing whispered orders. "Proceed at half speed." "Slower. Slower." "Stay close to the wall." "Pause and hide at the first sign of activity." "Scan for electrical fields."

"Can you brighten this transmission?" Shannon asked.

"The monitor has gamma controls, but you'll lose screen resolution," the lieutenant said.

He fiddled with the controls, brightening the scene. The gamma controls made a big difference. Suddenly we could see footprints and tire tracks on the ground.

Fifteen minutes after Scooter entered the cave, the robot started to detect sound waves. They were faint, but the robot registered them as human speech.

"Okay, Sergeant, here is a voiceprint. I'm bringing my robot back."

"Can you give me a visual feed of the men?" Shannon asked.

Still not looking at Shannon, the technician uttered a few inaudible words. Shannon repeated the question, and the man shook his head.

"The robot stays down there until I see people."

Looking around the cave from our Scooter's-eye point of view, I began to feel motion sickness. The fish-eye distortion left me dizzy, and I really had no idea what we were looking for.

"I don't see any people," Shannon complained.

"Sound carries well in caverns; they may still be a half mile farther in," the tech answered. "This is obviously the right chamber. You've located your target. I'm bringing my robot back."

"Not until I get my visual confirmation," Shannon snapped. "I want to know the best way to get to the enemy. I want to know how many men they have and how well fortified they have made their position. Most of all, I want to see how close Scooter can get to those Mogats before they start shooting. And, Lieutenant, I really do not give a shit if they hit Scooter. Got it?" Shannon said all of this in a single breath.

As soon as the robot heard voices, its self-preservation programming became active. Scooter moved at an unbearably slow pace, hugging closer to the wall than ever. The reduced speed was helpful. Scooter was several miles into the caves, and his path exposed tributaries and side caverns. Its slowing down gave us more time to study the video images.

Eventually, Scooter turned a corner and neared the spot where the Mogats had dug in. We could not see them, but we could see the dim reflection of distant lights on obsidian walls. The robot continued its slow roll forward, inching ahead like a scared mouse.

We heard the guards before we saw them. Scooter rounded a huge knob in a wall, and suddenly we heard voices echoing. The image on the monitor turned bright as a man stepped right over Scooter. The robot watched as two men walked away, swinging lanterns.

"They almost spotted him," the technician said. "Are you satisfied?"

"Not really," said Shannon.

"Get specked!" the lieutenant shouted. I thought he would recall his robot, but he made no move to pick up his microphone. We watched on the monitor as Scooter continued ahead for another few minutes, until the little robot reached a fork in the path. It paused and hid behind a rock, blocking most of our view on the monitor.

That time, even Shannon did not complain. Four men walked right next to the camera. One of them almost stepped on Scooter. They did not see the probe. They kept talking as they walked through the passage and disappeared into a tributary. Once they were gone, Scooter's self-preservation programming went into overdrive, and the little robot scurried in the opposite direction.

"Wh—" Shannon started to say something and stopped. He bent forward, practically pressing his visor against the monitor. "Can you roll the video signal back?"

The scene on the monitor ran in reverse.

"Stop," Shannon said. He studied the image and traced it with his finger. He scrolled the image forward and backward on the monitor. "Can you analyze this through other lenses?"

I looked over Shannon's shoulder and saw what he was looking at. There were two large metal cases; machines of some sort. A series of pipes ran through and around them.

"I have heat and sound readings," the tech said.

The heat reading was immense. The heat signatures showed yellow with a bleached corona. I didn't know what the Mogats used the machines for, but they were practically on fire.

"Can you ID this equipment?" Shannon asked.

The technician shook his head.

Shannon turned back to the monitor. "Has your robot left virtual beacons?" Shannon asked.

"Yes."

"All the way down?"

"Yes," the lieutenant said. "All the way."

"Can you upload that information to me on the inter-Link?" Shannon asked.

"No problem," the lieutenant hissed. A moment later, Scooter rushed from the cave and streaked right to the lieutenant, who picked it up and loaded it into its case.

"That's a magnificent robot you have, sir. The Navy needs more of them," Shannon said with a crazed laugh.

"Harris, I need to contact mobile command. I think we might be off this rock in another few hours."

CHAPTER
NINETEEN

"Dammit, Shannon!" McKay snapped. "What in God's name did you do? There's a lieutenant demanding a firing squad. A firing squad! He claims you assaulted him and threatened to shoot him."

I could not tell if Shannon had purposely included me in their conversation, so I listened in silence.

"In point of fact, sir, that would not be correct. I threatened to shoot Scooter."

"What the speck is Scooter?" McKay asked.

"The lieutenant's recon robot, sir."

"You threatened to shoot his robot?" McKay asked. There was a tremble in his voice, and I heard other officers laughing in the background. "Threatening Scooter is a serious offense, Sergeant. You may be looking at a long stay in the brig."

"Not meaning any disrespect, Captain, we need to settle that account later. I believe I have found a way to force the enemy to surrender."

"I'm listening, Sergeant." Gaylan McKay had an unnerving ability to read unspoken nuances in any conversation. "What have you got?"

My interLink connection went silent. Shannon might

have wanted me to hear him call Captain McKay, but the fine details would be on a "need to know" basis.

For the first time since I repeated the oath, I felt the weight and isolation of my armor. It wasn't that I cared about the plan. I cared about Shannon. I suddenly realized that Tabor Shannon, master gunnery sergeant and Liberator, was the closest thing I would ever have to family. Suddenly I felt cut off, trapped inside my helmet. I listened to the rhythmic hiss of my breathing. I became aware of claustrophobia causing my nerves to tingle. Strangest of all, I still felt glad to be a Marine fighting on Hubble. "God, what a mess," I said quietly as I considered my situation—a clone on a toxic planet fighting to protect the government that created him, then outlawed his existence.

"Harris, we're going in," Sergeant Shannon said, waking me from my momentary epiphany.

"How many of us?" I asked.

"This time it's just you and me, Corporal." Shannon switched to an open frequency. "Lee, you're in charge. Harris and I are going to do a little spelunking."

"You might want to leave the rifle stock behind," Shannon said, as we started for the cave. Not waiting for an explanation, I detached the stock and left it with Lee.

Shannon stepped into the cave and stopped to wait for me. His armor was coated with ash, but his visor was clean. "You should give your visor a quick wipe," he said. "You might not get a chance to do that later."

I pulled the swatch of cloth from my belt and wiped the glass carefully. As I entered the cave, I saw the bodies of the men Shannon and Lee had cut down. Two sat slumped against the walls as if resting, the others lay on the ground. One had died clutching his mask. If the gunfire didn't get you on Hubble, the atmosphere would.

Shannon waited for me to get a few steps closer, then drew his particle-beam pistol and pointed it at the wall. "I want to show you something," he said, and he fired a bright green bolt into the shiny black rock. The bolt bored into the wall of the cave. Slag and vapor poured out of the hole.

"Recognize it?" Shannon asked me.

"It's the shit from the trenches," I said.

"It's like being in an iceberg," Shannon said. "Make too much heat, and you will bring the whole damned cliff down."

"I don't get it," I said. "The rock melts into vapor?"

"It's the other way around, the vapor hardens into rock," Shannon said. "The vapor gets cold and hardens. That's why the rock looks so shiny; it's just hardened gas."

"Now you're a geologist?" I asked.

"Don't get smart, asshole," Shannon said. "Like I said before, I saw shit like this in the Galactic Center War. Since Liberators and Mogats are the only people who were at that little rumble, you can bet they know about it, too.

"Harris, I don't suppose the good lieutenant uploaded Scooter's data to you?"

I scanned for beacons, and a thin red line appeared on my visor marking the robot's path. There was nothing wrong with Scooter's self-preservation programming. The little robot had explored the caves hidden from danger by traveling in a groove along one of the walls. No wonder the Mogats had walked by the little rodent without seeing it. "Okay, I can read his beacon trail."

"That's good. If we get split, you'll need to find your way out on your own." Shannon started forward along Scooter's virtual trail. "You know those machines Scooter passed? Did you recognize them?"

I did not recognize the first machine, though it had looked familiar. I did recognize the second device. "The one on the left was a power generator," I said. "You planning on turning out the lights?"

"We're going to do a lot more than that," Shannon said. "The bigger machine is an oxy-gen." The term "oxy-gen" was Marine-speak for oxygen genitor.

"I don't think they know we took out the guys guarding this gate. As long as they didn't see Scooter, we should be able to slip up to the generators without too much trouble. I brought you along just in case, Harris. You get to run interference for me."

The ground, the air, and the walls in the cave were all shades of black. I had no sense of depth. Running my elbow against the wall as I walked helped me balance myself, but I constantly felt as if I might bump my head against one of the boulders that bulged from the low ceiling.

The Mogats had it worse than us, though. Not wanting to leave a telltale trail, they did not string lights along the cave. They had to find their way in and out using lanterns and flashlights. If guards came anywhere near us, Shannon and I would see the glare from their lights.

We walked softly, barely lifting our feet and hugging the wall with our backs. Though the darkness in the tunnel meant that we were alone, we kept our pistols drawn.

The path had an almost imperceivable downward slope. It bent and meandered around thick knots in the rock, and continued on its gentle incline, always downward, constantly downward. We moved through one long, straight stretch. When I looked behind me, it looked like the floor and the ceiling had merged. Seeing it left me momentarily dizzy, then I realized that the illusion was caused by my faltering sense of depth.

"Something the matter, Harris?" Shannon grunted.

"I'm fine," I said.

We would have lost our way in these caverns had it not been for Scooter's beacons. When I watched the monitor, I had not noticed how many capillaries led from the main path. The path curved around one wall, then another. It split and sometimes seemed to disappear entirely behind sharp bends. More than an hour passed before we rounded a corner and saw the first traces of light. "This is where it gets tricky," Shannon said. "Scooter was just ahead of us when it ran into the first guards."

Shannon stopped, and we knelt behind a rock to talk. "This tunnel leads to Mogat-central. Got it? The shaft with the generators is somewhere between us and them. That shaft is only big enough for one of us, Harris, so you're on watch while I speck with their equipment. Any questions?"

The cave was absolutely silent. Far ahead, I could see an odd-shaped circle of light. Its distorted reflection on the obsidian walls might have extended for hundreds of yards. My heart thudded hard in my chest, but the endorphins had not yet begun to flow.

"Once I'm through screwing with the equipment, I'm going to give you a signal, and you are going to run like your shitter's on fire. Don't wait for me. Just run, and I will catch up to you."

"You'll be cut off," I said.

"I'm getting out the same way Scooter did. This side tunnel loops back into the main cavern. I'll crawl through and catch up with you."

In the darkness, I could barely make out the shape of Shannon's green armor. His helmet looked like a shadow cast on those charcoal-colored walls.

"Sergeant?"

"What is it, Harris?"

"Why did you bring me? I've got less combat experience than anyone else in the platoon."

"You can't possibly consider Ezer Kri combat experience," he said in a harsh voice. "Harris, that's all any of them have . . . skirmishes. You're a Liberator, Harris. That makes you more dangerous than any of them. Now move out."

I climbed back to my feet but remained slightly crouched. By that time I had my finger on the trigger. I hated the idea of splitting up with Shannon. I felt like I was abandoning him, like I should go in the tunnel with him.

I passed the shaft with the generators and looked back in time to see Shannon crawling into it. From here on out, I could no longer navigate using Scooter's beacons. Scooter had gone no farther into the cave. That was the point where the little drone got scared and hid. From here on out, Shannon would be following the path blazed by the robot scout. I was in new territory.

Far ahead, the Mogats had set up some sort of temporary shelter. There would be thousands of them. The men who fried our patrol on Ezer Kri were probably somewhere up ahead. My finger still on the trigger of my particle-beam pistol, I moved on. Would Amos Crowley be there?

"How's it going?" I called to Shannon over the interLink. "Where are you?"

I looked around. "In a tunnel on the biggest shit hole planet in the galaxy."

"There are worse ones," Shannon said. "Now, where are you precisely, asshole?"

"I'm about forty yards from you. I found a good ridge to hide behind in case . . ."

"Harris?"

The part of the cave I had entered was about as brightly lit as a night with a full moon. Up ahead of me, I saw two bobbing balls of light that looked no bigger than a fingernail. Using my telescopic lenses, I got a better look—two men were walking in my direction. Both men wore oxygen masks and carried rifles. "Piss-poor excuse for sentries," I said.

"You see something?"

"Two men," I said. "They might be the ones who walked past Scooter."

"Pick them off before they spot you," Shannon said.

"Not a problem," I said, sighting the first one with my pistol. I took a deep breath, held it for a moment.

"They turned around." When I switched back to my telescopic lenses, I saw that they were walking away. From that distance, they were nothing more than gray silhouettes.

"Think they saw you?" Shannon asked.

"Not unless they're telepathic. How's it going with the equipment?"

There was no way the two guards could have heard me speaking inside my helmet, nonetheless they turned back in my direction. Shannon was saying something about one of the generators, but I stopped listening.

"They're coming back," I said, raising my particle-beam pistol. I kept my aim on the more erect of the two men. My hand as steady as the dead air in the cave, I pulled the trigger. The walls of the cave reflected my pistol's green flash, and sparks flew when my bolt struck its target. Knowing that I would not miss under such circumstances, I fired at the second man without waiting to see if the first one fell. My shot hit the second man in the chest, but it did not kill him. He flew backward against the wall. The man spun around to run and my second shot hit his oxygen tube. Flames burst from his breathing equipment, then snuffed out the moment the oxygen was gone. The explosion produced a brilliant flash and created a loud bang that echoed through the caves.

"What was that?" Shannon asked.

"The bastard's oxygen tube flamed," I said.

"Are you dug in?" Shannon asked.

The flange in the rocks behind which I hid was thick, but only three feet tall. I glanced ahead, then crouched as low as I could behind it. "They're coming," I said. I saw torch beams bouncing on a far wall.

"How many?"

"About a million of them," I said. "Wish I could use a grenade. How much more time do you need?"

A red laser bolt struck the rock in front of me. Sparks flew over the top, and I heard hissing as the laser boiled its way into the stone. Another bolt sliced across the top of my barricade, dumping molten slag and brown vapor over the edge. Remembering the way Amblin's helmet had slid from his body, I moved as far from the vapor stream as I could. Suddenly I felt the soothing warmth in my blood.

The Mogats weren't about to let me enjoy it. Shots began raining in my direction. So many shots struck the shelf in front of me that the black obsidian glowed red as laser bolts liquefied and hollowed it.

One of the people shooting at me began targeting the ceiling above my head, and slag and vapor poured out to the floor, just missing my shoulders. I started to peek around the corner of my barricade, and bullets glanced off the rock.

"I'm getting massacred out here!" I said to Shannon.

"It's tighter than I expected," Shannon said. "Hold them off!"

I could hear the Mogats yelling to each other. Their fire thinned, and I heard somebody running. I rolled to my right along the ground, fired three shots into the bastard without so much as a pause, and ducked behind a tiny ridge along the other wall. I moved just in time. The Mogats had pumped so much laser fire into the rocks on the other side of the tunnel that they glowed.

Reaching my hand around my new cover as far as I could, I fired blindly. They answered with a hail of laser and bullets. The ridge on this side of the cave was too small to protect me. I fired shots into the roof above them and backed up a couple of yards to a larger rock formation.

The Mogats did not see me back away. They continued to fire at the spot that I abandoned. I stole a glance and saw bubbles forming on the back side of the obsidian ridge as the center of the rock boiled red.

"I'm trapped," I said.

"I've got it, Harris. Run!" Shannon ordered.

As I turned to run, the thin light in the cavern flickered out. Light no longer shone from behind the Mogats. They were in total darkness, with only their flashlights and lanterns. Whatever Shannon had done, it doused their electricity. Once again I saw the world without depth through night-for-day lenses. For once I was grateful. I sprinted up the tunnel, laser blasts and bullets blindly spraying the rock walls behind me.

I reached the passage to the generators and saw a beautiful sight. Orange-red light glowed from the opening. It was not the flickering light of a struggling flame; it showed bright, warm, and strong. I got only a brief glimpse of Shannon's work as I ran past, but it was enough. White-and-blue flames jetted away from the oxy-gen, heating walls farther down the tunnel. Shannon had ignited a fire in the oxy-gen's piping, turning it into a torch. The flames carved into the obsidian walls. The surface of the rock was already orange and melting, belching thousands of gallons of vile fog.

I could not tell if there was a hunting party behind me. If there was, they weren't using flashlights—I did not see beams on the wall around me. Somehow I doubted that they were following me. More likely than not, they had run back to camp when Shannon turned out the lights.

Wanting to present the smallest possible target, I crouched as I ran. I sprinted around a bend and chanced one last look back. What I saw made me shutter. A thick tongue of vapor rolled out of the generator tunnel. Given a few hours, the vapor would flood the entire cave system. I had seen the way random laser fire had superheated the rock. The fire from Shannon's torch was not as hot, but it was broad and steady.

"Harris, are you out of there?" Shannon asked over the interLink.

"That shit's pouring out of that hole like a waterfall," I answered.

"Get moving uphill," Shannon said. "Meet me at the top."

I had not realized how much space we had covered. The path led on and on, and the slope no longer seemed so gentle now that it was uphill. My calves burned, and my pistol felt heavy in my hands. I found myself fighting for breath, then I thought about the Mogats trapped in the dark with their air supply cut off. "Dead or captured," I mused. For those speckers, that was one hell of a choice.

I continued up the slope, my run slowing into a jog, then a walk as I bumped my way forward. "Are you getting through that tunnel okay?" I asked Shannon.

"It's tight," he said. "But it seems to be getting wider."

"I wasn't paying attention when Scooter went through there," I said.

"Neither was I," Shannon said.

"I don't know how you figured this all out," I said. "They're not even following me. That vapor cut them off."

"Hang on a moment," Shannon said. "I need to concentrate." That was the last time we spoke. I walked around one final bend and saw the mouth to the cave. When I looked at the interLink menu in my visor, I did not see Shannon's frequency.

"Sergeant? Sergeant Shannon!" I called again and again. I called on the platoon frequency. I tried an open frequency. I turned around and shouted his name at the top of my lungs.

"Harris, is that you?" Vince Lee asked. "What's the matter?"

"I think Shannon is dead!" I said, wanting to go back to look for him. But I could not go back. I realized that. The vapor Shannon had unleashed had flooded the chamber behind me. It had probably flooded the tunnel around him as well. I imagined him crawling in the darkness of that narrow pass, struggling to get through a tight squeeze as he noticed the vapor creeping up behind him. Perhaps he was wedged in so tightly that he could not even turn to see the vapor until it had seeped around him. Whatever toxin that vapor held, it corroded its way through the rubber in our body suits, turning armor into a worthless exoskeleton. It ate through flesh and tissue. If I found Shannon, all I would find would be the hard stuff—the armor and bones, Everything else would be melted. God I hated Hubble.

A very comfortable cruiser landed near our platoon, and Captain McKay ordered me aboard. He wanted to introduce me to the colonels and commodores who would take credit for Tabor Shannon's tactical genius. Dressed in immaculate uniforms, the colonels and commodores showed no interest in me, but they allowed me to watch as they mopped up the battle.

Nearly ten thousand Mogats surrendered, more than enough for Bryce Klyber's judicial circus. Their quota met, the officers aboard the cruiser sent airborne battle drones into the caves.

The drones looked like little giant pie plates. They were about three feet long and a foot tall. Most of their housing was filled with a broad propeller shaft. They had particle-beam guns mounted on their sides. We called them "RODEs," but their technical name was Remote Operated Defense Engines.

The officers sent ten RODEs into the cavern. The little beasts hovered about five feet over the vapor, and the officers made a game of seeing who could fly the lowest. One swabbie flew his RODE too low, and the vapor shorted it out. Everybody laughed at him. There was a jolly atmosphere inside the cruiser. I could not think. The atmosphere inside the cruiser was suffocating me. I wanted to find a way to rescue Shannon. Even if he was dead, I wanted to pull his body out. I did not want to leave him stranded in a cave filled with dead Mogats. I asked if I could leave, but Captain McKay told me I had to stay.

Most RODEs are black, but the ones the colonels and commanders used were special. They had shiny gold chassis and bright headlights. They were not made for stealth.

"The angel of death, come to claim her victims," one of the colonels joked in a loud voice. I saw that he had a microphone. He was broadcasting his voice inside the cave.

Maybe if I got to Shannon quickly . . . Perhaps he was in the caves, breathing the Mogats' generated oxygen. I asked McKay a second time if I could leave, and he told me that the officers wanted me to stay.

The officers huddled around tracking consoles, watching the scene inside the cave through their RODEs' eyes. "Permission to go join my platoon?" I asked McKay.

"Denied," McKay said, sounding very irritated.

From where I sat, I could see one of the officers steering his RODE. I had a clear view of the monitor that showed him the world as his RODE saw it.

It took less than ten minutes for this officer to steer his RODE past the capillary that led to the generators. Thick fog still chugged out of it like viscous liquid. The RODE's bright headlight cut through the darkness with a beam that was straight and hard. It shined momentarily on the ridge I used for protection during the shoot-out with the Mogats. The obsidian walls sparkled in the bright beam, but the headlight was not powerful enough to penetrate the thick layer of vapor that blanketed the floor of the cavern. Whatever secrets lay hidden under that gas would remain concealed.

"I found one!" an officer on the other side of the cabin yelled. He got a giddy response from other officers, who wanted hints about how he got there so quickly.

The colonel closest to me had found a grand cavern. His drone flew laps around the outer walls of the cavern like a shark looking for prey. The officer began to search the fog for survivors, and it did not take long until he found his first.

Whatever chemicals made up the vapor were heavier than the atmosphere. The vapor was heavy; it melted flesh and circuitry. What other pleasant surprises could it hold, I wondered.

The RODE edged along the outer walls. It had a near miss as it dodged another RODE, and two officers shouted playful insults at each other.

A few Mogats had died while trying to pull themselves to safety, much the way Private Amblin had died in the trench. The colonel steered his way over to one of them for a closer look. The man's chest, arms, and head lay flat on a rock shelf in a puddle that looked more like crude oil than blood. The gas had dissolved everything below his chest except his clothing.

The colonel circled the camera around the dead man. Vapor must have splashed against the right side of his face. The left side seemed normal enough, but the skin had dissolved from the right side, revealing patches of muscle and skull. Brown strings, maybe skin or maybe sinew, still dangled between the cheek and jaw. His left eye was gone.

Then the colonel found his first survivor—a man in torn clothes perched on a narrow lip of rock. His back was to the RODE. His arms were wrapped around a pipe for balance.

"We'll certainly have none of that," the colonel said in a jovial voice. On the screen I saw a particle-beam gun flash, and the man fell from his perch.

The cruiser erupted with laughter.

"Watch this," another officer shouted. He, too, had found a survivor—a woman. He steered his RODE toward the woman in a slow hover, then shined its blinding headlight on her face. She screamed and tried to shield her eyes with her forearm, but managed to stay balanced on a narrow rock ledge. The colonel fired a shot at her feet. Trying to back away from the RODE, the woman stumbled and fell. Her face struck the ledge, and she caught herself, but her body had fallen into the pool of vapor that covered the floor. She tried to pull herself up, but the skin on her face and arms was melting.

The officers laughed.

"Captain, may I please return to my men?"

McKay looked around the ship. If the officers had ever known we were there, they had forgotten about us by then. "You are dismissed, Corporal," he said in a hushed voice.

Forty thousand Mogats landed on Hubble. We captured ten thousand as they fled the caves and another fifteen thousand died when our Harriers hit their ships. The rest died in the caves.

CHAPTER
TWENTY

First I was an orphan, then I was a clone, then I was both. Tabor Shannon had not been my father or my brother, but he had been my family. For a brief few weeks I belonged to a tiny and hated fraternity.

So where did all that leave me? I was the last member of a discontinued line of clones fighting to protect the nation that outlawed their existence. All in all, I thought I had it better than Vince Lee and the 2,299 other enlisted Marines on the *Kamehameha*. I knew I was a clone, and I knew I could live with that knowledge. It now seemed to me that it was impossible that they did not suspect their origins on some level, and they must have lived in fear of the fatal confirmation.

By the time we left Hubble, I had spent more than eighteen months on active duty without asking for leave. The idea sounded foreign when Vince Lee first suggested it.

"Hello, Sergeant Harris," Vince Lee said as he placed his breakfast tray on the table and sat down beside me. "Sergeant Harris . . . It almost sounds right. The next step is officer, pal. You could actually do it. Hell. You made sergeant in under two years."

"I did not ask for the promotion," I said. That was Lee, obsessed with promotions and success.

Lee smiled. "You were made for it. You're a Liberator."

"So?"

"Every Liberator I've ever known made sergeant," Lee said.

"Get specked." I knew he was joking, but he struck the wrong nerve. Though they gave me the field promotion before I left Hubble—that was why McKay took me to the cruiser— the paperwork did not get approved for another month. As with my promotion to corporal, I did not feel that I had earned it.

"Look, Harris, I know you miss Shannon, but you need to lighten up," Lee said. He spooned the meat out of his grapefruit half, then gobbled down two strips of bacon. "HQ reviewed the record before giving your promotion the go-ahead. You did what you could. Let it go."

I finished my orange juice and placed the cup on my tray. "I guess so," I said, in an unconvincing voice.

"Okay, well, I had an idea," Lee said. "You've got more leave stored up than any man on this ship. I've got a couple of weeks. Let's take some R and R."

"That doesn't . . ."

Lee put up his hand to stop me. "Look at yourself, Wayson. You're moping around. You should see yourself around the men. You're on a hair trigger. If you don't take some time to relax, I think you're going to shoot somebody."

"They just gave me a platoon. Do you think they'd let me take leave?" I asked.

"Harris, if they don't let you go now, they're never going to. This is the beginning of Klyber's war. Things will only get hotter from here. Mogats on other planets are going to rally around their dead."

"Not Mogats," I said. "Atkins Separatists. That came straight from HQ. We are no longer to refer to the group formerly known as Mogats by any name other than 'Separatists' or 'Atkins Separatists.'"

Lee was right about the Separatists' rallying. For a man who never followed the news, Vince Lee had an uncanny ability to read the winds.

* * *

"Two weeks," McKay snapped when I requested a leave of absence. "Two weeks of liberty? You only took command of your platoon a few weeks ago. This is not the time for you to take a holiday, Sergeant."

We stood in a small booth in the gunnery range. Looking through the soundproof window, I could see Lee drilling the remaining members of the platoon as they fired at holographic targets with live ammunition—bullets and grenades. The M27s and automatic rifles hardly made a sound, but the report of the grenades thundered so loud that it shook the booth.

In preparation for fighting the Separatists, we now shot at animated targets with human faces. The targets in the rifle range bled, screamed, and moved like living soldiers. I peered through the window to watch my men as McKay spoke. A holographic target materialized less than twenty feet from the shooting platform. Vince Lee fired once and missed. His second shot hit the target in its chest. The enemy screamed and vanished.

"You have four new privates on the way," McKay said, staring at me angrily. "One of them is fresh out of boot. Your new corporal has not even arrived. Who is going to command the platoon with you and Lee out?"

"I understand, sir," I said.

"When was your last leave?" McKay asked.

"I've never taken leave, sir," I said. "I had a few free days before transferring to the *Kamehameha*."

"And nothing since?"

"No, sir."

McKay sat on the desk at the far end of the room, his legs draped to the floor. "Corporal Lee says that you have . . ." he paused to consider his words, "concerns."

"Concerns?" I asked.

"You do not feel that you earned your promotion."

Good old Lee . . . diarrhea of the mouth, constipation of the brain. "The corporal was speaking out of turn, sir. When I have concerns, I am completely able to lodge them myself."

"I see," said McKay, sounding a bit too paternal. He looked right into my eyes, not challenging me, but observing.

"Lee says that you blame yourself for Sergeant Shannon's death."

"I never said that."

"Do you blame yourself?"

I felt my stomach turn and my palms sweat. I looked out the window and watched one of my men miss five shots before finally hitting a target no more than ten feet away. Sloppy shooting. He wasn't bothering to aim before firing rounds.

"I should have waited," I said. "I left him in there. And I gave away our position when I missed that shot."

"I saw the video feed, Sergeant. You did not miss."

"I was too loud."

"You hit a moving target from over a hundred yards in a bad light," he said, shaking his head. "Look out that window. Do you think anyone else in your platoon would have done better?"

"I should have aimed for a head shot."

"Do you think that was what killed Shannon? Do you think he died because the man's oxygen tube exploded?"

I watched another private. Three targets popped up a good sixty feet out from him. He hit all three in short order, never missing a shot. How could identical beings be so different?

I mulled McKay's question over in my head. Freeman had won the battle on Gobi. I'd just been along for the ride. Shannon had done all the work on Hubble, and I got him killed. I did not say that. I did not want Captain McKay to consider demoting me . . . maybe court-martialing me.

"Harris, he was dead the moment he touched Lieutenant Williams."

"Williams?"

"The tech with the robot," McKay said. "Williams might have been a prick, but he was a superior officer, and a Navy man at that. I might have been able to smooth things over if Shannon roughed another Marine, but Williams wanted blood, and I goddamned don't blame him."

I did not say anything.

Outside the command booth, Lee gathered the platoon. I could not hear him, but I could see him yelling at the men. Lee singled out one man and gave him a shove as he stepped into line. The man stumbled.

McKay saw none of that. He continued to look at me, not so much staring, but certainly studying me carefully. I glanced back at him, but just for a moment. He sighed. "I am going to grant your request, Harris. I'll assign Grayson from the Thirteenth Platoon to cover for you.

"Do you have any idea where you are going?"

"I haven't thought about it."

"I don't think Lee wants to waste two weeks of leave drifting around Scrotum-Crotch," McKay said. "We're going to pass a disc station in two days. I'm going to grant your request, on the condition that you take your leave on Earth."

"Earth?" I liked the idea. "I could visit the orphanage . . ."

"God, Harris, talking to you is more depressing than sitting through a funeral. Most of the officers on this ship visit a group of islands. I told Lee about the place."

McKay slid off the desk. "You've got two weeks, Harris. Don't waste them." He returned my salute and left the office shaking his head and muttering the word "orphanage."

The Scutum-Crux Central Fleet needed rebuilding. We had lost seven thousand men on Hubble. I noticed an eerie emptiness around our section of the ship. I saw vacant racks in squad bay, and the sea-soldier bar always felt empty.

After the nonstop rush of battle, life unwound at an uneven pace aboard the *Kamehameha*. The first weeks after the battle on Hubble passed so slowly. The two days after McKay granted my leave were a blur.

I put off packing until the morning we left for Earth. I drilled my men harder than ever the day before we left. I tried to combine the late Tabor Shannon's tirades and Aleg Oberland's intelligent doggedness in my orders. I think I pushed everybody beyond his limits. When one of my privates missed ten shots on the range, allowing a holographic target of a woman separatist to stroll right up to the stand, I screamed until spit flew from my lips. Shannon would have been proud. I removed the man's helmet, then I placed it over his head backward and hammered it down with my rifle butt. "Having trouble seeing through your visor?" I yelled.

Nobody laughed at my antics. The squad watched silently. I sent that same private to clean latrines during lunch and invited him to spar with me during hand-to-hand drills later that afternoon. That evening, I spied him practicing on his own in the rifle range. He showed marked improvement despite the two swollen black eyes I had given him earlier in the day.

Then, at 0500 the next morning, I woke from a deep sleep to see Sergeant Elmo Grayson dropping his rucksack beside my bunk. "What are you doing here?" I asked.

"What are you doing here?" Grayson answered. "Your ride leaves in less than an hour."

The blood surged to my head when I sat up too quickly. Still feeling sluggish, I swung my feet out of bed and forced myself up.

"Anything I need to know?" Grayson asked, as I pulled on my shirt.

I thought for a moment. "I've been drilling them on their shooting skills. Most of these grunts are pretty sorry shots. Take them to the range a couple of times per day. If they screw up, drill them again . . . especially the one with the two black eyes."

"Black eyes?" Grayson asked. "Maybe that's what messed up his shooting."

"Actually, they've improved his accuracy," I said. It was true.

Lee came into my office as I threw the last of my clothes in a duffel bag. "They don't hold shuttles for sergeants, you know," he said.

"I know," I answered as I slung on my shoulder strap.

The men sat up in their bunks and watched as we left. No one said anything, but they seemed glad to see me go.

Lee and I raced to the launch bay, arriving as a small line of men started entering the transport. We joined the queue, panting from our run.

Fifteen men, six in civilian clothing, boarded the flight. Lee and I traveled in our Charlie Service greens. My civilian shirt and denim pants waited at the top of my bag.

The entire flight, over sixty thousand light-years, took under an hour. As Captain McKay had said, the *Kamehameha* happened to be near a disc station. Once we entered the network, we flashed through eight sets of discs, ending up at Mars Station, where we boarded a five-hour flight to Salt Lake City.

The flight from Salt Lake City to the islands would be aboard a civilian airliner. As we disembarked in Salt Lake City, I looked at my ticket. The name of the final destination looked so foreign. "How did you say they pronounce this town?"

"Hon-o-lu-la," Lee said.

"Hon-o-lu-la? The second 'U' sounds like an 'A'? What the hell kind of name is that?"

From the window of the plane, the ocean around the islands looked like a luminous patchwork of aqua, green, and blue. Parts of the island matched Gaylan McKay's description— longs strips of beach and gorgeous forests. Other areas looked nothing like I expected. I saw a large city and long stretches that looked parched. A mountain range seemed to dissect the island. Thick rain forests ran along the mountain.

"It's beautiful," Lee said.

"Did you know it would look like this?" I asked.

"I heard stories," he said, staring out a window across the aisle. "Mostly from officers. McKay says Admiral Klyber always comes here on leave."

As the airplane began its descent, it flew parallel to the shoreline. We rounded a crater. I watched the scrolling landscape as the plane approached the runway.

Lee and I grabbed our bags before the plane touched down. We stayed in our seats with our bags on our laps. Heat, glare, and humid air poured into the cabin when the flight attendant opened the hatch. Squinting against the sunlight, I drew in a deep breath and felt the warmth in my lungs. Moments after leaving the plane, I felt sweat on my forehead.

Like so many places on Earth, Honolulu was a living museum exhibit. The airport was hundreds of years old, with thick concrete pillars and open-air walkways. It reminded me of the Marine base on Gobi. As we walked through the airport, I rolled up my sleeves. My shirt already felt moist under my arms. The heat felt great on my face and neck.

"Are you beginning to thaw?" Lee asked me.

I knew what he meant. Back on the *Kamehameha*, every room was climate-controlled. So was our armor.

Lee handled all of the logistics on the trip. He arranged our flights, found a place for us to stay, and rented the transportation—a beat-up buggy with a retractable cloth top. I was just along for the ride. "I hope you know where we're going?" I said as I chucked my bag in the back of the car.

"Don't sweat it, we have a map," he said, tapping his finger on the map window in the dashboard. "Besides, who could get lost on a little rock like this?"

We got very lost indeed. The twisting network of highways that ran from the airport led in all directions. None of the signs said "Honolulu." They had equally odd names like "Waikiki," "Wahiawa," and "Kaneohe," none of which meant anything to either of us.

I didn't mind being lost. We drove around with the top down, feeling the sun bake our shoulders. We passed beaches and streets lined with people. Over the last few months I had forgotten how to relax, but it was coming back to me.

Lee pulled onto the side of the road to look at his map. We were on the outskirts of an area called "Waikiki." Tall hotels lined the roads.

"Okay. If we are where I think we are, the beach is over there, just beyond those buildings. We will see it if we go down this street. And we can follow this street to Diamondhead."

"Look at that," I said. "It's a hotel for military personnel." Just up the street from us was a large hotel with a sign that said "Hale Koa. U.A. Military Temporary Residents." The building was not as elaborate as some of the towering structures around it, but the grounds were simple and pretty.

"Oh yeah, the Hail Ko. McKay told me about it."

"Hail Ko? How did they come up with these names?" I joked.

Locating the Hale Koa Hotel gave Lee the bearings he needed to find his way through town. As we drove away, I glanced back at the hotel. It looked beautiful. "Why aren't we staying there?" I asked.

"McKay suggested this other place," Lee said. "He sounded pretty sure of himself. I get the feeling he knows his way around Honolulu."

We drove through Waikiki, passing splendid hotels, streets packed with tourists, and crowded beaches. The road led us past parks and up a hill. There the road twisted back and forth as it followed the jagged coastline. At the top of the hill, we found streets lined with homes. Our pad was down one of those streets.

Lee had rented the house sight unseen based on Captain McKay's recommendation. The place belonged to a retired combat officer who rented it to him for $200 per day. McKay said that that price was cheap, and that was undoubtedly correct. The truth was that everything in Honolulu was cheap; the U.A. government subsidized the economy and encouraged off-duty military men to visit. Rooms at the Hale Koa, for instance, were free to enlisted men.

I half expected to find that Lee had rented a dilapidated hut. When we reached the rough-hewn stone wall that surrounded the house, I thought Lee had the wrong address. The wall was tall and thick and made of perfectly matched lava stones. He typed a code into the computerized lock, and the gate slid open.

"Vince, you got this for two hundred dollars per day?" I asked.

Looking as stunned as I felt, Lee nodded. We stepped into a perfectly manicured courtyard. A pond ran one length of the yard. Reeds grew in the pond, and fish swam near the top of the water, causing ripples on its smooth surface.

A tree with white and yellow flowers stood in the center of the small courtyard. I stepped into its shade, and for the first time since I had landed, I felt a cool breeze. "Lee," I said, "this is the prettiest place I have ever seen."

Mynx's eyes narrowed on its prey and its triangular ears smoothed back against its skull. It kept its gold and black body low to the ground, hiding in the brush as it prepared to pounce. The sinewy muscles in its haunches visibly tightened.

I leaned over and scooped Mynx up with one hand, and the cat purred as I lowered her into my lap. She had claws, this skinny feline, but she did not swipe at me. She stretched and made herself comfortable across my thighs, plucking gently at my pants with her claws. As Mynx curled up to sleep, her intended prey, a butterfly, flitted out of the garden.

"Careful, Wayson, you might get scratched," Lee warned as he joined me for a beer in the courtyard.

"The note in the kitchen says that Mynx is friendly," I said, absentmindedly stroking her back. She took a lazy swipe at my hand, but her claws were not extended.

"Don't say that I didn't warn you," Lee said in a singsong voice. He flipped the cap off the old-fashioned bottle. "To many days of absolute boredom."

I held up my bottle and nodded. Mynx, still lying across my lap, stretched her body and dug her claws into my legs again. I laughed, though it hurt a little.

Warm air, cool shade, cold beer, green plants, and garish flowers—it was paradise. "I don't imagine that life gets much better than this," I said.

"It beats the hell out of Hubble," Lee said.

I saluted that comment with my bottle, though it reminded me of my open wounds. We found beer in the refrigerator. It tasted sweet, but it was weak. I could never have gotten drunk on the stuff.

"Hubble," I said. "I was just starting to forget about that shit hole." I rubbed Mynx behind her ears, and she purred.

"I saw you packing," Lee said. "It looks like most of your clothes are government-issue. Want to do some shopping?" Unlike me, Lee owned plenty of civilian clothes.

"I'd like that," I said. Sweat had soaked through the long-sleeved shirt I wore on the plane. At the moment, I was lounging with no shirt.

"Either that or you can go around in your armor. That ought to attract some scrub," Lee said. "Scrub" was the term we used for one-night romances.

I looked down at the nearly sleeping cat on my lap. "Careful, Vince, or I might toss you a Mynx ball."

In many ways Honolulu was designed to accommodate vacationing military men. The store owners recognized every clone as a potential customer. As we walked past storefronts and street-side vendors, people looked at Vince and launched into sales spiels or tried to attract his attention by yelling, "Hey, soldier!"

"Liberators must have come here a lot in the old days," Lee commented. "They recognize you." He never appreciated the tightrope act that the neural programming performed in his head.

We followed heavy foot traffic into an alley marked "International Marketplace." "Waikiki Bazaar" would have been more appropriate. Once we entered the market we saw stands, carts, and small shops selling toys, tropical drinks, and gaudy clothing with overly bright colors.

Lee led me to a woman selling clothing out of a cart, which she kept shaded under a bright red canopy. The woman was tall . . . taller than me. She had long, blond hair that fell past her rather butch shoulders. The caked-on makeup around her eyes made her look old. Seeing Vince, she smiled daintily, and said, "Can I help you find something?"

"We're looking for shirts," he said.

"Oh, I've got shirts," she said as she batted her eyes.

"We'll have a look," Vince said.

The woman watched as I sorted through a bin of T-shirts with pictures of colorful fish. The shirts and shorts on her cart looked like they might fall apart after a single wash. I felt threads break when I picked up a pair of shorts and snapped the waistband.

"Two shirts for ten dollars," the woman said. "Five for twenty."

"That's cheap," I whispered to Lee. He apparently thought that I wanted help haggling. "Twenty dollars!" he gasped with such awful melodrama that I wanted to laugh. "Twenty dollars for this? C'mon, Harris. No one in his right mind would pay these prices. Every cart on this street is selling the exact same shit."

Twenty dollars for five shirts sounded good to me, no matter how poor the quality. I didn't want them to last my career, just two weeks.

The woman gave Lee a wily smile. "Eighteen dollars, but you buy now. If you leave, that price goes away."

"Is that a good deal?" I asked.

"I only know one way to find out," Lee said loud enough so that the woman could hear. "Let's go check some other stands."

"She said she wouldn't give us that price again," I said.

"Look around here, Harris. This place is filled with carts just like this selling clothes just like these." He spoke in a loud voice, making sure that the woman would hear. Even on vacation, Lee was political.

But Lee was right. The marketplace was crowded with stores selling bright shirts and shorts like the ones I was holding. And there I was, in my long-sleeved shirt and heavy and dark pants, sweating up buckets. Every shopkeeper in the International Marketplace would welcome me.

I decided to risk spoiling the deal. Purposely establishing eye contact with the woman, I tossed the shirts back into the bin and turned to leave.

"Twelve dollars," she barked angrily. "Twelve dollars for five shirts or three pairs of shorts."

"What do you think?" Lee asked.

"They're not great, but they'll hold up for the next two weeks," I said.

"You have shit for taste, Marine," Lee said.

"Get specked," I said.

"Okay, smart guy," Lee said. I did not like the mischievous smile that formed on his lips. He walked over to the woman and spoke to her in hushed tones that I could not hear.

"Mmmmm," she said, bouncing her head in agreement. She turned to me and winked, putting up a finger to ask me to wait for a moment. When she returned, she held five genuinely nice shirts all neatly folded. She handed me the shirts.

"What do you think?" she asked.

I looked down and saw a photograph at the top of the pile. The woman had given me a portrait of herself. In the photo, she had a sly, alluring smile. She wore a bright pink bathing suit that did nothing to hide her masculine shoulders.

"Looks like you found yourself some scrub," Lee said, choking down a laugh.

I looked at the photograph again and understood. The hips, the shoulders, the makeup . . . this was a man.

I handed the shirts and the photograph back. "My friend . . ."

"Leave my store," the woman said with a very male voice and an impressive air of dignity.

As we walked away from the cart, Lee laughed convulsively. I thought he might collapse on the ground. He clapped his hand on my shoulder and leaned his weight on my back.

"Go speck yourself, asshole," I said in a quiet voice. Then I thought about it and laughed. "Bastard," I said.

Lee started to respond, then gave up in another fit of laughter.

Despite Lee's sense of humor, I bought six shirts, three pairs of pants, and a pair of sandals before leaving the Marketplace. My entire wardrobe cost forty dollars.

At night, the streets of Waikiki took on a Roman Circus air. Rows of glowing red lanterns lined the streets. Strings of white Christmas lights blinked from every tree. Tourists and party-loving locals filled the sidewalks. Bartenders and sober-looking businessmen came to take advantage of them.

Lee walked over to a small tiki hut to purchase a drink. I watched him carefully, purposefully memorizing the look of his clothes. Half the crowd seemed to be made up of vacationing clones, and I was not sure how I would find him if we got separated.

When he returned, Lee had a yellow-and-green fruit that looked like a squat bowling pin. Holding the fruit with both hands, he sipped from a straw that poked out of its stem.

"What is that?" I asked.

"Don't know," Lee said. "The fruit is papaya, but I have no idea what they've poured inside it." He took a sip. "It makes you feel like your head is on fire."

A gang of boys stopped to watch Lee drink from that odd fruit. "What's their problem?" Lee slurred.

"Probably don't like drunks," I said.

"Oh," said Lee. "Me neither. You wanna try this?"

I did not know what was in Lee's drink, but I decided it would be safer if only one of us tried it. I led the way up the street, trying to keep Vince from bumping into people. It took a lot of work. A few more sips, and he could barely stand. Whatever else they put inside that drink, some of it must have come from Sagittarian potatoes.

A double-decker bus with a banner that said, "Free Historic Tour," came rolling up the street. Vince did not look like he could walk much farther, and I thought the night might go easier if I kept him off his feet. I waved, and the bus stopped for us. Our ride took us away from the crowded streets of Waikiki and out toward the airport. We drove past a harbor filled with boats and large ships.

"This is historic Honolulu Harbor," the bus driver said over an intercom.

"Oh, look at the ships," Lee said, moments before vomiting. The woman sitting across the aisle from us focused all of her attention straight ahead, completely denying our existence. The young couple in the next seat acknowledged us. Lee's vomit splashed their feet, and they turned back and glared.

When the bus stopped to let people walk around the harbor, I led Lee away from the tour group. No one seemed sorry to see us go.

We stopped on a bridge and watched swells roll across the top of the moonlit water. The salt air seemed to do Lee good. He took deep breaths and regained some strength, then threw up again over the top of the bridge.

"Pathetic bastard," I said as I patted him on the back.

This part of town was not nearly as crowded as Waikiki, but a steady trickle of pedestrians moved along the streets. "Are you up for a walk?" I asked Lee.

He did not answer. I took that for a yes.

Most of the buildings along the streets were dark. We passed a bar, and I heard dance music and noisy chatter. The farther we walked from the water, the more people we saw, until we reached a building that looked like an auditorium or maybe a movie theater. The sign over the door said, "Sad Sam's Palace" in foot-tall letters. Under the sign was a marquee that said, "Big-Time Professional Wrestling."

Dozens of clones in civilian clothing milled around the entrance. Some sat on benches, others lounged along the walls. Many of them had been on leave for a while and had bronzed tans. A few also had women tucked under their arms.

"Want to watch wrestling?" I asked Lee as I led him toward the door.

"Do we get to sit?" he asked.

"As long as you don't puke," I said.

Lee leaned on the pedestal of a bronze statue as I went to buy the tickets. When I returned, he said, "Sad Sam Itchynose," and laughed.

"What?" I asked.

"This is Sad Sam Itchy-nose," he said pointing to the sign.

I looked at the plaque. It said, "Sad Sam Ichinose, 1908–1993." "He must have been a famous wrestler," I said. "Are you okay now?" I asked. "Are you going to puke?"

Lee shook his head, but he looked awfully pale.

On closer inspection, Sad Sam's Palace reminded me of an oversized bar. The building was old, with chipped walls and no windows. We entered the lobby and found ourselves in a crowd waiting for the doors to open.

"What's wrong with him?" a clone in a bright shirt asked as we came through the door.

"He bought a fruit drink that didn't agree with him," I said.

"Hey, I did that my first night. They fill that specker with Sagittarian Crash. I'll never do that again," he said cheerfully.

"Is this wrestling good?" I asked.

"Best show in town," the clone said. "Just don't come on Friday night."

"What happens on Friday?" I asked.

"That's open challenge night," he said. I had no idea what that meant; but the doors swung open as he spoke, and the crowd pushed inside.

"We should get a beer," Lee said, as we passed the concession stand. He swayed where he stood. His jaw was slack, and slobber rolled over his bottom lip.

"You've had enough," I said. I wondered if I should take him home.

Thick red carpeting covered every inch of Sad Sam's Palace. Inside the second door, we entered a large, square theater with bleachers along its walls and a balcony. I estimated that a thousand spectators had come for the show— and the building was half-empty.

There was a small boxing ring surrounded by tables. The only lights in the room hung over the ring, but the glare made the room bright enough for everybody.

An usher asked for my ticket at the door. When I showed her, she smiled and led us to bleachers about a hundred feet from the ring.

"Think we could be any farther from the action?" Lee asked.

"Lee," I hissed, "these are good seats."

He squinted at me. "My head hurts," he said.

A man in an old-fashioned black-and-white tuxedo entered the ring carrying a microphone. "Laaaaaadies and gentlemeeeeen, Sad Sam's Palace is proud to present, Big-Time Wrestling."

The crowd roared. Lee covered his ears and moaned.

"For our first match, weighing in at two hundred sixty-five pounds . . . Crusher Kohler." A fat man with bleached blond hair, yellow tights, and no shirt strode to the ring, growling at people who booed his arrival.

"Weighing in at two hundred thirty-seven pounds, Tommy Tugboat." In came a man with balding black hair, dark eyes, and black swim trunks. The crowd cheered for this one.

Crusher? Tugboat? God, what kinds of names are those? I asked myself. I might have asked Lee, but he sat slumped forward with his head hanging.

We had mandatory judo and wrestling at the orphanage. I knew what wrestling looked like, and it looked nothing like this. For openers, this fight was in a boxing ring, not on a mat. Tugboat and Crusher ran face-first into the ropes then bounced backward as if the ropes around the ring were made of elastic.

The crowd roared.

Tugboat smashed Kohler across the mouth, and the guy staggered like a drunkard. Another punch, and Kohler fell to his knees. Remaining on his knees, he put up his hands and begged for mercy.

The crowd roared.

"They're faking it," I said. "They must be."

By the time it was over, both Tugboat and Kohler had stumbled around as if half-dead, only to suddenly recover. Tugboat once lifted the flabby Kohler over his head, no small feat, then dropped him face first to the mat. After both men had been so pulverized that they should have been dead, the match ended with a simple pin.

The crowd loved it.

There were three more fights. Each took about fifteen minutes. Each had men who looked to be near death, then came back to health and performed Herculean feats of strength. I did not believe a moment of it, but it was fun to watch.

When the last fight ended, the audience filed out quickly. Lee, however, still lay sprawled on the bleachers massaging the sides of his head.

CHAPTER
TWENTY-ONE

Honolulu was a city on an island called Oahu, which was part of the Hawaiian Islands, which was a state of the former United States on the planet Earth. Perhaps I should have known all of that. I studied geography in the orphanage; but consider, the galaxy had six arms. Each of which had thirty member planets. There were one hundred eighty member planets in the Republic.

Before serving aboard the *Kamehameha,* I had never heard of Ezer Kri or Ronan Minor. Hell, I had never heard of the Templar System before landing on Hubble.

My education was lacking in more than geography. The retired officers running the orphanage had left the term "transvestite" out of my education. They also neglected to mention professional wrestling.

Our small villa had a common kitchen, dining room, and den. It had two bungalows for bedrooms. Lee remained in his room late into the morning. Still hungover from that fruit drink concoction, Lee slept until 1000. I could hear him snoring as I drank a cup of coffee in the courtyard.

I fixed myself a small breakfast of fruit and fish and went back to the courtyard to eat it. Mynx came over and joined me. She curled up in my lap and made herself comfortable. As I scooped meat out of pineapple, the sneaky cat filched my fish and ran off with it. The slice was nearly as big as her head, but that did not stop her.

"Hey!" I yelled, for all the good it did me. Mynx hopped off the table, my fish hanging from her mouth, and paused to look at me. If I'd had my pistol, I might have shot that cat. Instead, I watched her leave with her tail sticking straight up in the air. I laughed and enjoyed a moment of complete relaxation.

That moment ended when I put on my media shades and searched for stories. A coalition from the House of Representatives was calling for the Linear Committee to reduce the military budget. "We have an unprecedented stockpile of weapons," said Speaker of the House Gordon Hughes, who represented Olympus Kri, a thriving colony a few hundred light-years from Earth in the Orion Arm. "We have more than twenty million clones on active duty, and the government keeps churning out nearly one and a half million more every year. The cost of supporting this build-up will pull our entire economy down."

Gordon Hughes of Olympus Kri appeared on the news quite often in those days. He wanted lower taxes, less military, greater territorial autonomy. He questioned the need of a U.A. Naval base on Olympus Kri and asked for a direct disc link with trading partners in the Sagittarius and Perseus Arms. In the House, Hughes was widely praised for his bold initiatives. In the Senate, they talked about the million-member march that the Atkins Separatists made to his planet's capital.

In a small sidebar, I read that the congressman from Ezer Kri challenged Hughes's ideas. No surprise there. Ever since the invasion, Ezer Kri had supported the Linear Committee on every issue. Had the Linear Committee called for a ban on oxygen, the honorable congressman from Ezer Kri would have supported it.

In another story out of Washington, DC, the Senate unanimously approved a bill calling for two hundred new orphanages. Open war between the House and Senate was nothing new. The Senate would naturally spin the request to sound like an attempt to help homeless children, but that would not fool anybody. The Speaker of the House called for fewer orphanages and the Senate unanimously thumbed its nose at him. Isn't that how it goes? As a product of the New Order orphanage system, and a military clone, I shared the Senate's view on the issue. So did somebody else.

I looked at the visual feed that accompanied the story. As the Senate leader announced that the vote had been unanimous, the camera swept the gallery to show senators and onlookers giving a standing ovation. The camera panned the VIP box. Most of the men in the picture wore civilian clothing; but there was a tall, skeletal man dressed in Navy whites. I stopped the feed. The picture was blurred, but the face was unmistakable. "What are you doing in DC?" I asked out loud. "I thought you were on the *Kamehameha*."

Klyber could have flown to DC quickly enough. Had he flown in for an important vote, or was there something else going on, I wondered.

"I don't feel so good," said Lee as he slid open the glass door of his bungalow. He did not look so good either. He stood in the doorway rubbing his head. His dark hair stood up in spikes, and he had huge sallow bags under badly bloodshot eyes.

"You cannot possibly feel as bad as you look," I said.

"I don't remember much. Did I do anything stupid last night?" Lee walked to his chair, then stood and stared at it as if deciding whether he was physically capable of sitting. He turned and dropped into the chair.

"Whatever you drank . . ."

"That fruit thing!" Lee interrupted. "I remember. That goddamn fruit thing." He groaned and rubbed his head.

"You got sick on a bus," I said.

"I don't remember a bus," Lee said.

"We went to wrestling matches," I said. "There was this place called Sad Sam's Palace, where they have fake wrestling matches in a boxing ring."

"Doesn't ring a bell," Lee said. He spent most of the morning moping around the house, trying to get his head straight. He seldom drank anything stronger than beer. Now I knew why.

By early afternoon, Lee became restless and wanted to drive into town. Neither of us had eaten lunch, and the idea of ordering a burger sounded good. The sun was up and hot, and I wanted to walk, but Lee insisted on driving.

The ocean glistened as we drove down to Waikiki. Lee wanted to put the top up and use the air-conditioning, but I vetoed him on that one. I wanted the heat of the sun on my head, and I liked the warmth, though I could have done without the humid air.

We left the car by a beach park and started to walk the last few blocks into town, but I heard the roar of the waves. "Let's check out the beach," I said.

"How about after lunch?" Lee asked.

"It's right over there," I said. I turned and started for the beach without waiting for Lee to answer. He followed, muttering words to himself that did not sound happy.

I took off my shoes when I reached the beach; the hot sand burned the soles of my feet. That part of the beach was almost empty. Sprinting past sunbathers, I wrapped my shoes and wallet into my shirt and dropped the wad in an empty spot, and trotted into the water.

The water was cold, but my body adjusted quickly. I loped forward through the shallows until the water was up to my waist, then I dived in. Lee followed me as far as the water's edge, but his willingness to continue vanished the moment he felt the water. He walked back to my shirt and shoes and sat down beside the pile.

The water was clear and bitter to the taste. The salt burned my eyes when I dived down for a look, but I kept my eyes open. There were fish all around me. I swam up for air, then dived to the bottom for a closer view. I saw small, silver fish and bright yellow fish that were about the size of my hand. A gentle current swept me farther out, and when I dived again, I could no longer reach the bottom.

The fish knew no fear. Thousands of red, green, blue, and yellow fish huddled together in a lazy cloud that barely parted when I swam too close. Even when I grabbed at them, they sped out of my reach but did not swim away. I stayed down too long and my lungs burned when I swam to the surface and gulped for air.

Back on the beach, Lee stood on the shore and waved at me. The current had pulled me a few hundred feet from shore. I needed to get back.

I took a deep breath and dived for another look at the fish. What I saw was far more exciting. A white silhouette passed sleekly along the ocean floor deep below me. At first I did not realize what I was looking at, but only for a moment. It was a very trim woman with short blond hair trailing behind her in a silky web. This woman had long tanned legs and she cut through the water with otterlike grace. She wore swim fins and a diver's mask, and with a kick from her perfectly toned thighs, she sprang forward over the coral reef.

The woman's face mask must have had an air supply because she held her breath for a very long time. In the time that she admired the coral shelf, I had come up for air twice and was about to swim up a third time. I would never have caught up to her had she swum away. Fortunately, she turned, looked at me, and came up with me. She broke through the surface just a few feet from me. She pulled off her mask and smiled. "And they said there was nothing dangerous in these waters."

We finished the preliminaries that quickly.

Kasara swam to shore with me. As we waded out of the water, I saw Lee. Still sitting by my shirt and shoes, his expression was a mixture of jealousy and hate. He picked up my shirt and trotted out to meet us.

I turned to Kasara. "I want you to meet Vince," I said.

Kasara smiled at Vince. She had a slightly mischievous smile—the big, unabashed smile of a child. I looked at her smile and her blue eyes and knew that my leave had unalterably changed.

She was about six inches shorter than I—about five-foot-ten. She wore a bright red bikini that contrasted sharply against her tanned skin. She had a flat stomach with just a hint of visible ribs and muscular definition. I had to concentrate to keep from staring.

"Vince, this is . . ."

"Kasara," she said in a soft voice.

"You don't happen to have a roommate?" Lee asked.

"As a matter of fact . . ." Kasara laughed. She looked embarrassed. "I'd better get back to her."

"What are you doing tonight?" I asked.

"What do you want me to do tonight?" she asked.

Clearly she was used to more experienced players than me. I pulled my shirt over my head and shoulders. "We just got here last night. Maybe you and your friend could show us the better spots."

"Show you around?" Kasara said with a grin. "That sounds fun." She pointed up toward the street. "See that two-story building over there?"

We were on the outskirts of Waikiki, well away from the luxurious towers and glossy hotels. The two- and three-story buildings that lined the far side of the street were wedged together like books on a crowded shelf. "Which one do you mean?" I asked.

She moved even closer until our bodies touched. In a moment, I would need to dive back into the cold water. Wrapping one hand around my waist, she pulled me so that I could see exactly where she was pointing. "You see that pink two-story building?"

"Oh," I said, feeling my legs go numb. I felt the side of her breast rub against my arm.

"Think you can meet us there at seven o'clock?" she asked, her voice sounding husky.

"Seven it is," I said.

"Don't be late," Kasara said, releasing me. I could barely stand. She, on the other hand, walked away down the beach as if nothing had happened.

"Not bad, Harris," Lee said. "I hope her roommate looks that good."

The sun set as we arrived at Kasara's hotel, but the sky remained bright for another two hours. The warm night air, so pleasant compared to the burdensome humidity of the day, was filled with the smell of the ocean.

Kasara stayed in a rattrap hotel with pink adobe walls and stubby, Moorish archways. The manager had plastered the walls of the lobby with advertisements for car rentals and island tours. "How much do you think they charge per night?" I asked Lee.

Lee was not listening. "Wayson," he said excitedly, "if the roommate is as good-looking as Kasara, I'll really owe you, pal."

Kasara and her roommate came gliding down the steps into the lobby. Kasara wore a short, white dress that stopped at the very tops of her thighs. Jennifer, her roommate, wore a green sundress. Kasara was the prettier of the two, but Jennifer was not off by much. I liked her dark brown hair and green eyes. So did Lee. He and Jennifer matched up well and started chatting almost immediately.

"You look beautiful," I said to Kasara.

"Thank you," Kasara purred, and gave me that young girl smile. As we turned to leave, she moved very close to me, and I felt an urge to put my arm around her waist. She rubbed up against me, and my hand seemed to slide around her of its own accord. She looked at me and beamed.

"Are you hungry?" I asked.

"Let's walk around," Kasara said. By that time, the street vendors had rolled their carts out along the sidewalk. A couple with two young boys was looking at a cart covered with toys. Vince and Jennifer paused in front of that cart, and he bought her a surfer doll. They seemed happy.

"I could get you one of those," I offered.

"You've got to be kidding, Harris," she said. From then on, I let Kasara do most of the talking. She told me about her job. She worked as a cocktail waitress on Olympus Kri. When I asked her what she thought about the row in Congress, she did not know what I meant. I asked her if she voted for Gordon Hughes, but she did not know the name.

She was just a girl who worked in a bar saving up tips for an annual vacation on Earth. She hated her job. She had a boyfriend back home, but did not like him much, either. We quickly established that she did not care about politics, professional sports, or novels. Movies and dancing, on the other hand, she talked about endlessly.

Kasara did not ask many questions, not even which branch Lee and I served in. I suppose she already knew my basic story. She might not have known if I was in the Army or the Navy, but she knew I was military and probably guessed that I grew up in an orphanage.

A little way down the road, I saw a familiar stand surrounded by flaming torches. "Hey, Vince," I called back. "This is where you bought that papaya thing last night." A crowd had already lined up around the stand.

"I want to try one," Kasara said, sounding excited.

"It practically killed Vince," I said. "He was still getting over it when we went to the beach this afternoon."

"Did you try it?" Kasara asked.

"I think it's mostly Sagittarian Crash," I said.

"Wayson, I work in a bar, remember? I can handle it. It's for tourists, probably half fruit syrup and ice cream. Let's get one."

I gave in and Kasara smiled and nuzzled her head against my shoulder. It reminded me a bit of Mynx, purring on my lap as she grabbed the fish from my breakfast. But Kasara was exactly the right height to fit against my chest, and I felt the warmth of her body. "Do too much of that, and we may have to make it an early night," I warned her.

She flushed. "Don't be too sure of yourself, Harris," she said, with a sheepish smile.

I wasn't. My heart was beating so hard, I expected my Liberator glands to start filling my blood with endorphins and adrenaline like they did in battle.

"What the hell do you think you are doing?" Lee gasped as we approached the fruit stand. "That thing wiped me out last night."

"We're going to split one," I said.

"It's your funeral, Harris," said Vince. "Jennifer and I are going to walk around a bit. Maybe we will run into you again later." Jennifer gave Kasara a friendly peck on the cheek, then Lee and Jennifer vanished into the crowd.

"How many?" the man running the cart barked as we approached.

"One," I said, then seeing Kasara's disappointed expression, I corrected myself. "Two."

"Four dollars," the man said, holding out his hand.

I paid.

Crash loses a bit of its bite when diluted with sugar. The fruit juice and ice cream might have made this drink sweet, but I still felt the nearly toxic alcohol in my blood. Kasara worked away at her drink slowly, taking little sips and talking cheerfully. The more she sipped, the more she rubbed against me as we walked. I would have proposed going back for seconds, but I was afraid it would kill her.

"This is so good," she said. "We make these at the bar, but it's not the same without fresh papaya."

By that time the sky had gone completely dark. Tourists of all descriptions now filled the streets. "Are you hungry?" I asked.

Kasara laughed. "Are you kidding? I just drank enough for two meals." As we walked toward the beach, we passed a bin with an open fire. Kasara tossed her half-finished fruit into the flames, and we both jumped when we heard the explosion.

"You want to sit and talk?" I asked.

"Talk?" she asked suspiciously, though I doubt she would have minded if I proved her suspicions correct.

We walked across the beach and sat down near the water. Waves rolled in stopping just short of where we sat. A cold breeze came in off the ocean. Leaning back on my elbows, I looked into a sky brimming with stars. Somewhere out there was the *Kamehameha*.

She placed her hand on my thigh and I knew that I did not know what was ahead.

TWENTY-TWO

I looked over at Kasara sleeping beside me and did not know what to do. I wanted more of what we had done last night, but I also wanted to get away from her. It might have been unknown territory for me, but it was certainly nothing new for her. I did not know if I had embarrassed myself.

She slept so soundly, and she looked like an angel as she slept. Her hair, straight and golden, was spread across the pillow. With her eyes shut and a slight smile playing on her lips, she looked sweet . . . almost innocent. She barely stirred, and I did not want to wake her.

I climbed out of bed and looked around my room. I would not describe myself as a naturally neat person, but as a military orphan and a Marine, I had been forced to maintain orderly quarters. From childhood up to the moment I set foot on Gobi, I had been subjected to weekly and sometimes daily inspections. If my bed was not made just right, if I did not fold my clothing properly in my locker, if the floor around my rack was not spotless, I was virtually assured KP duty or time cleaning the latrine. Kasara, apparently, did not have the same discipline.

Her dress was tossed over a chair in the corner of the room. Her shoes and socks were in two separate piles. Her bra hung from the top of my dresser. We had taken off our clothes pretty quickly the night before, but how had she managed to scatter everything like that? I thought about picking up after her, then decided against it.

Knowing that I might later regret the decision, I pulled my media shades off my dresser and went to the kitchen for a cup of coffee. Sitting down and taking a sip, I booted up my shades and scanned the pangalactic headlines. Klyber's judicial sideshow had begun. The ten thousand Mogat Separatists we captured on Hubble were now appearing in court on Ezer Kri.

The story included a quote from Nester Smart, the provisional governor of Ezer Kri. I was not aware that there had been a change. The story did not mention anything about Governor Yamashiro. There were several lengthy video segments from the courtroom floor. Every feed showed the same thing—male prisoners sitting in groups of four to ten at a time, remaining absolutely stone-faced as judges read the accusations.

I watched two of the feeds. I found it hard to concentrate; thoughts of the previous night kept clouding my mind. What I really wanted to do was wake Kasara and see what might happen, but I thought I should let her sleep for another few minutes.

I viewed one last clip. Just another judge reading the exact same four charges—sedition, assault against officers of the Unified Authority military, premeditated murder, willfully obstructing the law . . . The camera panned around the court to show the jury. And then it dawned on me. Not one member of the jury had black hair. Nobody had Asian eyes. No one in the previous video feeds had Japanese features, either.

I found a sidebar showing man-on-the-street interviews conducted in downtown Rising Sun. The streets looked empty, and the few people who gave interviews looked cosmopolitan.

The first time I read about Ezer Kri, the article said that the planet had nearly 12.6 million people of Japanese descent. The population of Rising Sun was over 80 percent Japanese. It would have taken one hell of an airlift operation to slip that many people off the planet. Later I searched for the latest demographic statistics from Ezer Kri. I found an article that was only one month old. There was no mention of a Japanese population.

"Damn, Wayson. You're reading the news," Vince Lee said in disgust.

"They've started the trials on Ezer Kri," I said.

"You need to get your head out of those shades," Lee said. "Kasara and Jennifer came as a package deal, and I am not going to let you speck this up."

Lee had a point. Bright sunlight shone through my kitchen windows. The curtains fluttered in a gentle breeze. I sipped my coffee and discovered that it had gone cold.

"You and Jennifer had a good time last night?" I asked.

"We did," he said. "From the sound of things, you and Kasara did okay. I promised Jennifer that we'd all drive around the island. Hope you don't mind."

"Sounds like fun," I said. I went to wake Kasara up. She and I had breakfast about forty minutes later.

We drove east, following the coast. The highway wound around bays and mountains, through small towns and wide-open countryside. Vince drove and Jennifer sat beside him. Kasara and I sat in the back. She nuzzled against me and occasionally stroked her hand over my thighs. She did not say much. She seemed wistful.

The coastal road led along the outside of dormant volcanoes. One side of the street was barren, the other side dropped straight down to the ocean, a fathomless mosaic of blues and greens. Kasara leaned forward and spoke to Jennifer. "Let's stop."

Jennifer put her hand to Lee's ear and relayed the request. He pulled into a scenic parking area overlooking the ocean, and we went to have a look.

I had seen enough from the car and didn't need to look much longer. Vince and Jennifer didn't care about much of anything. She held his arm and smiled. They talked happily. Kasara held my arm, too; but her thoughts were elsewhere.

Soon she would return home. She dreaded the idea. She was a girl who lived for one week out of every year—the week she spent on vacation.

Kasara stared down at the waves as they dashed against the black rock walls of the cliff. Wind blew her silky hair across her face. She did not smile, and her eyes seemed far away.

"The view is beautiful," I said, mostly because I was tired of looking at it and hoped to wake her from her trance.

"I could watch this all day," she muttered.

God help us, I thought, but I did not say anything. There was no peace in her face. The girlish smile that had so lured me had vanished. Without it, she was more beautiful than ever.

"Do you think there are fish down there? Wouldn't the waves kill them?" she asked.

"I don't know anything about oceans," I said, "but those currents look strong."

"We have an ocean on Olympus Kri," she said, prying her eyes from the view. She looked at me and smiled. It was not the same smile I had seen the day before.

"Does it look like this?" I asked.

"I've only seen pictures," she said. "I've never gone out to the coast."

She tightened her grip around my biceps. "You've probably seen all kinds of oceans."

"I've only been to four planets so far," I said. "One was a desert and one was toxic."

"Poor Wayson," she said. "I'm sure you've seen some amazing places. So exciting to spend your life on a ship traveling around different worlds." As she spoke, her thoughts drifted, and her smile became more pure. She reached an arm around my waist and we kissed.

"Seen enough?" I asked.

"Yeah," she said.

We turned toward the car. Vince and Jennifer were already there, watching us and talking.

"Hey," I said. "Vince, did you see that sign?"

The sign behind the car said "Scenic Area." Above the words was the silhouette of a man in a cape wearing a primitive war helmet with a fin along the top. It was the insignia of our ship.

"What's that doing here?" Lee asked.

Once we were alert to it, we spotted Kamehameha everywhere. He was on scenic signs and the sides of buses. There was a caricature of him on our map. Lee drove us to the spot on the way home. There, immortalized in an cast-iron statue with gold leaf, was King Kamehameha: "Conqueror of the Islands."

"No wonder all of those officers vacation here," Lee said. "The ship was named after a Hawaiian king."

The statue stood ten feet tall and stood upon a pedestal that added another five feet. I read the plaque at the base of the statue. Kamehameha had been a warrior king who paddled from island to island by canoe and conquered villages with spears and clubs. He was also a statesman. Once he finished conquering his island kingdom, he set up treaties with France, England, and the United States of America that played great nations against each other and ensured his primitive kingdom's survival.

This told me something about Bryce Klyber, too. The aristocratic admiral had selected our antiquated Expansion-class fighter carrier as his flagship because he liked the name. He liked the idea of the statesman warrior. He saw himself as both a statesman and a warrior, and he believed that his statesmanship ultimately differentiated him from the likes of Admiral Huang.

When we dropped Kasara and Jennifer off at their hotel in the midafternoon, Lee looked at me, and said, "Shit, now I'm stuck with you." He was joking, but the feeling was mutual.

We moped around the villa until 1700, then headed down the hill. The sun had not even begun to set. The last of the tourists still lingered on the beach, lying on the sand or wading in the shallows. In another hour the sun would go down, and even they would leave. Younger, trendier tourists would commandeer the streets once night fell.

We could not find anyplace to park, so Lee drove around the block while I went to find Kasara and Jennifer. As I entered the lobby, I realized that I did not know their floor or room number. I did not even know Kasara's last name.

"You're late," Kasara called from the second-story balcony. She was not much of an actress. She tried to sound angry, but she did a poor job of it.

I looked up. Kasara, wearing a sundress with an orange-and-red flower print, leaned over the rail of the balcony. Another Waikiki special, I thought. Her dress matched my shirt. "I'm half an hour early."

"Come on up," she said.

I skipped up the steps. Kasara's apartment bore a striking resemblance to my room earlier that morning—her clothes were everywhere. She had two pair of dress shoes, tennis shoes, and slippers scattered around the outside of her closet. Her clothes were on the bed and furniture. A bra hung from the knob on the bathroom door.

And there was more. I saw two sinks through the open bathroom door. One was littered with cosmetics, brushes, and toothpaste. The other was neat, with a simple toiletry bag leaning against its mirror. That must have been Jennifer's.

"You should have come earlier. We've been sitting around waiting for you," Kasara said, brushing some clothes from a chair as she retrieved her purse. She fixed those sparkling blue eyes on me, and I became oblivious to the clutter as well.

As we started to leave, Kasara loped off to the bathroom and closed the door. Thinking that was very sudden, I turned to Jennifer. "Is she okay?"

"You don't expect her to leave without touching up her hair?" Jennifer asked.

"But it was perfect," I said.

Jennifer shook her head. "Wayson, that girl spends two hours every morning doing exercises, touching up her hair, and putting on her makeup. Then she spends another thirty minutes making sure it's perfect before she leaves the hotel. But try to get her to clean up the room . . ."

It was Kasara and Jennifer's last night in Hawaii. Lee and I wanted to make a big deal of it. In many ways, it would turn out to be the last night of my vacation, too.

Kasara wanted to go shopping for trinkets. Jennifer and Lee wanted to get out of Waikiki. Both ideas sounded good. We drove to the Honolulu Harbor. There we found a mall that would be far less crowded.

Kasara went on a spending spree. In one store, she found hats with "I LOVE HAWAII" stitched across their bills in rainbow colors. She bought five of them "for the other gals at work." She also bought a case of locally made chocolates in the next store and canned oysters with cultured pearls in another. As we left, she saw a photo booth. Without even saying a word, she turned to me and rested her head on my shoulder, batting her eyelashes and pretending as if she was pleading for permission.

"What?" I asked.

She nodded toward the booth and grinned.

"Isn't that a bit dangerous? What will your boyfriend say?"

"I didn't tell you?" Kasara said. "We broke up."

"When did that happen?" I asked.

Kasara shrugged and smiled. She grabbed my hand and dragged me toward the booth.

"They broke up?" Vince asked Jennifer while we were still in earshot.

"They will when she gets home."

The thought of Kasara breaking up with her boyfriend left me both excited and scared. I ran my hands over my hair, trying to push it in place for the picture. Kasara slid onto the bench inside the booth and pulled me next to her. The people who designed the booth had kids or singles in mind. Even when I pushed in and squeezed against Kasara as best I could, my right shoulder still hung out of the door. We looked into a small mirror as lights around the booth flashed on and off.

Kasara let her hand slide up my thigh. I tried to ignore the jolt running through my body and look relaxed. "I didn't think nice girls did things like that," I teased as I stepped out of the booth.

"Nice girls don't," Kasara agreed. "Working girls on their last night of vacation do all kinds of things."

"What kinds of things?" I asked.

"You'll see." She stepped closer to me and stared deep into my eyes.

"I have to ask . . ." I said. "Your boyfriend . . . That wasn't because of me, was it?"

"You're so self-centered," she said, laughing. "You had nothing to do with it." I felt relieved. I also felt disappointed.

Something happened between Vince and Jennifer during the short time that Kasara and I spent in the photo booth. Perhaps Jennifer told Vince that she wanted to stay in touch with him, and he said he had other plans. Perhaps it was the other way around. They held hands for the rest of the evening, but I heard lags in their conversation and moments passed when they seemed reluctant to look at each other.

When we passed a stand selling the Crash and fruit drink, Kasara pointed. Jennifer, Lee, and I groaned. Pretending to ignore us, Kasara looked at the people waiting, and chirped, "Oh well, the line is too long, anyway."

"We haven't had dinner yet," said Jennifer.

Jennifer was the more sensible of the two. She did not flirt the way Kasara did, and she spoke less frivolously. Fun and flirtatious as Kasara was, I wondered what would have happened had Lee first met Kasara on the beach and I dated Jennifer.

We strayed into a courtyard in which people sold various kinds of foods from large, wooden carts. One cart had skewers of fruits, fish, chicken, and beef cooked over a charcoal grill. Kasara and I bought meat sticks and munched them while sitting on a bench overlooking the docks as Vince and Jennifer walked off to look for more options. We looked at ships and watched the sunlight vanish in the horizon.

"What's it like on Olympus Kri?" I asked.

"It's not like this," Kasara said. "The night sky is kind of like the day sky, only darker. We're pretty far from our sun, so it's cold and gray. I mean, it's not like we never see the sun. It's like a shiny patch in the clouds." She sighed. "We don't have a moon."

After our meal, we continued along the waterfront. I noticed that the sidewalks became more crowded. Men and boys were bustling up the street in droves. Then I saw the distant lights. "Sad Sam's Palace," I said.

"Sad Sam's," Kasara said. "I've heard about that place."

"We were here two nights ago," Lee said. "Didn't you say the fights were all fake?"

"You were there, too, weren't you?" Jennifer asked.

"He went," I said. "He just doesn't remember anything."

"I was drunk," Lee said. "That was the night I had the fruit drink."

Faked wrestling matches did not seem like something Kasara or Jennifer would enjoy, but they surprised me. "Can we go?" Kasara asked.

"You want to see the fights?" I asked.

I meant to ask Jennifer, but Kasara intercepted the question. "I've always wondered about this place."

"Are you up for this, too?" Lee asked Jennifer.

"Sure."

Lee and I shot each other amused smiles.

As we started toward the door, an old, white-haired man in a tank top called to us. He might have been a long-retired soldier. He had tattoos on his back and shoulders that looked ridiculous against his wrinkled skin. "Hey, you, you don't want to go in there." He had the gravelly voice of an old drill sergeant.

"We've been here before," said Lee, though he certainly had no memory of that last visit. I went to pay for the tickets, or I would have heard what the man said next. Unfortunately, I did not hear it until several days later. The man said, "You want to stay clear of the Palace on Friday."

Had I heard that, I might have thought twice about going inside. I might have noticed that as far as I could see, Lee and I were the only clones in the crowd. By the time I returned with our tickets, Lee had already told the man to mind his own business.

An usher led us to our seats. Coming late as we had, I expected to sit on the first or second balcony. Instead, the usher led us to the first floor. Threading his way around tables filled with screaming fight fans, he found an empty table just one row from the ring.

The venue had changed. Instead of ropes, ten-foot walls made of chain-link fencing now surrounded the ring. The fighters had changed, too. Instead of flabby men in colorful tights, the ring now held two large and muscular men.

"Are you sure they're faking this?" Lee asked. "It looks real."

One man grabbed the other by the hair and rammed his fist into the man's face several times. Blood sprayed. The fight ended a moment later when two medics carried the loser out on a stretcher.

"It wasn't like this last time," I said. "It was all headlocks and bouncing off the ropes."

A waitress came by our table between bouts and we asked her about it. "You came on Wednesday," she guessed. "That was Big-Time Wrestling night. Tonight is an Iron Man competition."

"What's that?" Jennifer asked.

The waitress smiled. "Open challenge, honey. Anything goes."

"Ladies and gentleman, we have your winner by knockout, Kimo Turner." The announcer raised Turner's arm and polite applause rose from the crowd. Considering Turner's impressive size and the vicious way he fought, I found the lack of enthusiasm surprising.

"Which branch are you boys in?" the waitress asked when she returned with our drinks. All of us ordered beer except Kasara, who ordered something fruity with layers of blue liquor and white smoothie.

"Marines," Lee answered.

"Where you in from?" the waitress asked.

"Scrotum . . ." Lee corrected himself. "The Scutum-Crux Fleet."

"You're a long way from home," she commented as she took the money for the drinks.

"Keep the change," Lee said. He was feeling generous. I was, too. It was a magical evening. We could feel the electricity in the air. In another twenty-four hours we would send the girls home, but not until we had made a complete night of it.

"And now, ladies and gentlemen, for the next preliminary match, please welcome once again, Kimo Turner." The audience applauded more readily that time. People shouted encouragement to the big man as he returned to the ring. Turner had a strong, rounded physique with bulging chest muscles, mountainous shoulders, and thick arms. I looked from him to Lee, a dedicated bodybuilder. Lee's arms and shoulders were more defined, but Turner looked far more powerful.

"And now . . . your returning champion, with a record of two hundred and zero in Sad Sam's Iron Man competition, Adam Boyd." The crowd went insane. Three stories of spectators began screaming at the tops of their lungs. Someone in the balconies began clanking a gong. Men stood on tables and whistled. The clamor was deafening.

Boyd entered the arena, walking a path that led him right past our table. A spotlight shone from the ceiling, and the people around us rose to their feet. Though he passed within five feet of our table, I had to stand to get a good look at him. The man I saw was nothing like I expected.

I had thought this undefeatable Adam Boyd must be seven feet tall and built out of bricks. Instead, an undersized and thin fellow with a receding hairline strode past. I would have had trouble believing that he was even five feet tall without seeing him measured.

"Key-riste! That's the champion?" Lee gasped.

"They're putting that little man in with that monster?" Jennifer gasped.

"The midget is the champion," Lee said.

The announcer left the ring, and the fight began. Boyd, whose head barely reached his opponent's shoulders, moved in warily. He crouched low, held his hands high in front of his head, and circled the floor rather than charging straight ahead.

Kimo Turner lunged straight in, throwing a massive punch that might have decapitated Boyd had it landed. The punch was slow. Boyd easily dodged it, but Kimo was a cagey fighter. The punch was a ruse. His body pivoted with the massive momentum of the missed punch, and he threw a back kick that should have hit Boyd in the chest or throat.

It was a smart move that did not work. Boyd had the reflexes of a demon. He dodged, shot in under the kick, and swept Kimo's other leg. Kimo fell. The crowd cheered.

Adam Boyd moved in for the kill without a moment's hesitation. He pounced on Kimo, drilling punches straight down around his eyes and jaw. The entire fight lasted less than one minute.

"Shit!" howled Vince. "Shit, shit, shit! I've never seen anything like that. That guy is a friggin' killer!"

I cannot accurately describe how the fight made me feel. It was like a challenge, as though Adam Boyd's abilities shook my self-confidence. "I think I like Big-Time Wrestling better," I said.

The announcer stepped back into the ring. "Ladies and gentleman, your winner, by early knockout, Adam Boyd." As Boyd and the announcer left the ring, the crowd roared. When they returned five minutes later, the applause became all the noisier.

"Ladies and gentleman," the announcer went on, "it appears we have been graced with a visit from the Republic's finest." Suddenly a blinding spotlight pointed at our table. I had to squint to see my own hands.

"Gentlemen, which one of you will represent the Scutum-Crux Fleet against our champion?" the announcer asked.

I looked over at Lee. In the glaring light, his skin looked white, flat white. He looked as nervous as I felt. We stared at each other for a moment, then Lee started to stand.

"Vince," Jennifer said as she reached for his arm.

"Sit down, Corporal," I said, pulling rank.

"Oh, come on, Wayson. Don't be like that," Lee said, sitting back in his chair.

"He said something about our Republic's finest, and that sure as hell isn't you, Corporal." I did not believe that, of course. But that Boyd character was fast and brutal. I'd sparred with Vince on several occasions. He was powerful but slow, and very predictable. He would have made an easy meal for this Adam Boyd fellow.

"You shouldn't do this, Wayson," Jennifer said. "You don't need to go up there."

"Kick his ass, Wayson," Kasara said. She clapped excitedly, and her face beamed. She loved the attention. I'd never seen her so excited.

"I think I do need to go," I said to Jennifer. Looking at her, I felt a pang of jealousy. Lee did not know it, but he had been the luckier one all along.

The spotlight followed me as I walked toward the ring, blinding me to everything outside its bright circle. I heard people applauding, but they sounded miles away. So did the announcer's voice. The bright lights above the ring made everything look black and white. The announcer, with his pale skin and black tuxedo, completed the effect.

Standing on the far side of the platform, Adam Boyd watched me calmly. The closer I came, the more things I noticed about him. From the steps along the side of the ring, I saw that his fingers ended in sharp points, almost like claws. *That's going to be a problem*, I thought. I also spotted the thick ridge of bone that ran under his eyebrows and into his hair. He was human, no doubt about that, but it was as if someone had engineered him for battle.

Once I stepped onto the platform, I found myself cut off from the rest of the world. I heard spectators shouting, but it blurred into a dull, indistinct roar. It sounded like waves on the beach. The announcer had already finished speaking and started out of the ring.

The flimsy shirt and shorts I had on would not slow me down in a fight, but they would offer no protection from Boyd's clawlike fingers. I looked at his claws, then expanded my glance to include the tightly muscled arms. There was a circular brantoo on his forearm. I only saw it for a moment, but I recognized the sweep of colors. "You're a SEAL?" I whispered to myself. Then the bell rang and thought turned into instinct.

Boyd immediately dropped into that cautious stance, his knees flexed and his clawlike fingers pointed right at me. His wide-set dark eyes fixed on my face and shoulders. He circled toward my left, moving so smoothly that he seemed to glide across the canvas.

My first instinct was to grapple. Growing up, I had studied judo and jujitsu. I'd won the orphanage wrestling title three years in a row. Boyd slipped around the arena so gracefully, however, that I doubted I would ever get close enough to knock him off his feet. Against that speed, my only chance was to keep him at long range, where he could not reach me. I jabbed with my left, keeping my right hand high to protect my eyes and chin.

Seeming to evaporate into the thick air, Boyd dodged my punch and lashed across my face with an open hand. Sharp fingers cut into my right cheek, just below my eye. Jumping back to get out of his range, I wiped the wound with the back of my hand. A thick layer of blood covered my knuckles.

That swipe across the cheek might have been a warning. Boyd could have just as easily sliced across my eye or throat. Even then, he paused a couple of feet away, allowing me to check my wound. I doubted he would be polite much longer.

I needed to rush the bastard after all. Win or lose, I needed to trap him quickly. If the fight wore on, Boyd could weave in and out, bleeding me dry until I could no longer defend myself. I looked into his brown eyes and assumed a boxer's stance with my fists high, guarding my face.

Boyd leaped forward with inhuman speed. Flinging himself at me, he suddenly veered to my right. I felt a white-hot pain across my face, but knew better than to check the damage. I had just been scratched above my right eyebrow, across the bridge of my nose, and down to the left side of my mouth. Blood started to pour from the gash on my forehead, stinging my eyes and blurring my vision.

With no other choice, I dived at Boyd, hoping to catch him off guard. Unsure whether I should keep my arms in front of my face for protection or grab for Boyd's knees, I kept my arms too low for protection and too close together for a good grab. I should have done one or the other; either would have been somewhat effective. Instead, I left myself open. Boyd swiped his talons across my forehead and pranced out of range.

Already out of breath, with my right eye swollen and stinging, I became vaguely aware of hooting and catcalls coming from the spectators. They could already see the fight coming to an end. So much blood had flowed across my right eye that I could not see through it. Boyd read the damage. He circled toward my right, working his way toward the hazy blind spot. I knew what he was doing, but I had no way to counter his move.

Perhaps, seeing the blood flow, Boyd had overestimated the damage he had caused. Though my right eye was blind, my sense of the ring was not. Hurt but not broken, I threw a blind backhanded fist that caught Boyd on the mouth and cheek. It was a powerful blow that left him temporarily senseless.

I spun into him, wrapping my arms around his chest. If I could throw him off his feet, I would take away his speed. We stood toe-to-toe, our chests pressed together. I cinched my arms around his and clamped them at the wrists. Our faces were so close we might have been kissing. As I heaved to lift him, I noticed that his skin was smooth, even under his eyes.

Small and compact, Adam Boyd weighed considerably more than I expected. I squeezed tighter. Straining my back and arms, I pulled him off the ground. I meant to throw him headlong into the cage walls, but he managed to slip his forearms around my back and stabbed those dagger fingers into my skin. I squeezed tighter and smashed my forehead down on the bridge of Boyd's nose.

Boyd was strong and fast, but he was not immune to pain. I had butted my forehead on the soft landing of his nose and felt the fleshy structure buckle under the force. When I saw Boyd's face again, his nose was purple and twisted so badly that one nostril pointed down and the other up. Blood gushed from both sides.

He did not give up. Digging his sharp fingers into my skin like corkscrews, he clawed into my back. His nails slit my skin and pressed into my ribs. He scratched deeper, twisting his fingers into the wounds. The pain and frustration made me scream.

I was losing blood and the pain sent white-hot flashes through my body. My head spun, but my thoughts remained focused. I reeled my head back and slammed my forehead back down against Boyd's badly crushed nose. His fingers loosened from my back. He was probably already unconscious, might even have been dead, but I did not wait to find out. I flipped the little bastard into the chain-link wall around the ring, smashing his face into it as hard as I could. His body slumped against the hard wire, and I dug my knee into his spine. He fell to the mat. Planting my knee across his throat, I threw three hard rights, battering the remains of his nose and left eye. A puddle of dark blood formed under his head.

My final punches were entirely wasted. Boyd did not move. He did not flinch or twitch. If an air bubble had not formed in the blood under his flattened nostrils, I would have thought I'd killed him.

Sighing heavily and taking no pride in what I had just done, I stood up. By that time the announcer stood in the ring. "Mary, mother of Joseph," he muttered, "I thought Boyd was going to kill you."

I started to say, "Looks like it was the other way around," but my knees buckled, and I swooned to the mat. The announcer quickly grabbed my hand and raised it. I heard the mob shouting hysterically outside the ring. Lights came on all over the arena, and I saw men hanging from the balconies. Lee ran into the ring and placed an arm under my shoulder.

"Vince," I said, unable to say any more.

"Wayson, that was amazing. Unbelievable! I've never seen anybody fight like that. No shit, Harris, you were friggin' amazing!"

TWENTY-THREE

I did not say good-bye to Kasara. On my way out of Sad Sam's Palace, I collapsed from loss of blood. Lee spent the morning driving Kasara and Jennifer to the airport and waiting with them for their plane. I spent the next two days drugged into peaceful oblivion with an IV needle in my arm.

Lee was in the room when I woke up on Sunday afternoon. "You going to stay awake this time?" he asked.

"Yeah," I said. "I'm awake."

"How do you feel?"

"Like my back is on fire." I could hear Lee, and I could see his blurred shape, but my sight remained fuzzy. "How long have I been out?"

"Going on three days," Lee said.

"Kasara?" I asked, feeling lower and lower by the second.

"She left two days ago," Lee said. "She wants you to call her. She was really worried about you."

I tried to sit up, but my blurred vision began to spin. I slumped back on my mattress, aggravating the lacerations on my back. I winced.

"That guy would have killed me," Lee said.

I thought about it. "He might have. He damn near killed me."

"He's damn near killed a lot of people," Vince said. My vision cleared as we spoke. I could see the features on Vince's face. I could make out details around the room. There were empty seats all around us, but Lee was sitting on the edge of my bed. We were in a hospital recovery room. There were empty beds on either side of me.

"The announcer said he had two hundred straight victories," Lee said.

I tried to sit up again. The tears along the small of my back stretched and I gritted my teeth. "I've had some time to think about that, too," I said. "My match might have been the little bastard's first fight."

"What are you talking about?" Lee sounded confused.

"Boyd didn't have any scars on his face," I said. "I got really close to him in that fight. He had baby skin—no scars, no cuts. Either he's so fast that in two hundred fights nobody ever hit him, or . . ."

"You think the announcer was lying?" Lee asked, slipping off the bed. The mattress bounced and I moaned. "Sorry. Want some water?" He picked up a plastic pitcher and poured me a cup.

"I think Adam Boyd is a clone," I said. "I think several Adam Boyd clones share that two hundred and zero record. Nobody could go two hundred fights in a ring like that without picking up scars."

"Two hundred wins and one loss," Lee corrected me. "You killed him last night. Maybe he doesn't scar. Wayson, having baby skin doesn't make you a clone. If it did, Jennifer would be a clone. I got really, really close to her and she didn't have any scars."

"Jennifer does not have a brantoo."

"What?"

"Boyd has a brantoo, right here," I said, pointing at my forearm. "He has the same brantoo the SEALs had on Ronan Minor."

"No shit," Lee said. "A midget SEAL clone. Why would they clone a midget?" We both knew the answer. We'd seen Boyd in action. Fast and small and agile, he was the perfect commando.

* * *

I had come on vacation to sort out my feelings, and that was pretty much all I did for the rest of my stay. I never left the hospital, never visited the beach. Lee wanted to stay with me, but I sent him away. It was my chance to think about undeserved promotions, friends lost in dark caves, and learning I was the last of my kind. My sort of misery did not love company.

I also needed to sort out what it meant to be a Liberator. Sergeant Shannon might have devised a cruel way to flush the Mogats out of their caves, but I doubt he wanted to massacre them. He was tough in drills, but hadn't I given one of my men two black eyes? And why had I assaulted the man—because he missed some shots? If Shannon had felt the same level of rage I had, he did a brilliant job of controlling it. Of course that could have been his religious side. From what I had seen, Shannon never missed Sunday services.

I continued to whale on Adam Boyd after I knocked him unconscious. Was I trying to kill him or was I just swept along by my own momentum? Maybe Congress was right to ban Liberators. What would a regular clone or a natural-born have done? I turned these thoughts over in my mind. Had Lee known about my maudlin musings, he would have regretted bringing me.

Nothing short of a medically induced coma could have protected me during the excruciating flight back to the fleet. Fortunately for me, we timed our trip around the fleet's movements. The *Kamehameha* was near the broadcast network, and our flight time was under ten hours.

My back hurt a little as they wheeled me out of the hospital. It hurt a little more when I climbed into Lee's rental car. I took some pain medication as we drove, and don't remember much after that.

By the time we got to Mars, I had run out of medicine. The transport from Mars was a military ship with stiff seats. I felt pinching in my back as I sat. What I did not realize was that that dull ache was actually a very acute pain that was masked by a slight overdose of painkillers.

"How are you feeling?" Lee asked.

"Not bad," I said. "I think I'm pretty well healed after all."

The transport struggled slightly as it left Mars's gravity. My seat shook, and I got my first hint that the medicine was beginning to wear off.

Lee looked at me. "You okay, Harris?"

I took a deep breath. My ribs expanded as I inhaled. It hurt. "I'll be glad to get back."

We approached the disc station. The lightning flashed and, of course, the transport shook. The shaking made my back hurt. We ended up passing through seven disc stations to reach the fleet. By that time, the small of my back felt swollen and some of the lacerations had begun to bleed.

As we approached the fleet, I looked out my porthole. "Lee. Lee, look at this. We must have boarded the wrong flight."

He leaned over me to have a look. "What are you . . ." Seeing what I meant, Lee stood up and opened the locker above our seats. He pulled out our flight information.

"Don't bother," I said. "I see the *Kamehameha*." The last Expansion-class fighter carrier in operation, the *Kamehameha* had a distinct profile in space.

As our shuttle glided toward the fleet, I could see four Orion-class star destroyers in the distance and the familiar sight of frigates circling like remora fish. Other ships floated about. I counted at least twenty Athens-class light missile carriers, oblong ships with diamond-shaped bows, hovering along one edge of the fleet. Five Interdictor-class battleships—bat-shaped ships that looked like miniature carriers—led the fleet.

"Looks like Admiral Thurston persuaded Klyber to expand the fleet. It's about time," Lee said.

I recognized other kinds of ships, too—ships I had heard about but never actually seen. We passed under a minesweeper—a short, sturdy ship that looked like a flying tunnel. Tiny communications ships buzzed around the fleet. The new ships had no armament at all, only large, retractable antenna arrays that pointed in every direction. Off in the distance, three huge barges sat perfectly still.

"I don't think Klyber had anything to do with this," I said.

"You can't order this kind of hardware without HQ's permission," Lee said.

As our transport landed on the *Kamehameha,* I told Lee about the news story I had seen. When I described seeing Klyber in the Senate, he shook his head. "And leave the fleet to an underaged outworlder?" He smiled. "Klyber wouldn't do that."

But we both knew that he had.

Under Bryce Klyber, the fleet ran efficiently. Under Thurston, it ran precisely. Prior to returning from leave of absence, I would have thought running efficiently and operating precisely meant the same thing.

When Lee and I reached the barracks, we saw a training schedule posted on the wall. The schedule had slots for the gunnery range, exercise, obstacle and field training, tactical review, and meals. Nights were generally open. With Admiral Klyber at the helm, sergeants evaluated their own platoons and trained them accordingly. Now that Thurston controlled the fleet, officers attended drills and gave out evaluations.

"Damn," said Lee. "Somebody is serious about this."

According to the schedule, the platoon was drilling when we arrived. Looking at that schedule, I felt a cold spot in my stomach. Yes, it addressed important issues like tighter discipline, but I could not ignore the gnawing feeling that officers had wrestled away my authority over my men.

"I wonder what else has changed," I said, as we went to stow our gear.

"Judging by this schedule, I don't think you are going to need to worry about marksmanship anymore," he said.

Maybe it was the emptiness of the barracks or maybe it was the pain in the small of my back. I looked around at the quarters. The beds were made, the lockers were neat. The air in the *Kamehameha* was dry and cool, and bright lights cast a dull glare in every inch of the room. I thought about the villa we rented in Hawaii. I thought about Kasara, her messy apartment, and the way she looked when I first saw her on the beach. I opened my locker, stowed my clothes, and saw my armor.

As I folded my duffel and placed it in the back of my locker, the clatter of boots cut through the silence. The hatch

opened and my men clambered in. I expected to see
Sergeant Grayson leading the group, so I was surprised
when a man I had never seen before bellowed out orders.
The man was a Liberator—First Sergeant Booth Lector.

Liberator clones, like Lector and me, stand just over six feet,
three inches tall—four inches taller than later models.
Something in Lector's demeanor made him seem even taller.
He seemed to fill the room. He had iron gray hair and a
bushy mustache that came down along the corners of his
mouth. His face, neck, and hands were covered with small
scars, including a bald strip through his right eyebrow. Seeing that particular scar, I became very aware of a similar one
I brought home as a souvenir from my fight with Boyd.

Upon seeing me in the office at the back of the barracks,
Lector dismissed the men. His mouth curled into a snarl, revealing two missing teeth. The Corps did not waste other
prosthetics on enlisted men, but even clones could get their
teeth replaced.

"Sergeant Harris," Lector said in a voice that was surprisingly high and stiff. "May I have a word with you?" He had
entered my office, a soundproof cubbyhole of a room with a
large window that opened to the rest of the barracks.

Glancing out the window, I saw the men in the platoon
gathering around Vince Lee. By the pats on the back and the
excited expressions, I could tell they were glad to see him.
This new sergeant had clearly worked them hard, and they
probably hoped that Lee and I would return things to normal.

Not all of the men came to see Lee, however. Several
younger-looking privates quietly stowed their rifles and armor. It was difficult to separate the new faces from the old in
an all-clone platoon, but I assumed these were replacements
who had arrived while Lee and I were away on leave.

"Sure," I said, feeling a bit off-balance. As I reached to
shut the door, Vince Lee, who had already changed into uniform, stepped into the office. He stood silently in the entrance.

"Perhaps we could find someplace more private to
speak," said Lector. "Why don't you come with me to the
gunnery range."

Standing behind Lector, where the sergeant would not

see him, Lee shook his head. His mouth hung slightly open, and his eyes fixed directly on mine. Vince looked nervous, but he need not have worried. I was not about to go to the range with this man. Lector's rage was primal and open.

"Look, Sergeant . . ." I realized that I did not know his name.

"Lector."

"Sergeant Lector," I said, "I just got back from two weeks' leave. Perhaps we can talk later."

"Excuse me, Harris," Lee broke in. "I'm sorry to interrupt. I heard that Captain McKay is looking for you."

"Maybe we can have that conversation when I get back," I said, glad to excuse myself. Lector gazed at me. There was an angry chill in his expression. He also had an unmistakable air of competence. Talking to Lector, I had the feeling that he was a man who accomplished whatever he set out to do, good or bad. I remembered how angry Shannon was the first time I met him, but Shannon was a cool breeze compared to Lector. Lector's anger seethed. It felt focused and vicious.

"We'll speak later," Lector snarled, turning sharply and leaving the office.

"That was scary," I said. I thought Lee had made up that story about McKay to help me escape Lector. That was not the case. Captain McKay really was looking for me. Stopping only to put on my cap, I left the barracks.

McKay worked out of a small office in an administrative section, two decks above our barracks. He was a young officer on the fast track. Few majors or colonels had offices so near the top brass.

But a lot had changed in the two weeks that I was away. Stepping off the elevator, I saw a small, wooden plaque on the door. The plaque was new and so was the name— "Lt. Colonel Stephen Kaiser." Not grasping the concept that McKay could have moved, I stood by the door puzzling the obvious. Kaiser opened the door. "Can I help you, Sergeant?" he asked.

"I was looking for Captain Gaylan McKay, sir," I said, feeling uncertain of myself.

"McKay?" he asked. "This used to be his office. I think they moved him two decks down."

"Thank you, sir," I said, with a salute.

Captain McKay had been knocked down. He now worked out of an office near the rifle range, in the Marine compound. "Like this office?" McKay asked as he opened the hatch to let me in. He made no attempt to hide the irritation in his voice.

"You've got a lot more space, sir," I said.

"Yes, it certainly is an improvement space-wise," McKay agreed, stepping back and allowing me in. "I've got more than twice as much floor space as I used to have." He looked around the room. I could not help but notice his sour expression. He pressed his lips together, and his eyes narrowed. "Couldn't ask for more space.

"Have a seat, Harris," McKay said, sitting down behind his desk. He stared hard at my face for a second. "You look like shit."

Without thinking about what I was doing, I reached up and rubbed the scar over my eyebrow. "I got in a fight, sir."

"A fight?" McKay said, sitting forward and looking concerned. "I hope I am not going to receive a misconduct report."

"No chance of that, sir," I said. "I entered an Iron—"

"You went to Honolulu, didn't you?" McKay interrupted.

"Yes, sir," I said.

"Didn't anybody warn you about going to Sad Sam's on Friday night?" McKay laughed. "You're lucky to be alive, Harris."

"Yes, sir," I said.

McKay smiled and leaned back in his chair. "One of the good things about being a Marine, Sergeant, is that you cover your scars with a helmet when you are on duty." He laughed. "I don't know who did that to your face, but I hope I never run into him."

"Yes, sir," I said.

"Do you know why I have been given this spacious new office?" McKay asked.

"No, sir," I said.

"It's a demotion," McKay said. "I've been moved down two decks and one million miles from command. I'm not sure if anybody has told you yet, but Admiral Klyber was transferred out."

I could understand the bitterness in Captain McKay's voice. Captain Gaylan McKay might have only commanded a couple of platoons; but under Klyber, he'd had access. He oversaw the color guard and had high-profile assignments. He attended briefings with generals and admirals. With Klyber no longer there to protect him, the officers that McKay had bypassed would make him pay dearly.

"Has Admiral Thurston taken command of all three Scutum-Crux Fleets?" I asked.

McKay laughed, and the full weight of his bitterness showed. "No. I'm not sure Klyber would have relinquished command to the boy. Admiral Huang is overseeing Scutum-Crux in the interim."

"Huang?"

"So far he's been running the Scutum-Crux Arm from DC." McKay seemed to take comfort from my shock. "Thank God for small miracles. I get the feeling Huang wanted this post all along. He and Thurston march in perfect lockstep. I think old Che Huang wanted Barry out and Thurston in before he took over. Now that he has what he wants, all we can do is sit back and see what he does with it."

"When did Admiral Klyber leave?" I asked.

"He was gone before we landed on Hubble," McKay said. "I did not hear about the change until a week ago. It's a different fleet now. Did you see the new ships when you flew in?"

"Yes, sir," I said. "I never thought I would see battleships in the Central Fleet."

"Yes," said McKay. "And minesweepers, and communications ships. You don't gin ships out of thin air. Huang and Thurston must have had them ready before Klyber transferred out.

"We got another present from Huang—new men. We're back up to two thousand three hundred sea-soldiers on board the *Kamehameha*."

"That's a step in the right—"

"And we have three new platoon sergeants. They're Liberators," McKay said.

"I met one," I said, "Sergeant Lector."

"That would be First Sergeant Booth Lector," McKay

said, rubbing the sides of his head as he spoke. "That one is a piece of work. He's probably the worst of them."

"The worst?" I asked.

"He took your platoon from Grayson a few days after you left. He came in the same day we got the new drill schedule. I don't suppose you've seen it."

"I saw it," I said.

"The drill schedule came down from Thurston's office. Admiral Thurston is an officer who never leaves anything to chance."

"Where did he find three Liberators?" I asked.

"Where did Admiral Thurston find the ships?" McKay asked, stepping out from behind his desk. He walked over to his shelves and looked at a model of the *Kamehameha*. "Where did he get the new ships? Where did he get the new officers? Harris, Thurston does whatever Huang wants, and Huang gives Thurston anything he needs. The bastards have an unholy alliance."

Turning back toward me, he added, "You need to watch your back around these Liberators, especially Lector. He's just plain nasty. Two of your men have ended up in sick bay after hand-to-hand combat training, and it turns out that both were sparring with him."

"How bad?" I asked.

"One had a dislocated shoulder. The other had a broken wrist. They both came in with concussions. Frankly, neither of them looked nearly as bad as you do."

McKay walked around his desk, then sat on the edge of it. "I'm afraid that I'm not going to be much help to you. Under the restructuring, I've been assigned to other duties besides your platoon."

"Understood, sir," I said.

"I've had a look at Lector's files," McKay said. "I'm surprised he hasn't been executed. Do you know anything about New Prague?"

I thought for a moment. The teachers at U.A. Orphanage #553 seldom talked about military crimes, but New Prague was too big to ignore. "That was the massacre, the one in which an entire colony was wiped out."

"Albatross Island?" McKay asked.

"The prison planet," I said.

"Did you ever hear about the uprising?"

"Every prisoner was killed," I said. "Even the guards were killed."

"Dallas Prime? Volga? Electra?"

"All massacres where U.A. forces lost control of their troops," I said. "Officers ended up in jail for those battles."

"Those were the first battles after the victory in the Galactic Central War. Those were the battles that convinced Congress to outlaw Liberators. Lector fought in every one of them. So did Marshall and Saul."

"Are Marshall and Saul the other Liberators?" I asked.

"Yes. Tony Marshall and Clearance Saul.

"I don't know where Thurston found three Liberators. It's almost like he collects certain kinds of soldiers. He's big on SEALs and Liberators."

"SEALs, sir?"

McKay returned to his seat. "Just before I got moved down hear, I heard that Admiral Thurston put in for ten full squads of SEALs. The way things are going, I think Huang has to be behind all of this, and that can't be good for either of us. I get the feeling that Admiral Thurston wants the remnants of Klyber's old fleet swept under the rug, if you know what I mean."

CHAPTER
TWENTY-FOUR

The *Kamehameha* separated from the rest of the fleet without any warning. One night I went to the rec room and watched the new ships through the viewport. When I returned the next day, all I could see was stars. Thanks to Thurston's mania for security, nobody knew where we were going. Even Vince's gym buddies were in the dark.

We spent three days traveling to the nearest broadcast disc station, during which time Command did not see fit to release information. My men started getting nervous. They were ready to fight, but they wanted to know something about the enemy. I had a hunch that we might attack the Japanese refugees of Ezer Kri. Huang and several politicians spent a lot of time trying to convince the public that these "ethnic purists" were a dangerous enemy. I did not think the Japanese were a threat and I did not want to hunt them down.

Under our restructured chain of command I no longer drilled my own men. Sergeant Lector ran the firing range and Marshall and Saul ran the training grounds. Needless to say, my platoon's performance spiked, and its morale dropped. Under Lector's guidance, our overall marksmanship score improved by 18 percent. Marshall and Saul coaxed an average of five seconds off the platoon's obstacle course times. But absenteeism rose, too. The men disliked drilling under the new Liberators. Some feigned illness. Two privates from another platoon showed up at sick bay claiming they had appendicitis. After an examination, the doctor determined they were fit. On the way back to their platoon, both men "stumbled." They limped back to the infirmary with broken ankles. I never heard if they broke their own ankles or if they were ambushed.

After passing through several discs, the *Kamehameha* headed into open space. We traveled for nine days before we finally received our briefing.

Captain McKay led our platoon into an auditorium for the session. I had never seen that particular chamber before. It was on the third deck, deep in swabbie country. No one turned us away, however. Twenty-three hundred Marines, all dressed in Charlie Service greens, filed into the semicircular auditorium, with its gleaming white walls and black, mirrored floor.

I did not recognize the Navy captain who conducted the briefing. A short, slender man whose red hair and ruddy skin contrasted sharply with his gleaming white uniform, the officer was undoubtedly part of Thurston's new regime. He paid little attention to us fighting men as we entered.

By the sound of things, I got the feeling no one else recognized the briefing officer either. A steady stream of anxious chatter echoed through the gallery. In the row behind me, a sergeant made a pointless attempt to quiet his men.

"Now listen up, sea-soldiers, and maybe we can teach you something new today," the captain called in a flat and well-practiced manner. He stood and switched on a holographic projector. The translucent image of a planet appeared on a screen above his head. The planet was shown in 3-D and seemed to bulge out of the screen as it rotated.

"Our subject today is real estate and how to protect your land against squatters. The Unified Authority owns the land." The captain broke every word into syllables and pronounced every syllable with equal emphasis. Rolling from his tongue, Unified Authority was pronounced "Un-if-ied [a half second pause] Au-thor-it-tay."

"The Unified Authority decides who uses the land. When

anybody steps on land without the express consent of the Unified Authority, they are squatters and trespassers. Do you understand me, sea-soldiers?"

The captain paused, giving us a chance to grasp his meaning.

"The planet you see twirling above my head is currently known as 'Little Man.' The reason I say 'currently known' is because the planet has not been colonized. When Little Man is officially settled, the Senate will rename it. But then, I am sure you all knew that."

Actually, I did not know that planets received new names when they were colonized.

The captain picked up a laser pointer from the podium and shined it into the image on the screen. The translucent planet turned solid wherever the red beam of the pointer touched. Some of the planet was covered with steel gray seas, but much of it was covered with green lands and dust-colored mountains. The laser pointer cut across the surface of the planet uncovering valleys and lakes.

"Gentlemen, Little Man has a breathable atmosphere. Little Man is the right distance from a star to grow crops. God made Little Man capable of sustaining life without help from Unified Authority science. We could land a colony on Little Man this very day and it would be self-sufficient within three years.

"Since our topic is real estate, sea-soldiers, I want you to know that this naturally life-sustaining atmosphere makes Little Man a very valuable piece of property. Do you understand me, sea-soldiers?"

"Sir, yes, sir," we shouted as a group.

"And they said you Leathernecks could not be taught," the captain muttered into his microphone.

"The only problem with Little Man is location." The screen dissolved into a map of the galaxy, with its six spiral arms. A glowing red ball showed on the outermost edge of the Scutum-Crux Arm. "Some of you sea-soldiers may not be familiar with astronomical maps. This is a map of our galaxy. As you can see, Little Man is located on the edge of the galaxy. In real estate terms, this is not a prime location." The captain pointed to the red ball with his laser pointer.

"The edge of the galaxy is called 'the extreme frontier.' For strategic reasons, the Unified Authority has not seen fit to settle the extreme frontier.

"It has come to our attention that squatters have trespassed on this valuable piece of property. Your government wants these extreme frontier trespassers evicted with extreme frontier prejudice.

"Do you understand me, Marines?"

"Sir, yes, sir!" we yelled, and we meant it. For all of his disdain and his condescending attitude, the captain knew how to communicate with Marines. Give us an enemy and aim us at said enemy, then let us do what we do best. Electricity surged through every man in the auditorium.

The image shifted to the surface of the planet. "This will be a land-op. The enemy has established a stronghold along the west coast of this continent. That means, sea-soldiers, you will launch your attack here." The pointer landed on a long stretch of beach. "You will establish a beachhead and force these squatters off our property. Do you understand me, Marines?"

"Sir, yes, sir."

"Once we have broken the enemy's backbone, we will proceed through these foothills, chasing the enemy inland. You will be provided with limited air support for that part of your mission." As the captain said that, a red trail appeared on the screen, marking the path we would take.

The map vanished from the screen and was replaced by the face of a middle-aged Japanese man with graying hair and wire-rimmed spectacles. "This is Yoshi Yamashiro. From what Captain Olivera tells me, you sea-soldiers have a score to settle with Mr. Yamashiro from Ezer Kri. For those of you with short memories, he is the man who looked the other way when one of your platoons was massacred.

"I may not be a Marine, but I understand that U.A. Marines always collect on debts. Is that correct?"

At those words the enthusiasm doubled. "Sir, yes, sir!"

"Sea-soldiers, the Unified Authority does not care if you

return with prisoners from this conflict. You are to carry out your duties with extreme prejudice. I should not have to say this to you Leathernecks, but I will. Do not hesitate to fire when fired upon. Do you understand me, Marines?"

"Sir, yes, sir!"

The briefing ended at 1800 hours. Lee and I stopped by the sea-soldier's bar on the way to the barracks. We found a table in the back and spoke quietly as we watched other men enter.

"Was I hearing things or were we just given permission to massacre everybody on that planet?" I asked, as the bartender brought us our beers.

"That's what it sounded like to me," Lee agreed.

"I may be mistaken, but isn't that considered a criminal act?" I asked.

"Shit, Wayson! We're trying to prevent a war. Those bastards ambushed a platoon. They shot down a frigate." He picked up his beer and downed it in two long swigs.

Never before had I noticed the dangerous side of Vince's programming. Vince Lee had received instructions from a superior officer, and he accepted those instructions without further examination. That was how his generation of clones was programmed to act.

"If the news of this massacre gets out, we may find our citizenship officially revoked," I said. "The Liberators who fought in the Galactic Central War were never allowed back into the Orion Arm for massacring prisoners on Albatross Island."

"I heard that they killed the guards," Lee said. "And how would that news get out, anyway? We're on the extreme frontier."

I knew about neural programming. Dammit, I knew that the new clones were programmed to take orders, but still I could not believe my ears. "You're not bothered by any of this?"

"Hold that thought," Lee said. He got up from the table and went to the bar. By that time, a pretty big crowd of non-coms and conscripts had drifted in. It took Lee nearly fifteen minutes to order four beers and return with the bottles.

"Okay," he said as he sat down. "I think you were just telling me your latest conspiracy theory."

"Get specked," I said. "Look, Lee, we're not going to do this drop in boats. If the plan is to trap and massacre the enemy, why not drop down on the land side of the foothills and chase the enemy into the sea."

"They're Japanese," Lee said. "Maybe they are good swimmers." He shrugged and downed his next beer.

"You think that's funny?" I asked.

"Calm down. Robert Thurston planned this invasion. The guy is a friggin' genius. He kicked Klyber's ass."

I put up my hand to quiet Lee. So many noisy Marines had come to the bar to celebrate by then that I could barely hear him anyway. But not all of the patrons were enlisted men. Captain McKay sat at a nearby table flanked by Lector, Saul, and Marshall.

"What is it?" Lee asked. He started to turn for a look, but stopped when I told him to sit still.

"It's McKay," I said. "He's sitting three tables from us with Lector and his boys." I had never spoken with Saul or Marshall, but they were cut from the same helix as Lector. The three ghouls spent their free time clustered together, speaking in quiet tones and bullying enlisted men. Just then, they were huddled around McKay.

"The *Kamehameha* was a better place before they transferred in," one of the privates from our platoon said as he joined us. "Got room at your table?"

"Have a seat," Lee said, smiling. His expression turned serious again quickly. "Those bastards are evil. I thought Shannon was bad. No offense, Harris, but you and Shannon are defective. Lector is the real Liberator. He almost killed a guy in Doherty's platoon today . . . sent him to sick bay with a dislocated shoulder and a broken collarbone."

"I don't think Captain McKay likes them," the private said. "I saw them come in together. McKay looked nervous."

Risking a quick glance, I peered around Lee and noticed the stiff way McKay sat in his chair. He stared angrily at Lector. Though all three of the new sergeants had the exact same face, I had no trouble telling them apart by their scars. Lector had that wide gash through his left eyebrow and a long, spiraling scar on his left cheek. Marshall had bald spots, probably the result of shrapnel, in his thinning white hair. Of the three, Saul might have had it the worst. The skin on his face was lumpy and blotched. He must have been burned in some kind of chemical fire. The scarring most likely covered his entire body.

McKay said something quietly. I could not hear him above the chatter in the bar. He placed his hand on the table and started to stand, but Lector placed a hand over McKay's and held him down. They traded more inaudible talk. Lector said something, and Captain McKay nodded. Lector removed his hand from McKay's, and the captain stormed away from the table.

Lee had turned to watch the exchange. "Look at them, Wayson," Lee whispered. "I'd kill myself if I were a clone."

"How you going to do it?" I asked distractedly.

Lee laughed. "I would not joke about that if I were you."

Apparently, Admiral Thurston believed one ship could handle our mission. The *Kamehameha* was almost alone in the quadrant. We had no accompanying frigates or cruisers; only one lone communications ship hovered nearby.

The logistics were simple enough. The *Kamehameha* carried fifteen armored transports, each of which could carry two platoons and supplies. Two trips per transport, and all twenty-three hundred Marines would be in position. My platoon, of course, got to land in the first wave.

As we prepared to take our place in the kettle, I found out what Lector and McKay were discussing in the bar. Captain McKay's command included the Twelfth and Thirteenth Platoons—Sergeant Grayson's. But it wasn't Grayson I saw at the head of the Thirteenth when I led my squad into the kettle. Lector paced the floor goading his men. Marshall and Saul sat at the stern of the ship.

"Harris." I turned and was surprised to see Captain McKay, wearing full armor with his helmet off, boarding the AT.

I saluted. "You're coming down in the kettle, sir?" This was the first time I had seen an officer ride with the ground fodder. Usually they stayed a safe distance away.

"Orders," McKay said, returning my salute. "Harris, you saw that they switched Grayson out of the thirteenth Platoon. Somebody placed all four Liberators in one company. I get the feeling they want to make a clean sweep."

"I get that feeling too, sir."

McKay signaled toward Lector with the slightest of eye motions. "Watch my back, Harris. I want to survive this mission. I don't want to die on Little Man."

"I will do what I can for you, sir." In my gut, I had the sinking feeling that it wouldn't be much.

We were both sergeants, but Booth Lector outranked me. I was just a sergeant. He was a first sergeant. In the noncommissioned ranks, Lector was just one step from the top.

"Okay, so now I am nervous," Lee said over a private interLink frequency. "What are Lector and Saul doing on our AT? What is McKay doing here? God, I hate Liberators."

"They shuffled the sergeants," I said. "And you are speaking to a Liberator."

"You're only a Liberator in theory," Lee said. "Lector's the real thing."

Several of my men removed their helmets and placed them on the floor. Judging by their expressions, I got the feeling that the grim mood had spread across the kettle. No one spoke. No one, that is, except Sergeants Lector, Marshall, and Saul. After liftoff, while the rest of the men quietly attached rifle stocks to their M27s or inspected the inventory in their belts, Lector and his friends continued to chat.

I sat with Lee in the back of the ship, whispering back and forth with him over the interLink.

"Why would McKay trade Grayson for those three?" Lee asked.

"I don't think McKay calls the shots anymore," I said. "He looked pretty nervous at the bar last night. He must have gotten a memo about the change in platoons right after the briefing. He probably took Lector to the bar to discuss the transfer.

"Remember when McKay tried to leave and Lector stopped him? McKay must have told them how he wanted to run things and found out that Lector and his pals had ideas of their own."

"You think they threatened him?" Lee asked.

"He's staying as far from them as he can. Lector probably said something about friendly fire or battlefield accidents."

"That cuts two ways," Lee said.

"It should," I agreed. Looking around the kettle, I knew that it did not. Standard clones were incapable of that kind of initiative; it was not in their programming.

A yellow light flashed over the cabin, warning us that we were broaching the atmosphere. The kettle shuttered. Men who were standing jolted forward but did not lose their balance.

Then the amber light turned red.

"What's that?" I asked.

"They must be firing at us," Lee said.

The men who had removed their helmets fastened them in place so that they would not smell the acrid ozone stench of the shields. In the vacuum of space, the shields were odorless. In an atmosphere, they burned oxygen and produced quite a stink.

The thick walls of the kettle muffled outside sounds. We heard the soft plink as bullets struck our hull. They must have been enormous bullets. The average M27 bullets turned to steam as they pierced the shields, but these shots had enough mass and momentum to tap the hull.

Whoever the "squatters" were, they had lots of firepower. Artillery shells burst all around us. All we heard in the kettle was a soft rumble as our shields disintegrated the shrapnel in the air. The bigger explosions created air pockets, causing our clumsy, armored transport to drop a few feet at a time.

The kettle shook violently. The lights flashed off, and we dropped at least a hundred feet before the lights kicked on again and the pilots regained control.

"They have a particle-beam cannon!" McKay yelled over the interLink.

"Take positions," I called to my men.

We were hit with another particle-beam barrage. That time, as we dropped, I heard the rat-a-tat sound of bullets striking the side of the ship. The shields were out, and bullets were hitting our unprotected hull.

There was a loud, hollow boom as a shell struck the top of the kettle, flopping the entire AT on its side. Two more struck. We were like a boxer who is out on his feet, taking shots with no way to protect himself.

In the flashing red emergency light, I saw a private jump to his feet and run toward the front of the cabin. As if out of nowhere, someone reached out a hand and smashed the man across the front of his helmet with so much force that the Marine fell to the floor. My visor identified Sergeant Marshall as he pulled back his M27 and knelt over the fallen man.

The lights came back on, and within moments, we were down on the beach.

The ATs landed in a row, their shields facing the bluffs at the top of the beach. The enemy's guns could not penetrate the barrier created by the shields—the only danger came from accidentally stumbling into them.

Under other circumstances the coastline might have been beautiful. A bright blue sky with puffy clouds stretched off to the horizon. We had landed on a beach with white sand and still, gray water. Ahead, through the electrified window of our shields, I saw sandy bluffs leading to coral rock foothills. The melting air in front of the shields blurred my vision, but I thought I saw men scurrying along the tops of the bluffs.

Then I heard the guttural growl of gunships. Two ships waddled across the sky, traveling over our heads and stopping over the enemy. They hovered in the air firing rockets and side-mounted chain guns. A huge explosion churned up a geyser of sand and a blinding green flash as the enemy's particle-beam cannon exploded.

Debris from the explosion flew in all directions. Concrete, dirt, and bits of rocks rained down around us. Fire burned at the top of the bluffs. The radioactive core of the particle-beam cannon might well have irradiated the enemy. The firefight seemed to have ended.

Though we did not have tanks with us, our transports

brought several cavalry units with gun-mounted, all-terrain vehicles—sprite four-wheel two-man buggies—with mounted chain guns and missile launchers. As the platoons organized behind the shields, the ATVs sped up the beach, kicking plumes of sand in their wake.

They drove in a zigzagging pattern, weaving toward the bluffs. When the first unit drove within a hundred yards of the hill, a single rocket fired. It was all so fast. I heard the hiss, saw the contrail, and the ATV vanished in a ball of flames.

The two gunships that had pulled back from the scene flew back and hovered over the area looking for targets. They continued over the area for minutes without firing. Whoever was down there was well hidden.

With no other options, we prepared to rush the bluffs. "Prepare for attack," McKay yelled over the interLink. The shield in front of our AT extinguished. For a moment I saw the distant hills clearly.

"Attack."

We started up the beach, running hard and kicking up loose sand. I kept my eye on the top of the bluffs, the enemy fortification. "Vince, do you see anything?" I called on a private frequency.

"If anybody's alive up there," Lee panted, "they're either wearing radiation armor or they glow in the dark."

The body gloves we wore under our armor would protect us from radiation poisoning, but technicians would need to neutralize the radiation before we could remove so much as a glove. In that kind of battle, radioactivity worked for us.

The gunships continued to float over the attack area looking for targets. They did not fire. Perhaps Lee was right. Perhaps some dying soldier flamed our ATV as his last act of defiance. As the first men reached the flaming, smoking remains of that ATV, gunfire erupted from the hillside.

"Drop!" I yelled over the platoon frequency.

Up ahead, machine guns fired so many shots into the first few men that their armor exploded, spraying blood and shredded plastic.

The gunships fired, but their shots were blind. The men on the ships must have been hunting human targets. Their heat sensors and radar would not locate motion-tracking drones.

"It's trackers," I said to Lee.

"It looks that way," Lee agreed.

"Think we can go around them?" I asked.

"It's not worth the trouble," Lee answered. "You watch, they're going to light up the hill."

As if on cue, the gunships fired incendiary rockets. One moment the bluffs were green and white, covered with sand and vines, the next they glowed ocher as chemical fires superheated the ground to well over eighteen hundred degrees. The flash heat vanished quickly; but wiring melted and munitions exploded as the bunkers at the far end of the beach turned into ovens. The air boiled with the crackle of bullets and the boom of artillery shells as the once-smooth ridge at the top of the bluffs convulsed into a jagged scar.

The problem with "lighting the hill" was that it took three hours for the heat to dissipate. Until the temperature went down, the most our ground forces could do was sit. Thurston sent Harriers and bombers to patrol the other side of the foothills, but the heavily forested terrain made flybys ineffective. We'd gone to Little Man to annihilate the enemy; but for the time being, all we could do was sit tight as the enemy fled to safety.

When we crested the hill, we saw the remains of a mile-long concrete bunker with yard-thick walls. With its ground cover blown to the winds, the concrete shell of the bunker lay exposed like a giant trench. Heat and explosions had blown the top off the structure, leaving a mazelike complex beneath. No other path was left for us, so we dropped down into the ruins.

I could not smell the outside world through my helmet. I sometimes smelled my own sweat after a long march or battle, but that was about it. Walking across the bunker's concrete floors, I thought I smelled death. It did not smell like burned meat. The dry and dusty scent of ash filled my helmet. Looking back, I am sure that I imagined the smell, of course I imagined it; but at the time, it seemed very real to me. The floor was littered with the cinder remains of wooden beams. It wasn't until we got deeper into the bunker that we discovered the bodies.

The charred remains of hundreds of men covered the floor in the center of the compound. There was no way to identify the bodies; they were scorched beyond recognition. They looked mummified, with all traces of hair burned away and skin that looked like parched leather. The fleshy, loose skin around their lips had shrunk, leaving their mouths with toothy grins. When one of my men accidentally stepped on a body, it crumbled into dust and bone beneath his boot.

"Think they're Japanese?" Vince asked, as we left a room in which four bodies had fallen on top of each other as if stacked.

"How could you possibly tell?" I asked. "What could these people have done to deserve this?"

Vince did not answer. That was the only reasonable response.

TWENTY-FIVE

"Harris, you're on guard duty," Lector said, as I climbed the ladder out of the bunkers.

"Aye," I answered, fighting back the urge to say more. I watched Lector swagger back to the front of the platoon, then switched interLink frequencies. "Lee, you there?"

"Sure," Lee said.

"Lector just gave me guard duty."

"That should be dull," Lee said. "Yamashiro will be light-years from here by now."

"If he was ever here," I said.

"Of course he was here," Lee said. He clipped his syllables as he spoke, something he did when he felt irritated. I knew better than to argue.

Thick forest covered the foothills ahead of us. Trees with green and orange leaves, so brightly colored they looked like gigantic flowers, blanketed the countryside. "Gather up," I called to my men, as we started for the forest.

The foothills stretched for miles. Beyond the hills, I could see the vague outline of tall mountains against the horizon. Somewhere between the forested hills and the mountains we would catch our enemy. "Let's roll," I said, after organizing my men.

Our course took us through the forest. The trees and boulders would have provided the right kind of cover for guerilla attacks. I scanned the landscape for heat signatures, but the trunks of the trees were ten feet in diameter. The rocks were thick and made of granite. I could not read a heat signature through such barriers. The light played against us, too.

Rays of sunlight filtered in through the trees. Bright, hot, and straight as searchlights, the beams of light looked like pillars growing out of the floor of the forest. And they were hot, as hot as a human body—nearly a hundred degrees. When I looked at one of the rays of light with my heat vision, it showed orange with a yellow corona on my visor, the same signature as an enemy soldier.

I pinged for snake shafts and found nothing, but that did little to calm my nerves. Fortunately, our scouts located enemy tracks. Hundreds of people had fled the bunkers, trampling ferns and shrubs as they rushed through the trees. Tracking the escapees posed little challenge, but the wilderness gave us other headaches. The overgrowth slowed our ATVs. Obviously, Harriers and gunships were out of the question. We had to send scouts ahead on foot. Five of our scouts did not return when we broke for camp that evening.

We stopped in a mile-wide clearing that would be easy to guard. At night, Little Man cooled to a comfortable sixty-five degrees. When I scanned the serrated tree line with heat vision, it seemed to hold no secrets. I saw the orange signatures of forest animals moving around the trees.

Every few hours, at uneven intervals, a gunship traveled around the perimeter of the clearing. I sat at my guard post, hidden behind a hastily built lean-to made of logs, clods of grass, and rocks, peering out across the flatlands at the trees. The night sky had so many layers of stars that it shone milky white. I realized that not all of the stars were in our galaxy. We were at the edge of known space.

A gunship rumbled over the treetops, its twin tail engines firing blue-white flames. Moonlight glinted on the ship's dull finish as it circled slowly across my field of vision. Traveling at a mere twenty miles per hour, it moved with the confidence of a shark circling for food. Switching the lens in my visor to heat vision, I watched animals flee as the gunship approached. A stubby bird, built a bit like an owl but with a seven-foot wingspan, launched from the trees and flew toward me. I could not see the color of its plumage with heat vision, and I could not see the bird at all when I switched to standard view.

Guard duty left me with plenty of time to roll evidence over in my mind. I did not think we were there to massacre Japanese refugees from Ezer Kri. They would not have had time to build the complicated bunker system on the beach.

The Morgan Atkins Separatists seemed a more likely target. I did not know how the Japanese could have gotten off Ezer Kri. They never could have traveled this far. I did not know what the Mogats would want on a planet like Little Man, but I knew they had transportation. They had their own damn fleet. Still, why would the Mogats colonize a planet that was so far from civilization? As I understood it, the Mogats never populated their own planets. They sent missionaries to colonize planets and attracted converts. But there was nobody to convert in the extreme frontier.

Just like Lee predicted, the night passed slowly.

We found three of our missing scouts early the next morning.

Packing quickly before sunrise, we continued through the woods. The trees in that part of the forest stood hundreds of feet tall. They stood as smooth and straight as ivory posts, with only a few scraggly branches along their lower trunks. Perhaps that was what made the scene so terrible—the almost unnatural symmetry of the primeval woods.

Walking in a broad column, we turned a bend and saw two dwarf trees with thick, low-hanging branches that crisscrossed in an arch. These trees stood no more than forty feet tall, but the spot where their branches met was considerably lower. A wide stream of sunlight filtered in around them, bathing them with brilliant glare and shadows.

Three shadowy figures dangled from the branches like giant possums. A quick scan of the forest floor told us that the bodies were our missing scouts. Each man's armor and weapon sat in a neat pile beneath his lifeless carcass.

We knew our scouts had died by hanging even before we cut their bodies down. The enemy had captured them, stripped them of their armor, and summarily executed them as war criminals.

"I want those trees destroyed," a major ordered, as we cut down the bodies. A demolitions man strapped explosives around the trunks. As we left, I heard a grand explosion and turned to watch as the forty-foot trees collapsed into each other.

The enemy had time to leave trackers along the trail, but trackers were ineffective in such rough terrain. They also left mines and a few snipers behind. The mines were useless; we spotted them easily. The snipers, however, used effective hit-and-run tactics as they targeted our officers. We began our march with fifteen majors and three colonels. By nightfall, two of the colonels and six of the majors were dead. When I saw McKay late that afternoon, he was surrounding himself with enlisted men.

"You holding up okay after that all-nighter?" Vince's voice hummed over the interLink.

"Bet I'm asleep before anyone else tonight," I said, unable to stifle a yawn.

Regrettably, Lee had not contacted me on a direct frequency. "You'd lose that bet," Lector interrupted. "You're on guard duty tonight."

"Sergeant, you cannot send a man on guard duty two nights in a row," Lee said.

"Are you running the show now, Lee?" Lector asked. I heard hate in his voice.

"Back off, Vince," I said.

"Wayson . . ."

"Stay out of this," I hissed.

On a private channel, Lee said, "I hate specking Liberators."

So did I.

We reached the edge of the forest in the late afternoon. There we discovered that our air support had been busy.

The still-unidentified squatters had built a town large enough for a few thousand residents just beyond the woods. It had paved roads and prefabricated Quonset-style buildings.

If they had put up flags, the place would have looked like a military base.

Our fighters struck during the night, shredding the town. I saw shattered windows, collapsed roofs, and melted walls. What I did not see was bodies.

"Sarge, do you think this was their capital city?" one of my men asked.

I did not answer. "Fall in," I said over the platoon frequency. "Get ready. If we're going to run into more resistance on this planet, it's going to start here."

The town was also a likely place to find out the "squatters'" identity. We would find computers in the buildings. Perhaps we would find more. With our guns drawn and ready, we organized into a long, tactical column with riflemen and grenadiers from Lector's platoon guarding our flanks.

We waded toward town. Lee's squad took point, moving cautiously in a group that included a rifleman, a grenadier, and a man with an automatic rifle. They moved in slowly, pausing by fences and hiding behind overturned cars. With every step it became clearer that the enemy had abandoned the city before our fighters attacked.

Most of the cars lay flipped on their sides, their front ends scorched from missile hits or fuel explosions. Smoke and fire had blackened the windows of several vehicles. I kicked my boot through one car's windshield in search of bodies but found none.

The first building we passed was a two-story cracker box with only two windows on its fascia. The facade was untouched, but a laser blast had melted a ten-foot chasm in a sidewall. Metal lay melted around the gaping hole like the wax bleeding from a candle. The heat from the laser must have caused an explosion. The windows of the building had burst outward, spraying glass on the street. Though I could not feel the glass through my boots, I heard it splinter as I walked over it.

The firefight began with a burst of three shots. Bullets struck the ground as Lee and his rifleman stepped around a derelict car. The bullets missed. Lee and his rifleman dropped back for cover and returned fire.

The enemy had taken position in the ruins of a building that might have been a latrine. Pipes wrapped the sides of the small structure, and its walls were thick. The gunmen opened fire. I could see muzzle flashes.

"Harris, report," Captain McKay ordered.

"We're under fire, sir," I said. "It seems like it's just a few men hidden in a latrine. We should have the situation under control shortly."

"Pockets of resistance," McKay said. "They're trying to slow us down. I'm getting reports of small firefights on every street. Let me know when you have the situation handled."

"Aye, sir," I said.

"Lee, how are you doing up there?" I asked, changing frequencies.

"These guys can't shoot for shit," Lee said. "Twenty yards away, tops, and . . ." He stopped talking as a long volley of shots ricocheted off the ground around him.

Bang. Bang. Bang. Bang. Bang. Five distinct reports, single shots from an M27 that cut right through the clatter of machine-gun fire. Lector's riflemen had flanked the enemy, slipped into the building behind them, and shot them in their hiding holes. One of the riflemen walked to a window and signaled that all was clear. His strategy was a textbook tactical advance.

"Enemy contained," Lector called in, over the interLink.

I spotted a stairwell that ran below ground on the other side of the street. "Lee, take my position."

"Where are you going?" he asked as he let his squad walk ahead.

"I see a door that needs opening," I said as I peeled off from the column with two of my men in tow. We ran across the street and took cover behind a brick wall.

The stairwell looked like it might lead to a bomb shelter or a subway station. It was wide enough for three men to run side by side. One of my men did a run by, peering down the stairs, then rolling out of range. He stood and took a position at the top of the stairs, signaling that the entry was clear.

There were no windows in the concrete walls lining the stairs, just a seven-foot iron door with an arched top. I ran down the stairs and hid by the hinged side of the door. One of my men took the other side. As I pulled the door open, he counted to five then swung in, sweeping the scene with the muzzle of his rifle.

"Clear," he said.

I followed him through the door.

"Jesus, Mary, and Joseph," the third man in my party said as he followed us into the structure. We had entered a tactical command room. File cabinets lined the walls. Several maps lay open on a table in a corner of the room. I checked the maps for traps, then leafed through the stack.

The first map showed the names and locations of every military base in the Scutum-Crux Arm. The next map showed a complex system of dots and lines overlaying a map of the galaxy. A sidebar showed an enlarged view of the Sol System. When I saw a red circle surrounding Mars, I realized that it was a map of the broadcast network.

"Don't touch anything," I said to my men. It was too rich a trove. It had to be rigged. We would leave it for the experts in Intelligence.

Captain McKay told me to nap while the rest of the men set up camp. I found a shaded corner between a tree and a stone wall. Removing my helmet, I lay on my side in the cool grass and let my mind wander.

I thought about that underground map room with its diagram of the broadcast network. There was nothing top secret about the disc locations, but seeing them charted in an enemy bunker made me nervous. Those discs served as the Unified Authority's nervous system. An attack on them could bring the Republic to its knees.

But why would anybody want to bring the Republic to its knees? The Senate allowed member states tremendous latitude. Breaking up U.A. infrastructure would end the ties of humanity that connected the various territories. Take away the Unified Authority, and the outer worlds would be forced to survive on their own.

In my mind's eye, I saw myself walking along a long corridor. Imagination turned into fitful dreams as I reached the first door.

* * *

Night had fallen by the time Lee woke me for guard duty. He led me to the edge of town and pointed to an overturned truck. "That's your station for the night," he said. He slipped me a packet of speed tabs. "I borrowed these from the medic. Don't use them unless you need them," he said.

I took my position hiding behind a crumpled-up bumper. Though I needed more sleep, I liked the solitary feel of guard duty. It gave me a chance to consider the day and play with ideas in my head. I had been on duty for two hours when Lector came to check on me. "See anything, Harris?"

"No," I said.

"Keep alert," he said. He lit a cigarette as he turned to leave.

"I don't get it," I said. I was tired and angry. I heard myself speaking foolish words and knew that I would later regret them; but at that moment, I no longer cared. "What the hell did I ever do to you?"

Lector listened to my question without turning to look at me. Then he whirled around. "You were made, Harris. That's reason enough," Lector said coldly. "Just the fact that you exist was enough to get Marshall, Saul, and me transferred to this for-shit outfit."

"I had nothing to do with it," I said.

"You had everything to do with it," Lector said. "You think this is a real mission? You think we are going to capture this entire planet with twenty-three hundred Marines? Is that what you think?"

I did not know what to say.

"They'd forgotten about us," Lector said. "Saul, Marshall, me . . . Nobody in Washington knew that there were any Liberators left. The brass knew about Shannon, but there was nothing anybody could do about him. Klyber kept him nearby, kept a watchful eye on him. Nobody could touch Shannon with Klyber guarding him. As far as everybody knew, Shannon was the last of us.

"Then you came along, Harris—a brand-new Liberator. You weren't alone, you know. Klyber made five of you. We found the others. Marshall killed one in an orphanage. I killed three of them myself. But Klyber hid you . . . sent you to some godforsaken shit hill where no one would find you. By the time I did locate you, you were already on the *Kamehameha*.

"I . . ." I started to speak.

"Shut up, Harris. You asked what's bothering me, now I'm going to tell you. And you, you are going to shut your rat's ass mouth and listen, or I will shoot you. I will shoot you and say that the goddamn Japanese shot you."

I believed him and did not say a word. I also slipped my finger over the trigger of my M27.

"The government hated Liberators. Congress wanted us dead. As far as anyone knew, we were all dead. Then you showed up. I heard about that early promotion and wanted to fly out and cap you on that shit hill planet. I would have framed Crowley, but Klyber transferred you before I could get there.

"Next thing I know, you're running missions for that asshole Huang. Shit! Huang was the reason we were in hiding in the first place. As soon as I heard that you'd met Huang, I knew we were all dead. Once he got a whiff of a Liberator, he would go right back to the Pentagon and track down every last one of us.

"And here we are, trying to take over a planet with twenty-three hundred Marines. This isn't a mission, Harris, this is a cleansing. This is the last march of the Liberators; and if they need to kill off twenty-three hundred GI clones to finish us, it all works out fine on their balance sheets. Clones are expendable.

"You want to know what I have against you, Harris? You are the death of the Liberators."

"Oh," I said, not knowing what else to say.

"Now watch your post," Lector spoke in a calm voice that made his anger all the more frightening. "We're pushing into that valley tomorrow. Whoever we're hunting on this god-damned planet, we'll find them in there." Having said his piece, Lector turned his back on me and left. He tossed the butt of his cigarette behind him. The tiny, glowing ember bounced and slowly faded.

Klyber had made five Liberators? Klyber had me sent to Gobi to protect me? It made sense, I suppose. When I thought of Booth Lector, I felt both sympathy and revulsion.

Tabor Shannon and Booth Lector shared the same neural programming, but it controlled them in different ways. Lector was addicted to violence and self-preservation. He was cruel and brooding. Shannon might have been a white knight, but I saw him as flawed. He lived his entire life on a quixotic mission to protect a society that despised him.

Earlier that evening, I had told myself that the Unified Authority bound mankind together. However, as I thought about it again, I questioned the benefits of being tied to mankind.

CHAPTER
TWENTY-SIX

Having slept for approximately two hours over the last two days, I felt sluggish and dizzy when Vince Lee led me back to camp. The ground seemed to shift under my feet, and I had trouble walking in a straight line. I considered taking the meds Lee had given me, but decided against it. Luding would keep me awake, but it would probably leave me jumpy when I needed a clear head.

And I definitely needed a clear head. The officers monitoring our progress from aboard the *Kamehameha* did not wait for sunrise before sending us into the valley. There was no trace of sunrise along the horizon when we grabbed our rifles and set off.

Walking in squads of five, we left the town and started into the valley. There the terrain came as something of a surprise. I expected grass, trees, and gently sloping hills. What I saw was a glacial canyon with steep, craggy walls. A well-trampled path led along the side of the canyon. The trail was wide enough for a squad or maybe a platoon, but not an entire regiment.

Observing the scene from the rim of the canyon, using my night-for-day lenses, I felt an eerie shutter of déjà vu. It was like returning to Hubble. The thick layer of fog on the canyon floor only added to the illusion.

"At least we won't need to go looking for the bastards," Captain McKay said as he moved up beside me.

Switching to heat vision, I saw what he meant. About two miles ahead of us, hundreds, maybe thousands, of orange dots milled around the valley floor.

"Look at them," I said. "Think that's what's left of the Japanese?"

"Obviously not," McKay said. "Whoever they are, they're waiting for us. They're dug in tight, armed, and waiting for us. Remember when I asked you to watch my back? I know you're beat, Harris, but if you have any Liberator fire left in you, get me out of this alive."

"Yes, sir," I said, though I had little hope to offer. If Lector planned on killing friendlies, his first bullet would have my name on it.

Our assault took place in three stages. As the sun rose over the far edge of the canyon, we "assembled." Our officers, the few who had survived the previous day's snipers, surveyed the field and assigned routes to each platoon. From there, as the rising sun melted the fog on the canyon floor, we traveled down the steep walls. That was the next stage of the assault, the "attack point." Then we fell into formation and made our last preparations.

The terrain was flat and empty. Jeeps, ATVs, and tanks would have been effective at that point, but nobody offered to airlift them in. Admiral Thurston wanted an infantry strike. With our light artillery preparing its positions, we started our advance.

A wide river must have once run across the valley. Its long, smooth, fossilized trail offered excellent placement for men with mortars.

Having left the artillery behind, we divided into two groups. The majority of the men formed a column that would attack the squatters head-on. One lone platoon would be assigned to move along the south side of the canyon and attempt to flank the enemy.

I was not surprised when I heard from Captain McKay. "Harris, your platoon is covering the flank."

"Who signed us up for that?" I asked, though I knew the answer.

"Lector recommended you. He's pretty much running this show. Everybody is afraid of him."

"Are you coming with us?" I asked.

"No," McKay said. He wished me luck and signed off.

A pregnant silence filled the canyon as the two-thousand-man column started forward. The squatters began firing long before the column was in range. Only snipers with special rifles would be effective at such a distance. The squatters had a few snipers, of course, but they seemed to be out of commission at the moment.

My platoon started its route just as our artillery units began lobbing mortars. The enemy had the tactical advantage of choosing the field, but our artillery soon battered their positions.

I led my men in a fast trot toward the south edge of the canyon. Hidden by a slope in the terrain, we slipped forward undetected. As we closed in, I hid behind some sagebrush and spied on the enemy position.

The main column remained just out of range as the bombardment continued. Shells exploded, sending swirls of silt dust and smoke in the air. Any moment now the shelling would stop, signaling the column to pin the enemy down while we closed in beside them.

Before we could attack, the squatters retreated. They abandoned their position and ran. I watched them from behind a sagebrush blind—thousands of men running toward distant canyon walls. I thought they were running from our mortars, but that wasn't the case.

Far overhead, another battle was taking place. Robert Thurston, the master tactician, had lied to us about everything. These "squatters" were Mogat Separatists; and while Little Man was not exactly Morgan Atkins's Mecca, the planet was a Separatist stronghold.

Giving us bad intelligence, Thurston landed our forces by the Mogats' weakest flank. With minimal air support and the element of surprise, we broke their defenses and chased their unprepared army. But reinforcements would soon arrive. Admiral Thurston, who viewed clones as equipment of no more value than bullets or tank treads, used us as bait to lure the Separatists into a counterattack.

As we chased Mogats on the surface of Little Man, four self-broadcasting battleships appeared around the *Kamehameha*. Thurston barely managed to raise his shields before they opened fire. With the dreadnoughts battering her shields, the *Kamehameha* headed toward a nearby moon.

The army that joined the Mogats at the far end of the canyon outnumbered us five to one. Their tanks and jeeps were forty years old. They drove antiques, we had the latest equipment; nonetheless their antiques would be very effective against our light infantry.

The Mogat army wore red armor. Red, not camouflaged, no attempt was made to blend in. They poured down the rim of the canyon like fire ants rushing out of an anthill, their armor glinting in the bright sunlight. Our officers were alert. The column quickly collapsed into a defensive perimeter by taking shelter behind the side of the riverbed.

"Holy shit," Lee screamed. "We'd better get down there."

"Hold your position, Lee," I said.

I frantically contacted Captain McKay. "Captain, I'm coming to get you out of there."

The Mogats were at the bottom of the canyon and coming fast. Poorly aimed shells from their tanks and cannons hit the ground well wide of their mark.

"Do they see your position?" McKay shouted.

"I doubt it," I said.

"Get your men out of here, Harris."

From where I lay, about three hundred yards from the action, the battle seemed to take place in miniature. I saw our men hiding in the dirt and the enemy running forward. The enemy looked poorly trained, but that would not matter with their numerical advantage.

The Mogat gunners figured out the range and their shells began pounding the riverbed. I saw a shell hit a group of men, flinging their bodies in different directions. Back behind the brunt, our light artillery returned fire far more effectively, hitting the advancing sea of enemy soldiers time and again. It didn't matter. There were far too many of them for a few shells to matter.

Squads of fighters and six destroyers raced to the *Kamehameha*'s aid. In the distance, the *Washington* and the *Grant,* ironically the two ships Thurston used to defeat Bryce Klyber in their simulated battle, remained stationed behind the cover of the distant moon. They had slipped in unnoticed two days before the *Kamehameha* arrived.

Self-broadcasting is a complex process that takes time and calculation. Thurston's ships counterattacked swiftly. Before the battleships could broadcast themselves to safety, Thurston's Tomcats and Phantoms swarmed them. His destroyers arrived moments later, blasting the battleships with cannons that disrupted their shields. The Mogats had enormous ships, but their technology was forty years old, and they did not have engineers who could update it.

The surprise attack succeeded. Two of the battleships exploded before returning fire. The third staged a weak defense, managing to demolish several fighters and dent one destroyer before exploding. The last Mogat battleship turned and ran. The officers commanding the lumbering ship could not have hoped to outrun the fighters. They must have thought they could buy enough time to broadcast to safety.

Closing in from the rear, a destroyer fired several shots at the battleship's aft engine area. The ship's rear shields failed, and several of its engines exploded just as it entered Little Man's atmosphere.

The Mogats poured into the valley like a tidal wave. They would not need stealth or weapons to flank our two-thousand-man invasion force—it almost looked as if they planned to trample us. But U.A. Marines do not give up without a fight.

"What do we do?" one of my men asked as I returned.

"McKay ordered me to retreat," I said.

Hearing that it was an order, my men immediately complied. Without a word, they turned and started back. Then Lee noticed that I did not follow. "Harris, what are you doing?"

"I want to get McKay out of there," I said. "I promised I would watch his back."

"Wayson, you have got to be joking," Lee said. "Take another look. He's probably dead by now."

I crawled up for one last look. I doubted that he had died yet, but his time was probably just about up. The Mogats had closed in on our front line and overwhelmed it. On one side of the battle, a group of about fifty men formed a tight knot and charged the enemy head-on. The tactic they took gave them the element of surprise. They broke through the Mogats' front line and pushed deep into their ranks. It was a gutsy move, but doomed to fail. As they fought their way toward an open field, they took more and more casualties. I did not stay to see if any of them survived the charge.

In the center of the battle, the Marines put on one hell of a show. Our riflemen pinned down pockets of enemy Mogat soldiers and our artillerymen lobbed a continuous arc of mortar fire. Despite their efforts, there was no denying the superiority of numbers. By the time I turned to follow my men to safety, it looked like half of our invasion force was dead or wounded.

"Can we go now?" Lee asked, sounding anxious.

I did not want to leave. Whether it was programming or upbringing, my instincts were to fight to the end. I sighed as I climbed to my feet. "Okay, Marines, let's move quickly!" I shouted, in my best drill sergeant voice. Most of my men were already a hundred yards ahead.

The air still rang with gunfire, but the amount of shooting had slowed considerably. By the time we reached the far end of the valley floor, I only heard the sporadic bursts.

We sprinted for the path leading up the far wall. The path twisted, and it left us more exposed than I would have liked, but I thought it would be safer than stumbling up the steep slopes.

By then we were several hundred yards from the battlefield. If we could just reach the top of the ridge, without being seen . . . "Stay low, move fast. Any questions?" I said to my men.

I led the way, rifle drawn, shoulders hunched, running as fast as I could. If there happened to be a few enemy soldiers at the top of the trail, I thought I might stand a chance of picking them off.

My lungs burned and my mouth was dry, but I had shaken off the fatigue I felt earlier that morning. The adrenaline rush of battle had woken me far more effectively than any meds ever could have. The muscles in my legs tingled and my head was clear as I continued up that dusty course at full speed.

The path started at a gentle angle, no more than ten degrees. A few yards up, however, it took a steep turn. I felt fire in my calves and growled.

I no longer heard gunshots, but what I heard next was far more frightening: the whine of ATVs. Turning a bend in the path, I paused and saw four trails of dust streaking along the valley floor in our direction.

"Move it! They're coming!" I shouted to my men. I swung my arms in a circle to tell my men to run faster, and I slapped three men on their backs as they ran past me. "Move it! Move it! Move it!"

The ATVs stopped a few yards from the base of the trail. As the last of my men ran past me, I saw four men climbing off their vehicles. They had rifles slung over their shoulders. "They'll never catch us," I said to myself as I turned and sprinted.

I was just catching up to Adrian Smith, one of the new privates who had transferred in while I was in Hawaii. He was a slow runner; I thought that I might need to stay with him to coax him on. That was what I was thinking as the bullet smashed through his helmet, splashing brains and blood against the side of the hill. The sound of the gunshot reverberated moments after Smith fell dead.

Ahead, up the trail, three more men fell just the same way. A single shot to the head followed by the delayed report of the rifle. The men at the base of the trail never missed a shot.

"Everybody down!" I yelled. "Snipers!"

They were using our tactics. The snipers pinned us down. Across the valley, hundreds of soldiers were headed in our direction. If we did not get up the ridge quickly, we would never make it up at all.

"Lee, take them up the hill," I called as I darted behind a rock.

"What are you doing?" Lee said.

"That is an order, Corporal."

Below me, one of the snipers saw Lee get to his feet. He swung his rifle. As he trained on the target, I shot him with a burst of rapid-fire. All three bullets hit the sniper before he fell.

Another sniper returned my fire. The other two picked off several more of my men.

I crawled along the ground, steadied my rifle, and rolled to one knee. Two of the snipers fired at me before I could squeeze off a shot. The third hit another of my men. In the background, I saw the Mogat army. They were almost here. Ducking out of their sight, I lobbed a grenade. The blast kicked dust into the air. I rose to have another look, then ducked back down quickly.

For some reason, the Mogats had stopped. Many were looking at the sky. Whatever had distracted them was not important enough to stop the snipers from taking shots at me. Three bullets zinged the ledge near my head.

I rolled onto my back, then I saw it—a dark gray triangle dropping quickly through sky. It looked like a capital ship, but capital ships were not designed to fly in atmospheric conditions.

Whatever it was, the triangle left a thick white contrail in its wake. The smoke billowed out in tight pearls that spread and congealed into a smooth strand of cloud. At first, the ship fell straight down, then it managed to catch itself.

And, as it flew closer, I noticed that there were dozens of smaller ships buzzing around it. From where I lay, the scene looked like a hive of bees attacking a bear cub as it tried to run away.

The valley seemed to shake under the echoing rumble of the big ship's engines. The ship was dropping lower and lower. The fighters that surrounded the ship continued to pick at it with lasers and rockets.

"Harris, get out of there!" Lee screamed. "That thing is going to crash."

Flames burst out of the front and rear of the ship as it dropped like a shooting star. A few bullets struck the ledge below me as I jumped to my feet, but I no longer cared. I sprinted as hard as I could, turning corners and skidding but staying on my feet.

The battleship slammed into the far end of the valley sending a shock wave, flames, radiation, and debris. Nearly one mile from the explosion, the shock wave hit me so hard that it tossed me through the air and into the canyon wall. The blast knocked the air out of my lungs, and my head rang with pain.

Dazed and barely able to stand, I continued up the path, fighting the urge to lean against the canyon wall for support. I could hear nothing except the sound of my breathing. The audio equipment in my helmet had gone dead. I was panting. My legs were tight. I placed my hands on my thighs and pushed, hoping it would help me run.

Below me, the canyon was consumed with molten fire. Looking down the slope was like staring into Dante's "Inferno." The battleship had skidded across the canyon, cutting a deep gash and spewing fiery fuel and radioactive debris in every direction. The very earth around the ship seemed to combust in an explosion of flame, smoke, and steam. I did not see any people in my quick glimpse, but I saw the remains of an upturned tank as it melted in that blazing heat.

Even one mile from the crash site, the heat from the fires would have cooked me alive if it hadn't been for my armor. For the only time in my career, I felt heat through my body glove.

As I reached the top of the trail, Lee and another man grabbed my arms. My legs locked and I started to fall, but they held me up. I could tell that they were trying to speak to me, but I heard nothing through my dead audio equipment.

Lee and the private lowered me to the ground. I fell on

my back and stared into the sky. Above me, a U.A. Phantom fighter circled in triumph. An entire regiment had been demolished; but for Robert Thurston, Little Man was a triumph indeed.

TWENTY-SEVEN

Growing up in an orphanage, I sometimes imagined that I had parents on another planet looking for me. In my fantasies, my parents kept a room on the off chance that I would someday return. The room would have a crib, a bicycle, and closets filled with toys. Until they found me, my parents would seal that room, entombing its contents. In my mind's eye, I saw the room as dark and filled with shadows. Dust covered the toys and crib.

Over the years, my childhood dreams were replaced by adult realities, and I forgot about that room until I returned to the *Kamehameha* with only six of my men. When I entered our vacated barracks, I experienced the very emotions that my imaginary parents would have felt whenever they visited my imaginary room.

Of the twenty-three hundred men sent down to Little Man, only seven survived. There were no wounded. That was the reality, and I kept on realizing it again and again.

Lee and I did not speak much when we returned from Little Man. We were not mad at each other, we simply had nothing to say. We returned to our living quarters with five privates in tow and the rows of empty bunks looked like a cemetery. You can shake a jar filled with marbles and never hear a sound. Take all but a few of those marbles out, and those last few will rattle around in the empty space. We rattled around corridors once teeming with Marines. We were the ghosts.

Captain Olivera allowed us to remain in our barracks, but he closed down the mess hall, the bar, and the sick bay. That meant we ate with the ship's crew, which might have been the most haunting part of having survived.

The first time we went to the upper decks for a meal was like stepping onto an alien planet. When the elevator doors opened, we saw sailors walking in every direction. Men talking, some shouting, others rushing past the door—I had forgotten what it felt like to be among the living.

I stepped off the lift. Lee followed. The hall fell silent. People slowed down and watched us. Nobody told us to leave. People simply stepped out of our way as we walked to the mess hall.

We arrived during the middle of the early dinner rush. Looking through the window, I saw men with trays walking around in search of places to sit. I heard the loud din of hundreds of conversations and remembered when our mess hall was equally loud. The noise evaporated as we entered the doorway. We were the only men wearing Marines' uniforms. Everyone knew who we were. I heard whispers and felt people staring, but nobody approached us.

I reached for a tray, and somebody handed it to me. "Thank you," I said. The man did not respond.

The battle on Little Man lit a fire in the public's imagination. "The New Little Big Horn" said the Unified Authority Broadcasting Company (UABC) headlines. Other famous massacres were also invoked. One reporter called it "a modern-day Pearl Harbor," an irony that would not have been lost on Yoshi Yamashiro, though I doubt the reporter recognized it.

The Pentagon served up an endless supply of details about the battle, milking it for every drop of public support. A briefing officer held a meeting in which he traced our movements using maps. The public affairs office released photographs of the captured map room. The Joint Chiefs gave the UABC profiles and photographs of the hundred officers who died during the assault. Captain Gaylan McKay, a promising officer in life, became a public figure in death.

The Pentagon did not release information about survivors, but somehow the press got wind of us. We were dubbed, "The Little Man 7." Probably hoping that the story would go away, the Joint Chiefs acknowledged only that "A fast-thinking sergeant had managed to evacuate six men from the field."

They did not release my name. I did not care.

Over the next six weeks, as the Pentagon released a litany of tidbits about the Little Man 7, SC Command ignored us as we rattled around the bowels of the *Kamehameha*. Once word was out about the survivors, I think the Joint Chiefs hoped that the public's interest in Little Man would cool, but it continued to grow.

As time went by, Lee returned to his weight training, and I became obsessed with marksmanship. I practiced with automatic rifles, grenade launchers, and sniper rifles, shooting round after round.

Lee and I went to the crewmen's bar almost every night. The sailors seemed used to us by that time. Some invited us to sit with them whenever we showed up. By the time our transfers came, Lee and I had almost forgotten about the animosity between sailors and Marines.

Having spent a month and a half hoping for the public to forget about the Little Man 7, Washington finally embraced us. In his capacity as the secretary of the Navy, Admiral Huang announced plans to bootstrap us to officer status. The thought of promoting a Liberator must have caused him great pain. Lee and the other men were transferred to Officer Training School in Australia. I was called to appear before the House of Representatives in Washington, DC.

The night before Lee and the others left for OTS, we all went to the crewmen's bar for one last gathering. We found that news of our transfers had spread throughout the ship. As we entered the bar, some sailors called to us to join them.

"Officers," one of the men said, clapping Lee on the back. "If someone would have told me that I all I had to do was survive a massacre and a crash to become an officer, I'd have done it five years ago."

Everybody laughed, including me. I didn't think he was funny, but more than a month had passed. In military terms, my grieving period was over.

"Lee and the others are shipping out tomorrow," I said.

"Congratulations." The sailors looked delighted. One of them reached over and shook Lee's hand. "I'd better do this now," he joked. "Next time I may have to salute you pricks."

"When are you leaving, Harris?" another sailor asked.

"Not for a couple of days," I said.

"I can't believe they're shipping all of you out," the sailor responded.

"What did you expect to happen to them?" another sailor asked. "Olivera needs to make room, doesn't he?"

"Make room for what?" I asked.

"SEALs," the sailor said, then he took a long pull of his brew. "Squads of them . . . hundreds of them."

Lee and I looked at each other. That was the first we had heard about SEALs. Until we received our transfers, we'd both expected to remain on the *Kamehameha* to train new Marines.

"That's the scuttlebutt," another sailor said. "I'm surprised you never heard it."

"Did you know that Harris is going to Washington?" Lee asked.

"We heard all about the medal," a sailor said. "Everybody knows it. You're the pride of the ship."

"A medal?" I asked.

"You know more about it than we do," Lee said.

"Harris," the man said, putting down his drink and staring me right in the eye, "why else would you appear before Congress?"

* * *

Lee's shuttle left at 0900 the next morning. I went down to the hangar and saw him and the other survivors off. On my way back to the barracks, I paused beside the storage closet that had once served as an office for Captain Gaylan McKay. Moving on, I passed the mess hall, which sat dark and empty. Not much farther along, I saw the sea-soldier bar. As I neared the barracks, I heard people talking up ahead.

"They mostly use light arms," one of the men said, "automatic rifles, grenades, explosives. That's about it. We can probably reduce the floor space in the shooting range."

"They're not going to blow shit up on board ship, are they?"

"I don't know. They have to practice somewhere."

Four engineers stood in the open door of the training ground. They paused to look at me as I turned the corner. I had seen one of them in the crewmen's bar on several occasions. He smiled. "Sergeant Harris, I thought you were flying to Washington, DC."

"I leave in two days," I said. "You're reconfiguring the training area?"

"Getting it ready for the SEALs. Huang ordered the entire deck redesigned. It will take months to finish everything." The engineer I knew stepped away from the others and lowered his tone before speaking again. "I've never seen SEALs before, but I hear they're practically midgets. That's the rumor."

As a guest of the House of Representatives, I expected to travel in style. When I reached the hangar, I found the standard-issue military transport—huge, noisy, and built to carry sixty highly uncomfortable passengers. The *Kamehameha* was still orbiting Little Man; we were nine miserable days from the nearest broadcast discs.

Feeling dejected, I trudged up the ramp to the transport. I remembered that Admiral Klyber had modified the cabin of one of the ships to look like a living room with couches and a bar. All I found on my flight were sixty high-backed chairs. After stowing my bags in a locker, I settled into the seat that would be my home for the next nine days. As I waited for takeoff, someone slid into the seat next to mine.

"Sergeant Harris, I presume," a man with a high and officious voice said.

"I am," I said, without turning to look. I knew that a voice like that could only belong to a bureaucrat, the kind of person who would turn the coming trip from misery to torture.

"I am Nester Smart, Sergeant," the man said in his high-pitched snappy voice. "I have been assigned to accompany you to Washington."

"All the way to Washington?" I asked.

"They're not going to jettison me in space, Harris," he said.

Nester Smart? Nester Smart? I had heard that name before. I turned and recognized the face. "Aren't you the governor of Ezer Kri?"

"I was the interim governor," he said. "A new governor has been elected. I was just there as a troubleshooter."

"I see," I said, thinking to myself that I knew a little something about shooting trouble.

"We have ten days, Sergeant," Smart said. "It isn't nearly enough time, but we will have to make do. You've got a lot to learn before we can present you to the House."

Hearing Smart, I felt exhaustion sweep across my brain. He planned to snipe and lecture me the entire trip, spitting information at me as if giving orders.

The shuttle lifted off the launchpad. Watching the *Kamehameha* shrink into space, I knew Smart was right. I was an enlisted Marine. What did I know about politics? I took a long look at the various ships flying between the *Kamehameha* and Little Man, then sat back and turned to Smart. Now that I had become resigned to him, I took a real look at the man and realized that he was several inches taller than I. An athletic-looking man with squared shoulders and a rugged jaw, he looked more like a soldier than a pencil pusher.

"Now that I have your attention, perhaps we can discuss your visit to the capital," he said, a smirk on his lips. "You may not be aware of it, but several congressmen protested our actions on Little Man. There's been a lot of infighting between the House and the Senate lately."

"Do you mean things like Congress passing a bill to cut military spending?"

"You've heard about that?"

"And the Senate calling for more orphanages?"

"Bravo," Smart said, clapping his hands in nearly silent applause. "A soldier who reads the news. What will they come up with next?"

"I'm a Marine," I said.

"Yes, I know that," said Smart.

"I'm not a soldier. Do you call Navy personnel soldiers?"

"They're sailors," said Smart.

"And I am a Marine."

Smart smiled, but his eyes narrowed, and he looked me over carefully. "A Marine who follows the news," he said, the muscles in his jaw visibly clenched.

"Yes, well, unfortunately, we Marines can't spend our entire lives shooting people and breaking things." I looked back out the window and saw nothing but stars.

"You'll find that I do not have much of a sense of humor, Sergeant. I don't make jokes during the best of times, and this is not my idea of the best of times. To be honest with you, I don't approve of Marines speaking on Capitol Hill."

"Whose idea was it?" I asked.

"You're considered a hero, Sergeant Harris. Everybody loves a hero, especially in politics, but not everybody loves you. There are congressmen who will try to twist your testimony to further their own political agendas."

"The congressman from Ezer Kri?" I asked.

"James Smith? He's the least of your worries. The last representative from Ezer Kri disappeared with Yamashiro. Smith is an appointee," Smart said. "If you run into trouble, it's going to come from somebody like Gordon Hughes."

"From Olympus Kri?" I asked.

"Very good," Smart said. "The representative from Olympus Kri. He will not take you head-on. You're one of the Little Man 7. Picking a fight with you would not be politic. He might try to make the invasion look like the first hostile action in an undeclared war. The question is how he can make Little Man look illegal without openly attacking you."

So I'm still a pawn? I said to myself. A hero who would shortly be among the first clones ever made an officer, and I was still a pawn . . . story of my life. I felt trapped. "Will you be there when I go before the House?"

"Harris, I'm not letting you out of my sight until you leave Washington. That is a promise."

Suddenly traveling with Smart did not seem so bad.

CHAPTER
TWENTY-EIGHT

"Do you know your way around Washington, DC?" Nester Smart asked. The way I pressed my face against the window to see every last detail should have answered his question.

The capital of the Unified Authority lay spread under a clear afternoon sky. With its rows of gleaming white marble buildings, the city simply looked perfect. This was the city I saw in the news and read about in books. "I've never been here before."

Our transport began its approach, flying low over a row of skyscrapers. I saw people standing on balconies.

Off in the distance, I saw the Capitol, an immense marble building with a three-hundred-foot dome of white marble. Two miles wide and nearly three miles deep, the Capitol was the largest building on the face of the Earth. It rose twenty stories into the air, and I had no idea how deep its basements ran.

"The Capitol," I said.

"Good, Harris. You know your landmarks," Smart said, with a smirk.

The architect who designed the Capitol had had an eye for symbolism. If you stretched its corridors into one long line, that line would have been twenty-four thousand miles long, the circumference of the Earth. The building had 192 entrances—one for each of the Earth nations that became part of the Unified Authority. The building had 768 elevators, one for every signer of the original U.A. constitution. There were dozens of subtle touches like that. When I was growing up, every schoolboy learned the Capitol's numerology.

I also saw the White House, a historic museum that once housed the presidents of the United States. The scholars who framed the Unified Authority replaced the executive branch with the Linear Committee. If the rumors were true, the Linear Committee sometimes conducted business in an oval-shaped office inside the White House.

A highly manicured mall with gleaming walkways and marble fountains stretched between the White House and the Capitol. Thousands of people—tourists, bureaucrats, and politicians—walked that mall. From our transport, they looked like dust mites swirling in a shaft of light.

"I can barely wait to get out and explore the city," I said, both anxious to see the capital of the known universe and to get away from Nester Smart.

"You are going to spend a quiet evening locked away in Navy housing," Smart said. "We cannot afford for you to show up tomorrow with a hangover."

Our transport began its vertical descent to a landing pad. Smart slipped out of his chair and pulled his jacket off a hanger. He smoothed it with a sharp tug on the lapels. Reaching for the inside breast pocket of the coat, he pulled a business card out and wrote a note on the back of it. After giving it a quick read, he handed it to me.

"There is a driver waiting outside. He will take you to the Navy base. Show this card to the guard at the gate. Also, your promotion is now official. Befitting your war-hero status, you are now a lieutenant in the Unified Authority Marines.

"You will find your new wardrobe in the apartment. I suppose congratulations are in order, Lieutenant Harris."

The White House had guest rooms, but I was not invited to stay in those hallowed halls. Those rooms were reserved for visiting politicians and power brokers, the kinds of people who made their living by sending clones to war. Spending the night in the barracks suited me fine.

The guards outside the Navy base were not clones. The one who inspected my identification had blond hair and green eyes. He looked over my ID, then read Smart's note. "You're one of the Little Man 7, right?" he asked. "I hear that you're speaking in the House of Representatives tomorrow. Congress doesn't usually send visitors out here."

"Yeah, lucky me."

"Officers' country is straight ahead," the guard said. "You can't miss it.

"Captain Baxter, our base commander, left a message for you. He wants to meet with you. You'll want to shower and change your uniform before presenting yourself. Baxter's a stickler on uniforms."

My driver dropped me at the barracks door. Carrying my rucksack over my shoulder, I found my room. The lock was programmed to recognize my ID card. I swiped my card through a slot, and the door slid open. It was the first time I had ever stayed in a room with a locking door. I considered that for a moment.

I had spent my life sharing barracks with dozens of other men. I heard them snore, and they heard me. We dressed in front of each other, showered together, stowed our belongings in lockers.

With the exception of my two weeks of leave in Hawaii, the "squad bay" life was the only life I knew. Now I stepped into a room with a single bed. The room had a closet, a dresser, and a bathroom. Smiling and feeling slightly ashamed, I placed my ruck down, walked around the room turning on a lamp here, dragging my finger across the desk there, and allowing water to run from a faucet. I took a shower and shaved. Nine days of travel had left my blouse badly wrinkled; but it was an enlisted man's blouse. In the closet, I found a uniform with the small gold bar of a second lieutenant on the shoulder. I dressed as an officer and left to meet the base commander.

"May I help you?" a civilian secretary asked.

I told her that I was a guest.

"Lieutenant Harris, of course," she said. "Please wait here." Watching me as she stepped away from her desk, she almost tripped over one of the legs of her chair. She turned and sped into a small doorway, emerging a moment later with several officers. That kind of reception would have made me nervous except that the officers seemed so happy to meet me.

"Lieutenant Harris?" a captain in dress whites asked.

"Sir," I said, saluting.

The entire company broke into huge, toothy smiles. "A pleasure to meet you, Lieutenant," the captain said, saluting first, then reaching across the counter and shaking my hand. "I'm Geoffrey Baxter." The other officers also reached across and shook my hand.

"Do you have a moment? Are you meeting with anyone this evening?"

"No," I said.

"What?" gasped another captain. "No reception? They're not putting you up in a stateroom? Outrageous! These politicians treat the military like dogs."

Baxter led me into a large office, and we sat in a row of chairs. As the receptionist brought us drinks, the officers crowded around me, and more officers strayed into the room. "I'm not sure that I understand. Were you expecting me?"

"Expecting you? We've been waiting for you," Baxter said. "Harris, you're famous around here." He looked to the other officers, who all nodded in agreement. "Your photograph is all over the mediaLink."

"My photograph?" I asked. "How about my men?"

"They're clones, aren't they? Everybody knows what they look like," an officer with a thick red mustache commented.

"Have you had dinner yet?" Baxter asked.

"I was going to ask for directions to the officers' mess," I said.

"No mess hall food for you. Not tonight," another officer said. "Not for you."

"I know you've just arrived, but are you up to a night out?" Baxter asked.

I smiled.

"I know a good sports bar," the officer with the mustache

said. The idea of a place with loads of booze and marginal food appealed to all of us.

Fourteen of us piled into three cars and headed toward the heart of DC.

The Capitol, an imposing sight during the day, was even more impressive at night. Bright lights illuminated its massive white walls, casting long and dramatic shadows onto its towering dome. Just behind the Capitol, the white cube of the Pentagon glowed. The Pentagon, which had been rebuilt into a perfect cube, retained its traditional name in a nod to history. Seeing the buildings from the freeway, I could not appreciate their grand size.

So many buildings and streetlights burned through the night that the sky over Washington, DC, glimmered a pale blue-white. The glow of the city could be seen from miles away. I could not see stars when I looked up, but I saw radiant neon in every direction, spinning signs, video-display billboards, bars and restaurants with facades so bright that I could shut my eyes and see the luminance through closed eyelids. I had never imagined such a place. Dance clubs, restaurants, bars, casinos, sports dens, theaters—the attractions never endled.

And the city itself seemed alive. The sidewalks were filled. Late-night crowds bustled across breezeways between buildings. We arrived at the sports bar at 1930 hours and found it so crowded that we could not get seated before 2030, did not start dinner until nearly 2130, and chased down dinner with several rounds of drinks.

The officers I was with held up at the bar better than the clones from my late platoon. Most clones got drunk on beer and avoided harder liquor, but Baxter and his band of natural-borns kept downing shots long after their speech slurred. One major drank until his legs became numb. We had to carry him to his car.

We did not get home until long after midnight. I did not get to bed until well after 0200. I'm not making excuses, but I am explaining why I did not arrive at the House of Representatives in satisfactory condition. Sleep-addled and mildly buzzed from a long night of drinking, I found myself leaning against the wall of the elevator for support as I rode up to meet Nester Smart.

The doors slid open, and the angry former interim governor of Ezer Kri snarled, "What the hell happened to you?" Dressed for bureaucratic battle, Smart wore a dark blue suit and a bright red necktie. With his massive shoulders and square frame, Smart looked elegant. But there was nothing elegant about the twisted expression on his face.

"I'm just a little tired," I said. "I had a late night out with some officers from the base."

"Imbecile," he said, with chilling enunciation. "You are supposed to appear before the House in two hours, and you look like you just fell out of bed."

"You mind keeping your voice down?" I asked as I stepped off the lift. Rubbing my forehead, I reminded myself that I was in Smart's arena. He knew the traps and the pitfalls here.

Smart led me down "Liberty Boulevard," a wide hallway with royal blue carpeting and a mural of seventeenth-century battle scenes painted onto a rounded ceiling. Shafts of sunlight lanced down from those windows. The air was cool, but the sunlight pouring in through the windows was warm.

"This is an amazing city," I said. "It must be old hat for you."

"You never get used to it, Harris," Smart said. "That's the intoxicating thing about life in Washington, you never get used to it."

As we turned off to a less spectacular corridor, Smart pointed to a two-paneled door. "Do you know what that is?" Smart asked.

I shook my head.

"That, Harris, is the lion's den. That is the chamber. Behind those doors are one thousand twenty-six congressmen. Some of them want to make you a hero. Some of them will use you to attack the military. None of them, Lieutenant, are your friends. The first rule of survival in Washington, DC, is that you have no friends. You may have allies, but you do not have friends."

"That's bleak," I said. "I think I prefer military combat."

"This is the only battlefield that matters, Lieutenant," Smart said. "Nothing you do out there matters. Everything permanent is done in this building."

Death is pretty permanent, I thought. I walked over to a window and peered out over the mall. It was raining outside. Twenty floors below me, I saw people with umbrellas and raincoats walking quickly to get out of the rain. Preparing to appear before the House, I felt the same pleasant rush of endorphins and adrenaline that coursed through my veins during combat. I had some idea of what to expect. Smart spent the flight from Scutum-Crux telling me horror stories, and I had every reason to believe the pompous bastard.

"Remember, Harris, these people are looking for ammunition. Answer questions as briefly as possible. You have no friends in the House of Representatives. If a congressman is friendly, it's only because he wants to look good for the voters back home."

The door to the chamber opened and three pages came to meet us. They were mere kids—college age . . . my age and possibly a few years older, but raised rich and inexperienced. They had never seen death and probably never would.

"Governor Smart," one of the pages said. "Did you accomplish what you wanted on Ezer Kri?" Taken on face value, that seemed like a warm greeting. The words sounded interested, and the boy asking them looked friendly, but Smart must have noticed a barb in his voice. Smart nodded curtly but did not speak.

"And you must be Lieutenant Harris," the page said as he turned toward me. He reached to shake my hand but only took my fingers in the limpest of grips. "Good of you to come, Lieutenant. Why don't you gentlemen follow me?" He turned to lead us into the House.

"Tommy Guileman," Smart whispered into my ear. "He's Gordon Hughes's top aide."

If Smart and I had been allowed to wear combat helmets in the House of Representatives, we could have communicated over the interLink. Smart could have told me all about Guileman. He could have identified every member of the House as an ally or an enemy. Since we did not have the

benefit of helmets on the floor, I needed to watch Nester
Smart and study his expressions for clues.

The House of Representative chambers looked something like a church. The floor was divided into two wide sections. As the pages led us down the center aisle, several
representatives patted me on the back or reached out to
shake my hand.

At the far end of the floor I saw a dais. On it were two
desks, one for Gordon Hughes, Speaker of the House, and
one for Arnold Lund, the leader of the Loyal Opposition. I
took my place at a pulpit between them and thought of Jesus
Christ being crucified between two thieves. Below me, the
House spread out in a vast sea of desks, politicians, and bureaucrats. Fortunately, I was not alone. Nester Smart hovered right beside me.

I had seen the chamber in hundreds of mediaLink stories,
but that did not prepare me for the experience of entering it.
A bundle of thirty microphones poked toward my face from
the top of the podium. One clump had been bound together
like a bouquet of flowers. Across the floor, three rows of mediaLink cameras lined the far wall. They reminded me of rifles in a firing squad. Later that day, I would find out that I
had been speaking in a closed session. The cameras sat idle,
and most of the microphones were not hot.

My wild ride was about to begin. "Members of the House
of Representatives, it is my pleasure to present Lieutenant
Wayson Harris of the Unified Authority Marine Corps. As
you know, Lieutenant Harris is a survivor of the battle at Little Man."

With that, the members of the House rose to their feet
and applauded. It was a heady moment, both intimidating
and thrilling.

"Do you have prepared remarks?" the Speaker asked.

"No, sir," I said.

"Quite understandable," the Speaker said in a jaunty
voice. "Perhaps we should open this session to the floor. I
am sure many members have questions for you."

Hearing that, I felt my stomach sink.

"If there are no objections, I would like to open with a
few questions," the leader of the Loyal Opposition said.

"The chair recognizes Representative Arnold Lund," Hughes said. Smart smiled. Apparently the meeting had started in friendly territory.

Above me, the minority leader sat on an elevated portion of the dais behind a wooden wall. I had to look almost straight up to see his face.

"Lieutenant, members of the House, as you know, the Republic has entered dark times in which separatist factions have challenged our government."

Nester Smart moved toward me and leaned close enough to whisper in my ear. "He's on our side," Smart whispered. "He is signaling us and his allies how to play this. He will try to shield you if the questions get hostile."

"As we all know," Lund continued, "a landing force was sent to Little Man for peaceful purposes. More than two thousand Marines were brutally butchered . . ."

"I am certain that history will show that these men died bravely . . ." The leader of the Loyal Opposition showed no signs of slowing as his speech passed the seven-minute mark.

"Were it possible, we should erect a statue for every victim of that holocaust." Lund waxed on and on about the innocence of our twenty-three hundred-man, highly armed landing party and the brutality of the Mogat response. He talked about the unprovoked attack on the *Kamehameha* and the good fortune that other ships happened to be nearby.

"Goddamn windbag" Smart whispered angrily.

"Lieutenant Wayson Harris is one of only seven men who survived that unprovoked attack," the congressman went on. "Fellow representatives, I would personally like to thank Lieutenant Harris for his valor."

Loud applause rang throughout the chamber, echoing fiercely around us. The shooting match was about to begin. Behind me, Hughes banged his gavel and called for order. "The floor now recognizes the junior representative from Olympus Kri."

An old woman with crinkled salt-and-pepper hair pulled back in a tight bun stood. She pushed her wire-frame spectacles up the bridge of her nose and spoke in overtly sweet tones. "Olympus Kri celebrates your safe return from Little

Man, Lieutenant Harris. I am sure the battle must have been a very grueling experience. What can you tell us about the nature of the incursion on Little Man?"

"The nature?" I asked.

"What was the reason you went down to Little Man?" the congresswoman asked. She leaned forward on her desk to take weight off her feet.

"Remember, you are an ignorant foot soldier," Smart whispered in my ear.

"Why did I go to Little Man, ma'am?" I repeated. "We went because that was where the transport dropped us off."

The soft hum of laughter echoed through the chamber.

The congresswoman managed a weak response. "I see. Well, Lieutenant, as I understand it, there were twenty-three hundred Marines on Little Man. That sounds like quite an invasion."

With that she stopped speaking. Perhaps she expected me to respond, but I had nothing to say. She hadn't asked me a question. An awkward silence swelled.

"Is it?" the congresswoman finally asked.

"Excuse me?" I asked. I looked over at Smart and saw an approving smile.

"Why did you invade Little Man?" she asked.

"I was not involved in the planning of this mission, ma'am."

"Twenty-three hundred units?" she persisted. "What reason were you given for sending so many men to the planet?"

"Ma'am, I was a sergeant. Nobody gives sergeants reasons. They just tell us what to do."

"I see," she said.

Nester Smart leaned over to whisper something to me, but the congresswoman stopped him. "Did you have something to add, Mr. Smart?" she asked.

"I was just advising Lieutenant Harris about the kind of information you might be looking for," Smart said.

"From your vast store of battlefield experience, Mr. Smart?" the congresswoman quipped. There was a burst of laughter on the floor. Smart turned red but said nothing.

"Lieutenant, I am merely trying to determine why so many Marines were sent to the surface of Little Man. I am not asking for an official explanation. You are a soldier in the Unified Authority Marine Corps. Surely you have some understanding about how things are done."

"It's not unusual for ships to send their complement of Marines to a planet, ma'am," I said.

"Two thousand men?" she questioned. "That sounds more like an occupying force."

"Ma'am, twenty-three hundred men with light arms is a tiny force. We keep more men than that on most friendly planets."

"I see," said the congresswoman. "Lieutenant Harris, I thank you for your service to the Republic." With that, she returned to her desk.

I recognized the next senator's face from countless mediaLink stories. Tall, with dark skin and a beard that looked like a chocolate smudge around his mouth, this was Congressman Bill Hawkins who represented a group of small planets in the Sagittarius Arm. Except for the telltale white streaks that tinged his hair, Hawkins looked like an athletic thirty-year-old. I'd read somewhere that he was actually in his fifties.

"Lieutenant Harris, I salute you for your service to our fine Republic," he said. He spoke slowly and in a clear, strong voice. Earth-born and raised, Hawkins had been a fighter pilot—his was the voice of one veteran speaking to another. He placed a foot on his seat and leaned forward. As he went on, however, his demeanor transformed into that of a politician.

"Lieutenant, perhaps I can assist my esteemed colleague from Olympus Kri," he began. Around the chamber, many representatives began muttering protests.

"Perhaps my esteemed colleague has not noticed that the lieutenant has already answered her questions," said Opposition Leader Lund.

"Certain questions remained unanswered," Hawkins said, turning his attention on Lund.

"This is supposed to be a presentation, not a board of inquiry," a congressman shouted from the floor.

"Order. Order!" Hughes said, banging his gavel. "Representative Hawkins has the floor."

"And I do congratulate the lieutenant," Hawkins said, looking over my head toward Representative Gordon Hughes. "Well done, Lieutenant Harris. But, in light of new information, certain questions must be answered."

"What information is that?" Nester Smart broke in.

"Oh yes, Nester Smart, good of you to escort the lieutenant," Hawkins said with a smirk. "After surviving a brutal battle on Little Man, it would be a shame if this fine Marine was lost in a dangerous place like the House of Representatives."

Laughter and angry shouts erupted around the chamber.

"Order," Congressman Hughes called. His booming voice stung my ears. "What new information have you acquired, Senator Hawkins?"

Hawkins reached down and pulled a combat helmet out from beneath his desk. "Do you recognize this, Lieutenant?" he asked.

"That is a combat helmet," I said.

"Your combat helmet, Lieutenant. One of my aides retrieved it from a repair shop on the *Kamehameha*. It appears that its audio sensors failed during the battle." Hawkins held the helmet so that everyone on the floor could see it. "We downloaded the data recorded in the memory chip of this helmet. The data shows that you acted most heroically, Lieutenant Harris."

"Thank you, Senator," I answered quietly. I knew something bad was coming, but I had no idea what it might be. My mind started racing through the entire mission. Would Hawkins accuse me of cowardice for abandoning Captain McKay? Would he call me a traitor for leading my men out of the canyon?

"Your mission, however, was about more than squatters," Hawkins said. "Congressman Hughes, with your permission I would like to show the chamber some excerpts from Lieutenant Harris's record."

"This is unacceptable!" blared the minority leader. "Mr. Speaker, this is a blind-side attack."

Hawkins's aides jumped to their feet and shouted in protest.

"Ironic," Hawkins said, putting up an open hand to silence his delegation. "That is the exact accusation I have against the men who planned the invasion of Little Man. We can view this record in a special committee if that is what my esteemed colleague wishes, but a committee investigation would require the testimony of all of the men who survived this attack. We would need them to verify that the records have not been altered.

"Today, we have the benefit of Lieutenant Harris's expertise. I think we should view his record while he is here and able to comment on it. If you like, Mr. Speaker, we can put it up to a vote."

Looking around the chamber, I could see that the majority of the people in attendance wanted to know what Hawkins had up his sleeve. Though I could not make out specific conversations, the tenor of the talk around the chamber seemed excited.

Hughes seemed to sense the excitement. "There is no need to hold a vote," he said. "I will allow you to show your information."

A large screen dropped from the ceiling behind the dais. By the faint glow that filled the chamber, I could tell that smaller monitors lit up on the representatives' desks.

"Do you recognize this scene, Lieutenant?" Hawkins asked.

"Yes," I said. I turned to Nester Smart for help, but he looked completely dumbstruck. "I was on guard duty the night before the battle."

The ghost of First Sergeant Booth Lector came walking through the undergrowth.

"So the battle was the very next morning?" Hawkins asked.

"Yes, sir," I said.

The video feed continued.

"What the hell did I ever do to you?" I asked from the screen.

"You were made, Harris. That's reason enough. Just the fact that you exist was enough to get me transferred to this for-shit outfit," said the ghost of Booth Lector.

The video feed paused.

"Who is this man?" Hawkins asked.

"Master Sergeant Booth Lector," I said.

"I know that, Lieutenant. I can read his identifier on the screen. I am asking about his relationship with you. What did he mean when he said that he was transferred because you exist?"

As I struggled to come up with a safe answer, Hawkins said, "Why don't you think about that question as we watch more of this video feed?"

"I had nothing to do with it."

"You had everything to do with it. You think this is a real mission? You think we are going to capture this entire planet with twenty-three hundred Marines? Is that what you think?

"They'd forgotten about us. Saul, Marshall, me . . . Nobody in Washington knew that there were any Liberators left. The brass knew about Shannon, but there was nothing anybody could do about him. Klyber kept him nearby, kept a watchful eye on him. Nobody could touch Shannon with Klyber guarding him. As far as everybody knew, Shannon was the last of us.

"Then you came along, Harris—a brand-new Liberator.

"You weren't alone, you know. Klyber made five of you. We found the others. Marshall killed one in an orphanage. I killed three of them myself. But Klyber hid you . . . sent you to some godforsaken shit hill where no one would find you. By the time I did locate you, you were already on the Kamehameha."

"I . . ."

"Shut up, Harris. You asked what's bothering me, now I'm going to tell you. And you, you are going to shut your rat's ass mouth and listen or I will shoot you. I will shoot you and say that the goddamn Japanese shot you.

"The government hated Liberators. Congress wanted us dead. As far as anyone knew, we were all dead. Then you showed up. I heard about that early promotion and wanted to fly out and cap you on that shit hill planet. I would have framed Crowley, but Klyber transferred you before I could get there.

"Next thing I know, you're running missions for that asshole Huang. You stupid shit! Huang was the reason we were in hiding in the first place. As soon as I heard that you met

Huang, I knew we were all dead. Once he got a whiff of a Liberator, he would go right back to the Pentagon and find every last one of us.

"And here we are, trying to take over a planet with twenty-three hundred Marines. This isn't a mission, Harris, this is a cleansing. This is the last march of the Liberators, and if they need to kill off twenty-three hundred GI clones to finish us, it all works out fine on their balance sheets. They're expendable.

"You want to know what I have against you, Harris? You are the death of the Liberators."

"I was a young boy during the days of the Galactic Central War, Lieutenant. I toured the devastation of both New Prague and Dallas Prime shortly after graduating OTS. Lieutenant Harris, I have seen the destruction that Liberators do. Are you a Liberator?" Hawkins asked.

I looked over at Nester Smart for advice. His eyes wide and scared, his face completely drained of blood, he took three steps back from me.

"Perhaps you have forgotten the mission of this body, Congressman." The voice was cold, direct, and final. I recognized it at once, but turned to check. Admiral Bryce Klyber stood alone at the far end of the floor. He stood stiff and erect, his legs spread slightly wider than his shoulders and his hands clasped behind his back.

Turning to look at Klyber, Bill Hawkins fell silent. Everyone on the floor became silent. I could sense their fear.

"The mission of this body is to represent the people. When representatives take it upon themselves to exceed their mission, they endanger the institution itself," Klyber said.

"And now, Congressman Hughes, if there are no more questions"—Klyber looked all around the floor, warning off anyone with the nerve to challenge him—"I suggest you propose a motion to recognize Lieutenant Harris's gallant service and dismiss him."

"I quite agree," said Lund, the leader of the Loyal Opposition. With Admiral Klyber watching, Hughes took an open vote.

Across the floor, Bill Hawkins's delegation exited the chamber. Ten minutes later, when Hughes tallied the vote, he noted that Hawkins abstained. The rest of the House, even the representatives from Olympus Kri, voted for my commendation.

TWENTY-NINE

I later found out that some of Nester Smart's allies closed the session to the media. They did not know what Hughes and his camp had planned, but they did not trust the honorable congressman from Olympus Kri. Closing the session, however, did not prevent leaks.

When I returned to the Navy base, I noticed a difference in the way the sailors responded to me. The evening I arrived, they clamored to meet me and shake my hand. Earlier that morning, as I rushed to meet Nester Smart, they couldn't wait to shake my hand and wish me luck. After the hearing, these same men took long furtive glances at me, ducking their heads and pretending to stare at the ground when I looked in their direction. They did not seem interested in speaking. When I approached two of my drinking buddies from the night before, they said they had business to attend to and walked away.

I went to the barracks to change out of my formals. I did not know how long I would remain in Washington, DC, or where HQ might transfer me. The only thing I knew was that I was no longer assigned to the *Kamehameha*.

When I checked my mediaLink shades, however, I found

three official communiqués for Lieutenant Harris and one
letter addressed to Wayson Harris. I read the letter first.

> *Congratulations, Wayson. You're a hero! I hear peo-*
> *ple talking about you at work. Nobody believes me*
> *when I tell them that you and I dated in Hawaii.*
>
> *Speaking of Hawaii, it's been months, and I have*
> *not heard from you. Jennifer says that you are doing*
> *well. Vince tells her about you in his letters.*
>
> *I am sorry that I was not able to say good-bye in*
> *Hawaii. I went by the hospital before I left. I think*
> *about you a lot. I had a very fun time and hope you*
> *did, too.*
>
> *Please write soon,*
> *Kasara*

I did not write to Kasara from the hospital. With all of the
excitement about Lector and the invasion of Little Man, I
mostly forgot about her. Now that I saw the message from her,
my memory came back with a rush of emotion. Funny. I didn't
think she meant much to me, but I felt lonely when I thought
about her. Nostalgia? Was it my heart or my testicles?

The first of the official communiqués was my transfer. I
had been assigned to serve under Bryce Klyber's command
on a ship called the *Doctrinaire*. Curiously, the *Doctrinaire*
was not attached to a fleet. I was to report for duty in three
days but had no idea where to go.

The idea of serving under Klyber again had great appeal.
I had not gotten a chance to thank him for rescuing me in the
House. He had slipped out the moment the vote was finished.

The second message was from Vince Lee.

> *Harris,*
> *You are a Liberator! Oh my God, how disgusting!*
> *News travels fast from closed sessions. And they*
> *thought your kind were dead, ha-ha!*
>
> *Hope all is well,*
> *Second Lieutenant Vince Lee*

Only an hour had passed since I had left the House. Did he hear about the entire session, or was my being a Liberator the only leak?

The third message came from Aleg Oberland, the teacher who ran the Tactical Simulations Center at the orphanage. It had been nearly two years since my last visit with him. Back then he had told me that my career would be set if I caught Klyber's eye.

Oberland's message was shortest of all—"Contact me."

At the end of his message was a command button that said "Direct Reply." Oberland appeared on the screen. "Wayson," he said, "are you okay?"

"You heard about it, too?" I asked.

He stared into the screen. "I'm in DC," Oberland said. "Does a busy Liberator like you have time for lunch?"

We met in a diner near Union Station. Oberland arrived before me. When I stepped through the door, I saw him waving from a booth.

"How are you feeling?" Oberland asked as he climbed out of his booth and shook my hand. He looked tired and worried. He looked into my eyes too long and too thoughtfully. He reminded me of someone visiting a friend with a fatal disease.

"I'm fine," I said. "Took a bit of a beating in the House, but I guess I should have expected that."

Oberland continued to stare at me as if he expected me to collapse on the spot. "Ever since Little Man, you're all anybody ever wants to talk about back at #553. I've been following the *Kamehameha* on the mediaLink. Ezer Kri was big news. So was Hubble!"

A waitress rolled up to our booth. I ordered a sandwich and a salad. Oberland only ordered a salad.

"I just about wrote you off when I found out you were sent to Little Man. You've been out to the edge of the galaxy."

"I just about wrote *myself* off on Little Man," I admitted.

"I came in last night," Oberland said. "What happened in there? I mean, I know you received a unanimous vote of commendation."

The waitress returned with our food, and we started eating. Picking at his salad, Oberland said, "The reports say there were several Liberators on Little Man."

"Four of us," I said, around a mouthful of sandwich.

"There was me, Lector . . ."

"Lector?" Oberland asked.

"Booth Lector. He was transferred to the *Kamehameha* a few weeks before we shipped off to Little Man."

"I know the name, Wayson," Oberland said. "I didn't know he was still alive."

"He's not," I said. "He died on Little Man. So did two other Liberators."

"Let me guess . . . Clearance Marshall and Tony Saul," Oberland said. "I finished my career on New Prague. I got there three weeks after the massacre. They cleaned up most of the bodies before I arrived, but I still found fingers and teeth on the ground. The first team on the scene cleared out the big stuff, the bodies.

"The Senate launched a full investigation into why so many civilians were killed. I conducted the Army investigation. We found out what went wrong. It was a platoon of Liberators—Lector's platoon. They destroyed an entire town, then they destroyed the next town and the town after that. By the time they finished, thirty thousand civilians had died. And it wasn't like they blew them up with a big bomb, either. I don't know why Congress outlawed Liberators, but I can tell you why I would. The people they killed on New Prague . . . they slaughtered them one at a time." Oberland pushed the rest of his salad away on his plate and shook his head. "I try hard not to think about New Prague."

"Must have been bad," I said, not knowing what else to say. They didn't teach us the details of that particular massacre in class. All we'd ever heard about was the number of victims. I wanted to ask how a single platoon managed to kill thirty thousand people in a single day; but looking at Oberland's grim expression, I decided to change the subject.

I told Oberland about Bill Hawkins producing my helmet. He listened intently, especially when I brought up the video feed.

"Hawkins should be more careful. Klyber is a powerful

enemy," Oberland said. "I imagine he is also a powerful ally. I don't suppose his appearance in the House was a lucky accident?"

"I don't think so," I said. "I just got transferred to his new ship."

"That makes sense. Klyber's involvement with Liberators was never much of a secret. We used to call them 'Klyber's brew.' Of course, we didn't say that in front of him . . . or them."

"Admiral Klyber told me that creating Liberators was the only black mark on his career," I said. "I get the feeling that he sees me as a way to wipe the slate clean."

"Pulling six men off Little Man was impressive," Oberland said as he started up his salad again. "Too bad you weren't able to pull an officer with them."

"You mean a natural-born," I said.

"Yes. Saving those clones was quite a feat, but it will take a lot more than saving clones to give Liberators a good name."

"I suppose," I said.

"I haven't heard anything about Klyber taking command of a new ship," Oberland said.

"My transfer didn't list a fleet, just a ship called the *Doctrinaire*."

"Klyber does not get involved with a project unless it is important," Oberland said. He looked at his wristwatch then stared out the window. I could tell he felt rushed. He drummed his fingers on table for a moment. "I want to ask you something. I've wanted to ask you this since the first time you walked into my simulation lab. Wayson, you always seemed like a good kid."

"Are you asking if I am like Lector?" I interrupted.

Considering my question, Oberland checked his watch and looked out the window again. Crowds of people had filed into the station. I had not noticed it before, but Oberland had a small overnight bag beside his seat. "I would never have allowed you in my simulations lab if I'd thought you were like Lector. But you have the same programming and the same genes."

"See these scars?" I pointed to my eyebrow and down my

cheek. "These aren't from Little Man. I never got so much as a nick on Little Man. These came from Hawaii."

"Hawaii?" Oberland said, clearly strolling down some old memory lane. I was afraid he would ask if I had gone to Sad Sam's Palace, but all he said was "I used to go there on leave."

"I got in a fight with a Navy SEAL. He was short, almost a midget. He came up to here on me," I said, running my pointer finger along my collarbone. "I've never seen anybody move so fast in a fight. And his fingers were like talons. He could have killed me right from the start, but he gave me a chance." I laughed a short, hollow laugh and paused to relive the fight in my mind. "The little bastard made a mistake, and I got the upper hand. I damn near killed him.

"You want to hear something strange? I think he was a clone."

Oberland shook his head. "SEALs are natural-born."

"That's the way of things, isn't it? Replace the valuable with the expendable. Get rid of the natural-borns with their relatives and their political pratfalls and exchange them for clones. You can tailor clones to fit your needs."

"I suppose that was what Klyber did when he made Liberators," Oberland said, in a tired voice.

"The best Marine I ever met was a Liberator, a sergeant named Tabor Shannon. He and I got drunk together the night that I found out I was a clone. You know what he told me? He said that being a clone meant that you never wondered about right and wrong. He said that we were man-made, and our commanding officer was our god and creator. That sounds bad when I think about massacres like New Prague, but this guy was nothing like Lector. I think Liberators make their own choices, just like everybody else."

"Wayson, I'm already late for my transport," Oberland said as he stepped out of the booth.

"I'm glad you came," I said. "It's nice seeing a friendly face."

I stood up and shook Oberland's hand. He grabbed his overnight bag and trotted out the door, pausing for only a moment to look back at me. Oberland, a small, trim man with messy white hair, blended into the transport station crowd and vanished. I wished that I could go with him and return to the orphanage. "Good-bye, old friend," I whispered to myself.

It turned out to be my day for meeting old friends.

I did not feel like returning to base and sitting around, ignored by Baxter and the other sailors, so I went to a nearby bar and found a small table in a dark corner where I thought no one would notice me. It was a nice place, more lavish than the sea-soldiers' drinking hole on the *Kamehameha*. The place had dim red lights that gave the beige walls a dark, cozy feel. During the quiet hours of the late afternoon, the bartender struck up conversations with the customers seated around the bar as he poured drinks.

I felt at home. The Earth-grown brew flowed freely enough there, and nobody looked like a politician. Everything seemed right in the universe except that I could not seem to get even remotely drunk. Then off-duty sailors started rolling into the bar. The first stray dogs showed around 1700 hours. By 1900, gabbing, happy swabbies filled the place. A few stragglers hovered around the counter swilling down drinks as fast as they could order them while dozens more crowded around tables swapping jokes and smacking each other on the arms. Sitting morosely in my quiet little corner, drinking my tenth or possibly fifteenth beer, I thought how much I hated this city.

Ray Freeman entered the bar.

I don't think anybody knew who he was; they just knew he was dangerous. Dressed in his jumpsuit with its armored breastplate, Freeman looked like he had come in from a war. He stood more than a foot taller than most of the men he passed.

Silence spread across the bar like an infection. Sailors stepped out of his way as he crossed the floor. Freeman walked through the crowd without stopping for a drink. He came to my table. "Hello, Harris," he said.

"How'd you recognize me without my helmet?" I quipped.

"Liberators aren't hard to spot," Freeman said. "At least that's what they're saying on the mediaLink."

"Neither are seven-foot mercenaries," I said.

Freeman sat down across the table from me.

"The chair isn't taken," I said. "Why don't you join me?"

"You were lucky to get off Little Man alive," Freeman said.

So much for small talk, I thought. "Thank you for that insight. Next time I get chased by ten thousand angry Mogats, I won't mistakenly think that I have everything under control."

With his dark skin and clothes, Freeman looked like a shadow in the dim ambiance of the bar. He smiled and looked around. "You should quit the Marines," he said. "Why don't you quit?"

"It's in my genes," I responded, pleased with my little joke. Freeman did not laugh, not even a chuckle. "You didn't come to Washington, DC, just to tell me to quit the Corps?"

By that time the sailors around the bar had forgotten about us. They joked, laughed, and told stories at the tops of their lungs. Freeman, however, made no adjustment to compensate for their rising decibels. He spoke in the same quiet, rumbling voice that he always used. "We could be partners," he said.

"What did you say?" I asked. "I didn't understand you. It sounded like you said I should become your partner."

"We'd do good together."

I paused to stare at him. Ray Freeman, the perfect killing machine and the coldest man alive, had just asked me to be his partner.

"Partners?" I repeated, not sure that I wasn't having a hallucination brought on from nearly twenty glasses of beer. "Go into business? With you?"

Freeman did not respond.

"Leave the Marines?"

"You weren't supposed to survive Little Man," Freeman said. "You may not survive next time."

"Next time?" I asked. I knew I could leave the Marines, but deep inside, I did not want to leave. Even after the massacre at Little Man and everything they put me through in the House of Representatives . . . even knowing that my kind was extinct and the people I was protecting wanted to end my life, I wanted to stay in the Marines.

"I can't leave the service. I'm a Liberator, remember? You can't drive spaceships underwater. I'm doing the thing I was made to do, and I can't do anything else." I knew I was lying. I could leave, but something in my programming kept me coming back for more.

Suddenly my mouth went dry. "Goddamn," I hissed to myself. Back when I was sober, I assured Aleg Oberland that I would not become like Booth Lector because Liberators made their own choices. But, faced with the knowledge that I would die if I remained in the corps, I wanted to stay where I was. My head hurt, and I started to feel sick to my stomach. I rubbed my eyes. When I looked up, Ray Freeman was gone, if he'd ever been there at all.

CHAPTER THIRTY

One sure sign of a high-security military operation is the means of transportation used for bringing in new recruits. I could have taken public transportation to Gobi. Military transports flew in and out of the SC Central Fleet on a daily basis. This transfer was different. On the morning I was supposed to transfer to the *Doctrinaire*, Admiral Klyber's new ship, a driver showed up at my door.

"Lieutenant Harris?" the petty officer asked, as I opened my door.

"Can I help you?" It was 0800. I was packed and dressed but had not yet eaten my breakfast.

"I'm your ride," the petty officer said.

"My ride? I don't even know where I'm supposed to go; I can't leave the station yet."

"You're transferring to the *Doctrinaire*," the petty officer said. "It's not like they run a shuttle at the top of every half hour, sir."

The petty officer loaded my rucksack into the back of his jeep and drove me out to the airfield. A little Johnston R-27 sat ready on the field. The Johnston was the smallest noncombat craft in military employ. It carried a maximum of twelve passengers.

I looked at the little transport. It was raining that morning. Beads of rain ran down the sides and windows. "I hope we are not going very far," I said.

"We'll put on a few light-years before nightfall," the petty officer responded. "That Johnston is self-broadcasting."

"You're shitting me," I said.

"No, sir," the petty officer said as he grabbed my bags from the back of the jeep.

"You have got to be shitting me," I said.

A pilot met us on the launchpad and opened the doors to the Johnston. He was a Navy man, a full lieutenant dressed in khakis. He looked at me and smiled. "I've heard a lot about you."

The petty officer placed my bags in the Johnston and saluted. "Lieutenant Harris does not believe this bird is self-broadcasting, sir."

I followed the lieutenant aboard. The Johnston was heavily modified inside. It only had four seats instead of the usual twelve. Used for both military and corporate travel, Johnstons had small galleys for long trips. There were no such amenities on that R-27. Behind the four seats, the rest of the passenger cabin was blocked by a cloth-covered wall.

The Johnston took off like any spaceworthy plane, using discrete jets to lift ten feet off the ground. We left Earth at a standard trajectory, flying at the standard MACH 3 speed. We had the usual quivers as we left the atmosphere.

Moments later, the petty officer shot me a wink as the tint shield darkened the windows. The air inside the cabin began to smell of ozone. Muffled crackling sounds seeped through the barrier at the back of the cabin. There was a bright flash, and suddenly everything was normal again.

"We're in the Perseus Arm now," the petty officer said. "Our base is a bit off the beaten trail, so to speak. Without a self-broadcasting ship, it would take you more than a month just to get to the nearest disc station."

According to Admiral Klyber, not since the United States developed the atomic bomb in the New Mexico town of Los Alamos, had a military project been conducted as covertly as the creation of the *Doctrinaire*. In many ways, Klyber's *Doctrinaire* reminded me of the Manhattan Project.

No one would ever stumble onto Klyber's shipyard by accident. Located on the outskirts of the Perseus Arm, the facility sat in the middle of the unsettled frontier. Spies could not trace the location because self-broadcasting ships leave no trail. Any research done on this facility stayed on this facility.

At first glance I found the shipyard unimpressive. It was big, but that meant little to me. I still thought that the *Doctrinaire* was part of a new fleet that Klyber planned to outfit with some new kind of cannon or faster engines—no big deal. As we approached the dry dock, the only thing I could see was the scaffolding.

When we got closer, I realized that Klyber was not building a fleet. All of that scaffolding was built around one colossal ship, a broad, wedge-shaped ship with bat wings. The ship was at least twice as wide as a Perseus-class fighter carrier. "What is that?" I mumbled.

"She's the biggest bitch in all of the six arms," the petty officer told me.

The petty officer led me out of the Johnston and told me to wait in the docking bay for further instructions. He left with my rucksack. A moment later, the pilot came by and patted me on the back. "Welcome aboard," he said, then he, too, disappeared.

I was not alone in the docking bay, however. The area was filled with engineers and workers. Technicians driving speedy carts raced between platforms, welding plates, placing circuits, and lacing wires. The area looked like an office building that had been framed but not finished. Strings of wires and aluminum ribs lined the inner walls. Uncovered lighting fixtures shone from the ceiling. The air ventilation system twisted over my head like a gigantic snake.

"Lieutenant Harris?" A young seaman approached me. He saluted.

I saluted back.

"Admiral Klyber sent me. He is waiting for you on the bridge. This way, sir," the seaman said.

"How long have you been stationed on this ship?" I asked, as we left the bay.

The seaman considered this question for several moments, long enough for me to wonder if he heard me. "Six months, sir."

"What do you think of her?"

"The *Doctrinaire*?" he asked. "She was made to rule the universe. If we ever leave the galaxy, it will be in a ship like this."

It took twenty-five minutes to get to the bridge. True enough, the *Doctrinaire*'s twin docking bays were in the aft sections of the wings, the farthest points from the bridge; but even so, the walk seemed endless.

"How big is she?" I asked.

"It depends on how you measure her," the seaman said. "It's two full miles from one wing tip to the other. That's the longest measurement. She has twelve decks, not including the bridge."

If there was an area that wasn't under construction between the docking bay and the bridge, we sure as hell never passed it. Half of the floor was pulled up in the corridors. Mechanics and engineers popped in and out of the uncovered crawlways like moles. The seaman took no interest in any of their work. He was a clone. All of the enlisted sailors were clones.

We took flights of stairs between decks because the elevators did not have power yet. The only lighting in one stretch of the ship came from strings of emergency bulbs along the floor. The engineers had not yet installed generators in that area, the seaman told me.

When we finally arrived on the bridge, I saw Klyber standing over two field engineers as they installed components in a weapons station. I read his restlessness in the way he micromanaged these poor engineers, going so far as to complain about the "inefficient" way they laid their tools out.

"Permission to come aboard, sir?" I called from the hatch.

The engineers, who were lying on their backs like mechanics working under a car, watched nervously from beneath the weapons station. Klyber, who stood in his familiar, rigid pose—hands clasped behind his back, legs spread slightly wider than his shoulders—spun to face me. His cold, gray eyes warmed quickly, but he still looked tired.

"Lieutenant Harris," he said. "Permission granted."

I saluted.

"That will be all, seaman." Klyber dismissed the man who had escorted me.

"Perhaps, Lieutenant, you would like a tour of the ship."

"I would love a tour of the ship, sir," I said. "I've never seen anything like her."

Klyber smiled, pleased to have his work appreciated. "I am rather excited about her," he said, sounding both proud and humble.

Having never visited the bridge of a capital ship, I had no point of comparison for the bridge of the *Doctrinaire*. When completed, the bridge would look more like an office complex than anything else. Rows of desks and computers stretched from wall to wall. I saw nothing even remotely resembling a joystick or a steering wheel.

Klyber led me out of the bridge. "The biggest difficulty in creating a ship of this size is finding a source of power. We needed dual cold-fusion reactors just to power the electrical systems."

"What about the engines?" I asked.

Klyber laughed. "That is another story entirely. That's not a function of size, it's a function of capacity and efficiency. We talked about making engines that were five times larger than the RAMZA engines used on Perseus-class carriers, but they're too inefficient. We have ended up allocating two-thirds of the ship to carry fuel."

"Is this a one-ship fleet?" I asked.

"Quite the contrary," Klyber said as he led me up a flight of stairs. "I will require a massive fleet of support ships to keep this juggernaut rolling."

We entered a glass-enclosed dome that Klyber identified as the observation deck. The outer skin of the tiny deck was one continuous window. I could see every corner of the ship from there. Engineers and builders in noncombat space suits stood on the scaffolding on the other side of the glass. I watched three men in weighted suits pulling a wagon along the top of the fuselage. Standing on the observation deck, I felt like I could see forever.

"I think I would be scared to come up here during a battle," I said.

Klyber heard this and smiled. "There's not a safer spot on this ship. These walls are made out of a plastic polymer. Not even a particle beam can hurt them. And beyond that . . ." Klyber pointed to two massive rings that encircled the ends of the wings on either side of the wedge-shaped hull. From a distance, the rings would make the *Doctrinaire* look like she was riding on bicycle tires.

The *Kamehameha* had shield projector rods—posts that stood no more than twenty feet tall and less than one foot in diameter. The rods projected flat force fields that could filter out large amounts of particle-beam and laser fire. The field fried enemy missiles.

"You have rings instead of rods?" I said. "Will they project your shields in any direction?"

"In every direction," Klyber said, with the knowing smile of someone who is about to reveal a secret.

"It's a new technology, Harris; the rings produce a curved shield that stretches all the way around the ship. No Achilles' heel gaps between shield screens."

"That is amazing, sir," I whispered.

Klyber probably did not hear me; he had already started down the stairs. We traveled down eight decks, staying in the center of the ship. The last flight of stairs ended in a glass booth overlooking a dark tunnel that stretched from the stem to the stern.

Hundreds of feet away, I could see balls of sparks where welders worked along the walls and ceiling of the tunnel. I pressed against the window and squinted. Off in the distance, I thought I saw pinpricks of light. "What is this place?" I asked.

"Flight control," Klyber said. "Each tunnel will have its own squad of fighters."

"Each tunnel?" I asked.

"There are four tunnels," Klyber said.

Other fighter carriers used a single flight deck for transports and fighters. This ship had two docking bays and four tunnels. As I considered this, Klyber continued the tour.

I still had not recognized the immense size of the project when Klyber brought me to the high point of his tour. We walked to the bottom deck of the ship and entered the biggest chamber of all.

The area was completely dark as we entered. Klyber tapped a panel beside the door and lights in the ceiling slowly flickered on. Like the tunnels, the chamber stretched the length of the ship. The ceiling was thirty feet high and the floor was at least a hundred feet wide. Every inch of space was filled by an enormous machine surrounded by catwalks riddled with walkways.

"What is this?" I said.

"This is the key to our success, Lieutenant Harris. The *Doctrinaire* is self-broadcasting. Once we locate the GC Fleet, we will be able to track it, chase it, and ultimately destroy it."

Admiral Klyber had an agenda. He wanted to bring his two creations together. He wanted to make the galaxy safe for the Unified Authority, and he wanted his Liberator and his supership to lead the charge. In his sixties, Klyber could see retirement approaching, and he wanted to leave a historic legacy.

As for me, I liked serving under Klyber. His paternal feelings toward Liberators gave me access I would never have had under other officers.

I spent one month on the *Doctrinaire* serving as the chief of security. Everyone in that section of the galaxy had a high security clearance. Except for cargo and parts that were brought in by our own pilots, no ships—friendly or otherwise—came within light-years of our position.

During my tenure as the head of security, I presided over an empty brig. (The only occupants were engineers who drank too much and became disorderly.) I requisitioned supplies. I also nearly forgot what it was like to be a rifleman in the U.A. Marines. Without knowing it, Klyber had domesticated me. I no longer remembered the electric tingle of adrenaline coursing through my veins or endorphins-induced clarity of thought. I was becoming an administrator. Police work did not agree with me; I was made for the battlefield.

Restless as I had become, I began looking for excuses to leave the ship. I accompanied engineers on requisition trips. When new personnel reported for duty, I insisted on briefing them. Klyber warned me that it was risky for me to leave the *Doctrinaire*. I should have listened to him.

Two new recruits waited for us at the galactic port on Mars. I went to brief the new officers, glad for an excuse to escape from the security station.

I sat in the copilot's seat of the Johnston R-27 as we self-broadcast from the *Doctrinaire* to the Norma Arm. From there, we traveled through the broadcast network. It was a new security precaution. Spies and reporters might become curious if they heard about a self-broadcasting ship appearing on Mars radar. Passing through the network only added ten minutes to the trip, though you might have thought it added hours to hear the pilots bitch about it.

Mars Port was in a geodesic dome used by commercial and military ships. As we landed, I looked at the rows of fighters standing at the ready.

"I'm going to refuel while you find the new recruits," the pilot told me.

"Sounds fair," I said. Crouching so that I would not hit my head on the low ceiling of the R-27, I left the cockpit and climbed out through the cabin door. The port on Mars was an ancient structure. There was a stately quality to its thick, concrete block walls and heavy building materials, but the recycled air always smelled moldy.

The U.A. never colonized Mars. The only people who lived there were merchants. A huge duty-free trade had sprung up around the spaceport—the busiest galactic port in the Republic. Selling duty-free Earth-made products proved so lucrative that retailers rented land from the Port Authority and built dormitories. Stepping into the Mars Port waiting area was like entering the universe's gaudiest shopping mall.

Many of the stores had flashing marquees and hand-lettered signs in their windows: "EARTH-MADE CIGARS,

$300/box!" and "SOUR MASH WHISKEY—100% EARTH-MADE INGREDIENTS." Travelers flowed in and out of the stores. Since Mars technically had no residents, everybody on the planet qualified for duty-free status.

I pushed through the crowd, ignoring the stores and the restaurants. Over the speaker system, I heard a woman's voice announce the arrival of a commercial flight, but I paid no attention. Our new officers would meet me in the USO.

The USO was empty except for a man refilling the soda bar. I was early—the trip in had taken less time than the pilot expected. I took a seat in the waiting room, amid the homey sofas and high-backed chairs. *Isn't that just how it goes in the Marine Corps,* I thought. *You spend 95 percent of your life sitting around bored and the other 5 percent fighting for your life.*

I was very tired and wanted to nap, but I fought the urge. My mind drifted. I thought about the security plans for the *Doctrinaire,* but those thoughts strayed into a daydream about how that great ship might perform in battle. In my mind, I saw the *Doctrinaire* flashing into existence near the GC Fleet, brushing destroyers aside as it concentrated its firepower on the GC battleships. I saw four squadrons of fighters spitting out of the tunnels and swarming enemy ships. God, it would be beautiful.

"Hello, Lieutenant Harris."

The voice sounded familiar and toxic. Admiral Che Huang, smiling so broadly that it must have hurt his face, sat in the seat beside mine. Behind him stood four MPs. "Surprised to see me?

"It was awfully nice of Klyber to send you. The way he's been hiding you, I had almost given up. Today must be my lucky day."

CHAPTER
THIRTY-ONE

In light of his feelings about Liberators, I expected Huang either to toss me in the Mars Port military brig or possibly shoot me and dump my body in deep space. Instead, he transferred me someplace where he could keep an eye on me—the Scutum-Crux Fleet.

Whether by coincidence or by design, the UAN *Ulysses S. Grant* happened to be patrolling less than one thousand miles from a disc station. Traveling from Mars to the deck of the *Grant* took less than ten minutes.

My new tour of duty started on a positive note. Second Lieutenant Vincent M. Lee met me as I stepped from the transport. He was made to wear the gold bar on his shoulder—well, maybe not made for it; but with his bodybuilder's physique, he looked like the ideal of how an officer should look.

"Wayson," he said in a whisper, rushing up to me and shaking my hand. "I half expected to hear that you were killed in a freak accident on the way here."

"How did you know I was coming?" I asked.

"It's all over the chain of command. Captain Pollard heard that another of the Little Man 7 was coming aboard and sent word down the line."

That didn't sound bad. It sounded like I had caught a break, like Huang possibly wanted to separate me from Klyber but didn't care much what happened to me beyond that. "You heard how I got this transfer?"

"Jeeezuz, Harris! Huang himself?"

"Yeah," I said. "The little specker looked like he was going to wet his pants he was so jazzed with himself. But if the worst he has planned is sending me here, maybe he's not so bad."

Having said that, I noticed a tense reaction in Lee's expression. His eyes darted back and forth, and his lips drew tight. "Harris, Captain Pollard wants to meet with you to discuss your orders. Maybe we can talk after that."

"That doesn't sound so good," I said.

"It isn't," Lee said. He led me down a long corridor toward the elevator to the Command deck. "I had to trade favors just to meet your transport. Huang wanted a team of MPs to escort you from the transport directly to the brig."

"You're taking me to the brig?" I had never visited the brig of a Perseus-class carrier. But I doubted it would be near the Command deck. The area we were passing through was pure officer country, all brass and plaques. Naval officers walked around us, some pausing to catch a quick glimpse of me.

"I'm taking you to Pollard's office. He was one of Klyber's protégés. He's doing what he can for you, but it's not much."

"You have enemies in high places, Lieutenant," said Jasper Pollard, captain of the *Grant*. "From what I can tell, Admiral Huang personally arranged this transfer."

"I'm not surprised, sir," I said.

"I would not assign a rabid dog to Ravenwood Station, Lieutenant."

"Where, sir?" I asked.

"Ravenwood. Have you been briefed?"

"No, sir," I said.

He shook his head, pursing his lips as if he had bitten into something sour. "Pathetic. How can they send an officer into action without a proper briefing? Under other circumstances . . ." Pollard walked to a shelf and selected two small tumblers. Using silver tongs, he placed three cubes of ice in each tumbler. "You drink gin?"

"Yes, sir," I said.

He splashed three fingers of gin over the ice. "I know about Little Man, of course. You must be one hell of an officer.

"I have also heard about your hearing before the House." He handed me a tumbler. "Leave it to those assholes to turn a medal ceremony into an inquisition."

Pollard downed his gin and jiggled his glass so that the ice spun. "Considering your record, you're probably a good choice for Ravenwood. You've got as good a chance of survival as anybody. Then again, I hate wasting a perfectly good officer on an assignment like that." He shot me a wicked smile. "Even a Liberator."

Sitting behind his desk with his hands on his lap, Captain Jasper Pollard looked too young to command a fighter carrier. With smooth skin and no visible gray strands in his brown coif, the captain looked like a man in his early thirties, though I am sure he was closer to fifty. "Let me tell you about Ravenwood. We've lost a lot of men on that speck of ice."

"Sounds bad, sir."

"We've kept a lid on the story. As far as I am concerned, if Morgan Atkins wants that planet, we should give it to him. We should pay him to take it. That goddamn planet is of no value, industrially or strategically. Apparently the big boys in the Pentagon have an itch about giving in, so they keep throwing men down that rathole."

He walked to his desk and sat down. "Ravenwood is on the inner third of Scutum-Crux, near the area where Scutum-Crux and Sagittarius merge. We never colonized it. It's too far from a sun. The goddamn rock is half ice, but it has an oxygen atmosphere.

"Anyway, the Navy set up a refueling depot on Ravenwood. It wasn't much—a small base, fuel, food, ammunition, emergency supplies. They stationed a hundred men there. It was one of those assignments. Get caught screwing some admiral's daughter and you might get sent to Ravenwood."

Or Gobi, I thought.

"The base went dark four weeks ago." Pollard raised his hands, palms up, to show confusion. "They did not send a distress call. For all we knew, they just blew up their communications equipment.

"So Thurston sent us to investigate. We found the base empty."

"It was empty?" I asked.

"Someone attacked it," Pollard said. "Someone broke through the outer wall. There was a fight. We found bullet casings and burns on the walls. What we did not find was bodies.

"Thurston ordered me to leave a unit behind to guard the place while he investigated. That unit disappeared the next day."

"How many men, sir?" I asked.

"A platoon," Pollard said in a hollow voice. At that moment he looked ancient and cold. "We don't know if they are dead. We never found bodies. We have recovered equipment and a few dog tags."

"This sounds like a ghost story," I said.

"It just might be that," Pollard said. "I'll tell you what I think happened, and maybe you'll wish it were ghosts. I think the Mogats are in Central Sagittarius. I think Ravenwood Station has a good view of their base. I can't prove it, but that is what I think."

We sat silently as a few moments ticked by. "How big a squad am I taking on this assignment?" I asked.

"You have a handpicked platoon. Good men. I'm sorry to lose them." He slid a thick personnel file across the desk. "Here's your mission profile. You have a few hours before you leave. I can loan you an office if you want to meet your men."

"Thank you, sir, but I think I'd rather place some calls."

"Huang sent a memo instructing me to make interLink and mediaLink facilities available for you. Admiral Klyber is your guardian angel, right? I think he wants you to contact Klyber. This is Huang's way of thumbing his nose at him. Now that you are in Scutum-Crux territory, there's not much Klyber can do.

"I'll give you that office. You're free to use the communications as you like."

* * *

The truth was that I was embarrassed to run to Klyber for help. I was supposed to be the head of security, and I'd let myself get abducted. God, I hated Huang. How long had that bastard been waiting for a chance to nab me? Probably since Ronan Minor. Admiral Che Huang, the secretary of the Navy, had spent more than one year looking for some way to cap me, a lowly grunt. I should have been flattered.

With three hours before my shuttle left for Ravenwood, and Lee waiting outside the office, I picked up the media-Link shades and toyed with the idea of writing a letter to Kasara. I wasn't really interested in her, but who else could I write to? So I tried to write to her and found myself struggling with every word. After less than five minutes, I deleted the letter and went out to grab a drink with Vince.

"How's the sea-sailor's bar on this boat?" I asked.

"Not as good as the one on the *Kamehameha,*" Lee said. "But it's got plenty of booze."

It was early afternoon; we had no trouble finding a table to ourselves. We sat in a corner and did not talk for almost a minute. "How is Jennifer?" I finally asked.

"She's good," Lee said. "We've traded a couple of letters since Hawaii, but I get the feeling she's moving on."

"Sorry to hear that," I said.

"You know Kasara is getting married next week, right?" Lee asked. He read my expression and knew the answer.

"I heard from her the day you went to the House," he said. Your speech was big news. She actually called me to ask if you were all right. I think she still has a thing for you; but you're off being a Marine, and her old guy is right there on her planet."

"And her fiancé was okay with her calling you to ask about me?" I asked.

"I doubt he knew. I get the feeling there are a lot of things he doesn't know, like the fact that his soon-to-be bride did more than get a suntan in Hawaii. Jennifer wrote me about it. She came home talking about breaking things off. That lasted about one month. Then she never heard from you. Next thing you know, Kasara is announcing she is about to get married."

"So we've both been dumped," I observed.

"Well, I never thought of Jennifer as marriage material . . . but damn fine scrub." He laughed.

"To damn fine scrub," I said, and we clinked our beers. And then we both became quiet again. This time the silence lasted longer.

"Harris, I don't know if anybody can survive in a trap like Ravenwood; but if anybody can, it's you. I wanted you to know that. I know you thought Shannon was the perfect Marine, but you're even better."

I did not know what to say. I looked at him and smiled, but inside I felt incredibly alone. "What about you, Vince? You made it. You were the first orphan to make lieutenant. Wasn't that the first step toward a life in politics?"

He shook his head. "Now that I'm here, I think I like it. I like life among the natural-born. I think I'm a career Marine from here on out."

Still the same guy, I thought. If any clone ever suspected his synthetic origins, it was Lee. And if ever a clone spent every waking minute trying to deny that suspicion, it was him again. And now he had landed himself in a position that truly did mark him as a natural-born . . . even if he was synthetic.

"A career man, eh?" I said. "You'll do one hell of a job."

I felt a sinking feeling as the doors of the kettle crept closed, blocking any hope of escaping back onto the *Grant*. The men in my all-clone platoon did not speak much as our transport took off. Two diligent Marines field stripped and cleaned their M27s. Most sat quietly staring into space. One fellow even managed to fall asleep. We had a five-hour ride ahead of us. I envied him.

A few minutes into the flight, I went to visit the cockpit. There were two officers flying the ship—a pilot and a navigator. "Could you turn down the lights in the kettle?" I asked. "I want these boys rested."

It was very dim in the cockpit. The only light was the low glow from the instrumentation. A soft blue-green halo glowed over the small navigational chart near the pilot.

Many of the energy and communications displays glowed white and red. "Want them all the way off?" the pilot asked.

"Can you give me ten percent luminance?" I asked.

"No problem, Lieutenant," said the pilot.

"Thank you. Oh, one other thing," I said as I turned to leave. "Could you call me before we land? I was hoping to get a look at the planet as we approach."

"No problem," the captain replied as he turned back to his control panel.

I closed the door behind me and returned to my seat. The pilot had dimmed the cabin lights so much that I could barely see in front of me. Dressed in green armor that appeared black in the dim light, my men looked like they were carved out of stone. A few conversations still smoldered around the cabin. Men spoke in whispers, hoping not to disturb comrades sleeping around them.

I dropped into my seat and thought about Hawaii and swimming in clear tropical waters. My eyelids fluttered, and my thoughts lazily floated into dreams, becoming more vivid and colorful. I felt myself floating in balmy currents, slowly rising and sinking in gently changing tides. I could see shapes moving just beyond my reach. As I concentrated on those shapes, I realized that I saw the bodies of men tied to the floor of the sea.

"Lieutenant."

A hand gently nudged my shoulder. I blinked as the dimly lit cabin came into focus. The navigator stood over me, speaking in a soft voice. "We're just coming up on Ravenwood now."

"Okay," I said as I stretched. My mouth was dry and filled with a bad taste. The stale air in the transport cabin had left my nose congested. I also had the dozen or so assorted aches and stiffnesses that come with sitting up while sleeping.

I entered the cockpit and got a quick glimpse of a gray-and-blue planet. I saw no hint of green on the planet's surface, just the black and gray of stone surrounded by the iron blue of frozen seas.

"Welcome to paradise," the pilot said.

"So that's what paradise looks like," I said.

"What did you expect?" the navigator asked.

"I've got a lock on the landing site beacon," the navigator said. "You'd better get back to your seat. We've got to prepare to land."

"There's an empty seat," I said, pointing to the copilot's chair. "Mind if I stay for the landing?"

"Suit yourself," the pilot said.

I peered out the cockpit door and noted that the lights had come back on in the cabin. Almost everyone would have woken up.

We were flying over a wide expanse of prairie. There were scabs of yellow-brown grass on the ground, but most of what I saw was a rock floor with patches of ice. Above the dismal prairie was a sky choked with clouds. In the distance, enormous mountains jutted out of the plains like great daggers that pierced the swollen sky. We did not travel as far as those distant cliffs. Our little fort sat by itself on a flat plateau. Its gleaming white walls looked insignificant, surrounded by thousands of miles of rock and ice.

As the transport approached, I was very pleased to see that Ravenwood Station was made of sturdy concrete and steel, and not just a prefabricated Quonset hut. Small, with thick ramparts and bulky architecture, Ravenwood Station was built to withstand a war. To my great relief, I noticed shield projector rods on its outer walls. If we could get the generators running, we would be able to seal the base off from all but the most violent of attacks. Considering the story Captain Pollard had told me, I doubted that the generators would work.

The AT touched down on a small pad just outside the walls of the station. Looking out the cockpit, I watched as our landing jets vaporized the thin sheet of ice that covered the cement. The ice turned into steam that rose along the hull of the ship. Moments later, two small streams of condensation raced down the windshield and froze in place.

"I've transmitted your security clearance code," the navigator said. "Your men can enter the base." I nodded, then turned back to the window in time to see the two doors made of seven-inch-thick metal slide apart.

The fortress was completely dark inside, but that was of

little concern with our night-for-day vision. I worried more about the condition of the outer walls than generators and power supplies.

I went to the bulkhead and called, "Marsten and Gubler." Two corporals came to the front of the kettle. "Leave your rucks. I need you to have a look around the base to see what works and what is broken."

They saluted and left.

According to their profiles, Arlind Marsten and Max Gubler were skilled field engineers. With any luck, their journeyman's knowledge would be enough to get the security, communications, and life-support systems online. Pausing only to pull their tool cases, they scrambled out of the transport.

"You boys," I said, pointing to the three privates. "Scout the outer walls, inside and out. I want a damage report."

As they started for the hatch, I called after them over the interLink. "Keep an eye open for weapons, armor, debris, anything that might give us a clue about recent battles. Got it?"

"Sir, yes, sir." They saluted and left.

"The rest of you unload this transport. Be quick about it. I want to seal the base by 1500."

Moving at a quick jog, the remaining Marines left the transport and crossed the landing pad. In Ravenwood's dark atmosphere, I noticed that their green armor blended beautifully against the ice and rock. If we were unable to get the energy systems running, if the security system was damaged beyond repair, we might still be able to take the enemy in an open-field ambush.

I watched my men hustling to unload the supplies. The boys knew the gravity of their situation. They would remain alert and disciplined. We had, I thought, a fighting chance.

A crackling sound reverberated along the station wall as a flood of bright light ignited around the grounds. In the brightness, I saw the dull sheen of frost on the walls.

"Lieutenant," a voice said over the interLink, "energy systems are up and running, sir."

"Nicely done, Marsten," I said. "I'm impressed."

"The power generators were in perfect order, sir,"

Marsten responded. "Gubler says the security and heating systems were damaged, but not badly. The energy rods are still intact. It's as if the last platoon powered the station down to prepare for us."

"I see. What is the condition of the shield generator?"

"Shorted out, sir. It's an easy repair. I think we can have it going in an hour."

"Really?" I asked.

"The communications system is a bust, though," Marsten said. "Whoever attacked the base made sure the occupants could not call for help." We all had mediaLink shades, but those were not made for battle. Using them left you blind to your surroundings, and a sophisticated enemy could easily jam their signal.

"Maybe they were making certain that future occupants would not call for help either," I said. "One last thing. I want you to check for radar. This used to be a fuel depot. It may have radar-tracking capabilities."

"Yes, sir," Marsten replied.

The area around the base looked clean when we landed. I would send a small patrol out to make certain of it. If the area was clean, and we could get a tracking system running, we might be able to track the enemy's landing. That was, of course, assuming they flew in. If they broadcast themselves in stolen Galactic Central ships, our radar would give us very little warning.

"Lieutenant," a voice came over my interLink.

"What is it?" I asked.

"We found out how they entered the base. You might want to see this."

I looked in the AT's cargo hold. My men had mostly emptied the compartment, but a few crates of supplies stood piled on a pallet in a far corner. "I'll be there in a few minutes. How bad is the damage?"

"There are a lot of holes, but the wall's still pretty strong. I think we can patch it."

As we spoke, a few men carried off the last of the supplies.

"Lieutenant Harris," the pilot's voice spoke over the interLink. "I understand that the cargo hold is empty."

"You in a hurry to leave?" I asked.

"This is my third drop on Ravenwood over the last two months, Lieutenant. As far as I know, the other teams are still here because no one came to pick them up. Yes, goddamn it, I am in a hurry to leave."

"Understood," I said. "Thank you for your help." I climbed down from the cargo hold and watched as the hatch slid shut.

"Cleared to leave," I said as I stepped away from the AT.

"Godspeed, Lieutenant. With any luck I will pick you and your men up shortly." There was no mistaking the lack of conviction in the pilot's voice.

I did not respond. Its jets melting a newly formed layer of ice, the boxy transport ship lifted slowly off the landing pad. It hovered for a few moments, then rose into the sky. Watching it leave, I felt an odd combination of jealousy and fear.

"Do you want us to get to work on the wall, sir?" one of the privates asked.

"Wait up, Private," I said, as I started around the base for a look at the damage. A thin layer of long-frozen snow covered the ground. My boot broke through its icy crust. I found my scout party examining the back wall—the wall farthest from the launchpad.

The wall was made of foot-thick concrete blocks coated with a thick plastic and metal polymer for added protection. Using a ramming device, or possibly just a well-placed charge, somebody had made seven holes through a thirty-foot section of wall.

"Can you fix this?" I asked.

"It shouldn't be much of a problem, sir. We have the materials, but, ah . . ."

"Private?"

"If the wall didn't keep the enemy out the first time, I don't see how patching it will make much of a difference."

"Point taken," I said. "Do what you can here and look for anything that tells us who made these holes and how they made them."

"Yes, sir."

"We did find these," the private said, pointing to an unexploded fractal-field grenade—a messy device that overloaded shields by flooding them with radioactive isotopes.

A couple of those bangers could certainly have shorted out the generators on this base.

"Son of a bitch," I said. The U.A. military stopped using those grenades decades ago, possibly even forty years ago. I picked the grenade up and rolled it in my palm, being careful not to touch the pin.

"You might want to be careful with that, sir," the private said.

"Private, this banger is forty years old. If it wasn't stable, it would have blown years ago." Just the same, I carefully replaced the grenade on the ground.

"While you're patching the walls, I want you to check the grounds for radiation. Let me know if the soil is hot, would you?"

"Yes, sir," the private said.

"I'll send some men out to guard you," I said. I did that for his comfort, not his safety. Whoever had attacked Ravenwood didn't care if we fixed the walls and started the shield generators. That much was obvious.

Everything I had done up to that point made perfect sense. In fact, it was obvious. If you inherited a base that had been ransacked, you fixed the holes and restored the security systems. The previous platoon would have taken the same precautions.

THIRTY-TWO

The war began on November 8, 2510. Hoping to find a response from Admiral Klyber, I went into the command office and slipped on my mediaLink shades.

NORMA ARM SECEDES FROM THE REPUBLIC

November 8, Washington, DC—Announcing that they had formed a new organization called the Norma Arm Treaty Organization, 27 of the 30 colonized planets in the Norma Arm declared independence from the Unified Authority.

Other territories may follow suit. There are reports that the Cygnus Arm has a similar treaty organization.

"Shit," I gasped. An entire arm of the galaxy had declared independence. If the Cygnus Arm followed, would Scutum-Crux be far behind?

I did not tell my men about the secessions. Knowing that a civil war had begun would hurt their morale and possibly weaken their resolve. In the new state of affairs, they would need to fight more than ever. With entire galactic arms declaring independence, the Navy would not waste time worrying about an all-clone platoon on an ice cube like Ravenwood. We were on our own.

While I read the news in my office, my men scoured the base for bodies and signs of fighting. We found them everywhere. Bullets had gouged and scratched many of the walls. Somebody had fired a particle beam in the building, too. We found places where beam blasts had exploded parts of the walls.

"Sir, I think you should see this," one of my men called.

"Where are you?" I asked.

"Squad bay," the man said, "in the hub."

Viewed from the top, Ravenwood Station looked like a square with an X connecting its four corners. The center of that X, the "hub," included the barracks, the rec room, the galley, and the latrine.

I found three of my privates in squad bay. One of them had noticed a dark stain on the floor. They had pushed the bunks out of the way for a better look and found that most of the bare, concrete floor was discolored.

"I don't think it's blood," I said. "Blood washes off clean."

"It almost looks like an oil stain," a private said.

"Whatever this shit was, sir, there was a lot of it," the first private said. "Most of the floor is stained."

"So did it evaporate?" I asked.

"No, sir. Somebody mopped up afterward."

"What?" I asked.

The private pushed a bunk out of his way and opened a service closet. Inside the closet were a coiled steam hose and some maps. The heads of these mops were thick and heavily stained towels that were stiff and purple.

"There are more stains, sir," another private said. The group took me on a tour of the base, pointing out crescent-shaped stains where past residents had most likely died.

From what I could tell, the unfortunate platoon before us made a stand in the barracks. Everywhere we went, we found scratches and gashes in the wall. The boys before us had not worried about conserving ammunition. They obviously had something more on their minds.

We stripped the sheets from the bunks and found that

most of the mattresses had a black stain running along one edge. Many had flash burns, and a few even had bullet holes. The last platoon had thrown their bunks on their sides and used them as barricades during the firefight.

As we examined the bunks, a corporal noticed something strange about the damage in the walls. Most of the shots were between three and five feet up, with only a rare shot having hit any higher. Marines, who are trained to shoot to kill, will normally aim at their enemies' chests and heads.

I went to the operations area, the northern corner of the fortress. The rest of Ravenwood Station had plastic-coated white walls and bright lights. Operations had black walls and no windows. The only light in the area came from the security screens and computer monitors. Lights blinked on and off on the banks of computers lining the walls.

It was there that I found Marsten and Gubler hacking into the station's many computer systems. Despite the cold, they had removed their helmets and gloves.

"Aren't you cold?" I asked.

"We've got the climate controls working. It's getting warmer," Gubler said. "We're already up twenty degrees." He pointed to a monitor that showed the base temperature at just under forty degrees. I looked at Gubler and saw that his face was pale; his lips had turned slightly blue.

"Yeah, warmer," I said. "How is it going with the radar system?"

"Up and running," Marsten said. "I may have already found something, too."

He went to a terminal and typed in some commands, bringing up a radar screen. "Now this may only have been an echo from something detected a long time ago; but as the system came online, I picked up a ship at the edge of our range. It was only there for a moment."

"So another ship might be in the area?" I asked. "Is it possible that the ship detected your scan and flew out of range?" I asked.

"I'm not sure why it would do that," Marsten said. "It was one of ours, a fighter carrier. Have a look."

Marsten typed some commands, and the screen fuzzed

for a moment. The time mark in the corner showed "11/8/2510: 1437." The screen froze.

"There," Marsten said, pointing to the very top of the screen. Outlined in green and white was the bat-winged shape of a U.A.N. fighter carrier.

"A carrier. Did you identify it?" I asked.

"No, sir. It moved out of range too quickly." Marsten stood in front of the scanning station, the glare from the screen reflected in a bright smear on his armor.

"Did you get any information?" I asked.

Marsten's forehead became very smooth as his eyes narrowed, and he considered my question. "I'll see what we can take from the radar reading."

I walked beside him and looked over his shoulder as he typed more information into the computer. A glowing red grid showed on the screen. He brought up the radar frame with the ghost ship, then isolated the ship. Numbers flashed on the computer screen as he plumbed the image for information. "You'll be able to see it more clearly if you take off the helmet," Marsten said.

"I need to stay on the interLink," I responded.

Marsten nodded. "This is the beginning of the scan. The ship was pretty far away." Strange numbers appeared on the screen. Leaning in for a better look, Marsten traced his finger along the screen. His finger looked green in the glare.

"That can't be right," Marsten said as he looked up from the screen. He turned to face me. "This may sound odd. It's probably a misread, but this ship is only twenty-two hundred feet wide. I mean, it's either a very large battleship or maybe an old Expansion-class fighter carrier."

This information should have come as a surprise, but it didn't. I felt a familiar chill run through me. "How far back in time can you go on radar record?"

"You want to know what the other platoons saw?" Marsten asked. "I can do that." He sounded both pleased and excited.

We had no information about the hundred-man Navy detachment that disappeared on Ravenwood. One moment they were there, and everything was fine. A week later they did not report in. Nothing is known about what happened during that week.

We knew more about the missing platoon. It disappeared within five hours of landing on Ravenwood. The commanding officer had checked in with Pollard every hour on the hour. Captain Pollard sent a rescue ship two hours after the final transmission. The ship took three hours to arrive, and by the time it did, the base was empty.

After a thorough search, Marsten found another slight echo that suggested inconclusively that an Expansion-class fighter carrier did indeed pass within radar range of Ravenwood Station sometime after the platoon arrived.

"Does that ship mean anything, sir?" Marsten asked.

"It might," I said.

"Do you think it's from the GC Fleet?"

I shook my head. "No. That fleet did not have any carriers."

"I'll keep on this," Marsten said.

"Okay," I answered, "I'm going to have another look around. Let me know if you find anything else."

All of the evidence pointed in the same direction, but I did not like where it was pointing. For one thing, if I was reading it right, our chances of survival were nil.

The one part of Ravenwood Station I had not yet visited was the vehicle pool. I called for a squad to meet me there.

"Lieutenant," Marsten said.

"What have you got?" I asked.

"The radar was running during the first attack. An Expansion-class carrier was in the area around the time of the attack. In fact, it was flying over the area when the radar was shut down."

"Was it the *Kamehameha*?" I asked.

"How did you know?" Marsten asked.

"Just an ugly hunch," I said. "You've done good work. Any chance you can search the security records? I need to know everything that happened in this base."

"Gubler already tried," Marsten said, now starting to sound slightly nervous. "The records were erased."

"Okay, you've done great. Thanks." I signed off.

Twelve of my men met me inside the motor pool, and we searched. If Ravenwood Station ever had tanks or ATVs, they were now gone. Except for tools, fuel tanks, and a lot of trash, the room was empty.

The floor and walls were bare concrete. We searched methodically, piling debris in the center of the room behind us. I found a few spent M27 cartridges and a line of icy footprints. Somebody had come in here with wet feet. Unfortunately, I had no way of telling the age of the footprints.

When it came to important discoveries, one of my corporals won the prize. "I've found a body!" he yelled over the open frequency. Everybody stopped what they were doing and went to have a look. The doors to the motor pool opened as more Marines came for a look.

"Where is it?" I asked as I looked at the far wall.

"He's buried in that corner, sir," the corporal said. He pointed toward the far corner of the room. Any lights that might have been in that section of the pool had either stopped working or been shot out. I switched on the night-for-day lens in my visor as I moved in for a closer look, but I need not have bothered. The corner was empty except for a pile of cans and rags; but growing out of those rags was the name, "Private Thadius Gearhart."

"Search it," I ordered, not knowing what we might find. The pile of trash was about a foot deep—too shallow to conceal a body. "The rest of you, get back to work."

As the others filed out of the motor pool, the corporal called out, "I found him. At least I have what's left of him."

The corporal held the broken front section of a combat helmet between his pinched fingers. The section included most of the frame around the visor and a jagged swath of the portion around the left ear. A few shards of glass remained in the visor.

Gearhart had been most likely shot in the face. The bullet would have entered through the visor, flattening on impact, and blown out the back of his head and helmet. If we examined the area more carefully, I suspected we would find bits of broken plastic along with skull and brain among the rags, cans, and trash.

The corporal swung the scrap of helmet as if he planned to throw it in the trash. "Stop," I said.

"Do you want this, sir?" the man asked.

"Take it to Marsten," I said. "Tell him that it's still transmitting an identifier signal and ask him if he can access the data chip."

Though Marsten was surely a gifted hacker, I had little hope that he would extract information from that data chip, assuming it was even in there. Combat helmets were complex pieces of equipment with optical movement readers, multiple lenses, interLink wiring, and more. It seemed like too much to hope for the read-and-relay data chip to be in that small section. Luck, for once, was on our side.

We did not find anything else of significance in the motor pool. As I left to return to the hub, I saw two of my men praying. "You do that," I whispered. "Why not." A few minutes later, Marsten contacted me.

"Lieutenant Harris, I think we got it rigged."

"I'll be right there."

"Rigged" was a good choice of words. Marsten had strung a full dozen wires into a small socket along the left edge of the visor. Gubler connected that rat's nest of wires into the back of a computer.

"The chip was damaged to begin with, and this is not the way these chips were meant to be read," Marsten said, by way of apology, as he turned on a computer monitor. "We won't get much, but we should get something."

Rather than a streaming video feed, we got a single image on the screen. It could only have been the last thing Gearhart saw as the bullet struck him. Jagged lines marked the screen where his visor had already shattered.

Gearhart must have been guarding the motor pool when the enemy arrived. The image on the screen showed three men climbing through holes they had bored—the holes my men were currently sealing back up.

I could see two of the men's faces. The third, likely the man who killed Gearhart, was hidden behind a rifle scope. One of the other men held a pistol in one hand as he pulled himself forward with the other. His clawlike fingers were wrapped over the edge of the hole.

"They all have the same face. Are they clones?" Gubler asked as he stared into the screen.

"Adam Boyd," I said.

"You know him?" Marsten asked.

I thought about the scars around my forehead and right eye. "We've met."

CHAPTER
THIRTY-THREE

Two years earlier, when I first reported to Gobi Station, I dreamed only of serving the Republic. My greatest ambition was the life of a Marine, but only twenty-four months later I no longer gave a damn about the Earth, the Unified Authority, or the Marines. Programming or no, I was done with all of it.

To me, the Unified Authority was people like Robert Thurston, who considered clones expendable. He was no more antisynthetic than he was antibullets. Both were supplies that could easily be replaced and should be used to strategic advantage. On Little Man, he sent twenty-three hundred loyal Marines to their deaths without a backward glance. And Ravenwood . . . Ravenwood wasn't a fuel depot, it was a training ground. Admiral Huang was using Marines as live targets to train his new breed of SEAL clones how to kill. I doubted that Huang knew that I had beat the shit out of one of his clones at Sad Sam's Palace, but I hoped that he did.

If only I could have peeked. One quick look at the old security tapes and I might have understood the SEALs' tactics. Screw superior numbers and the home field advantage, I wanted to know what methods the Boyd clones used, what weapons they carried, and what made those deep purple stains on the floors. But they had made sure that I could not peek. No one cared if it was a matter of life and death for my platoon; the important thing was that the SEALs have their training exercises. Peeking at past performances would be breaking the rules of their game.

If the SEALs stuck to their past schedule, they would attack within five hours of our entering the base. We spent three hours patching walls that the SEALs could easily breach, repairing systems the SEALs had twice destroyed, and gathering specks of evidence of past SEAL victories.

That was how the past platoons had played it, too. I needed to start developing new ways to play the game. The key, I thought, was not getting herded into a group.

The stains on the ground might not have been blood, but they represented death. Looking at the evidence, I reconstructed the last assault. The Boyd clones had circled the outer halls, killing off the stragglers and herding the rest of the platoon into squad bay.

There, with the last Marines using bunks for cover, the SEALs finished the battle. They massacred the platoon. They had done something awful, but I had no idea what it might have been.

In the waning minutes before the fight, I came up with an idea that might give us a small advantage. "Marsten," I called over the interLink, "kill the lights and close off the vents."

"Do you want me to shut off the heat?" Marsten asked.

"No, bump the heat as far as it will go. Just close the vents."

"The vents are in the ceiling, sir. It's going to get cold in here."

"That's what I want, Marsten. I want this base cold and dark. Do you have that?"

"Yes, sir," Marsten said in an unsure voice.

"I'm on my way to the control room. I'll explain when I get there," I said.

Next, I spoke over the platoon-wide frequency. "This is Harris," I barked. "I have given the order to power down the lights and turn off the vents. I want everybody to switch to heat vision. I repeat, do not use night-for-day vision, use heat vision."

An eerie, almost liquid, darkness flooded the halls as the lights went out. For the first few seconds, I did not see anything other than the heat signatures of the men around me. Their armor muffled their colors; instead of orange with a yellow corona, they were brown and red. Groping blindly, I found my way to a wall, then felt my way to the door.

"Begging the lieutenant's, pardon, sir, but I can't see a specking thing," someone complained over the interLink. "Can I switch to night-for-day?"

"No!" I shouted. "We're running out of time, and we cannot do what the last platoon did."

"And the lieutenant believes that fighting blind will help?" another man asked.

"You can bet the last platoon leader did not try that," another man quipped.

"Take a look at the ceiling, asshole," I said.

By that time, a faint orange glow appeared along the ceiling and the tops of the walls. It wasn't bright, but the air in the ventilation shafts was only getting hotter. Soon the heat signature from the shafts would give us a clear outline of every room. We could tell the shapes of the rooms and where we stood in them. We would see each other. We would have marginal lighting, and the Boyd clones would be entirely blind.

"Son of a bitch," one of the men said. "What is that?"

"Marsten is flooding the air shafts with superheated air," I said.

Looking through heat vision, the hall in front of me was long and black with no walls or floor but a flat, tan ceiling. I could see junctions where it intersected with other halls.

"Okay, everybody, take your positions," I said as I continued to the control room. "Get ready. Our guests should stumble in soon, Marines. I believe we have a debt to square with them."

"Sir, yes, sir!" they barked. I was using tactics I had learned from the officer who sent us to die on Little Man, and I felt angry at myself for doing it.

As I approached the entrance to operations, I saw the light chocolate-colored heat signatures from the ten men I had posted by the door. Some of them were kneeling with pistols drawn.

I also saw their identifier labels and made a point of calling each man by name. They saluted me as I approached. I returned their salutes. "Are you ready, Marines?" I asked.

They were.

"Sir, do you think this will work?" Gubler asked, when I entered the control room.

I meant to say that I did not know, but that I thought our heat vision would give us a slight advantage. I meant to tell him that I had once gone on a mission with a team of SEALs, and that they had gotten themselves blown up while exiting an empty campsite. I did not have the chance to say any of that, however. The attack started.

It began with a systems blackout in operations. Someone, somewhere, had managed to power down our systems, shields and all. The big screens around the operations room winked once and went dark.

"This is it, boys," I said over the interLink. "The attack has begun. Stay calm. Remember, with lights out and the heat on, you will see the enemy before he can see you. Now hold your positions."

I had placed men in every corner of the building, with the idea that they could call each other for help as needed. In the next moment, the SEALs turned that decision into a death sentence. A soft hum began ringing in my ears. "They're jamming the interLink!" I yelled at Marsten. He did not hear me. He stood three feet from me, and he did not hear my voice through my helmet. I watched him tap his helmet over the right ear.

What a choice they left me, my vision or my sight. I snapped off my helmet and motioned for Marsten and Gubler to do the same. With our helmets off we were now completely blind.

"They jammed the interLink," Gubler or Marsten said. In the darkness, I could not tell which one spoke. I heard panic in his voice.

"Pretty specking smart!" I yelled, not realizing that with their helmets off, both men could hear me perfectly well.

"The comms console is down," Marsten or Gubler added. "What do we do?"

"We do the same as everybody else," I said. "We hold our positions. You defend this room, shoot every SEAL bastard that touches that door." Since the power was off, taking that room would be a low priority for the SEALs. Marsten and Gubler had worked hard and pulled off miracles, but they were not combat grunts. Perhaps I could keep them alive by hiding them in the useless room.

"Where are you going?" one of them asked.

"I'm going to the motor pool. That's where they will enter the building," I said as I put on my helmet. It seemed, at that moment, that perhaps we had caught a lucky break. The power was off on the computers, but the ventilation system was still getting hotter. The ceiling above me looked dark orange through my heat vision.

Before leaving the room, I looked at Marsten and Gubler and tapped my visor. I meant to signal, "stay alert," but they thought I wanted them to remove their helmets.

I broke the seal on my helmet and yelled, "Stay alert!"

"Oh," one of them said.

"Goddamn useless techno-humpers," I said as I left the room. I had my helmet on. They did not hear me.

I'd posted eight men in every corner of the building, with an additional seven men inside the motor pool. Those seven men were our first line of defense. I went to join them.

I wanted to sprint down the corridor and through the living area. Made dizzy by my limited vision, the most I could bring myself to do was a fast jog.

I had not run far before I felt the first signs of fatigue. Perhaps the month I had served on the *Doctrinaire* doing administrative work had taken a fatal toll. Adrenaline shot through my veins, but I still felt weak. My heart pumped crazy hard, and my labored breathing sounded like the wheezing of a man who had run a marathon. I slowed to a stealthy walk as I reached the end of the hall, but I already knew I was too late.

The chocolate-colored cameos of men in combat armor lay on the floor before me. Three of the men lay in fetal positions, curled around their pistols. They had died near the door to the motor pool.

When I looked in the door, I saw that the entire floor was covered with multiple layers of green. The bottom layer was the coldest and darkest. It did not move. Above it was a light-colored fog that swirled and undulated. The scene looked like lime-colored mist rising out of emerald-colored water. Inside that dark green, I saw several splashes of purple. I had no idea what it was, but I did not enter the room. Something in that malevolent green color warned me away.

"Damn," I growled. "Damn!" My voice whirled around in my helmet.

Another body lay facedown in the hall beyond the motor pool. He must have been shot down while trying to run for help.

Seeing that, I did sprint. Running as fast as I could, I came to the storage area in the west corner of the base. I saw muzzle flashes as I approached. They appeared white in my visor.

I also saw three Boyd clones hiding behind a wall. Their signature looked orange with a yellow corona. They had something dark on their heads, probably night-for-day goggles. One of them pulled a canister from his belt. The bastards did not hear me coming, and I shot each of them in the head. Their dwarf bodies flopped to the floor, oozing blood that registered bright red in my heat vision.

Removing my helmet, I waved it around the corner so that my men would see my identifier. Then I stepped out with hands in the air.

"Lieutenant Harris?" one of the men asked. Without my helmet, I could not see a thing. I stumbled on a Boyd clone.

"How many did we lose?" I asked.

"At least seven," someone answered.

I nodded. I had already lost a good part of my platoon. "Marsten and Gubler are in the control room. If you can get to them, that will be the best place to fight."

"Are you coming, sir?" the voice asked.

"I'm going to see what I can do out here," I said.

"Aye, sir," the man said. I put on my helmet and saw him doing the same. Three brown silhouettes cut across the hub and ran to the control room. I hoped they would not run into any SEALs.

My battle instincts started to kick in. I could feel the adrenaline and endorphins, and my head cleared. The westernmost corner of the base was the machine room. I held my pistol ready and trotted forward.

The door of the machine room slid open, and I saw a flood of colors. The vents in the ceiling showed orange. The furnace generating the heat looked yellow. There I found more of that green mist. It seemed fresher this time; very little had darkened and settled on the floor. Whatever that green shit was, I wanted nothing to do with it.

The door on the far side of the machine room was open. Three Boyds stood right outside the door—short, slender orange silhouettes with yellow coronas. I could see the clawlike fingers. I capped the first two as the third one turned to face me. He was too late. I shot him in the shoulder as he spun. His momentum tripped him. As he fell, he tumbled into the green goo. His screams were so loud that I heard him through my helmet.

His heat seemed to charge the mist as he fell into it. It swirled around him, and purple liquid oozed from his body. It was not blood. The blood of the other two Boyds registered red in my heat vision. The liquid was purple and viscous. It seemed to seep from his body and did not spread on the floor.

Elite SEALs, the Republic's most deadly killing machines . . . They had to have been Huang's idea. How many trained killers would Huang send to annihilate a platoon of Marines? He would probably send a single squad against our three—thirteen of his men against our forty-two. Arrogant bastard.

I had no way of knowing how many enemy SEALs my men might have capped as they entered the motor pool. The battle might already be over, though I doubted it.

I needed to return to the control room. It all made sense. The herding tactic, the strange stains on the concrete floor and the mattresses—they were using Noxium gas—the gas that Crowley tried to use on us in Gobi. It was heavier than air. That was why the ducts that dispensed the gas on the elevators leading to the *Kamehameha*'s Command deck were built into the ceiling. The gas would form a fog along the ground—a fog that registered light green as it chilled and dissipated in the environment.

Hiding in the control room, using computer equipment barricades for protection, my men would be easy targets for a Noxium gas pellet.

I leaped over bodies as I ran toward the control room. If they had not jammed the interLink, I could call to my men and warn them. Ours was a battle against the senses—the SEALs left us deaf, we left them blind.

I rounded a corner and slid to a stop. On the ground before me lay the three men I had rescued outside of the storage area. They were dead, probably shot, but a thin green mist swirled like a swarm of flies near their bodies. The SEALs were dissolving the evidence.

The gas had not spread far. I knew that I should have backtracked around the motor pool, but I needed to get to the last of my men. I needed to warn Gubler and Marsten. Taking a meaningless deep breath that would offer me no protection, I edged my way around the walls of the room, never taking my eyes off the slowly melting bodies.

The panels on the far side of the hub slid open as I approached. The three Boyds standing on the other side of the door proved a lot more alert than the ones outside the machine room. I barely had a moment to drop to one knee before bullets struck the wall above my shoulder. I returned fire, hitting one of the three SEALs in the chest. I continued firing, but missed the other men as I hid behind the open door.

The Boyds had night-for-day goggles. I should have known that they would. As I prepared to spring out, I heard the muffled clink of something metal against the concrete floor. I was lucky to have heard it through my helmet. A few feet in front of me, a green cloud started to spread across the ground.

I had a brief moment to react. Jumping to my feet, I

lunged over the canister and into the open hall, shooting as I flew through the air. I hit one of the Boyds. But I landed hard, crashing face-first into a wall. Dazed, I rose on one knee, spun, and fired several more shots.

My head and shoulders stung and white flashes filled my eyes as I struggled to slide away from the door—away from the gas. I could see the jade-colored cloud rising in the darkness. Beyond it, I saw something that looked like a long, purple carpet across the floor of the corridor to the control room.

Something struck hard against the side of my helmet, knocking it off my head. I toppled to my elbows, barely conscious at all. I felt around the floor for my pistol but could not find it.

"You failed, Lieutenant," a high-pitched voice purred. "Your team is dead."

"Get specked," I said. Without my helmet I was completely blind, and there was a spreading cloud of Noxium gas somewhere nearby.

Out of the darkness, something grabbed the back of my armor and pulled me to my feet. The Boyd slammed me backward against the wall. I hit hard and fell back to the floor. I moaned and tried to crawl to my feet. The Boyd slashed his sharp fingers across my face, gouging deeply into my cheeks. He kicked me, and I slid across the floor toward the barracks . . . toward the gas. I started to sit up, but he knelt, his weight on my chest, and swiped another claw across my face. He pulled me to my feet, then shoved me backward.

My armor did not clatter when I landed. I landed on one of the SEALs I had shot a few moments earlier. Patting the ground behind me, I felt an arm and traced it. My hand reached the dead man's forearm as I felt myself being lifted. I felt my attacker slice his claws across my face a third time, and I fell to the floor.

I landed on the dead Boyd's arm, and there it was. I felt the bulge of a pistol under my back when I landed. Barely able to breathe through my badly ripped mouth, with blood pouring down my face, I turned on my side and grabbed the gun.

I felt weight on my shoulder. The Boyd stepped down on me, pressing his foot into my throat and allowing the sharp toe of his boot to dig into my jaw. I hoped he could see clearly as I raised the pistol and fired three shots up the side of his leg.

CONCLUSION

It was only a matter of time, really. The *Kamehameha* would wait for a signal from its SEALs. When the signal did not arrive, a second team of SEALs would come down to investigate. That team would find me bleeding and weak and finish the execution. The job was three-quarters done already.

Feeling around on the floor, I found my helmet and tried to switch to night-for-day, but my eyes twitched so erratically that I could not access the optical menus. I would spend my remaining hours of life lying blind on this floor, praying that the Noxium gas did not reach me.

When I awoke, I found myself on a narrow cot with a blanket pulled over my knees. I was in some kind of prison or cage, but the door was left open. I tried to sit up and bumped my head. My whole body ached.

"Still want to be a Marine?" a familiar, rumbling voice asked.

"Freeman? Is that you?" I asked. "How did you . . ."

"Klyber sent me to get you." Freeman called back. "He contacted me before they even escorted you off Mars.

"He left you a message. Check the shades by your bed."

There was a pair of mediaLink shades on the floor. It hurt to lean over the edge of the cage to grab the shades, but I forced myself to do it. My hands trembled too much to slip the shades in place. After a moment, Ray Freeman's giant hands pulled the shades from mine, and he slipped them over my eyes.

Freeman let me know that he found you. When I heard that Admiral Huang arrested you on Mars, I didn't know what to expect.

A lot has happened over the last few days. You may not know it, but the Cygnus, Perseus, and Scutum-Crux Arms have all declared independence. They call themselves the Confederate States. In response, the Linear Committee has shut down the House of Representatives.

We have a lot to discuss, Wayson. But for now, you must stay hidden. Huang thinks you died on Ravenwood, and you should do nothing to make him think otherwise.

Stay with Freeman. I have paid him to take care of you until I return.

I finished reading this and had an epiphany. I no longer cared. I did not care if Klyber wanted to protect me, and I did not care if his supership battered the Mogats into oblivion. Whether the Republic marched on to victory or burst into flames really did not matter.

I lay perfectly still for several minutes considering the message. "Was I reported missing?" I asked Freeman.

"Dead," he answered. "Corporal Arlind Marsten is missing. I switched your helmets."

"Marsten," I said to myself. "He was a good kid. Good with computers." I was sad to hear that he had died. All of them had died, I supposed.

"That means my military days are over," I said. "I'm dead, and Marsten is AWOL."

"I figure so," Freeman said.

"Are you still looking for a partner?" I asked.

The national bestselling authors
Sean Williams & Shane Dix

Geodesica: Ascent

The year is 2388.
Humanity has spread to the stars,
but the far-flung Arc Systems chafe under
the tight control of the Exarchs, post-human
AIs whose domination of Faster-Than-Light
technology gives them unsurpassed power.
Then the discovery of a vast hyperspatial
labyrinth known as the Geodesica
changes everything.

*"Some seriously cool space battles,
and one of the most mind-twisting
alien artifacts ever imagined."*
—Alastair Reynolds

Available wherever books are sold or at
penguin.com

New from Ace

Ironcrown Moon
by Julian May
0-441-01299-X

King Conrig has united the warring island of High Blenholme—but his enemies are plotting against him. Danger arises when word comes that the magical Trove of Darasilo has vanished from its secret crypt. In the wrong hands, it would seal Conrig's doom.

Cusp
Robert A. Metzger
0-441-01301-5

The year is 2051. An enigmatic entity has its own plan for human evolution, using the supercomputer known as CUSP—the first computer designed to run on the software of the human mind.

Daughter of the Desert
by Noel Anne Brennan
0-441-01394-5

The author of the acclaimed fantasties *The Sword of the Land* and *The Blood of the Land* brings readers this tale of a young noble-woman and a prince whose unlikely alliance must defeat the savage magic of a dangerous land.

Demon
by John Varley
0-441-14267-2

The satellite-sized alian Gaea has gone completely insane. She has transformed her love of old movies into monstrous realities. She is Marilyn Monroe. She is King Kong. And now she must be destroyed.